AN EXTRA ORDINARY LIFE

Blessings!
Rhoda G.
Penny

AN EXTRA ORDINARY LIFE

RHODA G. PENNY

TATE PUBLISHING
AND ENTERPRISES, LLC

An "Extra" Ordinary Life
Copyright © 2015 by Rhoda G. Penny. All rights reserved.

No part of this publication may be reproduced, stored in a retrieval system or transmitted in any way by any means, electronic, mechanical, photocopy, recording or otherwise without the prior permission of the author except as provided by USA copyright law.

This novel is a work of fiction. Names, descriptions, entities, and incidents included in the story are products of the author's imagination. Any resemblance to actual persons, events, and entities is entirely coincidental.

The opinions expressed by the author are not necessarily those of Tate Publishing, LLC.

Published by Tate Publishing & Enterprises, LLC
127 E. Trade Center Terrace | Mustang, Oklahoma 73064 USA
1.888.361.9473 | www.tatepublishing.com

Tate Publishing is committed to excellence in the publishing industry. The company reflects the philosophy established by the founders, based on Psalm 68:11,
"The Lord gave the word and great was the company of those who published it."

Book design copyright © 2015 by Tate Publishing, LLC. All rights reserved.
Cover design by Kristina Angela Igot
Interior design by Caypeeline Casas

Published in the United States of America
ISBN: 978-1-63306-725-7
1. Fiction / Biographical
2. Fiction / Medical
15.05.27

To my brother, whose life has touched so many lives.
He has brought so much joy and happiness to those around him.

ACKNOWLEDGMENTS

This book wouldn't be possible without the support of my wonderful husband and two children who encouraged me along the way.

I also thank Pat, my high school English teacher, who was there for me every step along the way.

Thanks to numerous friends who were a great support to me as I wrote this book.

Thank you to God for his blessings in my life which are too numerous to count.

PROLOGUE

PRESENT

PROLOGUE

Jenny rocked steadily back and forth in the squeaky forest green porch swing. She breathed slowly smelling the sweet aroma of fresh-cut alfalfa and the pink roses on the trellis by the porch steps. Gazing toward the rolling plains of the Midwest, she sighed, "Ah, the country. The quiet and peace of home."

Jenny had moved back to her Grandpa Rogers' farm home two years earlier. The white two-story farmhouse, built in the early 1900s and home to four generations of her family, was nestled on the hill several yards away from the main highway. The house had a wraparound porch with chipped gray paint on the floor and ceiling. White pillars supported the porch roof, but the floor with its loose boards sloped toward the lawn.

The yard was sprinkled with purple violets, dandelions, and the pinecones from the two blue spruce trees that towered over the house. In front of the porch was the dinner bell Grandma Trudy rang long ago to call the family to dinner. Jenny recalled how that dinner bell made lots of noise, yet she and her brothers, Matthew and Brad, had a hard time pulling it. It didn't stop any of them from trying. Matthew sure loved that bell more than anyone.

Across the driveway to her right, stood the old family barn with a huge hayloft covered by a roof with green wood shingles. A freshly painted white fence served to keep cattle in the barnyard. Jenny's heart was soothed by the familiar surroundings – the lush green landscape and the vast fields of corn and soybeans.

At sixty years old, Jenny had retired as an accountant from a firm in the city several hours away. Her husband, Ed, a professor at one of the state universities, had also retired early. They had moved back to be near Jenny's two brothers and her folks, Jed and Glenda Parker. Jed had suffered a massive stroke two years earlier, and Glenda had Alzheimer's disease. They now shared a room at the Oakwood Care Center.

Brad, Jenny's older brother, wearily stepped up onto the porch; his brown work boots were covered in mud from the cattle lot by the barn. Brushing the dust from his blue shirt and faded jeans, Brad sat down on the rocking chair near the swing. He took off his John Deere cap and wiped the sweat from his bald head and tanned face. Jenny noted that his rich, brown beard was now streaked with gray. He cleared his throat and said, "It's been a rough day."

"A good one, too, in a way," Jenny slowly replied. "I've been remembering the days when we were kids and shared so many pleasant times here with Grandpa Gordon and Grandma Trudy."

"Yep. We had many good times here. I've been remembering too, especially the day that forever changed our lives. Remember?" Brad thought back to the day over fifty-four years ago. The day was vivid in his memory. It was an event never to be forgotten. Brad rubbed his callused hands together as he recalled his childhood memories. Fifty-four years ago changed their lives forever.

PART 1

BIRTH TO TODDLER

CHAPTER 1

The sunlight shone through the sheer curtains of Jenny's bedroom window and warmed her face. Turning away from the light, she covered her face with the pale pink sheet that matched the walls of her room. Jenny kicked off the white chenille bedspread with pink flowers as she was awakened by the sunlight in her spacious room. She tossed in bed again and squinted her weary eyes at the maple bifold closet doors and her Barbie townhouse along the wall. She listened for the morning sounds of dishes clanking, Dad's deep voice, and the radio announcing the morning news. But it was so quiet, and the absence of these usual sounds made her break out in goose bumps as she shifted her body to a sitting position. Instead of smelling the pleasant aroma of pancakes on the griddle, she smelled nothing, and she sensed that something wasn't right. She slipped out of her bed and quickly changed into a tattered shirt and a faded pair of denim jeans. She crept down to her brother Brad's room and peered around the doorway. There was no sign of him, so she slowly stepped down the darkened stairway. The drapes were still drawn downstairs, and she now sensed that something was very different from the ordinary routine that she had grown used to when she first woke up every morning.

"Mom," she yelled, listening for a reply. Hearing nothing, she yelled louder, "Mom!" When there was no answer, Jenny's five-year-old body shook with fear as the goose bumps returned to her arms.

Jenny searched for her mom in the dark living room and family room and found them both empty. She walked toward the silent kitchen hoping to find her mom. Frightened now, she screamed, "Where is everyone?"

Grandma Trudy Rogers came out of the utility room and bathroom area off the large farm kitchen. Looking sternly at Jenny, she asked, "What's with all the screaming?"

Jenny felt bewildered that Grandma Trudy was at the house and no one else. She meekly stammered, "It's so dark. Where's Mom? I want my mom." She looked up at the stocky, sixty-two-year-old woman with tightly-curled, silver hair and a bold floral house dress that zipped up the front.

Grandma Trudy put her wrinkly arm around Jenny and tenderly spoke, "No reason to holler so. Your mom and dad left at six this morning for the hospital. She's having the baby, and you're going to be a big sister."

Jenny's spirit lightened. "The baby! She's having her baby!" Jenny shouted with glee and danced around in a circle.

"Go play, Jenny. I'll get you some breakfast. Brad already ate and is outdoors with Rick doing chores. What do you want?"

"Pancakes are my favorite, Grandma," Jenny told her merrily.

Jenny went into the living room where the golden drapes still covered the windows, and she sat on the long, tweed sofa. She imagined how the baby would be soft, cuddly, and fun.

As she opened the living room drapes, she wondered how long Mom and the baby would be gone before coming home. She looked out the window and down the steep hill at the highway where the heavy traffic was quickly passing by the house.

"Jenny! Come and get it! Breakfast is on!" Grandma Trudy hollered.

Jenny dashed into the kitchen and sat up to the oblong table with a red-checkered tablecloth. She inhaled a deep breath to smell the homemade, golden-brown pancake on her plate. She ate the first bite slowly as she savored the sweet, maple flavor.

While Grandma Trudy was folding clothes in the utility room, Jenny finished her pancake and rinsed off her plate.

Jenny went to the living room to watch Scooby Doo on the Saturday morning cartoons. As she watched Scooby and Shaggy eat a stack of sausages, she laughed. She went to the shelves of toys and picked out a Sesame Street puzzle to put together. Brad, her eight-year-old brother, came into the room.

"Whatcha doin' here?" he asked.

"Watchin' a cartoon and playing," she replied.

"Did you hear the news?" he inquired with a grin.

"Mom's havin' a baby today," she answered.

"Not only a baby," he teased, "but a baby boy. I know it."

"That's not true," Jenny spat. "You don't know that. I only want a girl, not another boy around here."

"We don't need another girl." He smirked as he left the room. A minute later, he peeked around the corner of the living room doorway. "Mom's havin' a boy! Mom's havin' a boy!" he teased.

"No she isn't!" Jenny argued. "She's having a girl!" She made a face at Brad and continued playing. She wondered if Mom was having a boy or girl.

Brad stepped into the living room after some time had passed. "We're goin' to Grandma's house soon. She's got work to do." Jenny turned off the television and disassembled her puzzle. Brad mischievously said, "I need a boy around here. Boys are superior to girls."

"Oh, please. Girls rule, not boys," Jenny smirked proudly.

"We have too many women around this place. I'm always stuck going with you, Mom, and Grandma. I'm outnumbered."

"Oh, I feel so sorry for you. Poor little Brad." She made a pouty face at him as she laughed. He picked up a pillow from the couch and threw it at her.

Grandma Trudy marched in and said, "Settle down you two. Your grandpa will be here any minute."

A few minutes later, Grandpa Gordon Rogers arrived in a rattly, late-sixties Ford pickup, with its rusty frame and livestock box; it mostly served as farm vehicle to transport baby calves and lambs to the barn. Grandpa Gordon hobbled slightly as he approached the house.

As he entered, he greeted them. "Hey, kiddos. Let's get Grandma home. We'll come back later if you need anything."

Brad shook hands with his grandpa and asked jokingly, "How you doin', Ole Timer?"

Gordon laughed and replied, "Feelin' old today, young man."

They all squeezed into the front of the pickup and headed to the Rogers' home place. The scent of freshly-tilled soil filled the air as farmers plowed the fields in preparation for spring planting. The rich, dark soil of the Midwest was a pleasant sight as the highway rolled along the rural landscape. Green pastures were scattered amongst the plowed fields filled with grazing cattle and newborn calves bounding with their tails high in the air.

As they pulled into the driveway, the children saw the Rogers' lavish, two-story home with a wrap-around porch. Grandma Trudy spent much of her day in the stylish home cooking for Gordon and his two hired men along with doing outside work, such as gardening and lawn care.

Gordon lived in this home where he had resided his whole life surrounded by memories of the Great Depression, his father's fatal car accident, and the tragic loss of his baby brother. Gordon lived a life full of adversity but with a spirit of perseverance.

Grandpa Gordon drove the pickup to the back door. Grandma Trudy and the children got out and went inside. They walked into the mud room where farm clothes hung on hooks and work boots sat on the floor against the wall in an orderly fashion. A white porcelain sink was mounted on the wall with Lava soap in a plastic dish and a towel on a roller to the left of the sink. Gordon and his hired men used this room to wash up before dinner.

Brad and Jenny climbed the three steps leading to the kitchen with its dark-blue linoleum floor and hand-constructed, white cupboards with silver handles. The spacious, burgundy countertop had Grandma's homemade sugar cookies sitting on paper towels. Upon noticing these cookies, the children licked their lips, and Brad begged, "May I please have a cookie? They are my favorite."

"Please, Grandma, they look so good," Jenny added.

"Wait until after dinner," Grandma Trudy commanded. She smiled and continued, "I'm glad you like them so well. They're your mom's favorite."

"I miss Mom," Jenny said sadly and frowned as she looked at the ground.

Grandma Trudy kissed Jenny's forehead and said, "You'll see her soon enough, sweetheart. Go play. We'll have dinner after a while."

Jenny and Brad ran out to the porch and chased each other around the old porch swing. They were careful not to run into the vine of roses on the trellis attached to the porch. While the children played, Grandma Trudy spent the morning preparing a dinner of roast beef, mashed potatoes and gravy, green beans, homemade bread, salad, and ice tea. She baked more of her sugar cookies with a dash of lemon flavoring.

At noon, Grandpa Gordon came in with his hired men, Clair and Buck, feeling hungry after a morning filled with cattle chores and other farm work. Jenny and Brad jabbed each other in the ribs sneakily to avoid being caught by Grandma Trudy throughout the noon meal. While everyone finished eating, Jed Parker, Brad and Jenny's dad, drove his green Ford LTD up to the back door.

He dragged his rugged, six-foot tall body to the door, weary from the early morning birth and the thirty-mile trip from the hospital. His sparkling blue eyes looked sad as he announced, "Glenda had a boy! He's twenty inches long and weighs seven pounds, five ounces. The birth went so fast that she almost didn't make it to the delivery room."

"What did you name him?" Grandma Trudy inquired.

"Matthew John Parker."

"Another boy, just what I need," Jenny grumbled and turned up her nose at Brad.

Brad began chanting, "Yahoo, it's a boy! I knew it!"

Usually soft-spoken and patient, Jed abruptly dismissed his children. "Brad, Jenny, I want to talk to Grandma and Grandpa alone. Go play."

They obeyed and went into the living room. They sensed that something wasn't right. While Jed whispered to Grandpa Gordon and Grandma Trudy, Jenny started back to the kitchen and stopped in the dining room when she overheard some serious, grown-up talk.

"Are the doctors sure?" Trudy moaned, "Can it be true?"

"The doctors are almost certain," Jed said sadly. "They noticed his ears are lower, his tongue is thicker, and his eyes are slanted. They had to draw blood from his heel. We won't know anything for sure until four weeks from now. The doctor talked so fast, I don't remember what he said they were checking. Glenda's taking it hard."

"You better get back to the hospital, Jed," Gordon suggested. "Glenda needs you now. We'll visit tonight, and Wilma can come over and babysit the kids." He patted Jed on the back.

Wilma had grown up in the same neighborhood as Grandpa Gordon and helped Grandma Trudy with babysitting and housework. She hired out to do domestic work for community families.

That evening, Wilma came out to the Rogers' home while Grandpa Gordon and Grandma Trudy went to the hospital. Her petite stature wasn't much taller than Brad's. Across her shoulder, she carried a brown canvas bag filled with games, cards, and crafts. Brad's and Jenny's eyes widened in awe as they saw the mysterious items in her bag. Wilma sat on the floor and played with them.

At six in the evening, Glenda's parents walked into the hospital room. They saw that Glenda's brown eyes were puffy, and her lips quivered. Gordon asked firmly, "What's going on?"

"They're concerned about Matthew's condition. There are many potential complications. We won't know for sure until another month, but the doctor said there are most likely going to be significant learning deficits."

Gordon breathed in slowly, thinking of what to say. "Glenda, I hope the tests turn out okay. Whatever we find out, we're a family. We'll deal with it!"

Glenda sobbed, "How could this happen?" Glenda was thirty-four years old. "This is all my fault. I'm too old to have a baby."

"You can't blame your age. Some things in life don't have a reason, Glenda. They just happen." Grandpa Gordon consoled her with a hug, and they sat with her for two hours. Finally, he said, "We have to get home to Jenny and Brad." Grandma Trudy and Grandpa Gordon kissed Glenda on the cheek then stopped at the nursery to admire the beautiful bundle snuggled in a blue blanket.

Grandpa Gordon said, "I don't know what's going on, but it sounds serious. Look at our sweet, new grandson. What could be wrong?" He wiped a tear from his eye and felt a lump in his throat.

"Our precious Glenda," Grandma Trudy cried. "The road ahead might be a rough one. It's so hard to see her in so much pain."

"It breaks my heart," Grandpa Gordon said. "Whatever is wrong, I'll have to be strong for her even though I'm worried about it."

"I know what you mean," Grandma Trudy sighed. "We have a long wait ahead of us."

CHAPTER 2

Three days later, Trudy and Jenny left early in the morning with Jed to pick up Matthew and Glenda from the hospital. Glenda sat in the lobby in a wheelchair with a nurse next to her. Her face was ghostlike and her eyes were red. With the assistance of Jed's strong arms around her, she walked unsteadily to the front seat of the car where eager family members were waiting. A nurse carried Matthew swaddled in a blue blanket and handed him to Jed once Glenda was settled in the car.

Trudy looked at Matthew and smiled. "What a sweet baby. Oh, the fresh scent of new life. Isn't it wonderful?"

Jenny sat in the back of the car and leaned up toward her new baby brother and scrutinized his tiny fingers, small body, and his soft face. He might not be so bad for a boy, she thought. I think that I can love him. What a cute, tiny person.

Jenny blinked away tears when she saw her mom's pale face and red eyes, "Mom, are you okay? You look awful."

Glenda noticed Jenny's fear. "I'm tired, honey, but I'm okay. I need some rest. Wilma will come down for a few days to help me take care of the meals and the house. She babysat me when I was little."

Jenny sighed and touched Matthew's tiny fingers, stroking them. She touched the softness of his cheeks. As she looked the new boy over again, she burst out saying, "He is the most handsome, adorable, sensational, sweetest, loveable, softest, and wonderful baby in the whole wide world." She spread her arms out wide. "I love my baby brother."

Tears trickled down Glenda's cheeks. Trudy patted Jenny's back and said, "You're already a good big sister."

"How are you doing, Glenda?" Jed's blue eyes glanced with concern at his wife.

"Okay," she said sadly.

As the grown-ups talked, Jenny continued to touch Matthew's soft cheeks and feel the tiny fingers. She touched his squishy nose, and Matthew squirmed a little as Jenny touched it.

"Let him rest, Jenny," Trudy spoke softly. "You've got plenty of time to admire him later.

"Okay," Jenny answered. "He's just so irresistible."

"I know, sweetie. You're so happy to see him. He needs sleep though."

When they arrived home, Jed carried Matthew to the bassinet in the living room. Glenda was going to sleep there for the first few nights to be close to the kitchen to make bottles when needed. The stairs of the house were so steep that she also wanted to stay downstairs until she gained her strength.

After settling the baby and Glenda into the house, Jed went out to do the farm work. Brad was in school and would come home in a few hours. The women let Matthew sleep in the bassinet and congregated in the kitchen.

"Wilma, will you please make the noon meal, wash laundry, do the dishes, and clean house while you're here? I have a menu written out for dinners."

"Whatever you need, Glenda. I'm glad to help out. I'm so sorry that you have to go through this. I can't believe how long you have to wait."

"I know you are. Thanks. I'm so grateful you're willing to help us."

Trudy said, "Ladies, I need to get home." She gave Glenda a big hug and said, "It's going to be okay." She turned to Wilma. "You're a lifesaver. We'll talk later."

Jenny tiptoed into the living room to peek at Matthew as he breathed slowly, motionless. She walked up to him, and she bent down to his ear and whispered, "I don't know why Mom's so sad right now. You must be a lot of trouble. I think you're wonderful, and I'll take good care of you. I love you, love you, love you." Jenny kissed his cheek softly, and she kissed his tiny hands." You're so soft and sweet. My brother. I'll love you always."

She heard Wilma whispering in the kitchen. "We'll pray for the best. We have to be patient and see."

Glenda cried, "But he may never be able to do much. We may not even have him very long."

Wilma wrapped her tiny arms around Glenda, speaking softly, "I'm here for you, honey." She patted Glenda tenderly on the back.

Jenny was confused. *What's going on? What are they saying?* She crept to the bassinet again and looked at Matthew. "I don't know what the secrets are, but you're going to be just fine. I love you very much." She kissed him again and left the room to go outside to play.

Brad darted off the bus at 4:00 p.m. and ran to Jenny, who was on the tire swing. Brad asked, "What's he look like? I'm so thrilled to have a brother."

"He's cute for a boy. But the grown-ups keep whispering and crying about him. I don't understand why."

"Grown-ups never make sense," Brad replied. "They're not like us."

"They are very serious about something, but I love Matthew already, even if he is a boy."

"I'm going to see him." Brad ran into the house ahead of Jenny. He found him lying in the bassinet. Matthew was stirring and moving his mouth while his blue eyes opened a bit. Brad teasingly said, "He looks handsome just like me." Brad patted himself on his chest.

"Oh, please," Jenny said. "He'll be ugly if he looks like you."

CHAPTER 3

Four weeks after Matthew's birth, Glenda and the adults continued having whispering voices in the household. Jenny didn't understand and wondered why the grown-ups had so many secrets to keep from her and Brad. She saw that her mom had changed from a bubbly, fun person to someone solemn with red, puffy eyes. Glenda stood at the sink doing dishes, oblivious to Jenny's and Brad's pleas to play a game or talk. Instead, she sang hymns from her childhood and stared out the window. All she could think about was the call from her doctor she received yesterday telling her that Matthew has Down syndrome. He did assure her that it appeared to be a minimal case, but there would be learning deficits and potential health issues. He had mild to moderate retardation. Glenda cringed at those words. Her beautiful baby wasn't going to be normal like other children.

Brad and Jenny discussed the change at home while they were outside on the tire swing. Brad suggested, "Mom might be tired from waking up in the night. Babies cry a lot, and Dad doesn't get up with Matthew. We don't know how often Mom's awake. She must be worn out."

"Yes," Jenny agreed. "We need to help Mom more so she gets rest. I don't want her so sad and tired. She doesn't play games with me anymore."

"Let's help her more in the house and not ask much from her. We can dust, sweep, and pick up our toys. Wilma's here, but she's here only for the mornings and dinner, and she won't be here for long."

"I love Wilma," Jenny declared. "She's fun to have around, but she can't play with us. She works so hard."

"Wilma's like our own grandma."

At noon that day, Gordon drove down to see how things were going since Glenda received the heartbreaking news about Matthew. He felt torn up inside, but he couldn't let Glenda know that. He had to help her come to grips and accept the situation. He walked into the back hall, then to the kitchen where he saw Wilma taking hot dishes from the oven.

"Good morning, Gordon," she said as she set rolls on a plate. "Are you here to see the grandchildren, or are you joining us for dinner? We have plenty of food."

"I'm here for both dinner and to see the children, but I also want to see how Glenda's doing after finding out about Matthew's disability."

"She's still weepy and disconnected," Wilma replied. "We're all shook up about it. I try not to say anything to upset her. It'll take time for her to accept things."

"Life gives us unexpected events. We need to be strong. I hope she comes to the point of realizing that we must accept it and press forward."

Wilma looked sympathetically at Gordon. "The church and community are all praying for you. Rest assured that we love your family and will be a support to all of you no matter what happens."

"Thanks, Wilma. Where's Glenda? I thought she'd be up by now."

"She's taking a late shower. She was awake several hours last night."

Gordon sat down and waited patiently for the meal to be served. Wilma set the table with fried chicken, mashed potatoes, cooked carrots, Jell-O and bananas, and homemade rolls. Jed and Rick, the hired hand, came in and washed in the back hall. Jed scrubbed his hands that were stained with grease and dirt from greasing the tractor and planter in preparation for spring planting. Rick hummed a Johnny Cash song in a deep voice that Jenny and Brad admired as he ran his hands through his brown, curly hair. At thirty-three years old, he had much strength despite his short, frail-looking physique.

"Children, time for dinner," Wilma called.

Glenda came into the kitchen with bloodshot eyes, her hair neatly combed around her face. She wore a brown blouse with khaki slacks and looked forlorn. "May I help you with something, Wilma?"

"You just sit down and relax. I've got everything ready."

Glenda saw the pan of freshly baked and frosted chocolate brownies on the counter. "I'll cut these into small bars."

Jed spoke, "Let's say grace." All but Glenda closed their eyes and bowed their heads. "Lord, thank you for this food and for all the blessings we have received from you. Amen."

Grandpa Gordon looked at Glenda. "Come join us, Glenda. We want to eat with you."

Glenda had her back to him and was busily cutting the brownies while humming a song.

He repeated, "Come and eat something. You need to have a meal with your family." Glenda stopped humming as she recognized his authoritative tone. She turned toward the table exposing her red, swollen eyes with dark circles beneath them.

Gordon continued gently and firmly, "Listen, I know you have been crying. I also know you didn't get much sleep last night. But, now that we know about his disability, we all have to come to terms with it and accept it. We'll be patient and love Matthew just as we love Brad and Jenny."

Glenda started sobbing, "But I don't know what will happen. I can't live with this."

"Yes, you can," Gordon said softly.

Jed added, "This is still quite a shock, Gordon. It's so unexpected. We have no knowledge or understanding of it."

"Jed, your patience will be a great asset. We'll hope for the best and keep our sights high." Gordon turned to Glenda. "You have not one, but three children to raise. Deal with this. Your mom and I are here for you. Wilma can help longer if needed. We can handle it."

Glenda looked down as Gordon addressed her and thought how she hadn't given much attention to Jenny and Brad lately. She had withdrawn into her own world of doubts and sorrow. Her dad was right when he said she had to make the best of this, but it seemed so unfair. For the sake of her own children, she had to stand strong. It was so difficult to handle, and she wished she could turn back the hands of time. She wished this had never happened, and that she had never had this child.

CHAPTER 4

September was cold and rainy and kept the farmers out of the field when they were eager to harvest the ripe crops. Matthew caught a severe cold that caused him to cough through the night for several days. It progressed to the point that he gasped for air when sleeping. Glenda made an appointment with Dr. Wilhelm, the family pediatrician.

The day after the call to the doctor, Glenda and Trudy drove to the office in the city. Dr. Wilhelm's reception area was filled with noisy, coughing children. Trudy snuggled Matthew in her arms as Glenda checked in at the reception desk.

Glenda sat down with Trudy and Matthew in the crowded waiting room. Soon a young, cheerful nurse dressed in all white from her cap to her shoes called, "Matthew Parker." She led Glenda and her son back to an examining room and took his pulse, blood pressure, and temperature. "The doctor will be right in to see you," she told Glenda sweetly.

Glenda noticed Dr. Wilhelm's dark, red hair and bright smile as he entered the examination room. The young doctor shook Glenda's hand and said, "Good to see you again, Mrs. Parker. How can I help you?" Glenda explained the details of Matthew's cough the past several nights. Dr. Wilhelm thoroughly examined Matthew and said, "I believe he has a respiratory infection. He'll need to be on antibiotics for ten days. He should stay home and not go anywhere until his symptoms improve. I also want to give him an elixir for the cough. If he's not better in one week, call my office. If he worsens, take him to the emergency room, and I'll come personally. I don't like the sound of his cough."

"Thank you, Dr. Wilhelm," Glenda said.

"Glenda, Matthew is a blessing," Dr. Wilhelm told her.

Glenda smiled slightly and didn't respond.

When Dr. Wilhelm handed her the two prescription papers and left the room, Glenda walked out to Trudy who was reading *Good Housekeeping* in the waiting area. Trudy held Matthew while Glenda paid for the doctor's visit at the front.

One week passed, and Matthew's cough persisted. There was no inkling of improvement. Glenda called Dr. Wilhelm. He told her to make another appointment for the next day. He said the receptionist would squeeze it into the schedule.

Again, Glenda, Trudy, and Matthew went to Dr. Wilhelm's office. He ordered blood work and a chest x-ray and prescribed a different cough medicine. "Go home and get some rest. We'll call you tomorrow with the lab results. That should give us some answers. If he needs a different medicine, I'll let the pharmacy know rather than have you come back to my office."

When Glenda got home, she collapsed on the couch in the living room. Wilma stayed all day to help with housework and babysitting. Gordon and Trudy came down in the evening to visit. Gordon played rummy with the children, and Trudy talked to Glenda about Matthew's condition.

"Is Matthew going to die, Grandpa?" Jenny asked.

"He's quite sick, but I think he'll be fine," Gordon comforted.

"He sure has been lots of trouble," Jenny said matter-of-factly.

Gordon said nothing and continued playing with the children.

During the next several days, Glenda often took a nap since Matthew continued gasping for air at night and kept her awake. She feared how serious his condition was and wondered if he would ever get better.

Jed offered, "Honey, I think you need to get out of the house. Let me watch Matthew while you and the kids go to church on Sunday."

Glenda let out a big sigh. "I'd love to get out and see our friends there. Thank you so much, Jed."

Jed stroked Glenda's cheek and ran his fingers through her soft, brown hair. He leaned forward and kissed her gently on the lips. "I love you, darling."

Glenda returned the kiss and wrapped her arms around his neck, holding onto him a while.

On the following Sunday, Glenda, Brad, and Jenny went to White Chapel Church. The church was a quarter mile from Gordon's farm home and served descendants of farmers who first settled in the community over one hundred years earlier. Glenda saw the white structure that resembled a one-room schoolhouse. She parked in the gravel parking lot surrounded by fields of corn and soybeans. Glenda, Brad, and Jenny entered the small sanctuary and sat in a wooden pew near Gordon and Trudy.

Flora, an elderly member, stepped up to the piano with the swivel stool and opened the hymnal to the first song. The congregation began singing "What a Friend We Have in Jesus," and Trudy sang enthusiastically in her off-key voice. Glenda sat peacefully and savored the opportunity of silence.

Dressed in his powder blue suit and brown loafers, Pastor Scott stood up to the oak podium with an engraved cross and large, red Bible on it. "Good morning. I'm glad to see everyone this morning."

"Good morning," the small congregation of fifty simultaneously said.

"I have a question for each of you. What does it mean to live a life pleasing to the Lord? How do we please him in the midst of trials?"

Glenda thought about how Matthew's birth and illness was a trial and burden in her life.

Pastor Scott continued, "God gives us events in our lives to help us grow closer to him. God gives us peace and wraps his arms around us to comfort us."

Glenda reflected about how God gave her a child that wasn't going to have a life like other children. She wondered how she could ever find any peace in that situation.

Ending the sermon in prayer, the pastor prayed, "Thank you God for having a plan for our lives. Be with us through life's fiery trials. Help us remember to seek you for comfort. Amen."

Pastor Scott dismissed the congregation and walked down the aisle to greet each of the members. The people smiled and shook hands with one another and bid each other a good week. Ruby, a petite, middle-aged woman with coal black hair, walked up to Glenda. Since Glenda hadn't shared with anyone outside of the family about Matthew's illness, she was surprised when Ruby snapped at her.

"So, where is that child of yours? Are you hiding him?"

Smiling sweetly, Glenda took a deep breath and meekly answered, "He has a cough and is unable to leave the house until it clears."

"I bet," Ruby countered rudely. "You're ashamed of him just like most parents are."

Glenda walked away and bit her tongue. She wondered what had possessed Ruby to speak to her like that. As she got the children into the car, she thought of the cruel words spoken to her and hit the steering wheel hard. She put on her sunglasses to hide the fury building inside her and drove home. Stifling tears, she mumbled, "Why, Lord? Why have you brought him into my life?"

At home, Glenda and the children changed from their church attire into clean farm clothes. Jed held Matthew gently in his arms as he coughed continuously despite all of the medications.

"Jed, Ruby asked me if I was hiding him. She was so rude."

As she sobbed, Jed put Matthew down and wrapped his strong, masculine arms around her and wiped the tears that streamed down her cheeks. He said, "People are going to talk and say things. We must ignore negative comments and do the best we can." He tenderly kissed her forehead and stroked his fingers through her soft, brown hair.

Jed got up and called Trudy. "I wondered if you two could come down for dinner. It would be good for Glenda to have company after what happened in church."

"Sure thing," Trudy replied. "We'll go to Chicken Haven and pick up some broasted chicken, coleslaw, and beans. Our treat."

"Thanks, Trudy. Sounds good. See you later." Jed hung up the phone. "Brad, Jenny, set the table with paper plates and cups. Grandpa and Grandma are bringing dinner from Chicken Haven."

"Yippee," Jenny shouted. "I can't wait."

"I get the legs," Brad teased as he set paper plates on the table.

"I want the legs," Jenny whined.

"I'm the oldest, so I pick first," Brad snickered.

"What about ladies first?" asked Jenny. "You need to be a gentleman and let me pick first."

"Oldest one rules," said Brad.

Trudy and Gordon arrived carrying the bundle of food in plastic bags and a gallon jug of root beer. The chicken tasted delicious with its crispy-coated skin and juicy meat. The special treat of root beer had a sweet flavor that was savored by everyone. After lunch, the children went outside to play, and Glenda filled her parents in on what had happened at church.

"Glenda," Trudy said, "I want you to know that Ruby's been thoughtless for years. She has no tact or consideration of others' feelings. I'm sorry you had to experience this."

Glenda sniffed, "I am not trying to hide him. I can't believe she would accuse me of that."

Trudy patted her on the leg. "I know, dear. Gossip is going to continue. That's the nature of people. It isn't right, but it won't change. You need to forgive her and let this go. I've had to forgive her many times."

Glenda was astonished and remarked, "You have?"

"Yes. It hasn't always been easy either, but I have learned that she can be most unkind. Remember, most of our church friends are gracious and loving."

With little strength left in her, Glenda felt numb from crying. *Why can't things be different? Why was he even born?* She shuddered and immediately dismissed her thoughts. A wave of guilt swept over her for questioning his birth.

Two days later, Matthew spit up in his crib in the night. Glenda gathered the velour blanket and replaced it with a handmade baby quilt. During the night, he had slept without one cough for the first time in weeks. Glenda awoke the next morning feeling rested from a full night's sleep and told Jed, "Just like magic. He slept soundly without one cough."

"That's good news. He's on the mend," Jed exclaimed.

"A breakthrough at last," Glenda said.

The next evening after Glenda washed the blanket and put it back in the crib, Matthew coughed so much, he was gasping for air. Glenda crawled out of bed and removed it. His cough stopped, and Glenda figured out that he was allergic to the material. She folded the blanket and stored it in the cedar chest.

CHAPTER 5

Although Matthew didn't walk by one year old, he crawled quickly all around the house. In fact, his agility and the strength of his arms was astonishing. One day, Matthew crawled across the kitchen carpet toward a flimsy portable cupboard. He grasped the handle of the metal drawer and swung up on the countertop. He reached for the higher cupboard door and stood up on the counter. He opened the door and smiled. Inside was his favorite box of cereal. He grabbed the cereal, and it fell all over the floor. Glenda chuckled and said, "Come on, my little monkey. Let's get you down from there." She wrapped her arms around him and set him on the floor.

Glenda returned to her sink full of dishes while Matthew kicked his feet and whined. Sneakily crawling back to the cupboard, he got himself up again and grinned. Glenda quickly shook the soap suds off her hands and hurried over to Matthew. "No. No. Stay off."

When Jed came in for dinner, she asked him, "What can I do to keep him off the counters? I can't get any work done. I'm getting him away from the cupboard dozens of times a day."

Jed rubbed his chin, thinking of a solution. "I know what we can do. It'll be inconvenient, but we'll have to put him in the play pen while you do your work."

"Won't work. He already climbs out of that."

"Hmm. We may need to put up a child safety gate to keep him out of the kitchen. I think that could work. When Jenny is home, she can watch Matthew in the family room. This will make things easier."

"I like that idea," Glenda said. "It should help."

They purchased a child safety gate and put it between the kitchen and dining room. Glenda placed two dining room chairs against the open stairway with its beautiful oak banister to keep Matthew from crawling up the steep stairs.

As soon as the gate was set up, Matthew pushed a chair against it, climbed on it, and jumped down on the kitchen floor. Glenda laughed as she thought how resourceful he was when he made up his mind to do something.

When Matthew saw the chairs blocking the stairway, he tried to squeeze his body underneath. Unable to get through, he climbed up on one chair and grabbed the banister. Using his upper arm strength, he hung on to the railing and swung his leg over it. He looked like a cowboy on a horse. He slid his body to the brown shag carpet and raced up the steps.

While Matthew was climbing, Jenny had been sock-footed on the oak hardwood floor acting as if she were an ice skater. She suddenly noticed Matthew at the top of the stairs and removed the chairs to get him.

Jenny couldn't carry him down the stairs. She yelled, "Mom! Mom! Come get Matthew!"

"What happened?" she questioned. "I thought you were watching him."

"He climbed over the banister. He got up there so fast, I couldn't catch up with him."

Glenda chuckled. "I cannot keep him out of anything. No grass will grow under his feet."

Jenny laughed with her mom. "He's a little daredevil."

Glenda agreed. "I hope he doesn't fall. He has no fear."

When Jed came in for the noon meal, Glenda told him all about the morning's events. He laughed heartily with her and responded, "He's quite a running bear." Jed slipped his muscular arm around Glenda's waist and kissed her tenderly on the lips. "He's sure agile and strong."

Jed removed the gate to open the doorway between the rooms. Hearing the hired hand Rick's voice in the back hall, Matthew crawled over to him and raised his arms. Rick picked him up and asked, "How's my little buddy today?" Matthew wrapped his small arms around Rick's neck and gave him a squeeze.

"Ick, Ick," Matthew said, repeating it over and over.

Rick grinned and said, "Matthew, I helped your dad feed cows today and worked in the shop." Rick set him down and found a seat at the table filled with the fixings of a dinner meant to satisfy a farmer's appetite.

Jed prayed, "Thank you, God, for the food and for the strength Matthew has. Thank you for our blessings. Amen." Matthew unfolded his hands and opened his eyes.

After dinner, Jed said, "Rick, I want to show you what Matthew did while we were outside today. He is quite a monkey. I'm calling him Running Bear. He is so quick and gets around wherever he wants to without even walking yet."

Jed showed Rick how the chairs were set up by the stairway and how Matthew climbed over the top. Rick beamed. "He sure is a running bear."

---*---

The summer when Matthew just turned two years old, Jed had made plans to transform a broken-down corn crib into a shop and garage area. He sat at his office desk and diagrammed how the crib with a leaky roof and rotting side boards would become a useful building. His sketch depicted the measurements of the structure to enable him to purchase accurate amounts of supplies for the project.

Step ladders were placed against the corn crib as Jed and Rick spent several hours a day nailing down metal sheets for the roof. The clanking sounds of nails being hammered filled the farmyard.

Every morning, Glenda baked a special sweet treat for a break from the monotonous labor the men were doing. She made a chocolate mayonnaise cake with white frosting and filled a Tupperware pitcher with iced tea.

Glenda called, "Jenny, help me get these snacks out to Jed and Rick."

"Why can't Brad do it?" Jenny complained. "I'm watching Matthew. We're playing here in the family room."

"Brad is with your grandpa today. Please come now," Glenda commanded.

Jenny slowly came out to the kitchen to grab the cups and pitcher. She wondered who would watch Matthew while they took out the treats, but her mom didn't seem too concerned. The two of them walked out to the men.

Glenda called, "Hey, guys, how are things going?"

"Great," answered Rick from the top of the ladder. "Do you have some of your goodies for us?"

"Yes," she replied. "I made a mayonnaise cake for you two. I thought you might be hungry. Why don't you stand here under this tree in the shade?"

Jed and Rick stepped down from the ladders and met Glenda under the cool shade of the tree. Rick gulped down two glasses of tea and took a bite of the rich, moist cake. Licking his lips, he said, "Mm. I love the chocolate flavor."

Jed agreed, "Glenda knows it's my favorite."

"Glenda, you sure know how to bake. Give this recipe to my wife."

While they were standing around talking about the shop construction, Matthew sneaked out the back door. Seeing the ladder propped against the corn crib, he ran over to it. Seeing no one around, he placed his hands on the rungs of the ladder and raced to the top.

As Glenda talked to Jed and Rick, she suggested to Jenny, "I think now is a good time for you to go in and check in on Matthew."

"Okay," Jenny said grudgingly. "I'll check on him." Jenny walked toward the house.

Jed switched the conversation back to the building job. "We should finish this floor for the storage attic tomorrow. Next, we'll put up the siding. If it doesn't rain, we should be done with the outside work in a week. The rest is no hurry." He looked around. "Where's Running Bear today? I haven't seen him since breakfast."

"He's in the house playing," she explained.

"Well, I want to see him and show him the work Rick and I've done out here."

Just then Jenny dashed out of the house. "I can't find him! I've looked everywhere in the house! He's gone!" she yelled.

"Jenny, you were supposed to watch him," Glenda accused.

"But, Mom, you told me it was okay to leave him while I helped you bring out the snacks for Dad and Rick."

"There is no excuse, Jenny. Don't sass me." Glenda welled up in terror.

"Calm down, Glenda," Jed ordered. "If you asked Jenny to help you, then she did nothing wrong. We'll find him."

She trembled in fear and felt a sense of panic. "It's all her fault that he's missing."

Rick shrugged his shoulders. Glenda was frantic with thoughts of Matthew running to the lane toward the heavily traveled highway. Jed spoke calmly to Glenda, "No need to turn your fear into accusing Jenny. She did what you asked. We'll look for him."

Glenda shrieked loudly, "We've got to find him. A car could run over him or…"

Rick hollered, "Matthew, where are you?"

Jed shouted, "Matthew!"

Red-faced and filled with anxiety, Glenda looked angrily at Jenny. Jenny couldn't believe her mom's unusual behavior and thought how it wasn't fair. *Mom asked me to come out with her. She's blaming me for something that isn't my fault. At least, Dad understands that.*

Jed and Rick checked the highway and hog lots but found no sign of Matthew. He was fast, but he could not have gone much farther than those places in such a short time. "Jed, I'll check the barn," Rick offered.

"Good idea." Jed turned to Glenda. "You owe Jenny an apology. You were out of line treating her so."

"She was irresponsible. Where's Matthew?"

"Calm down. You're making things worse. We'll find him."

Jed walked over by the ladder, looked up, and saw Matthew standing at the top.

"There you are," he said. "We've been looking everywhere for you."

Matthew smiled and looked proud of himself for going up the ladder. "Me up."

Glenda saw him and shouted, "Get him down from there! He could fall! He could get hurt!"

"He must have been there a while," Jed said amusedly. "He's agile, and the likelihood that he'll fall is slim. If you panic, it'll scare him."

Matthew said again, "Me up." He was bouncing his body up and down. Glenda listened to Jed, but she was anxious to see him get down from there.

Jed calmly climbed the ladder and wrapped his muscular arm around Matthew. As he held Matthew, Jed showed Matthew the tools they used and what they constructed. "Look what we've been doing up here, Running Bear." He gave Matthew a moment to look around and then said, "It's time to come down now so I can get to work."

Matthew responded, "Me up. Me do. Me do."

"Not with this, Matthew," he explained. "One day I will teach you how to use tools so you can be my right hand man. Come on down, buddy."

When Matthew climbed down, Glenda told Jenny to take him in the house. "Don't let him out of your sight again." Glenda went back into the house to do dishes and prepare the noon meal.

Jenny grabbed Matthew by the hand and led him to the house. She heard her mom speak calmer now that they had found Matthew safe and sound.

PART 2

AGE THREE TO PRESCHOOL

CHAPTER 6

During the summer when Matthew was three years old, the August temperatures reached one hundred degrees Fahrenheit. The Parker family packed for a trip to the sand hills of western Nebraska where Jed had worked as a ranch hand when he was a teenager. Jed's friends lived on a ranch seven hundred miles away and raised hundreds of cattle. Glenda filled a metal thermos with water, gathered pillows, and checked her packing list.

Already at six in the morning, Glenda loaded the car for the journey. Jenny awoke and saw Matthew running around the house chanting, "Me go. Go car." She wondered how he could possibly sit in the car.

"What's for breakfast, Mom?" Jenny asked.

"We're going to eat once we're on the road. Your dad likes big breakfasts, and he wants to stop at a full-service restaurant to eat."

"What do they have for breakfast?" Jenny asked.

"Pancakes, eggs, French toast, sausage, rolls, and more," Glenda answered. "I have to get back to loading now. We plan to leave in one hour."

After the Parker family piled into the car, Jenny and Brad restlessly began hitting one another with pillows. Matthew was sitting in the front seat between his parents. "Vacation's great," Brad yelled. "I get to torment Jenny for hours."

Glenda said, "Settle down, kids. We have a long trip ahead of us."

Jed explained, "Our first stop is breakfast. I heard about a small town café from some of my friends. Once we eat, we'll be on our way to Pioneer Town."

The family came to Brentwood, a small town with a well-known café that featured farmers' breakfasts. The restaurant looked full.

Jed said, "A busy restaurant is a sign of good food."

The small, rectangular building had a welcome sign posted on the faded entryway door. Inside, next to a revolving display of pies and cakes, a sign told customers to wait to be seated. A young waitress with blond, curly hair scurried past with a tray of food in her hands.

The hostess seated the Parker family at a long rectangular table and passed out four menus. "Your waitress is Cindy. She'll be over in a few minutes."

"I'm starving," Brad said. "I smell pancakes, bacon, and sausage. It makes my stomach growl."

"Look what that waitress is taking to that table. Scrambled eggs and waffles. Yum!" Jenny licked her lips.

The young blond waitress they had seen earlier was Cindy. She was bubbly as she asked, "What can I start you off with for drinks? Are you folks from around here, or are you traveling?"

Jed answered, "We just started out for a vacation to the sand hills of Nebraska. I used to live and work there. We're visiting friends and stopping at some places along the way."

Cindy smiled, "I grew up on a ranch in western Nebraska. I used to participate in the rodeo and do barrel racing." She turned to Matthew, "Do you like cows and horses? Are you excited?"

Matthew smiled and gave a thumbs-up. Jed replied, "This is the first vacation for the children. They have never been to a ranch before. I want them to see what it's like out there. It's so open and quiet."

"I miss it out there. It was a great place to be raised," Cindy replied. "Have a wonderful trip."

While waiting for their food, Matthew had his tongue out a little bit, which he could not help since his tongue was thicker than normal. Noticing two tables of children staring at Matthew and quietly snickering, Jenny asked, "Why are those kids staring at us like that?"

Glenda got a stern look on her face and said loudly, "That's because some parents haven't taught their children any manners. Some people are so rude."

One of the moms heard Glenda speak and got after her children for staring so much. She gave an apologetic look in the Parker family's direction.

The other mom turned up her nose and said, "Just look at them with that strange child. They don't belong in here."

Cindy brought out their food at the same instant that the comment was made. "I'm so glad to see you here. It isn't every day I meet people who are traveling to the same stomping grounds where I was raised. I hope you enjoy your meal and your trip." She patted Matthew on the shoulder. "You have a sweet family." She glared at the woman that had spoken so cruelly about them.

Jed got out the cash from his tattered brown wallet and reached for a $20 dollar bill. The manager came to the cash register. "My waitress said that there were some rude customers in here. I want you to know that this isn't typical of our community. We are friendly folk. My apologies to you. This breakfast is on the house, and I want to give each of the children a bottle of root beer for the road."

"We can't accept such a kind act," Jed refused. "We are hardworking, respectable folks and want to pay our bill."

"If you want to pay, then pay. But let me give your children each a root beer. You're a special family to care for your younger boy. Bless you all. Have a wonderful vacation."

Jed paid for the bill and graciously accepted three bottles of root beer. Jenny and Brad simultaneously said, "Thank you!"

Matthew grinned and put a thumbs-up and said, "Tanks."

"You're most certainly welcome," the manager said warmly. "The children have good manners."

"Thank you," Jed replied.

The morning dragged on as they drove along miles and miles of corn and hay fields. Hot wind blew into the car, providing little relief from the heat. With the exception of Glenda snoring and Matthew humming, the car was quiet. Jenny and Brad pointed silently at their mom, mocking her snoring.

Brad mischievously took his pillow and threw it in Jenny's face. "Stop it!" she hollered. "Leave me alone." She clenched the pillow in her hands and hit Brad in the side several times. "There, that serves you right."

Glenda stirred and mumbled, "Settle down, kids."

"Tell Jenny to knock it off. She won't leave me alone. She started it all."

"Jenny, leave Brad alone," Glenda said under her breath.

Jed wiped the beads of sweat from his brow and firmly said, "Knock it off." He stopped at a gas station in Davidston to fill up with gas. An attendant in a gray, one-piece coverall with the name Gregg sewn on it asked, "How can I help you, sir?"

"Fill 'er up, please," Jed requested.

Gregg pumped the gas, cleaned the windows, and checked the oil and tires. "I think you're all set," Gregg said when he was finished.

As they continued the monotonous journey, Jenny turned away from Brad while he opened his mouth wide and turned up his nose making snorting sounds. She kicked his feet, and he pulled off her brown sandals. Matthew tipped his hand to his mouth for a drink. Glenda poured the thermos cup half full of water and he took a sip "Ah, good," he said as he drank. With the little bit left in the cup, he tossed it behind him.

"Stop it, Matthew," whined Jenny. "Don't throw water."

Matthew laughed. "More, more," he said.

"No more, Matthew," Glenda said. "You've had enough."

"Mom, I want some water. I'm really thirsty," Jenny said while she mischievously looked at her younger brother. Jenny drank a smidgen and threw the rest on Matthew, getting his hair and shirt wet.

"Cool. Ah, good. Me like," Matthew said.

Glenda got after Jenny, "Don't get even with Matthew. You're the big sister and need to set an example."

At two in the afternoon, Jed pulled into Pioneer Town with its modern, two-story motel. They checked into their spacious room with two queen-sized beds and a cot. The simple décor and green shag carpet created a homey feeling. After unpacking, Jed remarked, "I'm hungry. Let's eat, then go into Pioneer Town."

Inside the motel, Matthew was jumping on the beds as if they were trampolines and leaping from one bed to another. Jenny bounced on one of the beds.

"Get down from there, and let's go eat," Jed ordered.

The Parkers viewed the various collections of antique tractors, cars, and farm equipment. The little village of pioneer buildings was similar to a park. Jenny led Matthew around to the buildings while Jed and Brad stood and talked about the early days of farming. Jenny's arm ached from Matthew pulling and yanking on her. He pulled loose of her hold and ran from one building to another.

Trying to catch up to him, she hollered, "Stop! Get back here!"

Matthew tried to duck underneath places that were blocked off with rope when Jenny caught up to him. "Let's go find Dad," she said panting for breath.

Matthew raced toward the black locomotive he saw in the distance. "No, you don't. You stay with me," Jenny said. He scurried in the direction of the train and quickly climbed inside it before Jenny caught up to him.

A father and son were inside blowing the whistle. When they stepped off the train, Matthew smiled and blew the train whistle several times. He bounced up and down in excitement.

"Come on, get down," Jenny pleaded.

"No. Me choo choo. Me like." He stood with his feet firmly on the floor and arms across his chest. Jenny tried to nudge him, but his body was heavy as lead.

A jolly, middle-aged man came on and said, "You really like this train, don't you?"

Matthew gave the man a thumbs-up and blew the whistle again, sending a shrill sound through the museum.

The man said, "I remember blowing that whistle when I was a train engineer. We warned people we were coming down the track."

Matthew smiled at this stranger. He pointed to himself and said, "Me do. Me choo choo. Me like. Choo choo."

The kind man smiled and said, "Maybe you can be a train engineer one day." He stepped down from the train.

Jenny slouched in the engineer's seat, leaned forward, and rested her head. She waited and waited, listening to Matthew blow the whistle.

At last, Jed and Brad climbed the train, and Matthew leaped into Jed's arms. He said, "Choo. Choo. Me do. Me like."

"Let's get you down from here, buddy. We have more to see," Jed explained as he carried Matthew off the train.

After a restful sleep, the Parkers loaded up the car for their journey to the ranch. Jed told stories of his ranching days. "We stayed in a bunkhouse with six other cowboys. We rode horses, rounded up cattle, and branded them."

"What is branding?" asked Jenny.

Jed explained, "Branding is what ranchers use to put their identity on the cattle. Each rancher has a special brand so that he knows which cattle belong to him. He heats a branding iron over a fire and places it on the animal's skin to make a permanent mark."

"Ouch!" Jenny yelled out. "That's awful. Ranchers are mean."

"No, Jenny. It isn't mean. It would hurt us terribly. But cattle are different. Cattle have thick skins. The hide is used to make leather products. It's not hurtful to the cattle at all."

"Cattle are real tough then," Jenny said. "What kinds of things are made of leather?"

Jed continued, "Many products are made from leather such as purses, furniture, and shoes."

Matthew attentively listened and clapped his hands. "Me go. Me see cow. Me like."

"I liked the freedom of being on a horse and being in the middle of nowhere. It was so peaceful. People are so friendly and laid-back."

"Can we ride horses there?" Brad asked.

"We'll see," Jed answered. "I don't know what Marty has for horses. I'll probably go with him to see the ranch again. Steve and Tara will have lots for you to play."

Matthew smiled and said, "Me cowboy. Me happy cowboy."

It was late afternoon when the Parkers drove into the long lane leading to the plain, white home with black shutters. Two eager children were peering through the window as the car slowly approached. Tara ran out first with her blond curls bouncing. She was Jenny's age and dressed in a pink hat and boots. Steve timidly followed his older sister. He peeked around her, revealing his blond hair and big blue eyes. Donna, the ranch wife, stood at the porch as she greeted the guests. She pushed up her black-rimmed glasses and opened her arms wide. "Welcome! Glad to have ya here!"

Jed's friend, Marty, walked bowlegged from the barn to the yard in his weathered Stetson hat and soiled clothing. "Jed," Marty said as they shook hands, "so good to see you, pal. Jed, you know my wife, Donna."

Jed nodded and smiled.

Marty continued, "These are my children, Tara and Steve."

Steve piped up, "Let's go play." The children ran to the yard.

Donna sweetly offered, "Glenda, would you like some lemonade? I'm sure you had a long, hot trip."

"I'd love some," Glenda graciously said. "That car's still hot with the windows down."

They walked inside the large kitchen where Donna served a glass of lemonade to Glenda. On the granite countertop, she set out plates, silverware, and napkins and stirred a crock pot of barbecued beef.

"You've gone to so much work, Donna. Can I help you with anything?"

"Let me see. You can get the lemonade and iced tea pitcher on the picnic table outside." Soon the two families were together sharing supper and stories.

"Jed," Marty explained. "I want to show you the ranch. Tomorrow night, we want to take your family into town to see the rodeo. We're so glad to have you here again."

"It's so quiet and relaxing here," Jed said. "I can hear myself think."

Marty replied, "We had adventures on the ranch when we were young, didn't we?"

In the morning, Matthew followed Marty and his dad to the stable and stroked the horses' manes. The horses neighed, shook their heads, and sniffed Matthew's hands. Matthew touched the damp softness of their noses. He watched Marty saddle up the horses. When Marty mounted one, Matthew bounced up and down, eager to get up on one himself.

Marty explained, "The saddles make it easier for us to ride. We put a foot in the stirrup here and swing our other leg around the saddle." Marty mounted the horse. "These are the reins. We use these to lead the horse. We click our heels to tell the horse to go faster, and we pull back on the reins to slow the horse down and stop it." Marty pulled on the reins.

His dad lifted Matthew up on a horse. "Put your hands here." Jed put Matthew's hands on the saddle horn. "Hang on real tight. Don't let go." Jed mounted the horse and sat behind Matthew.

As they rode across the ranch, Marty pointed out the windmills and creeks. The breeze of the fresh open air brushed against their faces. They dismounted at a wide, shallow creek to let the horses rest and drink. The men walked along the creek examining its eroded bank and steep sides. Matthew ran along exploring the waterway.

Marty saw a turtle and called to Matthew, "Come here, buddy. I want you to see this turtle. Feel its shell." Matthew came over to Marty. Marty knelt down and extended his fingers out to touch the hard shell. "See, Matthew. This shell is very hard. It protects the turtle from enemies. Did you see how the turtle put its head and legs inside when we touched it?"

Nodding his head and squealing in delight, he touched the surface of the shell. He took off and walked down the sloped bank at the edge of the flowing creek. Looking into the water, he saw fish and tadpoles swimming. He cupped his hands together and tried to catch a fish. He noticed something move on the bank and chased after it. He stooped down and enclosed the animal in his hands. He ran back to his dad, "Dad! Dad! Me get. See me get."

Marty asked, "What did you get, partner?" He saw Matthew's hands shaking.

Marty peeked between the fingers and saw a small, green frog. "You got yourself a frog. It wants to jump down. Frogs like to jump."

Matthew kept the frog in his hand. "Me keep. Me like."

Jed told Matthew, "We don't have anything to put the frog in."

Matthew saw the canteen draped over Marty's shoulder. He pointed to the canteen. "Do you want a drink?" asked Marty.

"No." Matthew lifted his hands to the canteen. "Me keep. Me keep."

"Do you want to take the frog home in the canteen?" Marty asked. Matthew gave a thumbs-up.

Marty unscrewed the lid and set the frog in the canteen. He looked at his watch. "We have a long ride back to the house. We better get back. Donna's grilling hamburgers for lunch."

Marty and Jed rode leisurely back to the house where Donna and Glenda were happily chatting, and the children were running around the house. Jed and Marty took the horses to the barn and unsaddled them. Matthew grabbed Marty's canteen and ran to Jenny.

Matthew held the canteen up to Jenny. "No! I don't want water." Matthew held it up to Jenny's face.

She sighed and said, "Okay, I'll take a drink of water." Jenny opened it and took a drink. She shrieked when a frog landed on her. Matthew shook with laughter. Donna and Glenda heard the scream and came out of the house.

The frog fell off Jenny's face. "It's only a little frog. No big deal," Glenda assured Jenny.

"It's gross and slimy. That wasn't funny!"

Matthew clapped his hands and smiled. "Me see you. Funny!"

Jenny stomped off to the house and washed her face with soap and water.

---*---

"Welcome, rodeo fans," the announcer said over the loudspeaker to the stands full of shouting spectators.

Matthew raised his hands above his head, clapping loudly for the cowboys. A bull rammed into a fence, stunning the spectators. Bullfighting clowns distracted the bull and chased him out of the arena. The crowd cheered wildly at the rider's bravery.

After the performance, the rodeo queen, clowns, and cowboys sat at a booth to sign autographs. Jed led Matthew to the booth where the queen sweetly greeted, "How'd ya like the rodeo?" Matthew gave her a thumbs-up. She signed, "To a real cowboy."

The bullfighting clown asked, "What was your favorite part?"

"Bull," he said. "Me like bull. Me on."

The clown shook Matthew's hand and said, "You sound like a real cowboy." He winked at Jed.

On the way back to the ranch, Tara said, "Chills went up my spine when the bull hit the fence."

"I felt my heart race," Jenny responded.

"I'm going to barrel race in a few years. I'm practicing already," Tara told her proudly.

"I don't see how they go around those corners and keep the barrels up," Jenny said.

"I'm roping calves with Dad when I get older," Steve said. "I want to ride bucking broncos."

The rest of the ride home was filled with comments about the rodeo events.

The next morning, Marty said, "I think you will like the western store and the gunfight in town. They have a gunfight every day in the summer months and stagecoach rides. The children will love it."

"I want to get Matthew some cowboy boots and a hat. The boots can slow him down. He takes off so quickly, we can hardly keep up with him," Jed told Marty.

"The western store has a variety of whatever you want. Their prices are reasonable. I think you can find something for the whole family," Donna explained.

"The gunfight and stagecoach ride sounds like a good time for the kids. They have never seen anything like it," Jed said. "This is definitely an Old West vacation."

"The town tries to attract tourists with the rodeo and western events. It draws thousands of people every year. The main street is designed to look like an Old West town with storefronts similar to those from the 1800s," Marty explained.

As the children came down for breakfast, Marty explained, "We're driving fifty miles into town for the day. We have some places to show you."

In town, they walked up to the crowded Main Street. Two men were shouting threats back and forth.

An evil-looking man shouted, "Sheriff, you can't get me!"

"Try me," dared the sheriff. "Let's see who's faster with the draw."

The two men turned their backs to one another and walked twenty paces. They turned face to face and drew their guns. Bang! Bang!

Smoke filled the air, and the gangster dropped to the ground.

The sheriff raised his hands triumphantly. "Another outlaw bites the dust," he shouted.

Jenny asked her dad, "Why did the sheriff shoot the man? Is he okay?"

"It's just pretend. They do this to show people what the Old West was like and how gunfights happened. The sheriff pretended to kill the bad guy. In the Old West, the bad guys robbed stagecoaches or murdered people. Gunfights were common."

"But it looked and sounded so real," Jenny said.

"The guns have what are called blanks," Jed told Jenny. "Blanks sound real. There are no bullets in the guns to harm anyone. Let's go to the stagecoach."

Over by the wooden sidewalk, a horse was tied to a hitching post. A stagecoach driver stood nearby waiting for customers. Jed and the children approached the driver. "I have a bunch of eager riders. Is it all right if my son and I sit in front here with you?"

"I don't see why not," the driver replied. "Hang on real tight." Once the children were loaded on the stagecoach, the driver went up and down the street.

Jed pointed to the storefronts during the ride on Main Street. The driver noticed Jed pointing to the saloon and said, "Be sure to stop there. It has the best homemade root beer in the country. A great treat on a hot day."

"Really," Jed said. "We'll have to stop. Our kids love root beer."

The driver dropped everyone off at the saloon where Marty, Donna, and Glenda were waiting. Matthew forcefully pushed open the saloon doors. They all sat at a long counter with stools and ordered the locally made soda. It was a sweet refreshment satisfying their dry mouths.

After the stop at the saloon, they strolled down the street to the western department store which sold hats, boots, ropes, saddles, and clothing. Matthew tried on a pair of brown boots and strutted around the store.

Marty said to Matthew, "We'll have you looking like a real cowboy."

Jed picked out a tan, velvety cowboy hat for Matthew. Matthew smiled and looked in the mirror as he tried it on. "Me like," he said. "Me cowboy." Matthew tried on a brown leather belt and looked at belt buckles. Jed showed him buckles with a cow, a rodeo bull, and a tractor. Matthew chose a silver buckle with a bull engraved on it.

As Jed paid for the purchases, Glenda asked the cashier, "Can my son put on his new items now?"

The cashier smiled and graciously replied, "He most certainly may."

Walking outside, many of the passersby tipped their cowboy hats in greeting. Several of the men said to Jed, "It looks like you have a future cowboy there, pal."

Jed replied, "I think he's a natural."

Matthew began walking with his head held high and tipped his hat as others greeted him. He mimicked the bowlegged walk of the cowboys he saw at the rodeo. He put his thumbs in the belt holes of his jeans and walked in long strides. The Nebraska trip stirred up a passion for cattle and the country.

CHAPTER 7

Jed drove his family to the outskirts of the city to visit his parents, Gary and Kate Parker. Jed eased the car across the rickety bridge to the small farmhouse. Grandma Kate was sitting on the three-season porch, which was furnished with wicker furniture. Brad and Jenny greeted Grandma Kate then rushed to the kitchen to get a glass bottle of Pepsi from the fridge. Their cousins, Derrick and Dale, joined them for a drink.

Gary sat in the recliner most of the time, looking gaunt and sickly. His robust stature had withered to a frail state with sunken cheeks and limp arms. Matthew crept up to Grandpa Gary and handed him a colorful picture of flowers and trees that he had made. Matthew tenderly patted his arm and said, "Papa. Me love me papa."

Grandpa smiled faintly and said, "That's good. Thank you very much. I love you too."

Grandma Kate took the picture and hung it on the shelf where she placed school pictures of her grandchildren. "This is very good, Matthew. You did a great job."

Grandpa Gary squeezed Matthew's hand and asked "Could you put a few M&Ms in my hand?" He told Jed, "He's a good boy. You have the patience to teach him many skills."

Gary raised his weak hand to his mouth and winced in pain as he bit down. "You okay, Papa?" Matthew sensed something was wrong.

"I'm fine, Matthew. Tell me about the farm."

Matthew made a motion with his hands like he was driving.

Jed explained, "Brad takes Matthew on rides out to the pasture on the three-wheeler. Brad lets Matthew steer it a little bit. Matthew likes seeing the cattle."

"Me big boy," Matthew said with his arms reaching up to the sky. Gary smiled weakly. He asked, "Do you have a cow?"

"Me do." Matthew pointed to the black shirt on Jed.

"Is your cow black?" Gary asked. Matthew nodded his head up and down.

Jed explained, "We bought several cows this summer. We let Matthew pick which one he wanted. The cows survived a tornado and were spooked by the storm. The owner didn't want to keep them after the storm."

Showing his grandpa his western shirt, belt buckle, and cowboy boots, Matthew said, "Me cowboy. Me cow."

Gary chuckled as he momentarily forgot about his pain and turned to Jed, "He can help you one day, Jed. He already likes the farm. He'll be capable of work. It would be a good place for him."

"You might be right. We'll see. I'm planning on teaching him everything I possibly can."

Gary replied, "That's the best thing to do. Let him reach his potential."

"There is some there," Jed added. "I want to help him achieve it."

Gary affirmed, "That's what I like to hear. You don't want to excuse his disability. See what he can do. It'll be more than you think."

Jed knew this was one of the last conversations he'd have with his father. Gary's diagnosis for advanced stage bone cancer was terminal, and the doctor believed he wouldn't live more than a month. Thoughts raced through Jed's mind how he wanted to share more memories, but this opportunity was almost gone. Matthew crawled onto Jed's lap and cuddled up to him.

One week later, Jed's father was admitted to City Hospital and felt weaker daily as he was nearing death. On Sunday, Jed drove the family to the hospital to visit Grandpa. Brad, Jenny, and Matthew went to a children's room off the main lobby of the hospital that consisted of a television and toys.

On the fifth floor, Jed asked the head nurse, "May I please bring my children up to see their grandpa one last time?"

"How old are they?" she asked gruffly.

"Four, eight, and eleven years old," Jed answered.

"They're too young to come up, but I'll make an exception this one time. Make sure they're quiet. We can't go around breaking rules for young ones to see patients."

Jed exhaled a sigh of relief and said, "Thank you so much. I appreciate it more than you can know."

"Go on," she snapped.

Jed came to the children's room and asked them to go up the elevator with him to see Grandpa Gary. "But we're too young," said Brad. "The rules say there aren't to be any visitors under twelve years old."

"We're going anyway," Jed said. "You're going to see Grandpa one more time."

They stepped on the elevator and rode up to the fifth floor. Jed explained, "The nurse said you can visit, but you must be extra quiet."

"Aren't we supposed to follow the rules?" asked Jenny. "I feel like a secret agent sneaking up here."

"You're fine, Jenny," Jed answered.

"We're the FBI," Brad teased. "We're on a secret mission and have to remain discreet."

Jenny looked at Matthew, put her fingers to her lips, and whispered, "We must be super quiet." Matthew nodded his head. Holding hands, they silently tiptoed down the hallway and watched for nurses. Matthew's boots made a soft, clomping sound. Jenny froze in place when she saw a nurse walk past them. The nurse smiled and winked at Jed.

They found Room 532. Grandma Kate stood up from the recliner next to Gary's bed and hugged each of the children. "My goodness, it is so good to see all of you. How are you doing?"

"Fine," Jenny answered.

"How are you, Grams?" Brad asked as he gave her a high five.

Grandma Kate's lips quivered. "Thank you so much for coming."

Matthew stepped up to his grandma and kissed her tenderly on the cheek. "Me love you."

Jenny felt nauseous when she saw Gary's lifeless body with wires and tubes connected to him. She looked at the ground and didn't like the sound of the IV pump and heart monitor.

"Brad, please take Jenny back downstairs. We'll be down shortly," Glenda said.

Matthew crept up to his grandpa and carefully stroked the tips of his fingers as if he was a fragile china doll. Gary smiled and was too weak to touch Matthew's tiny hand. Matthew said, "Me cow. Me work."

Gary looked at Matthew and closed his eyes. He fell into a deep sleep. He died a few hours after the visit from his grandchildren.

---*---

Neighbors stopped by the house and brought casseroles, sandwiches, and salads to show their sympathy. Arrangements were made for Wilma to spend the day with Matthew while the rest of the family attended the funeral.

A few weeks after the funeral, Jed and his brothers gathered at Grandma Kate's home to comfort her. Matthew walked quietly to the recliner where Gary usually sat and noticed he wasn't there. He searched the house and couldn't find him. He asked Kate, "Papa go? Papa no—" He pointed to the chair.

Kate's eyes filled with tears, and she felt unsure how to explain death to Matthew. She wasn't sure if he would comprehend it.

How could she explain that he'd never see him again? She stepped into the kitchen and stood at the sink with her back turned.

Brad led Matthew into the family room where they celebrated Christmas Eves and told Matthew, "Papa's gone. He's in heaven, and we'll never see him again."

"Papa no go. Me see him. Me Papa."

"Matthew, no more Papa. He's with Jesus in heaven. He was very sick and died. People get old and die."

"Me no die. No Papa die," Matthew obstinately continued.

Brad led Matthew to the storage shed to get out baseball equipment for a game just as Derrick and Dale joined them to play.

CHAPTER 8

When Matthew was four, he watched the Kansas City Royals on television during the summertime. One day, he went to the basement and brought up a bat, ball, and glove. The south side of the yard had three trees perfect for the bases. Matthew stood at home plate, which faced the barn and loading chute, positioned the bat in his hands, limbered up his body, and wiggled his hips. Jenny laughed when Matthew leaned his upper body forward and stuck out his rear end. "Okay, Sis. Me hit."

Jenny pitched the ball slow and out too far, yet Matthew swung at it. He got in his stance again mimicking the pros. "You're so funny. Here comes another one."

Matthew eagerly waited for another pitch while Jenny stepped closer and squinted her eyes from the sunshine. There was a cracking sound when the bat made contact with the ball, but it stayed at home plate. The next time, he hit the ball over Jenny's head toward the loading chute. As Jenny chased after it, Matthew ran past the trees to home plate three times. Jenny came back at last and cheered, "Good hit! You did it!"

Jenny threw the ball low, and Matthew leaned forward to hit, and it went smack on her leg. "Ouch!"

"You okay, Sis?" Matthew knelt down and looked at her leg. Me no hit you. Boo boo." He tenderly patted her leg.

"It hurts, but I'm okay. I wasn't ready for that. Good hit. You're getting better."

Matthew grinned and went to bat. He hit the ball between the trees across the driveway and ran the bases three times before Jenny retrieved the ball. When Jenny came back, he stopped at home plate. "Home run! Home run!" Jenny jumped up and down.

Matthew struck out and Jenny asked, "Can I bat now? You've done it the whole time."

"No. Me hit. Me do." He stood at home plate holding the bat firmly in his hands. Jenny grumbled and pitched the rest of the morning.

Glenda drove Jenny and Matthew to Grandma Trudy's home so she could help Jed with farm work.

Grandma Trudy told Jenny and Matthew, "When you get thirsty, you may choose a drink from the fridge. Be sure to shake the jug of apple cider or orange juice because the good stuff settles to the bottom. Does anyone want some now?" Jenny and Matthew both shook their heads no.

On the counter were fresh-baked sugar cookies that gave off a sweet scent. Jenny smacked her lips. "Mm. Those smell so good."

Matthew pointed to the cookies and said, "Mm. Mm. Me eat."

"Come sit down, and I'll get you one," Grandma Trudy commanded while she got two plates out of the cupboard.

Jenny's cookie melted in her mouth as she tasted the slight lemony flavor of the warm, soft cookie. Matthew devoured his and pointed to the cookies.

"I think one's enough for now," Grandma Trudy said. "I'll let you have another one after dinner today. Now, you two go outside and play. Get some sunshine before it gets too humid out there."

Matthew and Jenny hurried to the porch where they rocked back and forth on the swing. Matthew got it going so fast, it hit the siding of the house. "Stop it," Jenny scolded.

"Me like. Me do."

"No. Let's go do something else."

Jenny grabbed Matthew's hand and led him down to the yard where two trees were in a straight line. "Let's race. We'll run from this tree to that tree and back. We'll see who's faster."

Matthew ran all around the trees in the yard, laughing at Jenny trying to catch up to him. "No," she called to him. "We're going to have a race." Jenny grabbed his hand to lead him back to the tree. He got free from her grasp and ran toward the barn. One of the lots surrounding the barn had a bull in it, and Jenny knew Matthew was a climber.

Jenny caught him in her arms and pulled on him to go back to the yard. He felt like lead in her arms and wiggled from her grasp. She had an idea. "Matthew, let's go pick Grandma some flowers to show her we love her."

When Matthew gathered a yellow bouquet, he smelled them and turned his nose and chin yellow. "Me go Raw. Me go Raw," he chanted the nickname he had for Grandma Trudy. He walked up the porch steps and rapped on the door.

Wiping her hands on her blue apron, Grandma came to the door and looked surprised. "My, my. What have we here? They're beautiful. Thank you. I'll get them in water."

Matthew said, "Me like Raw. Me like."

Jenny and Matthew went to Grandma's house again the following day. Jenny led Matthew outside to the yard. "Let's race. Let's see who's faster." Matthew plopped himself down on the porch swing, rocking it back and forth. There was a loud thump as it hit the side of the house.

Grandma Trudy marched sternly out of the house and hollered, "What's that noise?" She looked around and saw Matthew clapping in glee. "Stop that," she barked. "Get off of there right now."

Matthew got wide-eyed, recognizing the stern tone in Raw's voice. He sprinted to the yard, running all around the trees and flailing his arms. Jenny panted for breath trying to catch up to him.

With two paper sacks in her hand, Grandma called, "Jenny! Matthew! I have a job for the two of you."

Racing up to Grandma Trudy, each one grabbed a sack. "Wait a minute, you two. Listen. Fill the sack with pinecones. I'll pay a quarter for a sack. When your sack is full, come get another one."

Jenny nodded. "I'll show Matthew what the pinecones are," she offered.

"Good," Trudy said. "I need to get dinner ready for you, Grandpa, and the hired men. If you need anything, come get me in the kitchen. Once I have everything in the oven, then I'll come out and do some games with you."

Jenny carried the sacks in one hand and led Matthew with the other. She bent down near the two blue spruce trees and picked up a brown, prickly pinecone. "Grandma wants us to put these in a sack. These are pinecones. Feel this one. Don't take them off the trees. Pick them off the grass."

Matthew hunched down and swept the cones up in a big pile with his hands. He threw his mound into the sack by the armful and quickly had the brown bag heaping full. They ran to the porch with their sacks full and grabbed a second bag.

"Good job, Matthew. See if you can fill the sack to the top." Jenny pointed to the top of the sack.

Grandma Trudy, dressed in her floral, bold-colored house dress marched out to the yard and told the children, "I want you to race from this tree when I say and go down to the tree over there, touch it with your hand, and run back here."

"Me run. Me run fast."

"Okay," she said. "One for the money, two for the show, three to get ready, and four to go!" Jenny and Matthew ran close to each other, but at the end, Matthew touched the tree first.

"'Gin, 'gin," Matthew chanted as he danced around the tree.

"Okay, are you both ready?" Grandma Trudy chanted the rhyme again.

Huffing and puffing, Jenny and Matthew sprawled in the grass under the shade of the tree. Grandma Trudy said, "You two look tired. Come inside for a drink."

Jenny spoke hoarsely, "I want apple cider, please." Grandma Trudy poured the drinks and served seconds.

Grandpa Gordon washed up for dinner and shouted, "Where are my munchkins?" Matthew and Jenny bounded into the kitchen and ran up to him. Grandpa hugged Jenny and swung Matthew up into his arms. Matthew laughed as his grandpa pressed his lips against his cheek and blew real hard. Matthew fidgeted and returned the kiss.

At the end of the meal, Matthew licked his lips and carefully wiped his face with his napkin. Jenny was finishing up when Matthew shouted, "Run! Run!"

"Wait, Matthew. I'm not done," Jenny responded.

"Run! Run!" Matthew went to put on his shoes.

"I'll go out with you a few minutes," Grandpa Gordon told Matthew. "I want to see how fast you run." He winked at Jenny. "Take your time, honey. I'll watch him until you get done."

Grandpa Gordon slowly walked to the yard and clapped his hands. "Let's see you run fast."

Matthew darted across the yard back and forth several times. He tired out and went to sit by Grandpa on the porch swing, pushing his weight to get it moving fast. "I bet you're trying to get this thing rocking hard," Grandpa laughed. "With my big ole body here, it's hard to move it very far."

"Raw. Raw stop me. Me stop. Me off."

"I heard about that." Gordon chuckled again. "It's fun to swing hard, but you need to listen to your grandma."

Jenny slammed the front door and squeezed between Matthew and Grandpa. Grandpa said, "I think Matthew's tired. Why don't you two go into the house and play quietly or watch some television. You can come back outside later."

"Sure, Grandpa," Jenny answered hesitantly.

"I'll tell you what, Jenny. I'll go in with you to get Matthew started on a television show. You can have some free time."

Jenny breathed a sigh of relief. "Thank you, Grandpa. I've been watching him all week."

"No problem, kiddo. You need a little break. Grandma and your mom get so busy doing their work, they forget to let you have some alone time. Everyone needs that."

Grandpa Gordon turned on the television and found reruns of a popular show. He settled into his big red chair and snuggled Matthew on his lap. Grandpa and Matthew dozed off from the steady rocking of the chair.

Jenny found an old trunk where Grandma Trudy stored Glenda's paper doll collection and childhood toys. She opened the box of dolls and dressed them in brittle paper clothing.

Grandpa woke up and rushed back to work. Jenny and Matthew went back outside exploring nature's treasures—anthills, birds' nests, and insects.

CHAPTER 9

The rain pelted hard on the windshield of Glenda's car. As she arrived at Trudy's home, Matthew and Jenny rushed to the house. The rain drenched their hair and clothing.

Matthew slipped off his shoes and restlessly raced around the house. He opened cupboards and slammed the doors.

Jenny rolled her eyes and slumped her shoulders. "Matthew, get back here," she yelled exasperatedly.

Matthew ran into the living room, "Me play. Me jump!"

Matthew went to the corner of the living room and sat on the piano bench. He gently pushed the keys and sang, "Me happy. Me big boy. Me play. Me happy. Me play."

He slid off the bench and climbed on Gordon's large, red rocking chair. He jumped up and down. "Whee! Whee! See me! Whee!"

"Get down," Jenny firmly told him.

Matthew ignored Jenny and jumped some more. He sat down and rocked until Jenny grabbed the chair and held it right before it hit the floor. Jenny scowled. Matthew got off the chair and climbed up on the long green couch. Running on it, he looked at the thick shag carpet. He stopped in the middle and dived to the floor. He got back on the couch and dived several more times.

"Matthew, stop!" Jenny locked her arms around his waist. They both tumbled on the floor.

Matthew quickly got back on his feet and opened the cover to the stereo and pushed the buttons. Music blared.

"Leave it alone. Grandma says we can't touch it." She grabbed him and tried to pry his body away from the stereo.

"Me play da-da-da. Me like. Me...," he said as he pointed to his ear. He was determined to get the record player started.

Jenny gave in and turned on the record player setting. She put a record of Guy Lombardo on the spinner. Matthew clapped his hands in glee and asked for more. "Me like." He pointed to a record of 1950s music. Jenny changed the album. The song "The Lion Sleeps Tonight" played. Matthew danced around to the music. He listened to a few songs, went over, and abruptly stopped the song. "Me stop," he said. There was a scratchy sound as he picked up the needle.

Grandma Trudy stomped into the living room and glared sternly at Jenny and Matthew. "You two stay away from the stereo. I heard a scratching sound all the way in the kitchen."

"Me like. Me..." Matthew shook his body and twirled around dancing.

"No more stereo," barked Grandma Trudy.

Matthew comprehended the stern voice. He knew Grandma was angry with him. He turned up his nose and mouth in irritation.

"Why don't the two of you find something else to play?" Grandma Trudy left the room.

Matthew sat sulking on the couch a couple of minutes. Jenny said, "Matthew, let me tell you a story. I want to tell you about Matthew and the giant."

Matthew snuggled up to Jenny on the couch. "Once upon a time, there was a little boy named Matthew. He went to the forest and found a giant. The giant captured Matthew and held him in his house."

Matthew's eyes became heavy, and he nodded his head downward. Jenny stopped the story and covered Matthew's motionless body with a blanket.

Glenda picked the children up around noon and took them home to lunch. By now the rain had turned to sprinkles. On the way to the car, Matthew leaped into the deep puddles near the driveway, splashing muddy water on his clothing.

"Time to go." Glenda grabbed his hand, and he released her grip. He ran swiftly and tripped, landing in a puddle. His clothing was soaked to the skin. Matthew's teeth started chattering as he shivered.

Glenda calmly said, "Matthew, let's get you home and changed into dry clothes." She grabbed his hand again and led him to the car.

Inside the car, Matthew told his mother, "Raw mad. Raw mad me."

"Why?" inquired Glenda.

"Raw mad."

"He was playing with the stereo and moved the needle while a record was playing. She came in and told him to leave it alone," Jenny explained.

"Matthew, you need to obey Grandma Trudy. She didn't want a record scratched."

"Me mad Raw. Me no like Raw. Raw mad me."

"It's okay. She loves you. I know you love her too."

While Glenda and Jenny prepared lunch, Matthew went upstairs for something. He went into the spare bedroom where some summer toys were stored. "Me no like Raw. Raw mad," he repeated. He looked in the closet and under the bed. "Ah. Me get Raw. Me mad."

He found a water gun and hid it under his shirt. He went to the upstairs bathroom and filled it with water. Holding the water gun upright so it wouldn't leak, he slowly crept down into the living room. A large picture of Grandpa Gordon and Grandma Trudy was sitting on a circular walnut end table. Matthew walked up to the picture and aimed the water gun at the picture and squirted several times. "Me no like Raw." He saw the water had leaked through the glass frame and moistened her picture. He went back upstairs, emptied the rest of the water, and put the water gun away. He was no longer angry.

Grandma Trudy and Grandpa Gordon came to have Sunday dinner with everyone two days after the incident at their house. Glenda and Trudy visited in the living room on the couch. Glenda noticed something strange about the picture that was on the end table. She looked at it from another angle, stood up and walked over to it. Something was wrong. It looked fine earlier in the week when she had dusted. She was a bit puzzled.

"What's the matter, Glenda?" Grandma Trudy inquired. "You look confused."

"I don't know what happened to this picture. It looks different."

Trudy took a look at it. "It's water stained. How did it get wet?"

"I don't know, but it's a bit discolored on your side of the picture," Glenda observed.

Jenny meekly walked into the living room while they were discussing what happened. Glenda saw her and asked, "Do you know anything about this?"

Jenny solemnly nodded her head.

"Tell me what you know," Glenda stated.

"When I was helping you set the table the other day and getting napkins out of the pantry, I saw Matthew carrying a water gun. I quickly set the napkins on the table. I peeked into the living room, and he was standing right there by the picture and squirted it several times because he was mad at Grandma for scolding him about the stereo."

"He squirted the picture with a water gun because he was angry?" Glenda was surprised Matthew would express anger.

"Yes, I think that's why because he said he didn't like Raw," Jenny replied. "May I be excused?"

"Of course, honey," Glenda answered.

Grandma Trudy, who normally was stern and strong, broke down in laughter.

"What's so funny about this?" Glenda questioned. "He ruined a nice picture."

"I know." Trudy laughed, trying to stifle it. "But we know now that he's quite expressive. It's a good sign that he's able to express anger in an innocent way. He didn't yell or have a tantrum. It's good for him to have some strong feelings."

Glenda relaxed and slightly chuckled. "He's aware of the feelings of others and his own feelings." She never said anything to Matthew about the picture. The picture continued to be displayed on the table as it always had been. It was a reminder that Matthew thought deeper than they expected.

CHAPTER 10

Aunt Pearl was Grandma Kate's sister. Pearl and her husband, Bob, lived in Oregon. They visited only once every year or two and came back for a visit to the Parker home. The Saturday of the visit, Jenny and Brad finished their chores an hour before Grandma Kate and the special guests were to arrive. They sat at the living room window where they watched for the school bus and watched as every car came down the highway.

At last, Grandma Kate, Uncle Bob, and Aunt Pearl drove the four-door Century Buick into the lane. Brad and Jenny jumped up and down shouting, "They're here! They're here!"

They rushed to the door waving their hands to greet them. Matthew stayed in the family room and played with his toys. He was unaware of the anticipation.

Everyone sat down to a festive table. The tablecloth was sky blue with dainty flowers on it. Glenda got out the best china from her wedding and clear crystal goblets for the drinks. She served a ham loaf, fried potatoes, green bean casserole, a relish tray, apple salad, and a strawberry Jell-o salad.

After the meal, Matthew withdrew into the family room with his toys while the rest of the family went into the formal living room to visit. Uncle Bob was animated in his stories about his own children. Matthew heard his laughter and playfulness from the family room.

Jed told the guests, "We traveled to the Wisconsin Dells. We went on a boat ride and hiked trails. The Indian Ceremony had authentic Indian dances. The Indians dressed in traditional clothing and danced around a bonfire. Drums were beating and bells on the moccasins were shaking. My heart pounded as they played the drums. The Indians yelled and chanted in their native tongue."

"I'd like to go down and dance with the Indians to wish for rain. We need some back home," Bob said merrily.

Brad and Jenny snickered. Brad teased, "We can try it and see if it really works."

In the family room, Matthew reached for the drum and headdress his dad had bought for him. He carried it into the living room. He scanned the room and sat down right next to Bob. He patted his mouth and told Bob, "Me woo, woo, woo. Me boom, boom, boom."

"Hey, buddy, do you like Indians?" he asked with a twinkle in his big brown eyes.

"Me woo, woo, woo. Me boom, boom, boom. You, Bob. You do."

"I will. How about you play the drum while I wear the headdress?"

"Okay. Me boom. You woo, woo." Matthew patted his hand across his lip again and chanted.

The ceremony began. Uncle Bob put the headdress on his head and was ready to be an Indian. "How do I look?" Everyone smiled. Matthew nodded his head and said, "Bob, woo, woo."

Matthew held the drum and started pounding it over and over. Bob stood up and danced like an Indian, patting his lips, saying, "Woo, woo, woo." He danced until the music ended.

Matthew stopped drumming and looked at Bob with amusement. "Me do. Me do woo, woo. You boom boom."

"Sounds like a great idea. My old body is tired of doing an Indian dance. I'll sit and play the drum."

Bob started hitting the drum rhythmically while Matthew put the headdress on his head and began dancing around the living room as if on hot coals. He made Indian noises and went up to Grandma Kate. He grabbed her hand. Grandma Kate got up and imitated an Indian dance. Then Matthew went to Aunt Pearl. She got up and danced. The evening was merry. When Bob finished, he said, "I haven't had that much fun in a long time." He laughed so hard he grabbed his stomach. "We'll soon find out if it brings us a good rain."

CHAPTER 11

The summer when Matthew was four years old was a typical summer on the farm. The bean fields needed to be walked to remove weeds. Jed hired a crew to walk the beans in the mornings. The crew consisted of approximately eight teenagers. The crew carried bean hooks to cut out the weeds such as milkweeds, button weeds, and sunflowers.

The afternoons consisted of putting up hay. A different crew was hired of all teenage boys. The hay was mowed, raked, and baled with a small baler. The boys rode on a wagon hooked to the 4020 John Deere tractor. One person drove the tractor, two boys put bales up on the wagon, and two boys stacked them. When the wagon was stacked full, the boys went to the barn. The hayloft door was down, and an elevator was propped up next to the barn. The elevator was powered by the tractor. The barn was hot, and bales came up fast. The boys at the wagon set the bales on the elevator as the crew in the barn grabbed and stacked them.

Glenda had plenty of extra mouths to feed during the summer. She furnished light lunches for the bean walkers and suppers for the hay crew. "Jenny! Matthew! Get your shoes on. We're going to Oakwood for groceries."

"Now?" whined Jenny. "I'm finishing the potholder I'm making for Grandma."

"Finish it later. We have many hungry mouths to feed. Jenny, when we get back, I want you to help make ham sandwiches and cookies."

"Oh, all right," Jenny said unwillingly.

Glenda drove to the local hub of Oakwood, which had a population of ten thousand. There were two grocery stores. Glenda went to Bee's Grocery for its sales and double coupon days.

Inside the store, Glenda told Jenny to push a second cart.

As Glenda and Jenny pushed the two carts, people shot them strange glances. Jenny shrugged her shoulders and her face flushed as people kept staring. Glenda filled both carts full of food and pushed them to the front of the store and waited patiently for the cashier.

Glenda got Matthew to stay by her side when she let him pick a special treat. He chose to carry a bag of M&Ms. She told him that he couldn't open them in the store because they had not paid for them yet. He shook the bag and stayed with Mom and Jenny. Matthew poked his fingers against the bag feeling the pieces of candy.

Glenda asked Matthew to put his tongue back in his mouth.

Matthew obeyed, but it still pushed out a little.

Glenda pushed up the carts to the cashier. She explained, "Both of these carts are one order. We have bean walking and hay crews this week."

The cashier nodded in understanding, "It's that time of year to get farm work done, isn't it? My older brother is putting up hay with a crew this week also. He looks forward to it."

"The young boys like the hard work," Glenda said. "We've never had any trouble finding a crew. We just ask around and get several willing young boys. I like to spoil the crew with home cooking."

The cashier smiled sweetly at Matthew and Jenny. "Do you help?"

"No," replied Jenny. "I do help Mom in the kitchen and help her take food out to the crew. I also watch my little brother."

"That's a big job," the cashier said. "He looks like such a nice boy."

"He is," Jenny replied.

At the next register, Jenny saw a boy her age glaring at them. She patted her mom on the shoulder and said, "Look at that boy, Mom. He keeps staring at us." Glenda tensed up and got a haughty look on her face. She turned her head and glared sternly right back at the boy who was staring. The boy's mom saw Glenda glare back at him and looked at Glenda apologetically.

"Why's he staring, Mom?" Jenny inquired.

Glenda spoke loudly so the people in the next aisle could hear, "Some people have never learned manners."

The cashier frowned and looked sympathetically at Glenda. "You're right. Some people don't have manners. It's so rude to stare."

Glenda fumbled to find the checkbook in her purse. She said, "People always stare. I get so tired of it." Glenda paid for the groceries, and a young, courteous teenager pushed the loaded carts of groceries out to the car.

As Glenda got into the car, she grew silent and muttered to herself, "Why can't people be more understanding? Will things ever get better?"

Jenny was bewildered. *What's Mom muttering about? Why do people stare?*

Glenda drove home and made preparations for the upcoming days.

CHAPTER 12

The Cloverville town council held a meeting to discuss plans for making the year's Christmas especially festive. Mayor Evans addressed the members, "Our community has been so faithful in supporting local businesses, they need more than window decorations and the tree displayed at the community center."

"What are you thinking?" asked Mrs. Vogel, a council member.

"I think we need a special event where families can come shop, listen to music, and have cookies. People who make homemade crafts can set up tables to sell items."

"Good idea," Mrs. Garrett replied. "I'll make sugar cookies and serve coffee and hot chocolate."

"I'll help," Mrs. Vogel offered. "I'll check with the Baptist church choir to see if they'll sing carols for us. Perhaps, the Lutheran choir can sing part of the time too."

"Those sound like some good suggestions. Thank you, ladies," the mayor said.

"Mary will probably offer a lunch special for the visitors at her cafe. She's had a booming business this year. She would love the opportunity to thank the community. And, I'm sure the businesses can have special discounts," Mrs. Vogel added.

"I'll contact people so we can have sales of homemade items," Mrs. Garrett said. "I know my brother makes birdhouses and wooden jewelry boxes. Mrs. Granger knits the warmest scarves and mittens. And, Mrs. Fisher embroiders such beautiful pillowcases."

"I like all these ideas, but something's missing." Mr. Evans sat quietly a moment, deep in thought. He snapped his fingers as an idea came to him. "I've got it. We need a visit from Santa Claus to give each child a small gift. We can fill a bag with some candy and a small toy. Gordon Rogers would make an excellent Santa Claus. I will call him as soon as we adjourn this meeting. I'm excited to give back to our community this Christmas. It's a small token of our appreciation. We'll meet in three days to confirm our preparations for the day."

When Gordon received the call asking him to portray Santa at the community center, he eagerly accepted. He thought this would be a small way to spread Christmas joy and offered to donate some of the candy and toys for the children.

The Saturday came when Christmas was being celebrated with caroling, and stores were open with special deals. The community center was decorated beautifully with an artificial Christmas tree standing eight feet tall with multicolored lights and garland around it. Gift bags for the children were wrapped in colorful Christmas paper and set under the tree. The aroma of chocolate and coffee filled the air. There was a food table with trays of decorated cookies available for the guests. A few vendors had goods such as flour-sack towels, knitted blankets, pot holders, and special crafts for sale.

Gordon slid the red velvet suit over his pants and shirt and tightened the black belt around his stomach that needed no extra padding. He put the red hat on his head, slipped the white beard over his face, stood in front of the mirror, and rehearsed bellowing, "Ho! Ho! Ho! Merry Christmas!" His hefty belly shook as he laughed.

As doors opened to the center, dozens of families came in, and the bright-eyed children lined up to see Santa Claus, who merrily roared, "Ho, ho, ho! Merry Christmas, everyone!" The children grinned in delight and enthusiastically waited in line to see Santa in his chair right next to the Christmas tree. As each child came and sat on his lap, he asked them what they wanted for Christmas. He laughed with them and presented them with a gift bag. The children thanked Santa and ran to their families with their gift bags. They excitedly opened their presents.

The next stop was the cookie table. The crowd lined up to select the appetizing cookies shaped in candy canes, wreaths, bells, Christmas trees, and snowmen. The frosting was skillfully spread on the cookies, and the sugars made them lots more tempting.

Glenda brought Brad, Jenny, and Matthew to the community center to see Santa. Brad and Jenny recognized him right away. Brad, now eleven years old, went brazenly up to him and sat on his lap. In his fun-loving way, he gave Santa a big list for Christmas.

Santa teasingly said, "We'll just have to see if you've been a good boy this year."

"Ah, Santa, you know I'm the best," Brad joked.

"Wait till Christmas and see what Santa brings you." He winked at Brad and handed him a gift bag.

Eight-year-old Jenny meekly went up to him and whispered, "Gra-, I mean Santa. I want a Barbie doll for Christmas."

Santa rubbed his beard, "Tell me, young lady, have you been a good girl this year?"

"I, uh, think so. I tried to be," Jenny said quietly.

"I'm sure Santa will visit you. Merry Christmas." Santa hugged Jenny and gave her a gift.

"Thanks, Gra-, I mean Santa."

Glenda said to Matthew, "Look who's here! It's Santa!"

Matthew turned his back to Santa and ran from him. He hid under a table and sat cross-legged.

Glenda nudged Matthew to go see Santa, but Matthew looked away from this man in the red suit. He had no idea that underneath the suit was his own Grandpa Gordon.

"Come on, Matthew," Glenda encouraged. "You're four years old. Santa wants to see you."

Matthew got out from under the table but kept as far away from the man in the red suit as he could. He went by himself over to the cookie table and carefully selected a sugar cookie in the shape of a bell. He told the server, "Tanks."

"You are so welcome, dear." Mrs. Vogel was impressed with the manners of this young boy who was disabled.

Jenny and Brad squeezed through a maze of shoppers as they looked at the various vendors. They searched for a special gift for their mom.

"Look," Jenny exclaimed. "This is perfect for Mom." Jenny held up an intricately stitched flour-sack towel. It had a design of a church that resembled White Chapel, the church they attended.

Brad observed the towel. "That looks like Mom. She'll love it!" He reached into his jeans pocket and pulled out some one dollar bills.

The vendor wrapped the towel in Christmas tree gift wrap. "Thank you so much," she said. "Have a Merry Christmas."

Brad and Jenny selected a cookie and cup of cocoa and found a place to sit. Carolers were singing Christmas songs. The voices were harmonious and created the perfect ambiance for the holidays.

A few hours later, Gordon returned home and collapsed in his red rocking chair in the living room. His chin fell to his chest as he snored.

Soon, Glenda stopped at the house so that the children could see Santa one more time. Matthew cautiously inched his way into the living room where he saw the man in the red suit. Matthew recognized Gordon's bald head and leaped up into his arms, wrapping them around his grandpa's neck. "Papa. Me papa."

Gordon jerked and opened his eyes. "Hey there, buddy. How are you?" Gordon reached for his hat and beard. When Matthew saw the beard and hat, he jumped off Gordon's lap and scrunched his small body under the piano bench.

Glenda was surprised that he was afraid. She had wanted to get a picture of Gordon being Santa with Matthew. She had taken a picture of Brad and Jenny with him in town. Gordon took off his hat and beard again.

Glenda called, "Look, here's Papa. Papa's here."

Matthew peeked around the chair and saw Papa. He jumped up into his arms again, giving him a great big blow kiss on his cheek. Gordon sneakily put his hat and beard on again. Matthew squirmed and tried to pry loose of his grip. Gordon held Matthew long enough to get a picture taken, but Matthew cried as Santa held him.

Then, Glenda took a picture of Gordon and Matthew with the red suit and the extra pieces removed. Matthew was grinning from ear to ear, showing his rosy cheeks and sparkling blue eyes. Glenda got a much happier picture of the two of them.

It was nearing the time for the Christmas program at White Chapel Community Church. A candlelight service was held in the small, country church one week prior to Christmas. Candles were placed in every window and lit right before the service. The congregation would each hold a candle.

Glenda volunteered to clean the church for the program. She packed the car with cleaning supplies and took Jenny and Matthew with her. The church had a hardwood floor and wooden oak pews with carvings on the ends. The pews, pulpit, piano, and swivel stool needed to be dusted. Each of the windows had to be polished. Glenda unlocked the side door of the church and walked up the steps to the sanctuary. She began dusting the floor while Jenny polished the furniture. There were three sections of pews and two aisles leading to the pulpit.

Matthew ran to the front of the church and sat on the swivel stool, spinning around and around. He hollered, "Whee! Whee!" The swivel stool got shorter as he spun around.

"Get off, Matthew," Glenda ordered as she continued with her work.

Matthew obeyed and sauntered up to the pulpit. He opened the red Bible and spoke, "God here." He put his index finger to his heart. He folded his hands and shut his eyes. "Pray God. Pray me. Pray sis. Pray Mom, Dad, Papa, Raw, Bad. Amen."

"That was a nice prayer." Jenny complimented.

As Jenny continued dusting the pews and piano, Matthew ran up and down the two aisles. He circled round and round. Glenda warned him, "No running. Walk."

Matthew went back to the podium and said some unintelligible words. He paced back and forth on the pulpit. He opened a hymnal and began singing.

When Glenda began spraying Windex on the windows, Matthew looked curiously at her. He thought the Windex bottle looked like a water gun.

Glenda set the bottle down as she polished a window. Matthew saw his opportunity and grabbed it. He ran around squirting it in the air. Glenda told Jenny, "You run that way. I'll go this way. We'll get him cornered."

Matthew kept running. Jenny chased after him. Matthew saw her and turned right smack into Glenda's arms. Glenda felt a vapor touch her cheek. She grabbed the bottle from Matthew's hands. "No. No water gun," she told him.

Glenda finished cleaning while Jenny entertained Matthew by playing the piano and singing "Silent Night" and "Joy to the World." Matthew mimicked the lyrics the best he could, making a joyful sound.

Glenda set candles in the sanctuary windows and on the pulpit. The cleaning was done for the evening.

At home, the kitchen smelled of pumpkin spices and sugar cookies made fresh for the evening. On the dining room table, presents decorated with bows were ready to load.

The cold winter winds howled fiercely the evening of the candlelight service. Trudy arrived one hour early to make coffee and chill cranberry juice in the old kitchen fridge. The concrete block basement with old tables and painted, wooden chairs was plain, yet it brightened as the church women arrived and covered the cracked countertop with Tupperware containers of sweet treats.

Pastor Scott arrived ten minutes early and lit each candle in the windows of the dark church. Each small glimmer of light shining in the darkness reminded him of how Christians were called to be the light in the darkness and how a small flicker shines brightly in spite of the dark. The glow had a calming and peaceful impact on each person who came into the church when given a candle. As the congregation looked in awe at the illumination in this simple church, Pastor Scott stepped up to the pulpit.

Flora went to the piano and accompanied "It Came Upon a Midnight Clear." As the members sang, Pastor Scott walked to the person closest to the front and lit that person's candle. That light was passed on and soon the congregation had lit all of them. He talked about the birth of Jesus and the humble beginnings of being born in a stable. Jenny visualized Grandpa Gordon's barn and the horse stalls he had, thinking about the hay up on top to feed the livestock. She thought being born in a stable would be dirty and smelly. But, it would be warm.

Jenny and her friends Linda and Susan sang "Away in a Manger." Some other children read poems about Christmas. Brad read the Christmas story in a deep, serious voice. That really surprised Jenny because he was normally so full of mischief, yet he read so expressively and captured the attention of the congregation. Matthew didn't have a part, but he sat wide-eyed, gazing at glimmering candlelight. He sat still through the entire service looking at the candles. He crossed his arms over his chest and frowned when it ended.

The members gathered in the basement as the women prepared serving trays with cookies and bars. The men set up folding chairs around the tables. Suddenly, one woman screeched loudly when she saw a scared little mouse scurry across the concrete floor. All the women laughed, and a merry joy filled the little basement.

The trays were set on a table for everyone to come and serve themselves. Presents were passed out to Sunday school students and the teachers. Pastor Scott received gifts from all of the generous families. After he opened each of the gifts, he spoke to the congregation, "Thank you. I'm humbled by the generosity of everyone. I'm honored to serve such a loving, thoughtful congregation."

The evening ended with a long-time tradition in which the elders gave each person in attendance an apple and a Hershey's candy bar. This ritual had started in the 1930s during the Great Depression when people didn't have much and so truly appreciated such simple gifts. Now, all these years later, the people of White Chapel looked forward to this tradition as they were reminded to find contentment in simple pleasures and the companionship of fellow believers.

CHAPTER 13

The car was packed full of packages and side dishes for the evening meal. The Parkers left for Grandma Kate's home on the outskirts of the city one hour away. The children wiggled and scuffled in the back seat. "Settle down," Jed's deep voice commanded as he drove.

Brad sneakily poked Jenny in the ribs causing her to squirm and yell. Matthew sat in the middle between his siblings, and Brad motioned for Jenny to push against Matthew. Brad nodded his head to start, and they squished Matthew.

Matthew felt his body being pushed. He said, "Okay, okay. 'Nuff. 'Nuff. No push me." Brad and Jenny were in alliance now. Brad tickled Matthew's neck while Jenny tickled his chin. Matthew laughed out loud and shouted, "Stop. No tickle."

When things settled down, Matthew put one arm around Jenny and one arm around Brad. "Me like Bad. Me like Sis. Me happy." Jenny laid her head on his shoulder, and Brad put his arm around Matthew. "Ah," Matthew said in delight.

They soon arrived at Grandma Kate's house. The children bounded out of the car, racing to see her waiting for her guests on the porch. She sprang to her feet and opened the screen door, thrilled for the company since her dear husband passed away and sang, "Merry Christmas, kids."

"Merry Christmas, Grandma," they chorused to her.

The children scurried into the house to see if Derrick and Dale, their cousins, were there. The children went back to Grandma's room. Derrick already had the tape recorder set up to record an impromptu radio program for everyone that the cousins created every year. The children sang two Christmas carols. Brad concluded the radio program with each one wishing Kate a Merry Christmas. Matthew shouted, "Me like Kate. Me like Papa."

Brad quickly stopped recording. He wasn't sure how Kate would respond to Matthew mentioning Grandpa Gary. He was concerned it might upset the festive evening. He intended to rewind the tape and erase the comment about Papa, but Aunt Lisa and Glenda called everyone to the table for supper. It was a tradition to have tacos and toppings, relish trays, salads, and sweet treats.

While the adults finished eating and caught up on events in one another's lives in the past few months, the children ran upstairs to play a spy game and hide-and-seek. A little later, Kate hollered to the children to let them know it was time to open gifts. Derrick and Brad went to get the cassette player. Everyone found a chair in the family room. Brad told Kate, "We have a special treat for you." He rewound the cassette and played the recorded program.

At the end, Kate heard, "Me like Kate. Me like Papa."

"What a delightful program. Every year it's so different. I keep every cassette. I listen to them from time to time," Kate told everyone. Her eyes filled with tears. "That's so sweet of Matthew to think of Gary." She wiped her eyes with a Kleenex, smiled, and announced, "Brad, Derrick, you are the oldest. Pass out gifts."

As Derrick and Brad passed out the gifts, Kate stepped up to the organ that sat against the wall of the family room. The family was always amazed that she could play without ever having lessons or reading music. She sat down at the organ and played two Christmas tunes. After Kate played, Matthew went to the organ and gently pushed the keys, making a soft sound. He clapped at himself and turned to the family and bowed.

Glenda came up to him, "It's time to open gifts now."

"No. Me play. Me like. Me good."

"You did a nice job, but it's time to see what you received from Dale and Grandma Kate."

"Me play. Me do."

Glenda sighed calmly and turned to find the gifts for Matthew piled neatly by a chair. She picked one of them up and brought it over to him. "See the pretty paper. The paper is so shiny and has stars on it. Let's open it and see what surprise is under here."

Matthew looked at the beautiful paper. "Okay," he agreed. He moved away from the organ and opened his gifts. He received a Fisher-Price village. He also received some building blocks and started playing with the new toys right away. "Tanks," he shouted to no one in particular.

At ten o'clock, Glenda called, "Kids, time to go home." Glenda hugged Kate and wished her Merry Christmas. Brad, Jenny, and Matthew hugged Kate and thanked her for everything.

Christmas morning was time to spend with Glenda's side of the family. Gordon, Trudy, Uncle Vern, and Aunt Phoebe were coming to the house for another Christmas celebration. The children were restricted from the living room where Santa's gifts were placed around the tree. They had to wait until the rest of the family came down from Grandpa Gordon's house. Uncle Vern and Aunt Phoebe lived six hours away at a university town. Uncle Vern was a professor of education. Aunt Phoebe was a fifth-grade teacher. They visited only two times a year, spring break and Christmas.

Excited to see what Santa had dropped off at their house, Matthew sneaked over to the living room doorway to peek at the unwrapped gifts Santa had delivered. Jenny caught him and pulled him back. "Wait."

"Me see. Me see," he pleaded. "Me happy."

"Not now. Come on and play."

Matthew was determined to get a sneak peek, but he went with Jenny to play Fisher-Price in the family room. Jenny turned on the television to a Christmas parade that was aired on a major network. She got engrossed in the beautiful floats and characters in the parade. While Jenny was mesmerized by the parade, Matthew sneaked out of the room. He stood at the edge of the living room doorway. He leaned his body over to get an early glance. He heard footsteps and quickly stood up. Glenda quietly came up to him. "What are you doing?"

"Me no know," Matthew answered.

"Well, you need to stay away from the living room. You get to see what Santa brought later."

"Okay," he complied.

"If you want an early taste of some goodies, join me in the kitchen. I'm frosting some Christmas cookies."

"No now," Matthew replied. "Me play."

Glenda went back to the kitchen to decorate her cookies and work on the meal. Matthew momentarily joined Jenny in the family room. He saw that Jenny was still immersed in watching the parade. He watched television a little bit, but he had one more opportunity to satisfy his curiosity. He tiptoed silently to the living room again, yet he knew better than to go inside. He bent forward and peered into the room. There was a life-like doll as tall as he was. He saw a Barbie Townhouse. He didn't see anything for himself. Disappointed, he quickly moved away from his spot so he wouldn't get caught again. He went to the kitchen to help himself to a cookie. From the variety of cookies, he chose a bell-shaped one with white frosting and blue sprinkled sugar. He bit into the cookie. "Mm. Mm." He rubbed his stomach in satisfaction and took a napkin and wiped a dab of frosting off his mouth. He ran into the family room to be with Jenny.

A knock was at the door. It was Uncle Vern and Aunt Phoebe, each carrying a box of gifts. Uncle Vern was a short, dark-haired man with a joyful personality who loved kids. Aunt Phoebe was blonde and slender whose voice had a ringing tone to it. She sang out, "Merry Christmas, everyone." It sounded like a song with every note held out. Jenny, Brad, and Matthew rushed up to them, jumping up and down. The kids grabbed Uncle Vern's arms.

"Hold on, kiddos. I need to take this box into the living room and get another one from the car."

Glenda came to the door and welcomed the guests, wishing them Merry Christmas.

Aunt Phoebe asked, "Is there anything in the kitchen I can help you with, Glenda?" She handed the box of gifts to Vern.

"I need to get the relish tray ready and the blue glasses out of the pantry. That would be a great help. I also need to set the table."

Phoebe followed Glenda into the kitchen to assist her. The children eagerly waited for Uncle Vern to find out what new game he had to teach them.

Uncle Vern shed his coat and hung it up in the entryway closet. Brad asked him, "Why did the circle turn into a square when it got out of prison?"

Uncle Vern answered, "I don't know, why?"

"It wanted to go straight."

Uncle Vern laughed, "Good one, Brad." He turned to Jenny. "How's school, sweetie?"

"Good. I'm in advanced math. My teacher's the best."

Uncle Vern patted her on the shoulder. "I'm proud of you. Keep up the good work."

Uncle Vern went into the kitchen to ask Aunt Phoebe if they had gotten everything. Matthew ran up to Vern again and reached his hands up to him. Uncle Vern hugged him again. "You sure are happy to see me, kiddo. I'm happy to see you too. Merry Christmas."

Matthew was flustered. He finally said, "Tick tock."

"The clock says it's ten," Glenda said, perplexed.

"No. No. Me tick tock."

Uncle Vern laughed loudly. "Do you want me to do the Matthew clock? Tick tock?"

Glenda was astonished that Matthew remembered that Uncle Vern did that. It was a special rhyme Uncle Vern had done with Matthew the previous March. She whispered to Phoebe, "I can't believe he remembers Vern and the clock rhyme."

"He retains whatever he learns," Phoebe said. "Some children who don't learn quickly have good retention once they learn something. That will be beneficial when he goes to school. He has a remarkable memory. He's so cute too."

"He's full of mischief and keeps us moving. He has brought us so much joy."

"You can tell that Jenny and Brad take good care of him too and have accepted him."

Glenda responded hesitantly, "They don't know yet. I didn't think they were ready to understand his disability when he was born. They have noticed people stare and that his tongue sticks out, but I haven't told them all of it."

"When do you plan on telling them? They need to know."

"I know," Glenda said guiltily, "but Jenny is so tenderhearted. She would have cried and cried about it. Brad wouldn't have treated him like a normal brother. He would have treated him like a china doll instead."

Phoebe sympathetically asked, "I can understand it's hard to explain his disability to them. Don't they ask about his speech?"

"Jenny has. She wondered why Matthew doesn't talk as much as other kids. I told her he just has difficulties with speech and will catch up."

"You know that may or may not be possible," Phoebe warned. "The kids are entitled to know before he goes to school. They won't change how they treat him."

Glenda looked down and focused on her decorating. She felt defensive at what Phoebe was telling her, even though Phoebe was right. It was just easier not talking about it anymore. One day, she needed to explain to the children about Matthew. "You're right, Phoebe. I think I'll let them know before he begins kindergarten. Otherwise, someone else will tell them."

"They need to be prepared. They need to be aware that not everyone will love and accept him."

A tear streamed down Glenda's cheek. She went to the sink and grabbed a paper towel. This was going to be difficult. She had adapted over the past four years. Talking about it would open up the door about her fears for Matthew's future when he would be away from them.

In the family room, Uncle Vern lifted Matthew into his arms and held him in front of him. Vern's fingers were interlocked, and Matthew was sitting on his hands. Uncle Vern swung Matthew back and forth like a pendulum singing, "Tick, tock, tick, tock, goes the little Matthew clock. Tick, tock, tick, tock, goes the little Matthew clock." He dropped Matthew down in front of him but did not touch the floor. "Boing! Boing!" He boomed. Matthew fell on the floor, rolling in laughter.

"Fun. Fun," he said.

Uncle Vern did the tick tock two more times. "Whew," Vern sighed as he put Matthew down. "That tired me out." He wiped his eyebrows. "I do believe you've gotten bigger since we did that last. You're a big boy now."

Matthew stretched his arms, reaching to the sky. "Me big. Me big boy."

"You sure are," Vern affirmed. "You are my big boy."

Matthew beamed and asked for more tick tock.

"No, but maybe later," Vern asserted. "I do believe that some other guests are here."

Grandma Trudy and Grandpa Gordon let themselves into the house. Grandma Trudy hugged each of the grandchildren. Grandpa Gordon gave each one a silly blow kiss as he wished them Merry Christmas. They all went into the living room except for the children who were waiting in the family room. Phoebe and Grandpa Gordon got their cameras ready to take pictures of the children when they saw their gifts from Santa.

The tree was surrounded with gifts and sparkled with silver tinsel and blue lights. The ornaments were homemade crafts and gifts from others. It was a simple décor that was filled with memories as each ornament told a story.

Grandma Trudy called the children to the living room. The children's eyes were wide in wonderment at the number of presents under the tree. Jenny was astounded at the sight of a Barbie townhouse and a beautiful doll the height of Matthew. It had movable arms and legs and a multicolored dress. Its long hair was auburn.

Brad saw puzzles and a Lego set. Matthew had a Fisher-Price boat and a garage for his Hot Wheels cars, but his attention went to the doll that was his size. He studied the doll as Jenny held it. It looked so real.

Brad began passing out packages while Jenny waited patiently and played with her Barbie townhouse. Matthew crept up to the doll and looked at it inquisitively. He touched its hair gently with the tips of his fingers. He stroked its cheek and moved the arms up and down. He lifted the legs and put the doll to a sitting position. He was puzzled by this doll. He grabbed the doll and held it in his arms and began dancing around the living room. He sang and swung it around and around. Everyone stopped talking and looked at him with amusement while he played with the doll.

"He has a new friend," Vern chuckled.

The gifts were opened, and Grandpa Gordon and Grandma Trudy had one more special gift for Jenny. They had it hidden upstairs in the spare bedroom closet. They brought it down. It was a doll bed made of maple wood and had a canopy covering the bed. The bed had a pink and white striped bedspread that matched the canopy. There was a small foam pillow and pink sheets with a small blanket. It was the perfect size for a few of Jenny's dolls. "Thank you, thank you, thank you," Jenny said. "It's perfect."

The women went to get Christmas dinner on the table while the men visited. The children played with Uncle Vern. Matthew had put the tall doll away. He was mesmerized by the fancy bed that looked the right size for him. He sneaked over to it. After pulling back the bedspread, he fluffed the pillow, climbed into the bed, and covered up in the bedding.

"Ah. Me sleep. Me bed." He was most content there several minutes before anyone noticed.

Jenny came into the room to get her doll. "Get out of the bed," she shouted. "It's for my dolls."

"You found a bed just your size," Vern said comically. "It fits you perfectly, but it isn't yours. Can you get out for me?"

Matthew pretended to be sleeping and made snoring sounds. He hid a smile and breathed deeply. A loud snort accidentally came out of his mouth.

"You're just pretending to sleep," Uncle Vern chuckled. "Let's do tick tock again."

Matthew arose quickly and left the doll bed unmade. He leaped over to Uncle Vern and said, "Tick tock."

Uncle Vern lifted him up and started, "Tick tock, tick tock, goes the little Matthew clock. Tick tock, tick tock goes the little Matthew clock. Boing! Boing!"

Both Vern and Matthew burst out in laughter. Vern went through it a couple more times when the women called everyone to the table for the Christmas dinner.

After everyone felt stuffed as a turkey, Vern took the three Parker children into the family room. While Vern played with them, Jed went into the living room, carried the doll bed out of the room, and hid it in Jenny's bedroom closet so Matthew wouldn't get into it again.

A little while later, Matthew went to the living room. He looked bewildered as he couldn't find Jenny's doll bed. He looked all around the tree, under the piano bench, and behind the couches. He searched the whole room, but there was no bed.

"Bed go? Bed go?" He paced around the room. "Me play bed. Bed go?"

Jed heard him and came up to him, "The bed is not yours. I put it away. It's too fancy for you to crawl into it. You're a big boy, not a doll."

"Me bed. Me like bed. Me go bed." Matthew put his hands to his face and closed his eyes.

"You have your big boy bed. That bed is not for you."

Matthew was determined to find that bed. He was upset that it had been taken away. Finally, Uncle Vern offered to play with the new Hot Wheels garage to see the cars go down the ramp fast.

"Voom," Matthew said as he made a gesture of pushing the car to help it go fast.

"Sounds good. Let's play," Uncle Vern kindly agreed. Matthew forgot about the bed for the day.

PART 3

KINDERGARTEN

CHAPTER 14

The summer garden kept Glenda working continuously. She had already canned sixty quarts of tomatoes and had frozen most of the green peppers for cooking later on in the winter. She pickled dozens of cucumbers in old stone crocks. Glenda boiled a pan of water on the stove to sterilize the glass Mason jars and lids. She set the clean, hot jars on a towel to cool. Dozens of quarts of pickle relish, Russian dills, and watermelon pickles were canned.

Sweet corn was plentiful. Glenda, Jenny, Brad, and Matthew went out to the corn patch and picked hundreds of ears. Glenda planned to freeze over fifty quarts. The first job was to get the corn husks off the ears. Matthew was a pro at husking the ears quickly and looking for bugs. He got off as much silk as he could and broke off pieces of corn that were damaged or not quite ripe and threw away ears that were infested with bugs.

Jenny's job was to scrub the ears of corn with a vegetable brush and get the rest of the silk off. If Glenda saw any silk left, she handed the ears back to Jenny to scrub some more. Glenda cut the kernels off of the cob and measured a certain amount into a large metal pan. She added real butter and half-and-half cream to the batch to make an even sweeter treat. The corn cooked an hour in the oven and needed stirring frequently.

Grandpa Gordon came on the first day of freezing corn with a time-saving tool. "I have a surprise for you, Glenda," he said. "I bought this electric knife from the hardware store. Ray said it's great for slicing turkey and corn on the cob. I think it will save you time and work."

"Thank you so much, but I don't mind cutting off the corn with the butcher knife. I'm fine."

"I'll try it out myself, Glenda. By the way, I'm caught up with my work, so I decided I would help you get this work done today and tomorrow, or however long it takes. You can use some extra help," Grandpa Gordon insisted.

"I suppose you cut corn so I can keep measuring, mixing, and stirring the corn in the oven. Then, when it cools, I'll have Jenny help me to hold open the freezer bags to measure one quart into each bag and put them in the freezer. Thank you so much for your offer to help, but I'll only accept it if I can send at least ten quarts home with you."

Grandpa Gordon was pleased with the deal. "You know I can't turn that down. Trudy and I love the recipe. It's so delicious."

"I suppose it isn't so great for the calories," Glenda commented. "But we work off the calories here on the farm."

"We sure do," Grandpa Gordon confirmed. "It isn't going to hurt us."

Grandpa Gordon plugged in the electric knife and began cutting the corn off swiftly. Jenny kept handing him more ears, then stepped outside in the yard where Matthew was husking. He was sitting at the picnic table with a paper sack full of ears. He set the green husks in one sack and the clean, fresh ears in another one. Jenny took the husked ones and handed Matthew another bag.

"How's it going, Matthew?" she inquired.

"Me do. Me good. Me good help. Yum. Yum corn."

"It's delicious," she agreed. "The corn Mom's making will let us have corn all winter."

"Me eat. Me corn," he said, yearning for the sweet taste of fresh-cooked corn.

"If I don't come out here as soon as you're done with this next sack, bring it to the kitchen. I have lots of ears to wash in the sink."

"Okay. Me sis like corn? Yummy?"

"I do. I'm impatient to try the recipe Mom's making. She'll let us have some tastes before she freezes it. She's making lots of it."

"Mm. Mm. Me come in. You call me."

"I'll holler out the window. Keep up the hard work."

Matthew flexed his biceps. "Me strong. Me work. Me do work."

"See you in a little bit."

Jenny walked into the kitchen where Glenda and Grandpa Gordon were deep in conversation above the noise of the electric knife.

"I hope that he isn't teased and bullied. I hope he makes friends and can have a school life that's happy," Glenda said, concerned.

"He'll do fine. I see Mr. Clark downtown at the cafe all the time. Matthew is the very first child with Down syndrome to attend Cloverville Community School. Mr. Clark says his teachers and staff are ready. He knows our family and knows you and Jed have raised him to be well-mannered and self-disciplined."

It pleased Glenda to hear that. "But what if he takes off? He's still fast on his feet even in those cowboy boots. I won't send him to school with tennis shoes. What if something happens, and he can't defend himself because he doesn't verbalize things well?"

"I'm sure Mr. Clark has taken these things into consideration. He wants his school to be one of acceptance and integration. He said children with disabilities learn better immersed in a regular school setting."

"His kindergarten and special education teacher are making a home visit on Monday before school starts on Wednesday. They want him to be all prepared for school. He's going to go half days like all the other children in kindergarten. He might explore everywhere. I know once he knows his way around, he'll stay where he needs to be. I'll warn the teachers how fast he is, and that he likes to explore new places. I know once he knows his way around, he'll stay with his teachers and class."

"It's good to give them a heads-up. He has learning difficulties, but he'll achieve his potential. The school will do everything they can. I have lots of faith in Mr. Clark. He also said that Miss Evans is a roll-with-the-punches kind of person. She is bubbly and accepting. Miss Wilson is a no-nonsense person, but she is tremendous."

Glenda put the first pan of corn into the oven and set the oven timer for one hour. Jenny was welling with curiosity. "Mom, what are you and Grandpa talking about? What's wrong with Matthew?"

Grandpa Gordon looked right at Glenda, signaling it was time to say something. Glenda nervously wiped her hands on the apron. "Glenda, it's time you let Jenny know."

"Know what?" Jenny asked curiously. "Is Matthew going to be all right? What's going on?"

"Your brother has some learning problems. He's healthy and very smart, but he cannot talk as well as other children his age, and he won't learn as quickly as they do. We knew all this at birth," Glenda calmly told Jenny.

"Why didn't you tell me?" Jenny cried.

Glenda got defensive. "I didn't think you'd understand when you were smaller. I just couldn't tell you."

"But he's my brother! I had a right to know!" Jenny spoke sadly to her mother.

Grandpa Gordon intervened. "It's okay, Jenny. You know now, but does it really matter? Are you going to treat him any differently now?"

Sniffling, Jenny answered, "No. He's a wonderful brother."

Glenda opened the oven door and stirred the corn. Glenda still felt it was her fault for having a child in her mid-thirties. She thought if she had had him in her twenties, this wouldn't have happened. However, the doctors had told her there was no explanation why it happened.

Grandpa Gordon observed that Glenda had her back turned. "He has a disability called Down syndrome," he told Jenny. "The only thing different about him is that he has an extra chromosome, and there is no cause for this other than it was a fluke. Chromosomes determine how we look. Since he has Down syndrome, he has the slanted eyes you noticed and his tongue is larger than ours. That's why he sticks it out when he's hot or upset. It's hard for him to keep it in all of the time."

"Is that why people have stared at us in the stores and on vacations?" Jenny asked, starting to understand.

"Yes," Grandpa Gordon said sadly. "Some people have never seen a child with this disability and don't know how to respond."

"I'm glad he's my brother. I love him and don't want anyone to make fun of him."

"Good to hear you say that, Jenny. Most of the community knows about him. I don't know about the kids in school. We have had positive comments from most people. There will be some, however, who will never accept him. That's because people fear what they don't know."

"I'm not afraid of him. He's kind and loving."

Glenda walked out of the room for a minute. Grandpa Gordon continued, "There's no reason for anyone to fear him. He's just like every little boy."

Jenny sat down at the dining room table in shock. She was upset that Mom had never told her about Matthew but even sadder that Matthew had learning problems. He sure didn't seem that different. He was full of mischief, but all boys were. She felt a protective spirit rise up inside of her.

Grandpa Gordon asked, "Any more questions?" He leaned over and gave Jenny a tender kiss on the cheek. "This is still very hard for your mom. Ask your dad or me anything about it. Your mom loves Matthew but has a hard time accepting it."

"Why would she be upset when he is such a great boy?"

"I don't know how to answer that. She loves Matthew. It takes a special kind of love that you, Brad, and your parents have for him. He is quite lucky."

Jenny stood up and went back to the sink to work. Glenda didn't come back for several minutes, and Jenny wondered why Mom had left the room. The oven timer went off. Glenda got the roaster pan of corn out of the oven and put in the next pan. Glenda stirred the corn and got out three small bowls. She distributed some corn to Grandpa Gordon, Jenny, and Matthew. Jenny hollered out the window to Matthew, "Come and try the corn."

Matthew finished husking the ear of corn he had in his hands and raced into the house, "Yummy. Yummy corn. Me want. Me eat."

When Jenny handed him a spoon, he tasted the warm, rich, buttery corn. He devoured his serving and asked for more. Jenny looked at her mom, and Glenda nodded in approval. Jenny went over to the roaster pan and scooped up another spoonful for him. He ate it in satisfaction and said, "Tanks." He darted out to the picnic table to husk more.

Grandpa Gordon complimented Glenda, "It's the best corn I have ever tasted."

Glenda smiled meekly and mixed up a third batch. Soon, it would be packaged for the freezer.

The next three days were filled with making corn to freeze. Grandpa Gordon came down each of those days to help.

CHAPTER 15

Monday came all too fast for Glenda. Two more days and the children would start another school year. This year was particularly hard for her. Matthew was going to start kindergarten.

Early that morning, Glenda was cleaning the downstairs to make it shine. Miss Evans and Miss Wilson were coming by at 11:30 for dinner and a visit with Matthew and the family. She wanted a flawless house that could pass a white glove test. This would be the first time a teacher had ever come over to the house for a visit. Glenda had a ham loaf in the oven along with baked potatoes and green bean casserole. She had made two Jell-o salads and brownies for dessert. There would be plenty of food for everyone; she made sure of that.

Jenny was helping clean by dusting the baseboards and furniture. She folded clothes and put them away. Since Glenda had the dinner in the oven and fridge, she scrubbed floors and cleaned the bathroom. She opened the windows to air out the house from the strong scent of cleaners. She lit a cinnamon candle in the dining room and one in the kitchen to give the house a welcoming aroma.

When Jenny was finished dusting, she had to make sure the toys were picked up and on the shelves against the wall of the small family room. Then, she had to take some Windex and clean the bathroom mirror and the one in the dining room. She finished chores and freshened up from her farm clothes into a new school outfit.

Glenda spruced up with a pair of navy blue slacks and a short sleeved shirt that resembled a sailor's shirt with its white and blue stripes. It had an embroidered anchor on the upper right hand corner of it. Matthew knew there would be special guests in the house. He put on his brown western shirt with the metal snaps, his belt, and buckle. He put on a new pair of jeans and his cowboy hat and boots.

A small, red compact car crept into the driveway. Glenda put her hands over her stomach. She hoped things went well. Jed and Rick came into the house for dinner and the visit. Jed was looking forward to meeting Matthew's teachers. Matthew jumped up and down. "Here! Here! Car here!"

Jenny shyly went to the door with her dad and Matthew. Jed greeted the two women. Miss Evans, the special education teacher, was short and plump with a kind face and a million-dollar smile. She was in her late twenties. Miss Wilson, the kindergarten teacher, was tall and slender with big blue eyes, short hair, and an authoritative posture.

"Welcome, ladies. I'm Jed Parker. This is our daughter, Jenny, our son, Brad, and our other son, Matthew. We're glad to meet you."

"It's our pleasure," smiled Miss Evans. "We're glad to come."

"Nice to meet all of you," said Miss Wilson. "You certainly have a beautiful home here."

"Thank you. We've lived here since Brad was three."

"It looks like we have a cowboy here," Miss Wilson observed.

"Me like. Me cow. Me bull. Me rope." Matthew formed his hands in a lasso.

"Those are sure nice boots," Miss Evans said. "I didn't know they made them for young children."

"It helps slow him down," Jed explained. "We have nicknamed him Matthew Running Bear because once he starts running, he goes fast. You'll find that out."

Miss Evans grimaced at the thought of chasing Matthew. She wasn't very quick herself. Miss Evans and Miss Wilson went into the family room with Matthew. Miss Evans sat right down on the carpet, sitting Indian style. Miss Wilson sat on the floor against the couch with her legs outstretched. The teachers asked Matthew what he liked to play.

"Me cowboy. Me cow. Me rope. Me hat." He pointed to his hat and the special buckle he had gotten in Nebraska.

"You're a sharp-looking cowboy," Miss Evans admired. "Do you ride horses?"

"Me one." He held up his finger to show one. "Me like."

Miss Wilson found a foam ball and tossed it to Miss Evans. They threw it back and forth and giggled. Miss Wilson saw a Fisher-Price airplane and pretended to fly it in the air. Matthew clapped with delight at their play. Miss Evans tossed the foam ball to Matthew. They played catch a little bit. Matthew was so impressed with Miss Evans that he plopped down on her lap and gave her a great big hug. "Me like you. Me call you?"

"I'm Miss Evans, but call me Miss E. Can you say Miss E?"

"Eeeee," Matthew repeated. "Eeeccc."

"Good job. I will be your teacher. You come to school in two days."

"Me see you. Me come see you. Me like you. Me happy."

"You'll love school," Miss Evans stated. "And your other teacher here is Miss Wilson. Let's call her Miss W." Miss Evans held up three fingers for w. She said, "W. Miss W."

Matthew followed Miss Evans's lead and, smiling, held up three fingers. "Double U."

Glenda and Jenny were setting the table when they heard the noise and laughter coming from the family room. Glenda walked in to call the ladies and Matthew for dinner. She was astonished to see how much at home these two teachers made themselves. She didn't expect both of them on the floor playing with the toys. She saw Matthew clapping and laughing. They spent dinner getting acquainted with one another. Glenda felt that the guests were not only teachers but new friends.

Later, Jed, Glenda, and Matthew went out to the farm to show them the cows. They all rode in the pickup truck to the pasture. Matthew and his new teachers sat in the back. Glenda sat up front with Jed as he talked out of the window to them, pointing to the cattle out on the grass. He stopped, and everyone got out. When Miss Evans climbed out of the back of the pickup, her foot squished into something soft and watery.

"Oops," she said amusedly, "I stepped in something." She looked down at the cow pie. She shrugged her shoulders and remarked, "That is part of the farm life, isn't it?"

Matthew found that funny. He said, "Eee, me do. Me icky."

"I got messy this time," she laughed.

"I've heard of stinky shoes, but this beats all," Miss Wilson said as she stifled a giggle. She plugged her nose as she stepped away from the gooey shoe. Then her own foot squished into a soft, smelly mound.

Miss Evans told Miss Wilson, "Serves you right for giving me a bad time."

The ladies both found some fresh green grass without any cow pies and wiped their shoes off the best they could. "This sure doesn't come off easily. Look at the side of my shoe," Miss Evans said good-naturedly.

"It'd better be all off of there before stepping into my car," Miss Wilson warned her. "I don't want the car smelling like cow pies."

"Oh," Miss Evans chuckled. "It won't hurt a thing."

"It isn't your car."

"I'll spray your shoes off at the hydrant," Jed said. "The hose has enough pressure to get you clean."

Back by the loading chute, Jed sprayed off their shoes. "There. That ought to do you."

The ladies inspected the bottoms and sides of their shoes. "Looks good," Miss Wilson said.

As the teachers got into the car to leave, Glenda offered, "You're welcome to come again. Perhaps you can come for supper and a game night. It would be good for Matthew, and we would like your company."

Miss Evans sweetly responded, "We'll have to do that. We'll see you in two days."

Once they left, Jed said to Glenda, "They'll be lots of fun and keep on their toes."

Glenda teased, "I hope they are able to keep better track of Matthew than they did their own shoes."

"I couldn't believe how good-natured they were about the farm and its mishaps. They made themselves comfortable right away. They're really down to earth."

Jed slipped his arm around Glenda as they walked into the house, both of them more hopeful about the school year ahead.

CHAPTER 16

Principal Leo Clark was sitting at his desk looking over his paperwork for a staff meeting in thirty minutes. He eagerly anticipated the start of the school year. He had high expectations for his staff and students. He wanted the school to be a community and a family as well as a place for quality education.

He had a reputation for being a "vulture." Behind his back, students made fun of him because they said he was out to catch them, yet they respected him and didn't want to go to his office to be disciplined.

As Mr. Clark sat in his office, his phone rang. "Hello," he answered. "Yes, Alice." His veteran secretary was on the other end. "Oh, I see. Now?…Can't it wait?…Oh, yes, all right. Send her into my office, but let her know I have only a few minutes until my first meeting." He hung up the phone reluctantly. Mrs. Pearson was in the main office and wanted to come back to speak with him.

"What's her dander up about now?" he muttered under his breath. He sighed and put on a poker face.

Alice, one of the school's secretaries, was Mr. Clark's confidant and full of cheer. She was a devoted secretary who was honorable in keeping confidences. Alice's sunny nature shone in the doorway of Mr. Clark's office.

"Mr. Clark, Mrs. Pearson is here." She turned to look at Mrs. Pearson. "You may go in and find a seat." She smiled pleasantly and went back to her desk at the front.

Mrs. Pearson stomped up to Mr. Clark's desk, towering over him, shaking her head and throwing her thick, blond curls away from her face. Mr. Clark stood and extended his hand to greet her. "Meredith, it's so good to see you today."

Meredith scowled and shook her plus-sized body in agitation. She urgently spat, "I hear you don't have much time, so I'm going to get to the point. I hear that monster child will be riding the bus this year and coming to school here."

"Who do you mean, Meredith?" Mr. Clark knew where this was going.

"That retard who belongs to the Parkers. We have a safe and superb school here. We don't need to blemish it with retards. He belongs in an institution or a special school for his kind."

"Hold on," Mr. Clark held his hand up to slow her down. "Do you mean Matthew Parker?"

"Indeed I do. He is a threat to the safety of the children of this school. He doesn't belong here. Children who are retarded don't belong in society."

Mr. Clark had enough of this woman's slanders. He was feeling himself fume inside but kept his cool on the outside, a skill he had learned from years of experience as a principal. He knew the Parker family well, was coffee buddies with Matthew's grandfather, and had heard stories about Matthew since birth. He suspected that there might be some resistance from some, but he wanted to make this experience a positive one for both the student body and Matthew.

Mr. Clark turned from the thoughts that flashed through his mind to Meredith. "Ma'am, I'm sorry to hear of your concern about Matthew. I do believe that you have not had any contact with him before?"

"Of course not," she spat out furiously. "I wouldn't speak to such a child."

"I see." He hesitated. "I will inform you that in education today, we are integrating and teaching children with disabilities.

We are embracing them rather than ostracizing them. Here at Cloverville Community School, we are welcoming Matthew with open arms. He's not a retard. He's a child who doesn't learn as quickly as other children."

Meredith shifted her weight again. "We are wasting our county tax dollars on someone who is incapable of learning. It's preposterous to educate the uneducable. I'll go to the school board about this."

"Meredith, the board has gladly accepted Matthew's enrollment. We are a close-knit community and care about his best interest and all of the children here. I have a meeting in a few moments with our teaching staff. I hope we are done."

"You haven't seen the end of me, Mr. Clark. I'm contacting a lawyer about my children's right to be safe at school. That child has no place here."

Smiling kindly, more relieved for ending the meeting than anything, he said, "Meredith, Matthew has every legal right to an education. Our schools don't discriminate against those with disabilities. You may contact a lawyer, if you wish. However, be cautioned to know that there are laws and rights in place that make it nearly impossible to remove him from school. We are in the 1970s. Whether you like it or not, that's the way things are today. Excuse me, I must get to my meeting." Mr. Clark looked at his watch. He was already ten minutes late.

Mrs. Pearson spoke bitterly, "I'm not giving up. You'll see that I will find a way, some way, to get him out of here. If you won't work with me, I'll find someone who will. I'm sure there are others who agree with me."

"I honestly haven't met any. Most people know and care about the Parkers," Mr. Clark told her impatiently now. "I really need to get to my meeting. Good day."

Meredith Pearson marched out of the office and slammed the door. She was going to show him. She wasn't going to let any law stop her. If that retard is allowed in the school, she decided she would watch his actions like a hawk and get him out of there one way or another. *This isn't over. Oh, no, this isn't over. I'll make sure of that.*

The two office ladies silently looked at their typewriters as Meredith Pearson departed the building.

"Whew," whispered Marie, the secretary who worked next to Alice. "She's on her high horse. I wonder if she'll ever come down from it. She's so nasty. Do you think she'll do all she can to get Matthew out of school?"

Alice looked somber, "Yes, she will. She thinks she's entitled to her way. She has always caused trouble, but this is the most determined I've seen her."

"Matthew's such a good kid. He's full of energy, but he deserves to be here as well as anyone else."

"If I can do anything to offset the negativity she is trying to spread, I will. The students here will like him and look out for him. Most of them anyway." Alice thought about the considerate student body. "Mrs. Pearson may have a few people agree with her, but most won't."

"Good luck. She's hard to fight," Marie said.

"She thinks her threats give her power. She needs someone to oppose her. Some of the parents will be too hesitant to cross her. They may not agree with her, but they won't stand up to her either. That's why she throws her weight around, by being threatening."

"This will be a challenging year," Marie replied.

"Yes, but we can handle it. Leo has a tough skin, and he stands up for what's right. He cares about the welfare of all our student body."

Mr. Clark entered the library where the staff was impatiently waiting for him. Miss Wilson jokingly spoke up, "We were about to leave. No show, no meeting. Just like college." The staff laughed.

"Deservedly so," added Mr. Clark. "I can only say I had a most unpleasant meeting that was difficult to leave. My apologies."

Mr. Morgan said, "Let's get this meeting going. I need to get to my classroom and get ready for the high schoolers."

"I agree. First, I do want to give a sincere welcome back to each and every one of you. I anticipate a sensational year with challenges and growth. As a staff, we need to keep our objectivity and show concern for our children."

The meeting went on for the rest of the morning. Mr. Clark put the encounter out of his mind for the time being. He put on his itinerary for the afternoon, however, to contact the school attorney. He wanted to give the attorney a heads-up on the situation with Mrs. Pearson. What prejudices and stereotypes this woman has.

It was one more day until the students arrived.

CHAPTER 17

It was the middle of August when the first day of school arrived. Matthew knew he was going to see the ladies who had visited his house. He woke up at 6:00 a.m. to get dressed in his cowboy clothes. He wore his denim jeans with a long-sleeved green western shirt. He wore his belt, but Glenda told him to leave his belt buckle at home. He sat down with Jed and Brad for a hot breakfast of pancakes and sausage. Jenny was still sleeping. Matthew was fidgety this morning. He smiled gladly as he ate, "Me go school. Me go bus. Me like."

"Be good. You're a big boy now. Listen to your teachers," Jed instructed.

"Okay," Matthew replied between bites of syrupy pancakes.

Jenny groggily came down the stairs and mumbled, "Mornin'" to everyone.

"Come and eat breakfast while it's hot," Glenda ordered.

Jenny sat down and ate breakfast. She then went to get ready for school. Matthew remained at the table and was attentively listening to Jed tell stories about his school life that captivated Matthew's attention.

When Jenny came back to the kitchen, Matthew joined Brad at the living room window to watch for the bus coming down the highway. The bus was to arrive at 7:15 a.m. The bus route was a long route since it drove on many gravel and dirt roads to pick up students for school. The bus ride would be about one hour in good weather.

Brad told Matthew in a protective way, "You sit with me today, Matthew. I want to make sure you're okay and follow the rules. You must sit down and no running on the bus."

Jenny whined, "I wanted to sit with Matthew. I'm his big sister. You aren't any better than me."

"I'm older and want to look after him. I also want to make sure he learns the rules," Brad explained.

Jenny saddened a minute. "I'll sit in front of you then. I'll help you keep an eye on him."

Brad saw the yellow bus from a distance coming toward their house. "It's here. The bus is here," he shouted. "Time to go, Matthew. We must meet the bus."

Matthew bounded out of the house like a fireball. The bus drove up the driveway and stopped in front of the sidewalk. The bus door opened. Mrs. Trent's pearly white teeth showed as she smiled at the children. "Good morning."

Brad and Jenny each replied, "Good morning."

Mrs. Trent continued, "And this must be our new rider, Matthew. Welcome, Matthew. Nice to meet you."

Matthew smiled shyly. He climbed the stairs of the bus and saw lots of seats. Only four people were on the bus. He raced to the vacant seats in the back. "Slow down," Brad asserted. "I told you not to run on the bus. We'll be on a long ride."

Matthew was already in the back seat. Brad sat next to him. Jenny chose the seat right in front of Matthew.

The bus started moving away from home. The ride was bumpy. Matthew started bouncing up and down in his seat in sync with the bus's motion. "Whee. Whee."

"Sit down, Matthew," Brad glared at him. "Sit."

Matthew squealed in delight. The bus stopped at many more houses and filled up quickly. The noise level elevated to a loud hum. Brad felt frustrated as Matthew went up and down. "Whee, whee," Matthew kept chanting. Some of the children laughed.

"He's cool," Mike, an upperclassmen, said. "He's having fun."

Brad smiled faintly. "Wait until I tell Mom when you get home," he said as a last resort. "Or I'll tell Raw."

Matthew looked at Brad wide-eyed. He sank down in his seat and sat still the rest of the way to school.

The bus had one empty seat as it drove up the school lane. Most of the seats had two students in them. The school was out of town and located on a gently sloping hill. When the bus drove toward the school, the first thing it passed was a pool of water with a fence around it. This was the lagoon for the school. It always looked like a swimming pool to young students. The school was atop the hill and was a large, square building where kindergarten through twelfth grade attended. It needed some extra space, so there were three mobile trailers near the main building. These trailers were for the kindergarten through third grade and special education classes. The units had olive-green siding. There were two carpeted classrooms in each one.

Matthew felt the bus stop and open its doors. The children piled out of the bus from the front seat toward the back. Matthew and Brad were the last to exit. Matthew saw Miss Evans first thing as he stepped off the bus. Brad held his hand and led him to Miss Evans. "Be good. Remember, Mom expects you to listen to your teachers."

"Okay," Matthew answered. He walked up enthusiastically and wrapped his arms around Miss Evans's stout frame and said, "Eeeee. Me see you. Me happy."

"Welcome, Matthew. Let me hold your hand and show you where we'll have class."

Matthew grasped her hand happily and followed Miss Evans to one of the trailers. Miss Evans's room was adjacent to the kindergarten room. Matthew would spend part of the time with Miss Evans in her special education room and part of the time with Miss Wilson in the kindergarten room. Miss Evans was going to go around with Matthew the first day.

On the way to the trailer, Matthew saw a large grassy field filled with playground equipment. His eyes noticed the teeter totter, the merry-go-round, the slides, swings, and ball field. He saw one thing that caught his eye more than any other. The monkey bars. Matthew pulled his hand from Miss Evans's hand. He ran determinedly in his cowboy boots straight for those monkey bars. She waddled after him panting for breath. "Matthew," she called. "Come back here. I need to show you your room."

Matthew ignored her calls. He kept running to the monkey bars. They were enclosed and shaped like a dome. He had never seen anything like them before. He got to the bars and quickly climbed to the top. "Me big. Me big boy," he hollered triumphantly.

Miss Evans awkwardly attempted to climb the top of the monkey bars. Matthew clapped with glee that she wanted to join him. "You come, Miss Eeeee. You come me. Me like up. Me see."

"Matthew, I'm coming to get you. Let's meet some new friends." She continued to climb the monkey bars slowly. Matthew braced his feet on the top bar and stood straight up and lifted his hands to the air.

Miss Evans gulped and hoped he wouldn't fall. She got within reach of him when he slid down on his bottom. He jumped down underneath the dome of colorful bars. Miss Evans spoke calmly to Matthew, "Come with me, Matthew. You can play here later."

"No. Me play. Me like."

"Matthew, we are late for games and play."

"Me go up. Me up 'gin."

Miss Evans spoke firmly, "I'll go inside and call your mom if you don't get out this instant."

He hesitantly crawled out of the bottom part of the monkey bars. Miss Evans reached for Matthew's arm to lead him to class. But Matthew took off again. He saw the swings several yards away. He ran like lightning and sat down. He started pumping his legs to go high. Miss Evans caught up to him and grabbed the linked chain. She stopped the swing. "Now, it's time to stop and go to class." She firmly grasped his arm as he got off of the swing.

He hugged Miss Evans tightly. "Me like you."

Miss Evans patted his back. He needed training about his schedule and where to go. It was going to take time and patience, but it was going to work out. *Good thing he has cowboy boots. I couldn't keep up with him as it was.*

Miss Evans led Matthew to the kindergarten room where Miss Wilson was instructing. The kindergarten room was a play haven. There were several small tables with chairs pushed up to them. Matthew scanned the room and saw a big desk, toy trucks, cars, blocks, crayons, paper, a toy kitchen, dolls, and cubbies. Miss Evans loosened her grip on Matthew. He headed right for the teacher's desk. He sat in the green swivel chair and spun around. He chuckled. The kindergartners were seated on the floor and smiled at Matthew. Miss Evans went over to him and said, "No. This is Miss Wilson's chair. Come to the floor with the other boys and girls."

"Whee." The chair whirled around again. The class laughed quietly. Miss Evans grabbed the chair and stopped it from spinning.

Matthew looked up at her and frowned. He tried to spin again and couldn't. He saw the class and sat down. Miss Wilson was reading a book to the boys and girls. Matthew sat down next to a sweet, blond, curly-haired girl named Stacey. Matthew reached out gently to touch the soft hair. Stacey felt his hand on her perfect blond hair and said, "No. Don't touch."

Matthew removed his hand and wiggled in his spot. Stacey put a finger to her lip to tell him to be quiet. Matthew sat still. Miss Evans observed how Matthew responded immediately to his peer group. Miss Wilson finished reading the book. Matthew stood up and applauded. The other students followed.

"Thank you, boys and girls," she spoke sweetly. "That was a good book, and I'm glad you enjoyed it so well. Please sit down."

The class followed directions, but Matthew continued to stand and clap.

He said, "Ree, ree."

Miss Wilson looked at Matthew and instructed the class to sit down at the tables. The students dispersed and Matthew followed a boy with a red plaid shirt and denim jeans. His name was Luke. He had a pair of tan boots. Luke had brown hair with freckles and smiled. Matthew hugged him. Luke sat down right next to Matthew.

"My name is Luke," he shared. "My mom told me about you."

"Hi, me Matt. Me like you."

Miss Wilson asked the students to count to five. She modeled counting to five with her fingers. She said, "One, two, three, four, five. Okay, class, say it with me this time."

The class followed. Matthew said, "One, two, one, two, one, two."

Miss Evans knelt down behind him, "Matthew, look at my hand." She held up one finger at a time. "One, two, three, four, five."

He watched her count with her fingers. "One, two," he said, holding up his fingers. "One, two, one." He smiled, pleased with himself.

Miss Evans made a mental note to herself to work on basic counting skills. He needed to be able to count to ten this fall. She saw that it was 9:00 a.m. It was time for her to take Matthew to her special education classroom. Miss Evans led Matthew through a small hallway to her room which had a round table and a kidney-shaped table with chairs surrounding them. She laid out three red paper cups on the table. She modeled, "One, two, three. Three cups."

"Water," Matthew replied, raising his hand and tipping it to his mouth.

"The cups can have water, but we are counting them now. One, two, three," she counted as she pointed to each one.

"One, two, one," he said and grabbed a cup. He walked to the sink, cup in hand. He turned on the water faucet and filled the cup full of water. He took a sip and dumped the rest. He saw a metal knob on the other side of the sink that had a hole in it. Matthew put his finger in it. He pushed a button while holding his finger in the hole. Water squirted all over his hand, face, and body. "Ah," he said, refreshed by the water. Miss Evans chuckled under her breath and showed Matthew how to use the water fountain. Matthew tried it again. He put his mouth down by the hole and pushed the button. Water squirted in his mouth and around his face.

"Come sit down," Miss Evans urged as she sat at the kidney table.

Matthew came bounding up to her and embraced her in a big hug. He signed, "I love you." Miss E. and Matthew continued to work on "one, two, three."

Soon it was recess time. Miss Evans went out with him. Matthew dashed out to the playground. He ran to the teeter totter and stepped on one end. He started at the bottom and walked up the slope. He kept his balance as he walked down the other side. Several fifth-grade boys, who were full of mischief, were astonished a kindergartner could walk along there without falling off.

Nick and Travis looked at each other wide-eyed. Nick whispered, "He's in big trouble doing that."

"Yeah," added Travis, "Wait until Mr. Clark hears about this. He sure is cool though. Most kids would fall."

Miss Evans had seen what happened. She asked Tricia, a fifth grader, to go inside and tell Mr. Clark there was a situation outside. In two minutes, Mr. Clark authoritatively marched out to the playground. He walked by Nick and Travis. "There's the vulture," Nick gulped. "Is this kid ever in trouble!"

Mr. Clark walked as close as he could to Matthew, who was standing in the middle of the teeter totter. He cleared his throat and firmly stated, "Matthew, get off of there right now." Matthew shyly eased off the teeter totter. He stepped down and gave Mr. Clark a hug.

"Yuck," Nick told Travis. "Why would anyone want to hug the vulture? He isn't nice at all."

"I don't get it," Travis replied. "He's brave. No one else wants to hug him."

"The weird thing is," Nick observed, "Mr. Clark has a smile on his face. That's odd."

"Tell me about it." Travis added, "I don't believe I have ever seen him smile. And that kid is in trouble too."

Mr. Clark walked toward the boys as he led Matthew around the playground to teach him the rules. The boys backed out of his way as he approached.

———*———

A shrill sound filled the air. It was time for the boys and girls to line up to go inside. Every teacher's class had its own line. The recess teacher was telling students where to stand this first day of school. Miss Evans looked to see if Matthew got in line. He wasn't there. She scanned the playground and saw him standing on top of the slide.

"Oh, my gosh," she muttered. Her heart began racing. She had to get to him before he fell off. Miss Evans rushed back toward the playground. She felt nervous and shouted to Matthew, "Get down! Get down!" Matthew heard the panic in her voice. He looked over to her. She came up to the slide. "Get off of there. You'll fall."

"Me okay. Me fine. Me like up."

"Get down NOW!" she yelled.

Matthew fearlessly wiggled on the slide. Miss Evans decided to take a deep breath and climb the ladder to the top. As she started up the ladder, a deep voice ordered, "Matthew, get down and come with me."

Matthew listened to Mr. Clark and immediately came down. He went up proudly to Mr. Clark. "Me do. Me up high. Me up. Me like."

Mr. Clark sent Miss Evans back to the kindergarten room. He walked with Matthew and discussed more rules of school. "Do not stand on that slide again. Do you understand?"

Matthew nodded his head up and down. He walked proudly back to the room with Mr. Clark. In the kindergarten room, Miss Wilson had the class sitting on the floor in front of her. She sat cross-legged along with the students teaching them a finger play. Matthew looked around and saw the sweet girl with soft, blond curls. He sat down next to her. He remembered to be quiet this time. The metal snap on his shirt sleeve came undone at recess. He looked down at it and fumbled as he tried to snap it. Stacey looked at him as he tried to figure it out. She leaned over and took his hand in hers and fixed the snap. Matthew told her, "Tanks." Stacey smiled sweetly at him.

Kindergarten went until noon, and the students went home on the buses. Matthew remembered Mrs. Trent and sat in the front of the bus this time since neither Brad nor Jenny was there to be with him. He felt more timid without them. The ride was less bumpy in front. Matthew studied the gears and levers the driver used, intrigued by how things worked.

The first day of the adventure was over. He was excited when the bus let him off at his house. Glenda and Jed both eagerly waited for him at the end of the sidewalk that led to the house. He got off with a big grin on his face. He hugged both of them. "How was the bus ride?" Glenda asked Mrs. Trent.

"It was fine. He is going to be all right." They visited a little bit since Matthew was the last kindergartner to get off. Mrs. Trent was a neighbor lady whose husband also farmed. They talked about the crops and the weather forecast, and then Mrs. Trent drove home.

Glenda took Matthew inside, and his dad joined them for dinner. After they ate, Matthew went outside with Jed. Jed worked at greasing some machinery and showed Matthew how he did it. Matthew watched intently and said, "Me do. Me do."

"Sure. Here." He guided Matthew's hands to grease the machinery carefully without getting it all over. Matthew was meticulous. Jed saw how well Matthew did, and he let him do more. From then on the afternoons became lessons that Jed had with Matthew to learn mechanical skills.

CHAPTER 18

Matthew eventually learned the recess rules and stayed on the playground. He learned the schedule for the morning and went right to his classroom without supervision when he arrived at school. The fifth grade boys were amazed at how Mr. Clark laughed more around Matthew and had no idea what magic Matthew worked on this grouchy man, but they were impressed. The boys watched Matthew come energetically running out to recess in his cowboy boots. The boys spoke to him, and Matthew put both thumbs up and said, "Ay."

During the second week of school, the kindergartners lined up for music while Matthew was in the bathroom. They left the room and followed Miss Wilson to the big building. She watched the class as they entered the music room in an orderly fashion and spoke pleasantries to Mrs. Phelps. She didn't look to see if all of the children had entered the classroom. As Miss Wilson turned to go to her room, Mrs. Phelps asked, "Is Matthew absent today?"

Miss Wilson looked confused. "He's here. He should be in the room with the others."

Mrs. Phelps studied the class. "I don't see him. Does Miss Evans have him?"

"I don't think so. He is supposed to be with the class. I'll go back to the room and check on it."

Matthew opened the bathroom door of the kindergarten room and didn't see anyone. He didn't know where everyone had gone, so he went to Miss Evans's room. She wasn't there either. He opened the door to step outside and didn't see anyone out at recess. *Where could everyone be?* He walked around the outside of the trailer. No one was there, and he didn't know what to do.

Miss Wilson came back to her room to find it empty and checked on Miss Evans. Her room was vacant. She was unsure where he went. She called on the phone to the office. "Is Matthew in the office?" There was a negative response on the other end. "May I talk to Mr. Clark? This is urgent."

"Mr. Clark speaking."

"Uh, I, uh, Matthew, he, uh, didn't make it to music. I don't know," she stammered, "where he is." She was talking louder.

"I'll be right over."

Oh no, not the lagoon! He could climb the fence and drown. Miss Wilson raced down the hill to see if he had run down there. Wondering where Miss Evans was, her heart was pounding and her head spinning.

While Miss Wilson was sprinting to the lagoon, Marie, the office secretary, contacted the janitors and cooks to search for him. The teachers in class were contacted but were warned not to alarm their students that a student was missing. The janitors checked the boiler room, every storage closet, and any hidden place they knew. The gym teacher searched the locker rooms with no success in finding Matthew.

Mr. Clark caught up to Miss Wilson at the muddy lagoon with its wire fence. Mr. Clark examined the exterior and remarked, "There are no footprints. That means he didn't come down here."

"Whew," Miss Wilson sighed in relief. "I don't know where he went, but at least he isn't in there. It had me scared to death, but where on earth can he be?"

Mr. Clark heard the sound of semi trucks and cars passing by the highway near the school. He told Miss Wilson, "Let's jog around the school by the highway and see if he went that way. I haven't heard any cars honk, but it's possible he could be standing nearby and not be seen."

The two of them ran around the school near the highway. Mr. Clark walked to the nearest trailer and called the office. "Alice, has anyone found Matthew?"

"No," Alice said sadly.

"Did anyone check the playground?"

"Yes, and he isn't there. We have lots of people searching. I'm scared for him. Where could he be?" Alice asked, feeling anxious.

"We'll keep looking for him," Mr. Clark said with determination.

Miss Evans met Miss Wilson and Mr. Clark outside of the trailer. "Mrs. Phelps has offered to keep the kindergartners in her room for extra music until we find Matthew."

"Good idea," Mr. Clark commented. "The more everyone stays put, the easier it will be to find him."

Miss Wilson vented at Miss Evans. "Where have you been? I tried to get you to help me."

"I was in a meeting with a new student's parents. I was unaware of this whole thing until the meeting was over. I'm sorry."

"You couldn't have known." Miss Wilson calmed down. "I thought he was with the rest of the class. He's been following Stacey and Luke everywhere. He must have taken off on the way to music. I can't think where else to look." Miss Wilson plopped down on the grass panting.

"This is like finding a needle in a haystack," Miss Evans stated. "Think of how Jed and Glenda are going to feel about this. I feel horrible." She breathed a few deep breaths. "We have to find him, but where else do we look?"

Mr. Clark dismissed himself. "It's time to call the police and report a missing child. I must also call Jed and Glenda. This isn't going to be easy. We assured them Matthew would be safe and in the best care." His thoughts went to the first meeting with them. If Mrs. Pearson gets wind of this, there will be trouble. He looked around the school grounds one more time. Was there somewhere he didn't have staff look? Where could he be? There had to be somewhere logical, somewhere so simple. He couldn't think.

Mr. Clark saw Mr. Taylor, the bus barn manager and mechanic, walk toward him. Mr. Taylor had not been informed about the disappearance. He said, "Mr. Clark, Bus 28 has a broken belt that needs to be fixed by the afternoon dismissal. I need to leave to get the part."

Mr. Clark gave his permission. "Of course, you may leave. Say, where do you think a young boy would run off to? We are missing a kindergartner."

"If I were a boy, I would hide in an obvious spot in plain sight."

"Like where?" Mr. Clark asked.

"Hm. I'd have to think like a little boy. I liked cars, trucks, fast things."

Mr. Clark thanked him and turned to go to his office to call the police. If there was any way to avoid this call, he would avoid it. He checked his watch; it was 10:30 a.m., one hour before the children would be loaded on the buses. He had an idea. The bus to take kindergarten students home was parked in its spot, ready to load the students. He walked toward it. The bus door swung open and then shut. It was rather early for the driver to be on the bus waiting. He walked closer to the door and saw a small figure in the driver's seat. Matthew was moving the blinker switch with one hand and had the other hand on the steering wheel. Mr. Clark knocked on the glass. Matthew ignored him. He knocked again and ordered, "Open this door."

"What are you doing on the bus?" he asked.

"No one room. Me no see. Me no see Miss E. No Miss W. Go. All go. Me go bus. Me go."

"You couldn't find your teacher?"

"No. Me come out." Matthew made a motion with his hands of flushing the toilet and washing. "Me no see. Go. Time go. Me bus. Me go."

Mr. Clark breathed a sigh of relief and patiently spoke, "It isn't time to go home yet. Let's go to my office and visit a little bit." Matthew quietly followed him to the office.

Miss Wilson and Miss Evans saw Matthew and were relieved that he was safe. "Where was he?" asked Miss Wilson.

"He was on the school bus," Mr. Clark explained. "He used his hands to explain to me that he was in the bathroom. He came out, and no one was there. He thought it must have been time to go home. It was a logical misunderstanding. We need to make sure he is in every line and arrives at every class."

Mr. Clark led Matthew into the office. "Alice," he said, "would you please call the janitors and staff that were looking for Matthew. He was found safe. It was all a mix-up that anyone could have had at this age."

"No harm done, then? I'm just so thankful he's safe. I was getting worried here sitting by the phone."

"I know. I'm thankful that I didn't have to file a report to the police. Thank goodness he didn't go to the highway. Glenda said he wouldn't go in that direction. I'm glad he didn't head to the lagoon."

"For land sakes, yes!" Alice exclaimed. "He is such a monkey. He could have climbed that fence in no time flat."

"Yes. I'm going to have him stay in my office until things settle down. It's been a long thirty minutes. It seemed like hours when we were looking."

Alice asked, "Do you want anything else?"

"Yes, get Matthew a juice from the kitchen. He should quench his thirst. He'll sit with me while I call his parents."

Mr. Clark had Matthew sit in a comfortable leather chair in his office. Matthew sat still and saw a Rubik's cube on his desk and recognized that Brad had one of those at home. "Me do. Me like."

While Matthew played, Mr. Clark took a moment to think how best to let the Parkers know about the morning. He didn't want to frighten them, but he wanted to be honest. He picked up the phone and dialed.

"Hello, Jed, this is Leo Clark. How are you today?"

"Good," answered Jed. "Is everything okay?"

"It is now, but I felt it was important to call you and let you know that Matthew was missing for a while."

"What?"

"The teacher took the class down to music. Apparently, he was in the bathroom when she walked the class to the music room. Matthew came out and was confused why the room was empty, and no one was around. He thought it was time to go home. He was found on the bus waiting to leave school."

"Oh," Jed was stunned and didn't know what to say. "Did this cause havoc today?"

Mr. Clark breathed deeply. "We, uh, were all very concerned about his whereabouts. It took a while to find him."

"I see," Jed stammered. "Why didn't the teacher wait for him to get in line?"

"All I can say is that he must have lined up and gone to the bathroom right before they left. I'm not sure. Neither is the teacher."

Jed wasn't angry; he was numb. His little Running Bear slipped right through their fingers. "Is this a chronic problem? Does he take off a lot?"

"The only other time he's has taken off was at the playground where we knew exactly where he was. The teachers were right on his heels. This is an exception, and that is why I wanted you to know about it."

"Thank you for calling. We'll talk to him tonight."

Mr. Clark hung up the phone. It went better than he expected. Jed wasn't emotional nor was he furious. He was calm and patient unlike many parents he called. Matthew sat in the chair, continuously turning the cube.

Alice came in with the juice and a cookie from the kitchen. Her smile shone brightly when she saw Matthew, "The cooks wanted you to have a special treat. They're glad you are okay."

"Me okay. Me go. Me time go."

"It's almost time but not yet," she said as she rubbed his back. He turned around and gave her a big hug.

"Me like you. Tanks."

"You're certainly welcome," she answered.

Mr. Clark talked to Alice and Marie. "You know, this is going to be a challenge. I don't want Jed and Glenda to distrust us. We are learning along the way. I'm confident things will be fine with time."

Marie timidly spoke, "It must be so hard to know that Matthew can run off like that. He's a loveable child, but it's a lot of work to raise him. They must be exhausted at times."

"They have lots of family support and are very fortunate to be a close-knit family," Alice defended.

"It still has to be tough. I don't think I could handle it," Marie said.

"We cannot control what happens, but we can control our responses," Mr. Clark answered. "I know many parents would feel burdened, but Gordon told me they were going to love him and teach him to reach his potential. Jed is a patient man and will teach him skills."

"I think it's a joy in disguise," Alice stated. "Matthew is young. We get to look after him and care for him. We'll watch him grow up here and see him learn and flourish to the best of his ability. He's already grown a lot."

Marie replied, "I have nothing against him, I just think it's a real burden to work with him. He's cute as can be, but how do parents deal with it?"

"We're all different. God chooses special homes for children with disabilities. He doesn't give us more than we can handle. Not everyone is suited for this blessing. It was hard for Glenda and Jed to accept at first, but they have embraced it now. We'll see good in all of this. Just wait and see," Alice optimistically told Marie.

"At least it isn't my problem," Marie said honestly.

Mr. Clark went into his office to do his administrative work.

CHAPTER 19

The Hearty Home Café was a quaint little restaurant that was a gathering place for the locals and had approximately twenty tables covered with vinyl tablecloths. The décor consisted of wall paintings that the school's art students created and displayed for the community to see. There was one long counter with six stools for individuals. Mary Smith, the owner, was a longtime resident and an amazing cook. Each day she offered two lunch specials and several varieties of pies and desserts on her small menu. Families packed into her establishment during the breakfast and lunch hours.

Mrs. Nora Daniels was sitting at a small booth waiting to have coffee with a friend. Nora taught second grade and had to talk with someone about the school year. She was so upset that this little Down syndrome boy was at school and thought he was nothing but a nuisance. She did not want to be his teacher in two years and wondered what was going on in this world. Why should teachers be expected to educate those who have no potential? And, the incident a few days ago, when he took off and scared everyone half to death, was unacceptable. She felt he belonged hidden at home, in an institution, or a special school with children of his kind like it always used to be.

The jolly, sixty-four-year-old waitress in a pale pink dress with a white lace apron and an order pad approached the table. "Can I get you anything while you're waiting?" she asked. "A cup of coffee, dessert?"

"What kinds of pie do you have today?" Nora asked.

"We don't have many left, but we have lemon, peach, and apple."

"I think I'll order a cup of coffee and a piece of lemon pie. It sounds delicious."

"It's the best pie in the region. I'll be right back with your order."

Nora retreated back into her own thoughts. She knew the Parkers, and they didn't have the skills to help this child. Nora was thirty years old and had lived in the community for only five years. She had married a man who worked in a nearby town as a supervisor at a factory.

The townspeople didn't know how shallow she was. In contrast, her husband relished the opportunity to visit with the locals on Saturday mornings at the cafe.

The waitress brought the cup of coffee and lemon pie. Nora thanked her and took one bite. This was the tastiest pie she had ever had. It was far better than any she had ever ordered from high-class restaurants.

Meredith Pearson came into the restaurant. The waitress said, "Good morning, can I help you?"

"I'm meeting a friend here." She looked around the room and saw Nora sitting at a booth near the back of the restaurant apart from the other clientele. She sat down across from Nora.

"Oh, am I glad to see you," Nora said. "This has been quite the year, and I feel like a minority. I cannot believe the things that have gone on since that Matthew Parker came to our school. He is nothing but trouble. He isn't fit to be there at all."

Meredith responded, "I knew it. I tried to talk to the principal before school even started. I told him I want him out of that school. I'm looking for a way to get him out of there."

Nora looked defeated. "It's an uphill battle to achieve, but I agree with you. Times are getting worse when we allow such children in our educational system. Ten years ago, you wouldn't have seen this coming. It's the downfall of our society. I knew you'd understand, Meredith. I just had to talk to someone."

"What happened? I want to hear all about it."

Nora Daniels told her about every instance at recess and the disappearance. She shared how the principal was so low key about it. She said that Miss Wilson couldn't even do her job and that the other teachers had no objections at all.

Meredith listened attentively, hanging on to every negative word that Mrs. Daniels had to say. "I'm so sorry that you have to tolerate being on a staff where this has become acceptable in education. It's the way of the times, but it isn't the way it should be. We need to revert back to the days when it was disgraceful to give birth to a retarded person. I will personally do whatever I can to get him removed."

Nora perked up as she heard Meredith say this. Before, she felt defeated on her perspective, but now she created an alliance with a person who made things happen. "Thank you. I'm glad someone else sees it the way I do. I feel so much better that we can find a way for this to happen. I love teaching, but I won't stoop this far beneath mediocrity."

Meredith stood, swaying her hips. "I'm glad we got together. Let's do this again soon." She smiled in satisfaction and left the restaurant.

Nora hoped Meredith never referenced her name to Mr. Clark. Information about children, especially special education students, had to remain confidential. There were laws to protect students and the staff. Nora finished her cup of coffee and dessert. She left a meager tip on the table and went to the cash register to pay the bill.

The cashier was Mary, the owner of the establishment. "How was everything? It was so good to see you. How is your school year going?"

Nora put on a phony smile. "Everything was fine," she said sweetly. "My year is wonderful. I have the best kids here. Families sure raise their children to be respectful and hardworking."

"I'm glad it's going well for you. We've heard such kind comments about you. The kids like you."

"Thank you," Nora said politely. "Have a great day."

"You too." Mary gave her the change and turned around back to the kitchen. She softly spoke to Delores, who was cooking. "Nora and Meredith were having coffee together. There's something fishy about that. I wonder what they're up to. You know, Nora has always thought she was above us. Something's up."

Delores nodded in agreement. "I know trouble's brewing. Those two make a nasty combination."

Mary agreed. "We will keep our eyes and ears open. It always gets around in no time in a small community like this one."

"Let's just tell the waitresses to pay close attention to them."

"Agree. Now, let's get cooking. More customers will be in for noon dinner."

CHAPTER 20

By October, Matthew had adjusted well to school and learned what the teachers expected. His speech was slow, and it was decided to teach him more sign language to express things he couldn't articulate. Stacey and Luke sat with Matthew during class, art, music, and assemblies. Matthew often put his arm around Luke and Stacey. He said, "Me friends."

Stacey was a sweet motherly girl whom the other girls admired, and she gave Matthew lots of attention. Luke and Matthew shared interests in rodeos, the farm, tractors, and baseball. Luke and the other boys began including Matthew in recess games like baseball, soccer, and kick ball. Matthew kept up with the boys, using his physical strength to compete.

Nick and Travis, two of the fifth-grade boys, were humored by Matthew's antics and thought he was so cool. The boys watched for him as he came out to recess. This was the first year Mr. Clark seemed patient and happy.

Nick saw Jenny at recess with big news to share. "Jenny, you won't believe what Matthew did this time."

The fifth-grade boys reported all the Matthew news to her. Jenny was a bit tired of hearing all about it, but she sighed and listened to Nick's story.

"Cody had to go Mr. Clark's office because he wasn't listening in class. He saw Matthew sitting in Mr. Clark's chair."

"So?" Jenny responded. "He goes to the principal's office several times a week."

"Yeah, but he was sitting *in* Mr. Clark's chair, and that isn't all."

"What?" she asked impatiently.

"Matthew was holding a flyswatter in his hand and was hitting the desk. He even swatted Mr. Clark."

"Are you sure?" Jenny asked in disbelief.

"Yeah. Cody told us about it." Nick laughed. "He sure is brave. Imagine, swatting the principal. And, he wasn't even in trouble. Mr. Clark only thanked Matthew for trying to get the flies out of his office and asked for the flyswatter back."

"So what did Matthew do?" she asked.

"Oh, he listened to Mr. Clark. You know how it goes. When Mr. Clark talks, kids do what he says, even when he is asking nicely."

Jenny shivered a bit and went off to play with her friends. Matthew was becoming quite the talk of the school. At least it wasn't mean. *Was it only because of his naughty ways? Did they really see the personality she saw and loved? Time would tell.*

Miss Evans took Matthew to the big building to run errands with her. She taught him how to ask the secretaries for copies for a worksheet, find her mailbox, and pick up her mail. Matthew politely opened the door for Miss Evans and other girls who entered the building and office.

One day at noon, when Miss Evans was taking Matthew into the building to get her mail, the high school students were lined up against the wall waiting for lunch. Alice sat at a small table with a hole puncher and punched the paper lunch tickets of each student in line. "Hey, gang!" Alice yelled out to the students. "Keep a straight line and behave yourselves back there." She laughed boisterously. "Good to see y'all today."

Matthew was strutting down the hallway where the high schoolers were lined up. He was dressed in his cowboy attire and proudly came toward the line. Alice was sitting at the table and saw him coming. She stood up and told the high schoolers, "Excuse me, guys and gals. I need to say hello to my good friend,

Matthew." She opened her arms wide and gave Matthew a big hug. "This is my friend, Matthew. He is in kindergarten and new to our school. Some of you know him already."

The high schoolers watched Alice and listened to her while she continued, "Everyone, say hello to my buddy." Several of the students waved or shouted hello to him. Alice let go and returned to punching tickets. Matthew turned to the friendly high schoolers and put his two thumbs up and said, "Ay." Matthew walked past the line of students and several of them put out their hands to give him five. He whipped his hand up and slapped the hands to give the high five.

Glenda was delivering her cut-out sugar cookies for a Halloween party. She arrived at school during the recess break. She was walking from her car toward the classroom when she saw the boys and girls outside and thought she would sneak a peek at how things were going. She didn't know what went on during recess and feared him getting treated cruelly.

The same day that Glenda brought the cookies, Miss Wilson dismissed the kindergarteners for recess. Matthew hurried out to the playground and tripped over his own feet and fell to the ground. A large group of big boys crowded around him. Glenda watched what they were doing and walked closer to the playground, wondering what happened. When Matthew didn't get up, the boys huddled over him.

She heard voices saying, "You okay?" "Can we help you up?" "Are you hurt?" "Can you get up on your own?" "How did it happen?"

The huddle dissipated. Matthew sat up and brushed off his clothing. He stood up and grinned. "Me okay. Me down." The boys smiled and Cody suggested, "Let's race you to the monkey bars."

There was small Matthew and a group of big boys all running toward the monkey bars. Glenda felt a sense of calmness seeing him at recess. She went to the classroom where she saw Miss Evans and Miss Wilson talking and set down the cookie container.

"Oh, Glenda, thank you so much for the cookies for our party. They look delicious," Miss Wilson said as she peeked under the lid of the container.

"Thank you. I was glad to make them. I always enjoy baking."

"It's good to see you," Miss Evans greeted.

"You too. I thought while I brought these, I'd ask you how Matthew is doing." She told them what she saw on the playground.

"That isn't any surprise," Miss Wilson answered. "The boys in that class are the nicest boys and were the best kids in kindergarten. They've liked Matthew from day one."

"Is there anything else you can tell me?"

"Let me see," Miss Evans added. "He has adjusted to the expectations of school. He is well-accepted by his peer group. He has taken a strong liking to Stacey and Luke the most, but the girls mother him almost too much. They're a bunch of mother hens." Glenda smiled in relief as she heard the good news.

Miss Evans continued, "Alice introduced him to the high school students, and they were taken with him. They genuinely like him. You know how he walks with attitude in those cowboy boots. He draws lots of attention."

"Yes, I know," Glenda smiled.

"He's a very neat eater, very particular, in fact. He is always well-groomed and clean. He is doing great. It's good for him to be with his peers."

"Oh," Miss Evans put in, "he opens the doors for me and other girls in the school. They love it. He has learned such good manners."

"I'm so pleased to hear that. We've worked hard on manners at home. He has never been a messy eater."

"He's past other children in that area," Miss Wilson said. "I wish all children had learned manners like that before coming to school. You can tell your family has worked with him."

"My main concern, Glenda," Miss Evans sadly said, "is his counting to ten and the alphabet. I'm working daily on it. Sometimes, I seem to be making progress, and then it seems soon after, he forgets what he just knew. This is common, but I hope to get that taught this year."

"We can practice at home. Brad takes him out to the pasture and can count cows with him."

"Whatever you can do to support his learning at school would be really appreciated."

Glenda and the teachers were ending their conversation when the kindergartners came in from recess. Matthew took off a light jacket and hung it neatly in his cubby. Stacey and Pam led him to the carpet where the class always sat right after recess. Luke and Brian asked if they could sit by Matthew, but the girls declined the offer.

Glenda excused herself and went to the car. She felt a sense of peace again. On her way home, she ran the morning's visit over and over in her mind. The kids accepted Matthew, and he had a good personality. He might not learn as fast and talk very well, but he was getting along fine. Glenda felt so honored to have him as a son. He was truly heaven-sent. Life wouldn't be the same without him.

CHAPTER 21

It was a mild day for December, and Matthew was dismissed from Miss Evans's room to go outside for recess. When he walked across the trailer to the kindergarten room to get his coat from the cubby, he saw that the room was empty. He decided to investigate the room while no one was watching. There was the blackboard with dusty chalk on the ledge. He scribbled some marks on it and drew a smiley face. Then he saw some Play-Doh on a shelf and opened two containers, mixed them into a ball, and squished it between his fingers. A Tupperware canister with graham crackers inside sat on the teacher's desk. He picked it up and pulled on the lid with no success. Studying the canister some more, he lodged his small fingers under the bottom, pulled up, and off came the lid. He reached inside for a cracker and munched on it.

Leaving the lid off, he walked around the desk to where the drawers were. He opened the middle drawer of the desk and saw nothing much except pens, pencils, and paperclips. In a side drawer of the desk was a shiny metal piece with a rope on it. There were several other objects in the drawer, but Matthew kept investigating the metal object. He picked it up and fit the rope over his neck. He held up the shiny piece and saw a cork ball inside, so he shook it to get it out. It didn't come. He felt the smooth sides of the metal, let go of it, and it fell down to his chest. This was a new treasure. He went to the cubby, slipped on his jacket, and went out toward the playground. As he went out, he remembered that the recess teacher wore one of these things and that it was a whistle that made a shrill noise. Teachers put it to their lips to get the attention of those at recess.

Matthew got to the outskirts of the playground where students lined up to go inside. Matthew stood tall and started blowing, one blow after another. Students started running to line up. Mrs. Daniels, whose back was turned, heard the noise, looked at her watch, and saw there were ten minutes of recess left. *Why is that whistle being blown?* she wondered. She turned around and saw students in line. She was astonished when she saw Matthew blowing the whistle repeatedly, pacing back and forth in front of the lines.

Nick asked, "Matthew, are you the teacher today?"

"Me blow, me like," he answered.

Cody asked, "Where'd you get that?"

Matthew shrugged his shoulders. The fifth-grade boys came up to him. Travis said, "Matthew, you'd better put that away before the teacher comes."

The boys laughed at Matthew blowing the whistle and didn't see the recess teacher. Students began pushing and yelling in line when the teacher stomped up to the front. She hollered, "Go back to play. We have a few minutes left." She flung her arms in the direction of the playground.

Mrs. Daniels quietly said, "Give it back to me, you troublemaker."

Matthew took off running with the whistle bouncing up and down on his body. Three fifth-grade boys offered to help get the whistle. Travis and Nick chased after Matthew calling, "Come back. Come back."

Matthew kept racing away from the boys and peeking back at them. He smiled at this game. Jon was coming toward Matthew and tried to block him, but Matthew dodged past him. The boys continued chasing him.

Mrs. Daniels furiously blew her whistle as the students on the playground continued to play. She blew again, but the students had deaf ears. She stomped out to the swing sets, teeter totters, and monkey bars and yelled at the top of her voice, "Line up, recess is over!"

A few students heard her and ran toward the lines. Mrs. Daniels circled around the playground, shouting to line up. The fifth-grade boys chased Matthew all over, gave up, and lined up. Mrs. Daniels silenced the students and sent them into their classrooms.

Matthew finally came up by his class and blew the whistle again. His classmates looked back and stifled their amusement. Matthew saw the attention he got and blew the whistle several more times.

Mrs. Daniels asked Nick, one of the fifth-grade boys, to get Mr. Clark. Soon, Mr. Clark appeared on the playground.

"I don't know what to do with him. How can I get this off him?" she shouted angrily.

"I'll take care of it, and you go back to your class. Thank you, Mrs. Daniels."

She walked away in an angry huff. Mr. Clark saw her reaction and was glad the other teachers were patient. When Matthew saw Mr. Clark, he tucked the whistle under his jacket with the string still showing.

"Hello, Matthew," Mr. Clark said deeply. "How are you?"

Matthew smiled and gave a thumbs-up. "Okay."

"Matthew, come with me to my office a few minutes." Matthew walked next to Mr. Clark.

"You okay. Me like you."

"You're a good guy too, Matthew. We need to talk a little bit though."

Mr. Clark and Matthew entered the office where Matthew sat down in the comfy leather chair. He bounced up and down until Mr. Clark looked him right in the eye. Mr. Clark offered him a drink of water or juice. Matthew nodded his head. When Mr. Clark had Alice bring in a glass of water, Matthew saw Alice's radiant smile and jumped up to hug her.

"How are you today, buddy?" she asked.

"Me okay." He signed "I love you" to Alice. He gulped down the water. Alice went to get him some more.

Mr. Clark sat patiently as Matthew drank another cup of water. He finally asked, "What's around your neck?"

Matthew felt the rope around his neck. He pulled out the whistle from beneath his jacket. "Me blow. Woo. Woo."

"Where did you get that?"

Matthew wasn't sure how to say it, so he pointed to the office desk. He got up and walked around to Mr. Clark and pointed to a drawer. "Me see. Me like."

"May I please have it now? You need to get back to class."

Matthew nodded his head, lifted the whistle off his neck, and hesitated. He held it in both hands, studied it, and slowly reached out to hand it to Mr. Clark. He pulled back suddenly and blew the whistle. Mr. Clark rubbed his ears. The sound was annoying inside the office. Matthew blew one more time and smiled in satisfaction. He dropped the whistle to the floor and scurried down the hall.

Some upperclassmen were coming toward him. Ted, a burly wrestler, smiled and said, "Hey, Matthew. Give me five."

Matthew held his hand up and slapped Ted's hand. Amber, Ted's friend, said, "He's so cute."

Ashley added, "He is always up to something."

Shortly after Matthew left, Mr. Clark came down the hall and asked, "Have any of you seen Matthew?"

"Yes," Amber answered, "He went that way." She pointed down the hallway in the direction Matthew went.

"Thank you," Mr. Clark said.

"Matthew must be in big trouble. Mr. Clark is in a hurry," Ted observed.

"Remember," Ashley informed them, "that a few months ago he was lost and panicked the teachers."

"How do you know?" Ted was curious.

"My mom is a first-grade teacher. She said he was on the bus sitting in the driver's seat ready to go home. He thought it was time to go. It gave everyone quite a scare. They are keeping a close eye on him."

Ted said, "He's probably given Mr. Clark a scare or two."

The high schoolers laughed and walked to their class.

Matthew raced all the way back to the kindergarten room. The teacher was surprised to see him so soon. She told him to sit down and color the paper at his table space. He sat down and neatly colored the picture in front of him. A few minutes later, Mr. Clark appeared and scanned the room. He was relieved when he saw Matthew sitting quietly at the table. Matthew saw Mr. Clark and waved then knowing he was all right. Mr. Clark waved back and left the room.

Back at the office, Alice asked, "Did you find him?"

"Yes. He went back to where he was supposed to be. Thank goodness. He knew where to go this time."

"Well, there's never a dull moment around here, and you're getting workouts at work. You should be in great shape." She winked at Mr. Clark.

He smiled weakly. "I think I need a pair of dressy tennis shoes rather than these loafers. I could run faster. I can't keep up with him. No wonder they nicknamed him Running Bear. Can you imagine how fast he would be in tennis shoes?"

"No one would ever catch up to him." Alice stood up as Mr. Clark went to his office and filed some paperwork. She decided to screen his calls and give him a break.

After school, Mrs. Daniels called Mrs. Pearson on the phone. "The morning was such chaos, thanks to you-know-who. He caused nothing but trouble and made the recess time a zoo. He wouldn't follow directions and ran away from me. He causes more harm than good."

"It doesn't surprise me. How long can Mr. Clark bear this? He can't put up with it forever."

"He told me to go on back to class while he took care of the boy. That boy listens better to Mr. Clark, but he does one thing after another. It's trouble, I tell you, trouble."

Mrs. Pearson replied, "I know the day will come when he'll hurt someone, and I'll be there complaining. This needs to be stopped before someone gets hurt. If he is that wild, there is no doubt he's incapable of controlling his fists or body. What will be next?"

"I'll be right in the office if I see anything," assured Mrs. Daniels. "I'm keeping my eyes open. I only see him at recess now. As he gets older, I'll see him more. I only hope he's gone by the time he reaches my room."

"I want him gone this year," Mrs. Pearson said determinedly. "He doesn't belong here. Keep me updated on any more news."

"You know I will. I've had enough of this."

Mrs. Daniels hung up the phone. *Just wait. Wait until I catch him doing something. He will pay. Oh, he will pay.*

Mr. Clark called Matthew's mother. "Hello, Glenda. This is Leo Clark. How are you today?"

"Fine," Glenda answered reluctantly.

"Glenda, I'm calling to inform you that Matthew took a teacher's whistle and ran all over the playground blowing it." He stifled a laugh.

"Oh, my!" Glenda exclaimed.

"Students lined up early when they heard the whistle," Mr. Clark chuckled.

"That's terrible," Glenda said.

"We noticed he mimics what others do. It wasn't a big problem."

"Are you sure?" Glenda asked.

"I called to let you know about it. He's quite a character."

Glenda smiled, "We know he is. Thank you. We'll talk to him about leaving things alone that aren't his."

"That would be good. Thanks for all your support."

"We want him to behave," Glenda replied.

"Your support makes our job so much easier. Have a great day." Mr. Clark hung up the phone and visualized Matthew running around the playground blowing the whistle. He smiled to himself.

In the evening, Glenda called her sister, Phoebe. "Phoebe, you won't believe what Matthew did today."

"What?" Phoebe asked curiously.

"He took a whistle from the teacher's desk and blew it at recess. The students all lined up when they heard him blow it. He wouldn't hand the whistle over right away either. Mr. Clark didn't seem too concerned, but I need to talk to Matthew about taking things that don't belong to him."

"If he likes the whistle so much, I'll order one from the school supply company and have it sent to you." Phoebe giggled.

"Oh, no. I don't want a whistle blown at home all the time."

"Think about it," Phoebe explained, "If he uses it at home, he won't want it at school. The novelty will wear off."

"Good idea, but my ears won't tolerate the noise," Glenda said half-heartedly.

"Tell him to blow it outdoors. He'll follow your directions."

"We'll try it. I'll look for the package in the mail," Glenda said thankfully.

A few weeks later, Matthew got his own whistle. He blew it continuously at home for about one week. Then, he put it away and never blew it again.

CHAPTER 22

Alex was a blond, freckle-faced boy with a bit of a slur to his speech. He and his brother rode the bus every day and were on before the Parker children. One day, Alex told Jenny that a bad old dog was running around the neighborhood.

"It's white with black spots. That blamed thing wanders around homes near us. The dog growled at the Daltons. They threw a stick at it, and the dog looked like it was gonna attack."

"That's so scary." Jenny felt chills.

"The darned dog came to our house too. We chased it away. My dad said if that thing comes our way again, he's going to shoot it."

"Oh my, he shouldn't shoot the dog," Jenny said.

"We don't want an old stray coming on our property and hurting us."

"Are you sure the dog's that bad?"

"Sure is. It keeps trying to hang around where it doesn't belong. It's feisty, I tell ya, feisty."

"Oh my. I'll tell my mom and dad as soon as I get home after school today. I don't want that animal around us."

"It's a mean thing, that's for sure," said Alex.

The bus pulled up to the school and unloaded the students.

While Alex was telling Jenny about the dog, Glenda was outside that March morning for gardening preparation since the winter snow had melted. She saw a white dog wandering along the shoulder of the highway near their property. Glenda didn't like stray animals. They had a tendency to be unpredictable and possibly have rabies. She yelled to the dog, "Shoo! Go on. Get outta here."

The dog slowly passed their property. She didn't know where it went, but a few minutes later, she saw the dog lingering around at the bottom of the driveway. She tried to shoo it away again.

When Matthew got home, she went out to the pasture to help Jed. A cow had gotten out due to a broken fence. Jed drove Glenda and Matthew out to the pasture near the house. Mom told him to stay in the pickup and not to get out at all.

Matthew opened his lunch bag and got out a ham sandwich with mustard wrapped in plastic wrap. As he ate his sandwich, he heard a snarl. As he was sitting in the back of the pickup, he saw an animal, white with black spots, growling and showing its sharp teeth. Matthew ignored the animal and continued eating. Mom told him to stay in the pickup and not to get out at all. He looked the dog in the eye. The dog still growled. Matthew whispered, "Okay, baby. You okay."

The dog stopped growling at the gentle voice. Its ribs were showing, and Matthew picked a small bit off the sandwich for this stray dog and threw it on the ground. The dog flinched and began sniffing the ground then ate the piece and licked its mouth, barking for more. Matthew gave the dog the rest of his sandwich and watched the dog devour it. Matthew checked his lunch bag and found a buttered blueberry muffin, some sliced apples, and two sugar cookies. He threw them on the ground. After eating, the dog whimpered and lay on the ground, resting. Matthew hung his arm over the pickup and kept it as still as a statue. The dog cautiously walked up to him to sniff his hand. Matthew didn't move at all as the dog sniffed some more and licked his hand. It tickled so much that Matthew jerked from laughing. The dog backed off defensively from the sudden movement, then eased slowly up to him and sniffed again. Matthew felt his hand getting moistened but remained still.

Matthew moved to the back of the pickup and reached the handle, letting down the back end gate. The dog came up to Matthew and rubbed its body against his legs. Matthew slowly reached his hand down to touch the dog's stiff, short fur. Wagging its tail, the dog became less edgy and leapt up next to Matthew in the pickup. Matthew put his arm around its neck and held it. The dog relaxed in his arms as he stroked its neck and back.

Jed and Glenda got the fence fixed and came back to the pickup and saw Matthew sitting comfortably with a dog snugly pressed up against him. Glenda noticed this was the same dog that she had tried to chase away and couldn't believe her eyes. She looked at Jed and said, "What do we do?"

He shrugged. "We could keep it. It really takes to Matthew, and we could use a second dog. Is this the same dog the neighbors have been complaining about that is so mean?"

"It is," she whispered. "I tried to chase it off this morning. Look at that. Matthew won't let it go. He adores it."

"Her. It's a female dog."

Glenda walked up to Matthew, and the dog growled protectively. Jed looked amazed. "She's already guarding Matthew. She'll be good for him."

"I suppose so."

They decided to keep the dog and named her Mitzi.

CHAPTER 23

In April, Glenda and Jed were to meet both Miss Evans and Miss Wilson with Mr. Clark on Friday at 10:00 a.m. for a conference while the students were in gym class. Glenda hoped Matthew was gaining some skills throughout the year.

The day of the conference, Jed and Glenda arrived at the office fifteen minutes early and were pleasantly greeted by Alice. "How are you two today? I tell you, we sure love Matthew. He has been a nice addition to our school."

"Thank you, Alice." Glenda said hoping that this was a sincere comment too after some of the dealings they had with him.

Alice's phone rang. They heard her say, "Yes, they are here. They've been waiting a short time. You want me to send them in? I'll do that. Yes, I'll see if they want coffee or water. We'll be right in."

She turned to Jed and Glenda, "Mr. Clark wants you to meet in the board room where there's more space. I'll show you the way. The teachers are on their way down. Come with me." She led them down the hall to the board room where there was a long rectangular table with twelve chairs. Jed and Glenda sat down at the elegant, walnut table. Alice left to get Jed a coffee and Glenda some water. Jed nervously tapped his fingers on the table, and Glenda twisted her hair.

"Where should we begin?" Mr. Clark thought out loud. "Let's start with social skills. Matthew had some troubles taking off earlier in the year. He's done well this semester. I agree with you both when you told me a while back that he likes to explore his environment first, then settles down. That has proven to be true. We needed to give him time to feel out his surroundings. His curiosity is a great sign. Miss Evans, would you fill us in on how his math and reading skills are?"

She checked her assessments. "He has achieved the goal of counting to ten. He still doesn't know his alphabet. Sometimes, he says part of it and other times, he seems to have forgotten it. He is good and meticulous in art. Mr. Rich says Matthew has ability with visual work. He's able to excel in copying a picture and following the directions given. In gym, Mr. Snyder noticed that Matthew has much strength and keeps up with the other children. He demonstrates positive relationships here, and the kids accept him and actively include him. Socially, the student body likes his happy and polite personality. He's the center of attention with some of our upperclassmen. He hugs people often."

Glenda interrupts, "That is something I would like to slow down. I don't want him hugging so much. I think he needs to learn to shake hands instead."

Mr. Clark intervened, "I understand your concern, Glenda. It's quite typical for Down syndrome children to be affectionate. I think you're saying that you want him to limit who he hugs."

"Yes. I don't want him overly affectionate. He needs to learn to limit that."

Miss Evans jotted some notes on her paper. "I agree. We can make that a goal."

"He has impeccable manners and is very organized. He doesn't like messes," Miss Wilson said. "He's improved in his speech, but it's often difficult for others to understand him. However, some of the students who are with him every day know what he's saying."

"Things are looking up," Mr. Clark confidently spoke. "We do need to go over his goals for the rest of the year and beyond. First, Miss Evans stated in her report that she would like him to be able to count to twenty and begin some basic addition. Second, she noted that she would like to see him learn the alphabet by the end of the school year."

Miss Evans spoke, "Yes. I'd like him to work toward that. I want him to consistently say his alphabet and recognize the letters. He's able to write his name now. We shortened it to Matt to make it easier."

"We're thrilled that he was potty trained before kindergarten," Miss Wilson added. "We learned that children with his disability often aren't potty trained by school age."

Glenda was amused by this and spoke frankly. "He learned fairly young. Actually, he potty trained earlier than Jenny. I never was concerned about him that way."

"Also," put in Miss Evans, "he has no health issues, such as heart disease. So many Down syndrome children are born with problems with their hearts. Some have surgeries at a young age, and the heart problems go on their whole lives. Matthew is robustly healthy."

Jed spoke up, "We're so thankful for that. We count our blessings all the time. The pediatrician said if he hasn't had any problems by now, he'll most likely not have any during childhood."

Mr. Clark looked pleased. "He's one fortunate child. It's evident that you work with him every chance you can and have high expectations for him."

"His disposition is very good-natured. We're honored to have him in school." Miss Evans smiled widely.

Jed shared, "I'm working with him on mechanics. He tends to catch on quickly. I'll continue this through the summer."

Mr. Clark was impressed. "That might be his niche one day. He may achieve more in mechanical skills. However, we'll teach him all we can.-I think he'll learn. It must be on his own timetable. We're all different with various strengths and weaknesses. I'm enthusiastic for the upcoming years of his education."

Jed shook Mr. Clark's hand and said, "Thank you so much. All your work is much appreciated."

Glenda added, "We're so thankful he's getting along so well."

Mr. Clark replied, "You're most welcome. We're happy to have him here. Have a great day."

As Jed and Glenda left the school, Glenda breathed a sigh of relief. "That went much better than I thought. I'm glad he gets along so well."

"I know. I'm glad too," Jed whispered back.

Birthing season for the cows was in full force. On the weekends, Brad and Matthew went out to the pasture to check on cows that had given birth to baby calves. The farm had a white metal shed where the new calves were kept with the cows. There was a pen for each cow and calf with fresh straw spread on the ground to provide warmth for the newborns. Matthew was given his very own Brahma cow that had been in a tornado.

It was late Saturday morning when Brad and Matthew drove out to the pasture to get a cow and newborn calf into the calving shed. Matthew gently walked up to his cow as she stood still and let Matthew pet her black hair. His cow nuzzled her head against him and licked his hand with her rough tongue, making Matthew laugh. He took off his hat and put it on her head as she stood still and didn't shake it off. She let Matthew put his arms around her and hug her.

Brad and Matthew stopped at the shed to spread a bale of straw in the pen, then they went across the pasture where Brad had earlier found a newborn calf. It was weakly standing on its legs and reaching for milk from its mom's udder. Brad and Matthew watched as the calf got its first drink of milk. As the calf received nourishment, it stood stronger. When the calf finished, they walked the cow and calf to the shed. Brad opened the gate to the pen to let them in and fed the cow. The brothers walked light on their feet back to the lush, green pasture, soaking up the rays of sunshine on this beautiful spring day. Brad looked around at the other cows in the pasture, scanning for signs of new life. As they walked, Matthew started singing, "A, B, C, D, E, F, G, H, I, J, K, L, M, N, O, P, Q, R, S, T, U, V, W, X, Y, Z."

Brad turned to Matthew singing away. His little brother repeated the alphabet song several times. "Uh, Matthew. I…uh… let's get the three-wheeler back to the house. Would you sing that song for me again?"

He couldn't believe his ears. Matthew perked up even more and sang the song again and again. Only a week earlier, Mom and Dad had a conference and were told he didn't know his alphabet. Brad was so elated he couldn't wait to get to the house to tell Mom.

He came back to the house yelling, "Mom, Mom, you won't believe it!"

Glenda ran to the door with her hands full of suds and urgently asked, "What is it, Brad?"

"Matthew. It's Matthew." Brad was panting.

Glenda looked at him in bewilderment as Matthew walked right past her. He looked fine to her. "What are you talking about?"

"He sang his alphabet. Not once, but over and over. He didn't miss a letter. He started singing out of the blue. We were walking in the pasture. I couldn't believe my ears."

"It's amazing. Miss Evans said they hoped he'd know the letters in order, but didn't know if he'd be able to do it this year."

Jenny walked into the room. "What's going on?"

"Matthew sang the alphabet song out in the pasture. Isn't that a surprise?" Glenda felt so joyful.

"He did it! He did it!" Jenny cheered and jumped up and down. "I need to go and congratulate him."

Jenny went to the family room where Matthew was playing with his Fisher Price. She gave him a great big squeeze. "You're so smart!! You know your alphabet! You're my super duper smart brother." Jenny held out her hands to Matthew, and they danced round and round in a circle as he sang.

Out in the kitchen, Glenda told Brad to go out and tell his dad while she got on the phone and called Trudy and Kate. She also called Miss Evans at home. Miss Evans was flabbergasted. She said, "Maybe I need to make a visit to your house to hear him. This is great news."

Glenda said, "You're welcome to visit anytime. This is quite an achievement."

The day went on with Kate and Trudy calling their friends. Big news spread fast through Cloverville as family and friends celebrated this landmark in Matthew's life.

CHAPTER 24

Summertime! Matthew was six years old and had finished kindergarten. He tagged along with Jed during much of the day. Jenny, eleven, kept busy helping Glenda with gardening, cooking, canning, and housecleaning.

Brad was fourteen years old, participated in many of the farm chores, and drove the farm equipment. He had learned how to disk and plow. He fed the livestock and mowed the lots. He used a corn knife to chop down weeds around the garage and buildings. He worked long days on the farm doing fencing, haying, and cultivating.

Whenever Jed and Brad drove to the cattle lot to feed the livestock, Matthew climbed into a bunk and swung his body into the feed wagon, plopping down into the mound of powdery corn. He had a small shovel in his hand and dug in the ground corn as if he were on the beach digging in the sand. Granules of corn flew everywhere creating a cloud of dust. He helped fill the bucket with corn, but he felt it was a game. Brad and Jed emptied bucket after bucket into the bunks.

One day when they finished, Jed said, "It's time to go to the wheat field. I need to see if it's dry enough to harvest. I'll do a moisture test. As hot as it's been, it should be ready." During the hot summer months, Jed combined a small wheat field. He raised a bit of wheat for soil conservation and to replenish the supply of straw to bed the baby calves.

Jed went to the wheat field and collected a sample for the test. He went into the house and told Glenda, "Looks like we're ready to combine the wheat." He turned to Matthew who was putting dishes away and said, "Running Bear, come with me."

Matthew bounded out of the house and climbed like a spider onto the combine. He and his dad went to the small wheat field. Jed held Matthew on his lap and said, "Here, hold the steering wheel. I'm gonna lower the front to get us started. You get to steer the combine."

"Me do." Matthew looked in front of him at the endless stalks of wheat. The combine cut the wheat leaving a short stubble of stalk on the ground.

"You're steering good and steady," Dad complimented him.

The combine filled to capacity and needed unloading. Jed drove it to the truck parked in the field nearby. "This wheat needs to be unloaded. I lined up the combine to the truck here. I want you to watch as I move this lever to move the auger. Then, I'll get the wheat movin' from the combine to the truck."

Matthew watched as the wheat emptied out of the combine through the auger and into the truck. Soon, the combine was empty. "Perfect. Let's get back to harvest."

Once all the wheat was harvested, Brad raked the straw, letting it dry in the sweltering heat. The next day, Jed baled the straw into small bales and loaded them into the calving shed.

After wheat harvest, Jed constructed a tree house right outside the Parker home. He nailed four boards on the tree and built a platform seven feet above the ground. Due to other demanding summer farm projects, he didn't get it enclosed. Matthew climbed up to the platform, taking his Hot Wheels along. Mitzi, the mutt, curled up under the shade of the tree, patiently waiting for Matthew to come back to her. When Matthew climbed down, Mitzi stood and rubbed against Matthew's legs. He said,

"Shake. Shake." When he released her paw, she jumped on Matthew with her paws reaching his shoulders. "Sit. Down. Sit." Matthew pointed his finger down. Mitzi obeyed and wagged her tail. "Good dog," he praised. Mitzi was Matthew's constant companion. She went wherever Matthew went. If he was in the house, she rested in the yard near the side entry door. Matthew's companion was quite protective of him, and he took care of her basic needs.

Jenny came outside and mischievously sneaked to the water hydrant and pulled out the long hose. She pulled up on the lever, and water flowed forcefully. Stretching the hose to the yard, she sprayed Matthew and Mitzi, drenching them with water. Mitzi barked and cowered away. Matthew chased Jenny and yanked on the hose. Jenny stumbled and dropped the hose on the ground, and Matthew picked it up. Chasing her, he soaked her hair and clothing to the skin. She ran for the hydrant and finally turned it off. Both of them looked as if they'd been swimming at the pool in their farm clothes, but they were laughing.

Matthew spent hours with the cows. His cow, Bonnie, recognized him whenever he was in the pasture. She stood perfectly still for Matthew. He spoke in quiet whispers to her.

Matthew woke when the sun rose and slept when it was sundown. He learned some number, letter, and color recognition by reading the tags on cattle. There were different colors for different ones. Each tag had a letter and number. He quickly caught on to the names of these numbers.

Jed taught him how to fill the three-wheeler with gas. Brad took Matthew on three-wheeler rides several times a week and let Matthew drive on his lap. The fresh, clean country air was liberating. Life was good.

As the summer came to an end, Matthew continued to help husking sweet corn. He was taught how to peel cucumbers. Matthew also helped Glenda and Jenny pick tomatoes from the garden.

Matthew was thrilled to begin first grade. He started watching for the bus several days early. Each day, Glenda told him that it was almost time to start school but not yet. The first day of school came at last.

PART 4

ELEMENTARY

CHAPTER 25

School began smoothly Matthew's first grade year. His teacher was an old family friend named Mrs. Benson. Her parents were good friends with Gordon and Trudy. Mrs. Benson knew Matthew was exceeding expectations socially and was accomplishing more academically than they thought possible. Yet, he was still way behind his peers. Matthew didn't take off exploring anymore nor did he stand on recess equipment. She anticipated the year to go well with Matthew in her class.

Matthew attended first grade all day and rode the bus to and from school. One day September day, Matthew was sitting behind Tiffany Pearson. The bus ride was bumpy as it crossed railroad tracks and hit potholes. Tiffany was standing while the bus was moving when it hit one of the many bumps on the route. She lost her balance and dropped to the aisle floor. Matthew knelt down and asked, "You okay?"

Tiffany was horrified by the fall, and when she saw Matthew, she screamed at the top of her lungs. "You! You pushed me down!"

Matthew asked her again, "You okay?"

"Get away from me, you retard. Look what you did to me."

She stood up and winced at the dirt that soiled her clothing. She brushed her clothes, but the sticky dirt from the bus floor stained her pants. The bus stopped at her house. She marched to the front and tattled, "That retard pushed me and look at me. Look what he did to me."

Mrs. Trent, the driver, calmly said, "I'm sure it wasn't deliberate. You were standing up when you weren't supposed to."

"But I have never fallen when I'm standing," Tiffany argued. "I was pushed."

Mrs. Trent was not letting her off the hook. "Tiffany," she spoke firmly, "I'm always asking you to sit down. It's against the rules to stand on the bus. You were not following the rules."

"So what? I was still pushed."

"Are you sure about that?"

"Mm hmm. He shouldn't be on this bus!" Tiffany arrogantly stepped off of the bus flipping her blonde ponytail in defiance.

Alex eased up to the front of the bus. "Mrs. Trent, Matthew wasn't near Tiffany. The bus hit a bump, and she fell."

"Yeah," Van added. "She fell right when the bus hit the bump. Matthew leaned down after and asked if she was okay. He never touched her."

"Thanks for letting me know, boys." Mrs. Trent went home and immediately called Mr. Clark.

The next morning, Mr. Clark got out forms for an incident report. He had asked Mrs. Trent to stop by in the morning and fill one out. He also had spoken with Van and Alex. He wrote down the details they shared and had Alice type out the report for him to read again. He proofread the report and filed it in his special file. Beads of sweat trickled down his forehead as he took a white handkerchief and dabbed it off. He knew he would be hearing from someone this morning.

Alice was diligently typing the school newsletter when she heard the office door open and slam shut. In front of her was a stocky woman with her thick hair flowing down to her shoulders. She marched into the office and fumed. "I need to see Mr. Clark this instant."

"I'll have to call him and see if he's available."

Mrs. Pearson impatiently ranted, "I don't have time for you to call him. I need to see him right now."

She charged past Alice's desk to Mr. Clark's office. Alice quickly tried to call Mr. Clark. "Uh, Mr. Clark, you have a visitor."

As soon as Alice announced it, Mr. Clark saw Mrs. Pearson push her way into his office. He had heard the fuss before Alice even called. Mr. Clark politely greeted, "Good morning, Meredith. So good to see you today. Would you please have a seat?"

"Don't good morning me," she seethed. "You must know why I'm here!"

"Please sit down," he offered, "and let's discuss whatever is on your mind as two reasonable adults."

Mr. Clark sat down in his chair while she towered over his desk. She breathed fire like a dragon as she spoke. "Yesterday, Tiffany came home filthy. She was crying and wailing that Matthew Parker pushed her down on the bus and held her down."

"Did she tell you that?"

"Yes. She was so upset. Her hair was tousled, her clothes stained. I tried to clean them, but the stains didn't come out. How can you even allow a child in our school that would do this to another person? I want him off that bus!"

"How did she say that Matthew happened to push her down?"

"She said that he was sitting right behind her and forcefully threw her down in the aisle of the bus. As I've said, he's nothing but trouble. A retard doesn't belong on the bus."

Mr. Clark opened a filing cabinet next to his desk and thumbed through the folders. He stalled for time as he searched for the incident report. He pulled out the report and read through it while Mrs. Pearson scowled at him angrily. She crossed her arms across her chest and didn't say a word.

He put on his spectacles as he flipped through the report. He looked up at Meredith and explained, "I have an incident report that was written immediately after a call I received last night and a meeting I had this morning. The report states that Tiffany Pearson has been repeatedly asked to sit in her seat on the bus. She continued to stand in the aisle while the bus was moving. We've talked about this before."

"I see no reason why this has anything to do with what happened," she replied defensively.

"I see exactly how this relates. She has continuously refused to follow the bus rules."

"Mrs. Trent lets the kids do whatever they want on that bus. It isn't Tiffany's fault that Mrs. Trent doesn't make them sit down. Nobody follows the rules of that bus."

"This is not a discussion about Mrs. Trent. We are here to talk specifically about what happened yesterday. Mrs. Trent recalls the bus hitting a big bump. She heard a thud on the bus and looked back. Tiffany had fallen on the floor. Next, Tiffany screamed. We have two witnesses to verify that Matthew was nowhere near Tiffany. He was sitting in his own seat keeping his hands to himself."

"That's a bunch of hogwash," she yelled. "He purposefully pushed my baby down. He's nothing but trouble. I cannot allow this to go on for the sake of my children and all children."

"The only thing that Matthew did was kneel down and ask her if she was okay. There's not a problem in having a child show concern when another child gets hurt. That's all that happened."

"My daughter would never lie."

"Sometimes, we speculate about what happens. She may have thought it impossible to lose her balance after all of this time and wanted to blame it on someone else. It's true no one, not one child, so much as touched her. She lost her balance and fell. Several others can verify that."

"That isn't true. And people are always standing up for Matthew. They'd lie to keep him out of trouble."

"No one has any reason to lie. I can make a copy of the incident report for you if you like. If you'd feel better, we can ask Tiffany all about it together. I think that would be a good idea."

"What good would that do? She doesn't need to repeat it again."

"As you wish. Would you like a copy of the report?"

"No, I only want him out of this school. If you won't take care of this yourself, I'll contact my lawyer."

"I'm sorry you feel so strongly about this issue. I won't discipline a child who's done nothing wrong."

She stood up. "You'll see. You'll see that I will take care of this. I'll make sure he's out of here. He's been here too long. And Mrs. Daniels agrees with me. We've talked since last year. She's told me all about his escapades. Believe me, she doesn't want him in her classroom and wants him removed from this school." She turned and marched out of the office.

Mr. Clark sat down and massaged his forehead and temples. During the meeting, he was calm on the outside but fuming on the inside. He also needed to have a meeting with Mrs. Daniels this week about her breaking confidences in regard to students. She needed to be reprimanded for this.

He walked toward the front reception area and motioned Alice to come immediately to his office with paper and pen. Alice picked up on his cue and casually went to his office. She quietly shut the door behind her.

Mr. Clark spoke in the softest voice possible since the walls had ears and told her to take notes as he explained the encounter. Alice wrote down all of the information. "And," he concluded, "I want you to get our school attorney on the line so I can tell him what happened. I want to know what we may need to do on our end here. I want you to call Mrs. Daniels's room and tell her to meet me after lunch. I can have you or Marie fill in for her while

I have a little chat with her. She's been unprofessional, and I don't like it."

"Anything else, Mr. Clark? A cup of coffee? An aspirin?"

"Get rid of Meredith Pearson. Just kidding. I know we can't, but she won't even look at Matthew with an open mind. She thinks he's nothing but trouble. I know people used to feel this way, but many people have erased their stereotypes since he's been at this school. She won't look at who he really is. She desperately wants him removed from school."

"I'm thankful we don't have more people in our school who feel the way she does."

"I know. I'm writing a disciplinary warning. I'll check with our school attorney on how to proceed, but if Mrs. Daniels continues telling confidential information, she'll be on a forced leave of absence; then if it continues, she'll be disciplined further. We cannot violate our students' rights to confidentiality."

"She's showing a different side to herself this year."

"It isn't tolerable. This is unprofessional behavior."

"I'll be right back with your report, sir."

"Alice, you're the greatest. I trust you and can confide in you. Thank you for all you do."

"You're certainly welcome, sir."

Mrs. Pearson drove to Oakwood to Hall Law Firm. If the school principal wouldn't take her seriously, then a lawyer would. She had to do something. She had waited too long to let this go.

She walked into the office up to the reception desk. The office had a small waiting room with six black leather chairs. The receptionist smiled brightly and asked, "May I help you?"

"Yes, I need to see Mr. Hall right now."

"Let me check his schedule." The receptionist looked down at a calendar on her desk. "I'm sorry, but he has no openings this morning. I can make an appointment for you on Thursday if you like."

"I demand to see him now! This cannot wait!"

"If it's that urgent, perhaps you need to contact the police. I'm so sorry, but I'm unable to squeeze you in this morning. As I said, his calendar is full."

"Did you hear what I told you? I need to see him now."

Mrs. Pearson had had enough of this cheerful receptionist. She bullied her way past the desk and back into the law offices. She read the names on the rooms and found a gold engraved name plate with the name Ben Hall, Attorney-at-Law. She turned the knob and charged into the room. She saw Mr. Hall behind his desk and two clients with him. The three of them gasped at Mrs. Pearson's intrusion.

The receptionist timidly followed her. "I apologize, sir. I tried to get this woman to make an appointment. She forced her way back here and is most persistent."

"Apology accepted," Mr. Hall said with formality. "I understand." He politely spoke, "Good morning, ma'am. As I can see, you must feel a sense of urgency, but please wait ten minutes while I finish up with these clients. Let me show you a room next door where you can wait."

Mrs. Pearson felt a wave of relief. Someone would finally listen to her. She would at last get somewhere. Mr. Hall made her feel so at ease and confident. She'd get her way with him.

Mr. Hall and his clients looked quizzically at each other. "Excuse me, folks. I'll get this woman settled so we can conclude our day's business." Mr. Hall stepped out into the hall and opened an adjacent door. "I'm sure you'll find this very comfortable while you're waiting. I'll be right back."

A few moments later, he reentered the room. Mr. Hall shook Mrs. Pearson's hand. "Hello. What's your name?"

"Meredith Pearson."

"Nice to meet you, Meredith. What's so urgent today?"

Mrs. Pearson smiled and calmly told him about her daughter. "And," she concluded, "I'm so concerned about the well-being of our student body that I want Matthew removed from the school. After all, he belongs in an institution."

Mr. Hall listened intently and took down detailed notes. He asked her, "Are you sure of the facts? Is this exactly what happened?"

"Of course it is. That's why I can't endure this anymore."

He sighed, took off his glasses, and rubbed his eyes. Finally, he said, "I promise you that I'll check into how I may represent you. This may take some time. I need to find out what Matthew's legal rights are. Children with disabilities are protected legally. I'll do all I can to investigate this. I'll contact you as soon as I find out anything."

Mrs. Pearson felt pleased that he would help the best he could. She shook his hand. "Thank you so much, Mr. Hall. I'm so glad I came to see you."

Mr. Hall knew Leo Clark and how he ran the school. If the incident was as serious as Mrs. Pearson had said, he wondered why she would need to ask a lawyer to help her. Mr. Clark was a reasonable man. He felt there must be more to this story and decided to call him that afternoon. He reviewed his notes. He had heard of schools integrating special education students more and more over the years. He also knew there were laws passed to protect the rights of these children. Mrs. Pearson seemed impatient, but while he listened to her, she seemed sweet enough. Still, he felt that something about her didn't add up. He put his thoughts about the visit aside and continued with his appointments.

Alice informed Mr. Clark that Nora would meet with him at two o'clock and that Mr. Snyder would return the students to class.

"Thanks, Alice." Leo looked up from his notes. "I don't look forward to this meeting."

"I know," Alice agreed.

Nora Daniels entered the office. Alice kept on busily typing. Marie, however, greeted her. "Hello, Nora. I'll let Mr. Clark know you're here."

"Thanks, Marie," Nora said sweetly.

Marie called Mr. Clark. She turned to Nora and said, "He's ready to see you. Go on back."

Nora walked back to the office. She saw a stern look on Mr. Clark's face, similar to the one he gave his students when they were disciplined. She wondered why he looked so serious. Mrs. Daniels sat in the chair across from his desk.

"Hello, Nora," he spoke firmly. "I want to let you know upfront that this isn't an easy meeting for me."

"What's wrong, sir? Is it something with my class?"

He cleared his throat. "No. I need to talk to you about what it means to be a professional in this school."

"Sir, I do my best to be professional. I don't know what you're talking about."

"Nora, it has come to my attention from a source in the community that you've been sharing confidential information about Matthew Parker. It also has come to my attention that you have spoken in a negative light about him, in fact, resorted to name-calling."

"Wherever did you hear such a thing?" she asked.

"I have learned of this from a very reliable source." Although he didn't always trust Meredith Pearson, he knew she was in alliance with someone on staff to get Matthew removed from the school. Also, the ladies from the restaurant had mentioned the two of them having coffee dates.

"I don't know what you're talking about," she denied.

"Really? Shall I review some things that have come to my attention?"

"Sure, I have nothing to hide."

Mr. Clark read from his report quoting information that Mrs. Pearson told him. He didn't tell what he had learned from Mary and Delores. He bluffed by saying, "I have other names of people who are also aware of your desire to get Matthew removed from this school."

Nora Daniels turned pale. She couldn't believe that Meredith would disclose their private conversations.

"I see you don't have much to say. I'll say right now that I'm letting this go as a warning for you. If it ever happens again I hear you have shared a confidence with a community person, or if you ever try to find ways to remove a special education child from this school, then you'll be strictly disciplined. Do I make myself clear?"

Mrs. Daniels was feeling light-headed and faint. She weakly responded, "Yes, sir." She tried to recall anything she had said to Mrs. Pearson.

"Do you deny any of the information that I obtained?"

"No, sir."

"I have found your behavior to be most unprofessional and, quite honestly, malicious. If this ever occurs again, be aware that it will be found out, and I'll take action to terminate your employment."

Mrs. Daniels stiffened but showed no emotion. She knew Mr. Clark meant what he said. She was in deep trouble and needed to watch her step. She hoped for a miracle before he came to her classroom. She haughtily held her head high as she went back to her classroom.

Mr. Hall, the lawyer, called the school at 2:15 p.m. Alice answered the phone. He asked to speak to Mr. Clark. Alice informed him that he was in a private meeting and was unable to be interrupted. Mr. Hall thanked her and didn't leave a message. He decided to call later.

After school, Nora Daniels called Mrs. Pearson. She asked to meet her at the café at 4:00 p.m. When they met, Nora Daniels smiled sweetly and talked softly even though she was furious with her friend for sharing their private conversations. She said, "I wanted to let you know that I had a meeting with Mr. Clark concerning Matthew."

"Really? Whatever about?" Mrs. Pearson was on the edge of her seat.

"I was told that I've been spreading stories about him and want him out of the school."

"No!" Mrs. Pearson looked taken aback. "Where did he get such an idea?" she asked innocently.

"He didn't tell me. But I have it in my file now that I've shared confidential information about a special education student. Their rights are strongly protected. If Mr. Clark hears about it again, I'll be sent on a leave of absence indefinitely."

"That's absurd. Where are teacher rights today?"

"I'm not able to discuss anything about him anymore. I wish I could. I can only say I'll do everything in my power to catch him doing wrong to prove he needs to be out of there."

"I have news for you too," Mrs. Pearson sneered. "That child pushed my Tiffany down on the bus. Mr. Clark didn't believe a word of it. He had witnesses that said she fell when the bus hit a bump. You know who those are, friends of the family. People are always standing up for him because he's different. Community people all in it together, including the students, the principal, and the bus driver. They look out for that child. So, I have taken it upon myself to contact a lawyer and see if Matthew can be removed from school on the basis of being unfit and a detriment to the safety of our children."

"Hm. I think that might be a way to go forward with this. It just might work."

"My attorney is looking into it. He's such a handsome and genuine man. I trust him."

"I hope you get somewhere. I have to watch my step now. I don't want him there in my classroom next year. I'm the only second grade teacher."

Mary, the waitress, was seated in the next booth filling napkins and salt and pepper shakers. The ladies were unaware she was there, and she overheard the whole conversation. She was friends with Mr. Clark's wife. Mr. Hall, the attorney, was her son-in-law. She waited until the ladies left the restaurant and excused herself to the other workers. She went home immediately and called both men. She filled them in about what she learned at the café.

CHAPTER 26

The first quarter of school was already completed, and there was no school the last Friday of October due to a teacher's work day and conferences. Harvest was full steam ahead, and the farmers were out with their combines and trucks working out in the fields. The orange, red, and yellow landscape was beautiful.

Matthew woke up at 6:30 a.m. and came downstairs with his brown western shirt tucked into his blue jeans and his shiny silver buckle. His hair was combed neatly when he entered the kitchen and sat down for breakfast. Glenda was in her quilted housecoat standing at the stove. A warm, rich scent of pancakes filled the air. Glenda asked Matthew to bring his plate to the stove. Matthew's mouth was salivating for the taste of the golden pancakes.

"Tanks, Mom. Mm, good," he said rubbing his stomach in pleasure.

Brad and Jed sauntered in while Matthew was eating. He saw Brad in his farm clothes and thought Brad should be dressed and ready for school. Matthew asked, "You do? You no go?"

Brad saw the perplexed expression on Matthew's face. "I'm going out with Dad to feed cattle and to help harvest."

"No. You go school."

"Matthew, today is a day off. Teachers are working, but the kids don't go."

"No. Friday. Me go school. Me see bus come."

After Matthew ate the rest of his breakfast, he walked to the window to watch for the bus. Glenda came up to him and reminded him, "Matthew, there's no school today. You get a day off."

"No. Me wait bus. Me go school." He crossed his arms across his chest and sat firmly in his chair.

"The bus isn't coming today. You can watch, but it won't come."

"Too come. Bus come. Get me. Me go. Me school. Me see Miss E."

Glenda wondered how long he would sit there and wait. She went back to the kitchen to clean up from breakfast. It was 8:20 a.m., a little more than one hour after the bus normally came, and Matthew continued waiting patiently for the bus to arrive.

Jenny sleepily came down the stairs yawning and stretching her arms. She squinted her eyes to peer at the clock. She said, "Mom, why didn't you wake me up sooner? I slept in too late."

"There's no school today, and I wanted to let you catch up on rest."

"I wanted to be up earlier. Hey, where's Matthew? Did he go outside with the guys?"

Glenda smiled and let out a big sigh. "He is sitting and waiting for the bus. He's has been there quite a while. He won't listen about there being no school. He thinks because it's Friday, he's going no matter what."

"That's silly. Why is he waiting so long?"

"He is determined to go."

"I'll go check on him." Jenny went to the living room where Matthew sat perfectly still and waited. She gave him a good morning hug and said, "Hi, Matthew. What are you doing?"

"Me see bus. Bus come. Me go school. Me see bus come."

Jenny looked out of the window. "I don't see the bus. Mom said there's no school today. Let's play UNO or Candyland. I'd like to play with you. But first I'll eat a quick breakfast."

"No. Me stay here. Me see bus. Come bus."

"Have it your way. I'd be tired of waiting."

Jenny went out to the kitchen where she was served two pancakes. She reflected about how she could coerce Matthew to get away from that window. *Mom has said try to get his mind off what he's doing. What's that called? Re…Re…Redirection. That was it. She said to redirect him to a different task. I'll have to try that.*

Jenny went back to Matthew and asked him to find her some colored pencils so she could draw. He went and got Jenny the colored pencils and some blank paper. She sat at the dining room table and drew a pumpkin. "What can you draw for me?" she asked Matthew.

He got a brown pencil and drew a tree using the orange and yellow pencils to add leaves. He took a green pencil and added grass, and when he finished, he ran to the kitchen to show Mom. "What do we have here?" Glenda asked.

"Me do. You like."

"I can't wait to get another one." She kissed his forehead.

Matthew raced back to the table and drew a cow and a house. He spent some time drawing until Jenny brought out the Candyland game. "Let's play a game," she suggested. "I like this."

"Okay," Matthew agreed and selected a playing piece and set the cards on the game board, eager to play.

While they were playing, Jed came in and said, "Hey, Running Bear, come with me on the combine."

When Matthew heard this, he jumped up and down, "Bine, bine, me." He held his hands like steering a vehicle. "Me up. Me way up. Me like."

Jed took Matthew out the rest of the morning. While they were in the combine, Jed let Matthew move the levers and steer.

CHAPTER 27

Mr. Hall decided he was well overdue in calling Leo Clark about the bus incident. Mrs. Pearson had contacted him a few weeks ago. Mary Smith had called him about a conversation that Mrs. Pearson and the second grade teacher had had at the local café. What a coincidence, that his mother-in-law owned the establishment where the two ladies met, so he learned several details about her desire to get Matthew out of the school. He deliberated calling Mr. Clark, but he represented his client and had to at least check into it.

Alice answered the phone, "Good morning. How may I help you?"

"Good morning. This is Ben Hall, attorney-at-law. I'd like to speak to Mr. Clark please," he said smoothly.

"Of course, Mr. Hall. I will put you through right away."

Leo Clark was in his office, contemplating what Mary had told him about a conversation she had heard between two women at the restaurant. He needed to keep a close eye on Mrs. Daniels unacceptable, vindictive behavior.

The phone rang. "Mr. Clark speaking. Oh, yes, put him on. Thanks, Alice." She transferred the call to his office. "Yes, Ben. How can I help you?"

He listened intently to the meeting Mr. Hall had with Mrs. Pearson. When Mr. Hall got done explaining the scenario, he also told about the conversation Mary had heard at the restaurant.

"Ditto. She told me the same thing. I was just thinking about it. What do you make of it?"

"I wanted to know what happened on the bus that day."

"I'll get out the signed incident report." Mr. Clark searched for the file on his desk. He read the report to Mr. Hall. "By the way, I offered to talk to her and Tiffany together to ask questions. I think Meredith persuaded her children to blame Matthew for anything. She wants him in a different school. She'll grab at any straw to accomplish this."

"It sounds like I have no reason to pursue any legal action. I didn't think you would let off anyone for a serious infraction. You know the school business and run it well. Your reputation is flawless. I'll keep my ears open, and I'll check into the legal rights of children with disabilities since I'll have complaints again."

"Thank you, Ben. I have already contacted the attorney who represents the schools and rights for children with disabilities. But, it would be good for local professionals to keep up to date on their rights. This whole interaction with Mrs. Pearson is about her anger toward integration."

"I agree now that I know the whole story. Thank goodness we live in a world that protects the rights of all children. Good to talk to you. We'll be in touch."

Leo Clark bid Mr. Hall good-bye and called Alice into his office. He confidentially told her about the call and the two women in alliance with one another. He said, "We need to keep our eyes and ears open. I'm disappointed in one staff person. She has done enough damage and more will come. I can't believe this. Two people…two people out of the whole community who won't adapt and accept. We can't change them, but we can stop them from causing harm."

Alice sighed. "I would take one thousand Matthews over one Mrs. Pearson. She's impossible."

"I know. I have to be diplomatic, but with her, it's hard. She thinks she will get her way, but she has me to deal with. I have contacted attorneys myself. There's no proof to her claim on the bus. On the contrary, her story doesn't match other witnesses."

"Goodness," remarked Alice. "You'd think she has better things to do than this."

"Apparently she doesn't. Thank you, Alice. You're the backbone of this school. What would we ever do without you?"

Alice teased, "Do you want me to quit, so you can find out?"

"No, we'll keep you around a few years. Have a great day." Mr. Clark felt more lighthearted after their conversation.

Matthew liked to be expressive with his feelings toward others by hugging them. Jed and Glenda were concerned he might offend students and staff by hugging them too often. They decided it was time to teach him physical boundaries with others.

One Saturday at dinner, Jed announced, "Matthew, we don't want you to hug so much. You're a sweet, loving boy, but hugs are saved for family. We know you care about others, but don't hug everyone."

"Me like. Me hug you." He gave his dad a great big hug.

"Thank you. I like to hug you too, but hugs are special. I like Pastor Scott, but I don't hug him. I like Mrs. Trent, but I don't hug her. I save hugs for special occasions and my family."

Jed said, "Brad, stand up. You're Matthew. I'm someone you met. Hello, I'm Jed." Brad extended his right hand out for a handshake. The two firmly shook hands.

"Hi, I'm Matthew. Nice to meet you," said Brad.

Matthew watched carefully. Jed said, "When you shake hands, it's important to give a good firm handshake." He released his hand from Brad and shook Matthew's hand. "Feel how I'm giving a firm one? That's how you do it. No hugs, just shake. Now let's play a game. Everyone line up and shake each other's hands. And be firm."

Glenda, Jed, Brad, Jenny, and Matthew walked around and greeted one another with a handshake. "Wow, that's firm," Brad exclaimed. "Attaboy."

"You are so strong," Glenda said. "Feel those muscles working." Matthew flexed his muscles and did the Hulk stance.

Matthew liked the handshake game. "Shake. Me shake. Me tough. Me." He flexed his biceps and felt his muscles.

"You can show people you're strong," Jed chuckled. "That's better than a hug."

Matthew shook Jenny's hand again, "Ouch," she whined. "That hurt."

"You okay? Me no hurt you."

"I'm fine. You just squeeze too hard."

"Not too tight, Matthew," Jed explained. He showed him a shake that was too hard and a firm, yet gentle one.

Matthew asked Jenny, "Me tough? Touch me. Me muscle."

Jenny complied and felt his arms. "Those are rock solid muscles. You're strong. They keep getting bigger."

The Parkers rehearsed the handshakes for several minutes.

At church, Pastor Scott welcomed the small congregation. He opened the service with prayer. "Dear Lord, thank you for this day. Thank you that we are able to gather together this fall day. We celebrate you, oh Lord. We celebrate one another and the fellowship we have. We share our faith in Christian love. Help us remember every day that we live for you. We are to be the light in the darkness by loving others the way you love us. Let our conduct reflect our love for you. Every day is a gift from you. You have a purpose for each of our lives. Amen." Matthew was sitting in the pew with his hands folded in front of him and head bowed down as Pastor Scott prayed with the congregation. The congregation opened their eyes and looked at him.

Flora, the pianist, stepped up to the piano and sat on the swivel stool. She opened the hymnal and began playing "What a Friend We Have in Jesus." Grandma Trudy sat in the back row, singing joyfully off key. The Parkers sat in front of Trudy and Gordon. Ten other families gathered together in this small sanctuary.

When the song was over, the pastor lowered his hand to signal the congregation to sit down. He talked about how God is not only to be worshipped on Sunday. God is to be in every aspect of our lives. He talked about how everyone has a purpose in life to honor God.

Flora played two more hymns, and Pastor Scott ended the service with a closing prayer. He stepped down from the front and walked down the aisle. The congregation greeted one another and visited. Walter, an old friend of Gordon's, came up to Matthew and put his hand on Matthew's shoulder. Matthew remembered the skill they had practiced. He reached out and shook hands with Walter. Walter remarked, "That's a good firm handshake, Matthew." He continued to hold his hand. Matthew then went up to each person and shook hands as he said hello.

On the way home, everyone clapped and shouted, "Good job. Great handshakes."

"Me love sis," Matthew said as he hugged her.

"I love you too. I'm okay to hug. You can always hug me."

In the afternoon, Brad turned on a Michael Jackson record. Matthew began dancing and shaking to the rhythm. He was standing in sock feet on the dining room floor and slid back, imitating the moonwalk. Brad and Jenny clapped and joined him until the record was over.

CHAPTER 28

Laura and Michele were two second grade friends who played together daily at recess. Laura asked Michele, "Do you want to go with me to the teeter totter?"

"Sure," Michele answered. "Let's go."

They darted to the teeter totter and started going up and down. Michele felt like she was about to fall off. She bounced way up in the air. When she reached the bottom, she hit hard.

"Ow!" yelled Michele. "Don't be so hard."

"Sorry. I didn't know I did anything."

"Well, you did. Stop it!"

Laura snapped, "I will stop it!" When she was at the bottom, she dropped the teeter totter and stomped off to the long line of children waiting to go up the slide. The teeter totter landed so hard that Michele's mouth hit the bar along with her hands and stomach. A steady flow of blood oozed from her mouth, and she shrieked loudly. Michele slid off the seat and sat on the ground, crying all alone. Although it seemed no one saw her, Matthew noticed her on the ground when he was on the top of the monkey bars. He quickly climbed down and darted across the playground as he said, "Hurt. Girl hurt. Me help." He saw Michele with blood on her face and knelt down. "You okay? You boo boo?"

Mrs. Benson finally arrived at the scene and examined her mouth. "Well, sweetie, good news. No teeth are broken. I believe you bit your lip when the teeter totter came down. Go to the nurse's office and get cleaned up."

Mrs. Benson and Matthew helped Michele stand up on her feet. She tried to smile at Matthew, but her lip was already swelling and her speech was slurred. "Thank you."

Matthew looked forward to lunch every day when he saw his friend, Bobby, a high school senior, washing dishes. The dishwasher room was noisy, making it difficult for them to talk. Each day, Matthew waved to his older friend, and Bobby raised his eyebrows in greeting since his hands were busily stacking clean trays. One day, Matthew saluted the greeting, amusing Bobby.

Bobby always wore a smile and was well-liked by his peers and teachers. He flourished in sports, built strong relationships with his teammates, and was captain of the football team. No one knew the well-hidden secret that his father was an alcoholic and had a fiery temper when he drank. One morning, Bobby's dad had come home in a drunken state, throwing things and yelling. Bobby was concerned for his mom's safety, but she encouraged him to go to school anyway. He looked back at his home full of turmoil when he got in his car and drove off to school. He masked his concern and pretended nothing was wrong.

Matthew saw Bobby while he was in lunch line. His buddy was carrying a stack of clean lunch trays from the wash room to the main kitchen area. He was crossing the hallway where children were lined up for their lunches. Matthew looked at him and sensed something wasn't quite right with him today. He knew he was to shake hands only with his friends, but he stepped out of line to where Bobby was walking. He reached up to Bobby's tall slender frame and gave him a big hug. Bobby's eyes moistened. "Thanks, buddy. You have no idea how much I needed that today. You're a great pal."

Bobby walked back to the wash room, took a deep breath, and blinked several times. He stepped back inside and started stacking clean trays. *No one else had a clue how I was feeling. How could Matthew sense it? How could he possibly know what I needed?*

A week later, Matthew sat down at the lunchroom table with David, Luke, Brian, and Melvin. The lunch consisted of hot dogs, French fries, green beans, peaches, and a cookie. Melvin picked up a fry, covered it in catsup, and threw it in the air. It landed on David's tray. He picked it up and threw it back at Melvin, getting catsup on his shirt. With a reddened face, Melvin squeezed the slimy peaches in his hands and mashed them in David's green beans, splattering juice on all the boys. David lifted his milk carton and poured milk on Melvin's French fries.

Bobby went to empty the garbage from the cafeteria. He saw the first French fry thrown into the air. As Bobby got the two garbage bags changed and tied, he continued to watch the scenario.

Melvin and David threw food back and forth, soiling their clothing and spilling food all over the table. Food dropped onto the floor. The food on the trays was mixed together like a stew. Since Matthew got green beans in his peaches, he picked them up and put them back on Melvin's tray where they belonged.

At this point, Mrs. Daniels was at the table. She only saw Matthew picking up the green beans. "What is going on here?" she asked sternly. "Matthew, what have you done?"

Melvin lied, "We were minding our own business when Matthew started messing with everyone's food. Look at the mess he made." He glared a warning glance to the other boys.

Judging hastily, Mrs. Daniels ordered, "Matthew, come to the principal with me. You are in big trouble."

Matthew obeyed and followed her down to the office. She bellowed to Mr. Clark. "See. I knew he was untrainable. He made a mess of his tray and other trays at lunch."

"Mrs. Daniels, can you calm down and tell me what happened?"

"I saw Matthew with a handful of green beans. He threw them on top of Melvin's tray. The area was a complete mess. I asked the boys what happened, and Melvin said that Matthew started a food fight. The other boys just sat there and didn't do a thing."

"Now, now, Mrs. Daniels. Did you see Matthew make the whole mess?"

"I saw him put the green beans on Melvin's tray. The other boys wouldn't think to behave in that way; only a child like Matthew would do this."

Mr. Clark thought of her harsh words and earlier conversations he had with her. Nora had already been written up for her unprofessional behavior. He remained silent a moment as he thought of Matthew's behavior patterns of neatness and manners. Mrs. Daniels's story didn't add up. He knew Mrs. Daniels would be quick to judge and blame Matthew for anything. Mr. Clark got a notepad and wrote down notes. He asked her the names of all of the boys at the lunch table with Melvin and Matthew. He wanted to ask the boys themselves what had happened. As for Matthew, he would keep him there a few minutes.

Once Mrs. Daniels left, Mr. Clark tapped his pencil on the notepad and glanced at Matthew. Mr. Clark twisted his mouth in bewilderment and leaned back in his chair, rocking back and forth. He called Alice. "Please bring me a cup of coffee and an aspirin. I have a throbbing headache."

"Yes, sir," she complied and turned to Matthew. "Hey, sweetie. Let's go back to Miss Evans's room. She has some work for you to do."

"Oh, Alice, stop by the cafeteria and see if there's anyone who saw what happened. I want to get to the bottom of this. The sooner, the better."

"Of course," she said. "Do you need anything else?"

"Yes, an afternoon without any more people in my office. But that isn't likely to happen," he added sarcastically. He rubbed his forehead and temples. He kept out his notepad.

Bobby finished his shift for the day. He was stacking his last batch of clean trays when Mrs. Daniels marched Matthew out of the cafeteria. Melvin and David weren't taken with him, and he wondered why. Bobby dried his hands and removed his white apron when the elementary students were dismissed to class. He heard Melvin bragging to the boys, "Ha! Ha! Matthew's in trouble. He's going down for my mess. Ha! Ha!"

Luke frowned. It wasn't right for Matthew to get into trouble for someone else. He walked down the hallway feeling guilty that he didn't speak up.

Melvin bragged loudly, "I got someone to take the blame. Ha! Ha!"

Bobby didn't like the brazen words he heard, and his nostrils flared. He felt a sense of urgency to speak with Mr. Clark. He rushed down to the office rather than to class. As Bobby raced around a corner, he collided with Alice who was on her way to the cafeteria. "Excuse me, Alice. I'm sorry," he politely said as he panted. "I was in a hurry and didn't see you."

"Slow down, Bobby. What's the rush?" she asked.

"I need to talk to Mr. Clark. It's urgent. I saw a food fight and heard something. I need to talk to him."

"I'll go with you and let him know you need to see him right away. I was on my way to the cafeteria to see if anyone knew anything about this."

Bobby walked down the hallway with Alice. "I can't understand some people's attitudes. Matthew was blamed for something he didn't do. Mrs. Daniels didn't even attempt to find out the truth. What kind of teacher is she?"

Alice bit her lip and was professional enough not to say anything.

"I thought teachers were supposed to be open-minded and tolerant of all students."

"They're human, Bobby. They have weaknesses like anyone else."

Mr. Clark heard a knock on his door. "Yes?"

Alice smiled cheerfully at him and said, "I have a student who needs to talk to you."

Mr. Clark gave Alice a curious look. "Really? I hope this is a good visit. I sure could use it."

"I think you'll be pleased," she grinned. "It's Bobby, who works in the lunchroom."

"What does he want?"

"You'll have to find out for yourself," she teased.

"Okay, send him in," said Mr. Clark, his mood lightened up by Alice's teasing.

Alice winked at Bobby as she let him in the office. Bobby confidently sat down in a soft leather chair. He leaned forward to speak to Mr. Clark. "Hello, sir."

"Ah, Bobby. How can I be of service to you today?"

"Well, I have something I think you need to know. I couldn't wait until later. I'm late for class, but this is important."

"Really? What could be so important that you aren't in class?"

"I witnessed a food fight in the lunchroom. I was getting the garbage and saw the whole thing." Bobby recalled the scenario for Mr. Clark and told him about what he heard Melvin say.

Mr. Clark sat quietly and shuffled some papers on his desk after hearing Bobby's story. "That answers several questions I had about this. Does anyone else know?"

"Yessir," Bobby replied. "Luke and Brian were also there. They didn't do anything."

"Thank you for coming and telling what you saw." He shook Bobby's hand and added, "Stop by Alice's desk. She'll write you a pass to excuse you from being late to class. Bobby?"

"Yessir."

"We're lucky to have you in our school. You're such a mature young man and stand up for what's right."

Bobby's face flushed. "I wouldn't have it any other way, sir."

"See you later." Mr. Clark called, "Alice, please call Mrs. Benson and have her send Luke and Brian to the office. I need to talk to them."

"Certainly. I'll get right on it."

While Mr. Clark waited for Luke and Brian, he felt relief that Matthew hadn't started anything. He was angry with Melvin and Mrs. Daniels. Melvin had wrongly blamed Matthew for something that he himself had done. Mrs. Daniels hadn't attempted to find out the truth. If he inquired about it, he knew she would say it was an honest mistake. She would claim that Melvin had no reason to lie. However, Melvin had been the leader of pranks and mischief in the school the past year. It was no surprise that he was the instigator. He couldn't change Mrs. Daniels's prejudiced attitude. The friendship between her and Mrs. Pearson was a problem, but the school didn't have enough evidence to take action against Mrs. Daniels. The good thing was that the community was beginning to see Mrs. Daniels for her true colors, and her judgmental outlook was beginning to surface. News spread around Cloverville how she looked at Matthew with disgust and felt farmers were filthy people even though many held to high moral standards and strong Christian beliefs. She was too highbrow for this community where people cared for one another despite diversity of abilities and economic status.

Luke and Brian entered the office looking somber. Luke knew it was wrong not to speak up to Mrs. Daniels about Melvin and David doing the whole thing, but he didn't want to cross Melvin. Melvin was a bully and would get back at him during recess. He also didn't like how Melvin bragged about getting Matthew in trouble. It wasn't fair. Now, here he was, in Mr. Clark's office. He knew he had to tell the truth, or Mr. Clark would call his parents. He didn't want to get into trouble at home.

Brian looked over at Luke. He had thought someone else would tell Mrs. Daniels what really happened. He had wanted to speak up, but he was too shy to say anything. He didn't like what happened at lunch at all. He knew Melvin was wrong to shift the blame to someone who could barely talk. Here he was now waiting for Mr. Clark to talk to him. He hoped he wasn't in trouble and shifted in the chair. He had never been to the office before.

Mr. Clark scanned the boys' faces. He saw them fidget and look down at the floor. He called Alice and asked her to bring the boys sodas and some cookies from the break room. Luke and Brian looked astonished. *Why would the principal be so kind when they were asked to come down?*

Mr. Clark sat back in his chair and put his feet on the desk and arms behind his neck. He began, "Boys, I'm glad to see you. First, I want you to know that you're not in trouble. In fact, I need your help. I learned about something at lunch, but I don't know the whole story. I thought the two of you could fill me in since you were sitting with Melvin, Matthew, and David. It would be most helpful to have your assistance."

Alice brought in a small paper plate with homemade chocolate chip cookies and a soda for each of the boys. Their eyes widened in pleasure at the sight of these treats.

"Help yourselves, boys," Mr. Clark encouraged. "Thank you, Alice."

"Thank you!" exclaimed Luke.

"Thank you," said Brian meekly.

"Now, boys," Mr. Clark continued. "I want you to recall every detail that occurred. Please be totally honest with me. I would appreciate that. The treats are for your help. I don't often have students assist me in my job, but today's an exception."

Luke began telling every detail about Melvin and the food. Brian sat shyly and nodded his head in agreement. When Luke finished telling the story, Mr. Clark asked, "Do you have anything to add, Brian?"

"No, sir. Luke told it exactly the way it happened." Brian breathed a sigh of relief.

"Thank you, boys. I appreciate your vivid recollection of this. You are to be commended for your honesty and courage. I know it's hard to say anything in front of the person causing trouble, but we cannot let someone pass the buck in our school. You may go. Thank you. I'll give your parents a call."

Both boys looked at each other in alarm. Mr. Clark laughed. "I'm calling them to let them know that you both are great boys. They should be proud of you." The boys exhaled in relief.

It didn't happen very often that Mr. Clark called for a good thing. He usually called parents when the children got into trouble.

Mr. Clark scheduled a meeting with two more boys.

"Nora, you've been in my office already this year. I want to ask you again. What can you tell me about the food fight?"

Nora rubbed her hands together. "I, uh, I saw Matthew have some food in his hands and put it on Melvin's tray. The trays, table, and floor were a disaster. I've never seen such a mess at school."

"Did it occur to you when there was such a mess that others might be involved?"

"Melvin told me that Matthew did all of it. I had no reason to question it."

"Nora, two boys were in my office a while ago and told me Melvin and David caused the whole thing. Why didn't you ask the others at the table what happened?"

"It was an honest mistake, sir. No one spoke up after Melvin told me what happened," she said apologetically, knowing that her job and her career might be in jeopardy.

"Next time you drag a student down to my office, make sure you know the whole story. Lately, you have not exhibited professional objectivity but rather have acted out of prejudice. This must stop. Good day."

Melvin received a one-day in-school suspension.

CHAPTER 29

The summer after Matthew's first grade year was quite stormy. Thunder boomed loudly and lightning flashed through the sky. The local radio program was often interrupted by a weather warning that there was a severe thunderstorm warning and a tornado watch. This night was no exception. The sky was filled with dangerous bolts of lightning.

Jed and Brad came through the back door, soaked to the skin. They both removed their drenched clothes and changed into dry ones. Jed looked out the window at the thick sheets of rain hitting the ground and lightning piercing the sky. "This is the fifth severe storm system this summer," Jed observed. "Glenda, get out the two kerosene lanterns and matches. I'll find a couple of flashlights. This is going to be a bad one. We might lose electricity. I think it's worse than the others."

Glenda opened the bifold doors of the pantry and reached up to the top shelf where two silver-colored kerosene lanterns were stored. She set each one on the table and lit them. Just then Matthew came into the kitchen and saw the lanterns. He turned off the lights and said, "Dark. Dark. Me like dark. Me like." He pointed to the lanterns with their small glimmer of light that radiated through the kitchen.

When a crack was heard close by, the dryer stopped turning, and the refrigerator motor moaned. The electricity had gone out. The radio announcer came on the air, "Stay indoors. We are in a severe thunderstorm warning with large hail likely. There's a chance for a tornado. Please be ready to take cover. Get inside and stay away from windows. Keep posted on local storm updates."

Jed watched as large branches broke off of the trees from the high winds. Lightning hit a tree a few yards from the house; the sound caused the children to shudder. The rain came down swiftly, washing soil from the driveway.

The whole family sat down in the dim light around the kitchen table and waited for more weather announcements.

Suddenly, there were loud knocking sounds all around, like baseballs hitting against the house. Everyone rushed to the dining room picture window and saw large, icy chunks falling to the ground. More branches fell from the trees and covered the yard with sticks. The ice chunks were several sizes ranging from pea size to some that were the size of golf balls.

When the storm passed, Matthew got a paper cup from the pantry and stepped out into the yard. He saw some very large branches on the ground and carefully stepped over them. He gathered several pieces of ice of different sizes in his cup, but one really caught his eye. He picked up the piece that was as big as a tennis ball and brought it to the house.

"What are you doing, Matthew?" asked Jenny.

"Me ice. Me pop."

Jenny peeked in the paper cup and explained, "That's hail. That came down from the sky. It isn't ice for drinks."

"Ice. Me ice. Me get pop."

"No, don't use that ice for pop. It's dirty. You want ice from the freezer, not this. It came from the bad storm."

"Me okay. Me do. Me ice. Me pop. Me." He tipped his hand up to his mouth and pretended to get a drink.

"No!" Jenny got louder. "No! Don't use this!"

Matthew hurried into the kitchen searching for a can of pop. He opened the can and poured it into the cup of hail. Jenny yelled, "Stop it! Stop it!"

Glenda came into the kitchen and asked, "What's going on here?"

Matthew started putting the cup to his lips while Jenny explained, and Glenda tried to snatch the cup from his hands. Matthew held on tight and pulled back so hard the pop spilled on his shirt and all over the floor. "Icky. Icky. Pop all gone. No me pop. All gone."

"Go change your shirt, Matthew. I'll get you another glass of pop," Glenda kindly said. She picked up the sticky ice and saw the chunk that was as big as a tennis ball. "Look at this," she looked amazed. "I've never seen hail so big. I'll hide it in the freezer and show Dad later."

Jed had gone outside to see the damages of shingles blown off the roof and branches in the yard. Some of the crops were lost from the hail.

The electricity was out for several more hours, and everyone sat around the kitchen table playing cards, waiting patiently for the lights to come back on.

Matthew wondered where the ice went. The following day, he helped clean up the sticks in the yard and worked diligently at getting the sticks put on a trailer to be hauled away.

There were no other storms as severe as this, but there were many nights when the lights went out. Matthew enjoyed the evenings of dim light. He didn't mind the storms at all. He got so used to it, that he often requested suppers at night in the dark with only the lantern for light.

CHAPTER 30

Kate Parker especially cherished visits from her sons since Gary had passed away three years earlier. Jed and his brothers planned a surprise birthday party for her with a potluck dinner. Each family was responsible for bringing plenty of food and table service. Kate's brother in-law, Victor, and his wife, Betty, were coming along with great-grandma June and several friends.

Jed arranged to have Edith, Kate's best friend and neighbor, take Kate shopping while the guests arrived at the house to set up the food and decorations. On the Sunday in July, Jed called Edith. "Hello, Edith. We'll be leaving from home in fifteen minutes. Are you ready to pick up Kate?"

"I'm picking her up in thirty minutes. If we get done with one store, I'll make an excuse to go to another one. She won't suspect a thing. Trust me. Your mom's easy to fool. She loves shopping and chatting with me."

"All right, we're trusting you to help pull this off. Have fun."

"Oh, I'll have fun doing this. Kate deserves it. She's been so lonely."

"We want to lift her spirits. She'll be surprised."

"See you later. Have a safe trip up here."

Outside at Kate's house, picnic tables were covered with colorful floral vinyl tablecloths. Pitchers of iced tea and lemonade were already set on a table along with silverware and napkins.

"Hi," Glenda greeted.

"Hey there," Lisa said.

"Good to see you," Lesley said. She checked her watch. "We'd better get this table set. She'll be here any minute."

"This will be a surprise for sure," Glenda said as they arranged the food on the picnic table.

While the adults prepared for the pot luck and visited, the seven grandchildren, including Jenny, Brad, and Matthew, played badminton by the white fence separating her lane from the front yard. Brad saw a car coming and shouted. "She's coming! She's coming!" Everyone came out to the front and got ready to yell "Happy Birthday." Edith drove slowly and stopped the car.

Kate noticed several dozen people in her yard and stepped out of the car, hearing, "Surprise! Happy Birthday!"

She put her hands over her mouth and said, "My goodness! What is this?"

"Happy Birthday, Kate! We're here to celebrate it with you," Lisa said.

"I never imagined such a party!" Kate walked over to the food table. "My, look at all that food. You went to too much work, gals."

One by one, guests lined up to the food line, choosing from several main dishes, relishes, salads, and desserts. While waiting, Matthew gave Kate a big hug, "Me love Grandma." He stooped down, wrapped his arms around her lower legs and picked her petite body right up off the ground.

"Oh my, you're strong. Please put me down before I fall on you." She laughed heartily and turned to the guests and said, "My, he's strong."

Matthew flexed his arms and showed his biceps. "Me tough. Me pick you up. See me muscle."

Kate good-naturedly said, "You sure are." She felt his biceps. "My, those are big muscles. It must be all that farm work your dad has you do."

"Me like. Me work. Me dad. Me help him."

She gave him a big hug. "I know you do." She kissed both of his cheeks tenderly. " I love you."

As the grandchildren went through the food line, Kate remarked, "I'm so happy to see everyone. What a surprise! And Matthew picking me up was even more surprising." She circulated around to all of the guests and received warm wishes for her birthday.

After the daughters in-law cleaned up the leftover food and washed dishes, the adults gathered at the picnic tables where Kate opened gifts. Kate opened a mug that said, "Thirty-nine again."

"That's perfect," she exclaimed. "How'd you find something with my age on it, Lesley?"

"The clerk at the card shop helped me find it. It seemed perfect for you." Lesley laughed.

The children set up square wires in the grass and got out wooden balls and clubs. The object was to hit each ball through the wire squares with as few swings as possible. "This is like golf," Jenny observed.

"It's called croquet, and it's a very old game," explained Brad. "Our great-grandparents played this with friends."

"It's tough to get the ball through these wires," Jenny complained.

"Easy. Me do. Me okay," Matthew said. "See me. You do." Matthew hit the wooden ball through the wire.

Jenny clapped for him. "Good. You made it look easy."

"Let's get a Pepsi," Derrick suggested, after the first game.

"Sounds good. My throat's dry." Brad wiped his forehead and neck with his shirt.

Each one of the cousins got a glass bottle of Pepsi from Kate's fridge and opened it with a bottle opener. Matthew chugged down his bottle when he saw Kate holding pictures of family and showing them to her guests. Matthew knelt down, wrapped his arms around her legs, and picked her up in the air again.

She grabbed onto the table nearby. "My, you startled me this time." She smiled kindly at him.

"Matthew, don't pick people up," Glenda told him firmly.

He flexed his muscles again. "No fall. Me muscle. Me okay."

"You're strong, but don't pick Kate up again," Glenda repeated.

When it was time to go home, Brad teased Kate, "How old are you, Grandma?"

"I'm thirty-nine again," she teased back.

Brad laughed. "And how many years have you been thirty-nine?"

She hesitated and looked at the ceiling, calculating. Brad thought he would get a response from her, but she lit up and laughed. "You sneaky one. You're trying to trick me to figure out how old I am."

Brad snickered. "I already know your age, Grandma. I'll keep it a secret."

"You better," she teased back. "I'm thirty-nine again. That's good enough for people to know."

The surprise worked. Kate told everyone as they left, "I don't believe I could have any better day than today, except if Gary was here. You have made my birthday so special. Thank you so much. I'll never forget it."

CHAPTER 31

Matthew followed Jed around the farm during the summer months. He rode with his dad to the cattle lots and climbed into the wagon with ground corn. His legs sank into the feed like into slow moving quick sand. He had a bucket and used a wide shovel to scoop the ground corn. Jed grabbed the bucket, carried it on his shoulders, and walked in the center of the bunks where cattle were lined up on each side waiting to be fed. Jed gave Matthew the empty buckets, and Matthew filled them up again. Matthew's feet felt heavy as lead as he lifted them out of the corn.

"Scooping feed makes you strong," Jed told Matthew. "You're my strong Running Bear."

Matthew flexed his muscles and said, "See me muscle. Me tough boy."

"You are. I see the muscle getting bigger every day."

"Me good. Me help you. Me happy cows."

Matthew calmly eased up to baby calves after they were born and held them as Jed tagged their ears. When out with the cows, Jed pointed out to Matthew, "Look, that cow has a green tag. Its number is twenty-eight. There's a red tag with the number fifty-seven on it." Matthew studied each tag on the calves' ears and soon named the colors and numbers of each one.

On Sundays, Jed and Brad went to each pasture to count cows and calves to make sure none got lost. Matthew counted with them as they drove through the pasture to find each one.

During hot days, Matthew sat on Jed's lap in the John Deere tractor. Matthew held the steering wheel tightly as he drove. Jed accelerated the tractor and told Matthew where to drive. Jed drove him to the stack of big bales and backed up the bale carrier to a large bale.

"Okay, here's the lever to drop the carrier. Move this for me. Good job. Watch me back the tractor up to the bale. When I get the hay, I want you to move the lever to raise it up. Then, we'll take the hay to the cows." Matthew pushed the lever hard. "There you go. It's easy, isn't it?"

"Me help. Me hay cows."

"Next, we're going to repair fences."

"Okay, me tough. Me help."

"The posts are heavy. Someday, you'll be able to lift them, but not today. We'll let you hand us tools and hold the posts in the holes," Jed said.

Mitzi followed Matthew to the field while the men worked on fences. Matthew stooped down to her and stroked her soft fur. In the afternoon, Matthew sat under the cool shade of an elm tree with Mitzi snuggled up by his side with one arm around her. Matthew climbed the tree house and sat on the platform. Mitzi's front paws scratched the tree as she barked and wagged her tail.

"No you come. Me. No you. Me down soon. You stay. Me play. You okay." Mitzi got down and curled up in a ball under the tree house. When Matthew came down and went into the house, Mitzi walked by his side and waited by the door until he came back outside.

Jenny asked, "Will you come with me? I want to talk to you."

"Me go out. Me see dog. No you."

"Please. Just a few minutes."

"Little bit. No more. Dog see me."

Matthew and Jenny sat on the couch in the living room. "Matthew, it's time to learn to say 'I.' Can you say that?"

"I," said Matthew.

"Good, now say 'I go. I play.' Say it for me."

Matthew nodded his head. "Me go. Me play. Play dog. Play ball."

"Try it again. I run. I eat."

"Me happy sis. Me run. Me eat. See mom. She cook. Me eat."

Matthew ran to the kitchen to get a fresh-baked chocolate cookie then ran back to Jenny with a mouth covered in chocolate.

"You have a chocolate mustache." Jenny chuckled.

Matthew licked the chocolate off his mouth. "Mm. Good. You eat cookie. Yum." He rubbed his stomach and smiled.

"I want to try one more thing, and then you can go outside with Mitzi. Okay?"

"Okay."

"We go see Grandma Trudy today," Jenny said.

"Raw. Me see Raw. Me like Raw."

"Her name's Grandma. Say it. It's Grandma Trudy like Grandma Kate. Let me hear you," Jenny instructed.

"Grandma Kate. Her nice lady. Grandma Trudy."

"Wonderful. Now, who are we seeing today?"

"Raw. Me see Raw. Me happy see Raw."

"No! No! It's Grandma Trudy."

"Raw. Me see Raw."

"I think it's time for you to go out and play with Mitzi. We'll try it again later."

Jed saw Matthew come out of the house. "Matthew, I want you to come to the shop with me. I have something to show you."

"Me come you. Okay."

Mitzi walked between Matthew and his dad. She lay down in the shop in front of the fan.

"Here are my wrenches. Look at all the different sizes. This one says three-eighths. Here's one that says nine-sixteenths. See the numbers here? You look at these numbers when I ask for a wrench."

Matthew looked at the numbers Jed showed him. "Me see. See numbers."

"Take this wrench and tighten the bolt. This is how you turn it. If you go the wrong way, the bolt will get loose and come off."

Matthew set the wrench on the bolt and turned it, yanking so hard, he gritted his teeth. The bolt barely moved, but it was tighter. "You did it. Thatta way, my boy." Jed patted him on the back.

Matthew flexed his muscles and said, "Me tough. See me muscle."

"You'll be quite a help."

Mitzi was right at his heels, watching him every minute he was outdoors. Jed taught Matthew how to fill fuel tanks and wash windows of the tractors, car, and pickup. He showed him how to check the oil and air pressure. Matthew learned well from Jed's patience and the time he took to show Matthew things.

CHAPTER 32

It was October of Matthew's second grade year, and Glenda brought him home from another doctor's appointment. She went to the sink and washed the heavy iron skillet and wooden spoons. When she finished dishes, she checked on Matthew in the living room where he was resting comfortably all wrapped up in a green blanket. "How're you doing, honey?"

Matthew answered in a hoarse voice and pointed to his throat. "Me owie. Hurt bad."

She patted him on the back. "You'll get better. It will take some time."

"Me go school. Me see Miss E. Me friends."

"I know you miss them. I'm sure they all miss you too. Miss Evans called and asked how you're doing. I told her you had medicine to take and needed lots of rest."

"Me okay. Me see TV."

"You rest and enjoy the TV. I'll be back in a few minutes to check on you and bring you some chicken broth to sip."

Glenda felt sad to see Matthew struggle so much with infections this school year. The doctor said it was typical for kids his age to go through this. As she went back into the kitchen, Jed came in for a mid-morning break and asked, "How did the doctor's appointment go?"

"He needs another round of antibiotics. This is the third prescription this fall. Dr. Wilhelm says this is chronic tonsillitis and believes it'll keep recurring. Matthew feels so miserable. The chicken broth helped, but he's so ready to feel comfortable swallowing regular foods without soreness."

"So, is there any way to help him? What does he suggest?"

"Dr. Wilhelm believes the sooner Matthew gets his tonsils and adenoids out, the better. He said there will be fewer infections, and Matthew will breathe easier from the adenoids coming out. I can't see him having surgery."

"I see. It sounds like it will significantly help him though. Most kids today do get them out. It isn't any big deal."

"I have to call his office today if we want the surgery. There's time available next week. He's already checked the surgeon's schedule. I don't know how he'll handle the surgery."

"Glenda," Jed spoke gently. "He'll be healthier with them removed. It isn't good for him to have so many infections. I think we need to think about what's best for Matthew. How long will he be in the hospital?"

"The nurse said the surgery is normally done in the morning. He would stay overnight and come home the next day. I'd stay there with him, of course."

"That's best. I don't think you have anything to worry about. It's never fun to see someone have surgery, but this is a minor surgery. It's surprising that Brad and Jenny never had this done. Jenny sure has been sick enough over the years."

"Hers was never chronic tonsillitis. I hope he can handle it."

"Look at it this way. He hasn't had to have heart surgery the way most Down syndrome children have. We haven't had health issues with him. He's quite healthy. Having tonsils out is so common. I think you should call as soon as possible and get it scheduled."

"I guess so. He's so miserable. I don't know how to tell him."

"We just tell him that he's having surgery to make his throat all better. He'll understand that. We can tell him the doctors will have him take a long nap while they work on him. And he'll get lots of ice cream and milkshakes."

"Jed, you're so wonderful. You make it sound like something to look forward to rather than a surgery."

"He has to see it as easy as possible. He'll be brave. We'll be there for him."

Glenda laughed. "He's a character, that's for sure. It will be interesting if you're right."

"His disability hasn't affected his courage. Look at school. You were so worried about how he'd get along. We know he won't be a scholar, but he's learned so much. The teachers are awesome there."

"Especially since Mrs. Daniels resigned. Mary told me she tried to get Matthew removed from the school because he had a disability and said such horrible things. Mary has been telling everyone the best thing for our school was her resignation. Matthew has a wonderful teacher this year. Mrs. Wiegman is strict but so happy and caring with the children."

Jed thought about Mrs. Wiegman who transferred from fourth grade to second grade. Her husband raised cattle and farmed crops. She moved to the area for her first teaching job and got married not long after she moved to Cloverville. Mr. Wiegman was a reserved and kind man whose family had lived in the area for generations.

Jed asked, "What goodies do you have today? We are mighty hungry. We are heading out to the field to harvest right after break."

"I have some oatmeal caramel bars in the freezer. I'll get some out for the two of you." Glenda went to the upright freezer in the utility room. The bars had an oatmeal base that was baked first and melted caramel and chocolate chips were spread across the middle. An oatmeal crumb topping was sprinkled on top. She filled a pitcher with iced tea to take out to the shop where Rick was waiting. As soon as she served the two men, she called Dr. Wilhelm.

Matthew had stayed home from school until the surgery day arrived. It felt scary to Jenny knowing that while she was at school, Matthew would have surgery. Brad teased Jenny, "Matthew's going under the knife today."

"Yuk, don't say that," Jenny pleaded for him to stop.

"He is. What do you think they do? The doctor goes into his mouth and slices off those tonsils. It will be all bloody and gross," Brad taunted.

"Knock it off. I don't want to hear it."

"Well, it's true. The doctor will have this sharp knife and other tools on a tray that the nurse holds."

"I don't want to think about it. Leave me alone, Brad."

"Hey, most of my friends have had their tonsils out. It happens all the time."

"I don't want you talking about knives and blood and all that stuff."

"You're so wimpy, Jenny. It's just life."

"Yeah, but it's our brother who's going in for surgery. I hope he'll be all right."

"He will be," Brad confidently answered. "We get to see him tonight after school."

Jenny crept up to Matthew carefully and smothered him with several kisses on the cheek. "I love you. Take care. I'll see you tonight."

"Me okay. Me love sis. Me okay."

Brad called, "The bus is coming. Good-bye, buddy. See you tonight. Good luck."

Matthew smiled weakly. He didn't understand what the fuss was about. Brad and Jenny rushed out of the house to meet the bus.

"Good morning, kiddos," Mrs. Trent greeted cheerfully. "How's your brother? I haven't seen him for some time now."

"He's going to have surgery on his tonsils this morning," Brad explained.

"I'm scared for him," said Jenny as she looked somber.

"I'll say a prayer for him. He's in the Lord's hands now. Don't you worry."

"Thanks, Mrs. Trent," Brad replied. "You're the best."

"You're welcome. Focus on school today. He'll be fine."

Jed drove Glenda and Matthew to the hospital. Glenda explained to Matthew, "You're going to take a long nap and get your tonsils out. This will make you get much better. You'll get lots of ice cream and shakes the first few days. Then you'll feel great again. Do you understand?"

"Me do. Me good. Me okay. Me tough."

Jed dropped Glenda and Matthew off at the hospital entrance where Glenda began the check-in for the surgery. Hospital staff gave Matthew a wheel chair, and the three of them sat in the surgery waiting area thirty minutes before they called his name. The nurse attendant pushed the wheelchair through the surgery doors. Glenda fidgeted during surgery. Gordon and Trudy came.

"It's okay, Glenda," Gordon told her. "It won't be long. He's going to be so much better."

"I know. It's hard to see him go back there. We're so lucky that he hasn't had more health problems than this. We're blessed," she acknowledged.

"Yes, we are," Trudy agreed. "He's quite strong physically and very active."

They waited patiently. Finally, Dr. Miller came out in his green scrubs and mask removed. "Jed, Glenda, surgery went well. I want him to wait in recovery about thirty minutes before you see him."

"Thanks, Dr. Miller." Jed shook his hand. Then, he slipped his arm around Glenda.

"I can't wait to see him," Glenda said.

When Matthew awoke from surgery, he saw his parents and grandparents and smiled at them. He was groggy and thirsty. He didn't speak because it was too painful. Trudy stayed with Glenda and Matthew. Jed and Gordon left to do farm work and planned to come back in the evening to visit again.

Glenda was sitting in a plaid recliner next to Matthew's bed. Matthew was watching the *Brady Bunch* on the television mounted on the wall. He was dozing in and out as he watched. Glenda was reading a magazine. She often looked at Matthew to see how he was doing.

Jed brought Brad and Jenny to see Matthew. Jenny's stomach felt queasy being in the hospital. She thought about the gruesome explanation Brad gave her in the morning. She didn't like seeing anyone in pain. Blood was so horrible. Brad missed Matthew so much and wanted to tease him about having an easy day off from school. Jed brought a card that was sent home from school. Mrs. Weigman had the class sign the card for Matthew. Jed also brought other cards that had been sent by mail.

"How was school?" Glenda asked the children as she got up out of the recliner chair.

Jenny replied, "Fine. Lots of kids asked about him."

Brad added, "It was good. The teachers sent their get well wishes, and I saw Mr. Clark. He told me to tell you that he misses him."

"That's so thoughtful of everyone," Glenda said. "So many caring friends."

Matthew heard their voices and opened his eyes. He smiled as he saw his family. Jenny came up to him and held his limp hand. "You're so lucky. You're going to get all of the pudding, ice cream, and shakes that you want."

He closed his eyes again. Brad added, "You get any flavor that you want. But save some chocolate ice cream for me. Don't eat all of it. I want some too." Matthew nodded an okay.

"Everyone was asking about you today, Matthew. You're missed. Even Mr. Clark wondered when you'll be back. How are you? How's your throat? Does it hurt?"

Matthew opened his eyes, pointed to the inside of his mouth, and nodded his head.

Glenda asked Jed, "What did you do for supper?"

"We haven't had it yet. The kids wanted to stop at Pizza Parlor."

"That sounds delicious," Glenda commented. "They gave me a supper here. I had an egg salad sandwich, carrots, peaches, and a cookie. Thanks for doing that."

"You know that I'm no cook. We can't wait to have you both home tomorrow. We miss you," Jed said as he slipped his arms around her.

"It gets boring here. I try to keep myself occupied, but I can only do so much. I went down to the gift shop while Matthew rested."

"I think we need to get going. The kids need to get to bed for school tomorrow. It's already getting late for them."

"Brad, Jenny, let's say good-bye and get some pizza."

Matthew perked up a bit. He opened his mouth to say something. He rasped, "Me go. Me pizza."

Everyone chuckled. "Not tonight, Matthew," Jed said. "We'll take you out as soon as you're able to eat some."

Matthew hoarsely repeated, "Me go. Me pizza." He rubbed his stomach. "Mm."

"Later," Brad said. "Rest up tonight and we'll see you tomorrow after school."

"Bye, Matthew," Jenny sadly said as she turned and left. "We love you."

Matthew soon ate again and had a full recovery. The tonsillectomy eliminated the infections. Matthew slept quieter at night with his adenoids removed.

CHAPTER 33

The winter after Matthew had his tonsils out was blustery and snowy with the blowing snow and drifting roads. The main highways were top priority for snow plows, but as the plows removed snow, the strong winds blew drifts over the roads again. School was closed for three days in a row due to the blizzard conditions. When the highways opened for travel, the country gravel roads remained snowy.

On the first day back to school after the storm, it was still below zero degrees wind chill. The Parker children were excited to be going to school and were tired of being cooped up in the house. Even though they were bundled in their winter attire, Jenny and Brad noticed their feet were quite cold. The bus was frigid despite the heater being turned on high. Jenny kept wiggling her toes to see if she could feel them. She asked Matthew, "Are your feet okay? Are you cold? Wiggle your toes to try to stay warm."

"Me brrr. Me toes. Me brrrrr."

"I know," she continued, "Wiggle them and keep moving. It'll keep your blood pumping. I can't warm my feet."

"Me do. Me okay. Tanks, Sis. You okay?"

"I'll be okay, but it's so cold and windy out. The heat's on the bus, but it doesn't get warm enough."

The bus turned onto the gravel road with steep snow banks drifting the sides. Mrs. Trent drove down the narrow, cleared path. A car was approaching, and Mrs. Trent pulled to the right of the road to give the car room to get past the bus. When the car drove by, Mrs. Trent tried to steer back toward the center, but the tires spun. She attempted to back up, but it was no use. The bus was stuck in the snow.

The car's driver looked into his rearview mirror and saw that the bus was still sitting along the side of the road. The driver, Zach Turner, was on his way to work at the factory. He went to the nearest driveway and turned his car around. He parked behind the bus and turned on the hazard lights. Zach walked up to Mrs. Trent, who was reassuring the children that help would be sent. He waved his hands to get her attention. "Is everything okay? Can I help you?"

Mrs. Trent nervously laughed. "I can't get the bus out of this snow. I'm stuck. I need to call the school and have them bring out another bus. I'm more concerned about the children. It's so cold on the bus."

The students fidgeted and wiggled to warm their bodies.

"We're freezing," Alex whined. "What's going to happen to us?"

"We're going to die!" Tiffany Pearson shrieked. "I want Mommy!"

"I can't feel my nose. It's frozen," Jenny said.

"I'm catching pneumonia," another student said, shaking.

Zach told Mrs. Trent he would go home and call the school. Zach had five students pile into his car and took them to his house. He sent his wife, Sandy, to pick up more students. She came back to the bus and picked up six children including Brad, Matthew, and Jenny. Zach and Sandy transported students until every student was off the bus.

Zach and Sandy were both silver-haired and in their fifties. They lived in a modest two-story home with red shutters and awnings. Sandy invited the students into the family room where wood was crackling in the fireplace. Students huddled around closely to feel the warmth on their bodies. Soon, they dispersed to the kitchen booth, chairs, and couches. Sandy prepared hot chocolate, apple cider, and homemade cookies to sooth their shivering bodies.

Sandy engaged the students in activities by inviting them to the game room that consisted of an air hockey table, ping pong table, and board games. The children felt at ease as they soon forgot the cold they felt.

"Sandy, you've done too much. We really appreciate this. I can't thank you enough. What would we have done without you?" Mrs. Trent expressed thankfully.

"It's no problem. I think if it were my children or grandchildren, I hope someone would help them out. This weather has been so frigid and these side roads are treacherous."

The doorbell rang, and the school mechanic, Mr. Taylor, was there. The new bus was parked in the driveway and warm. Mrs. Trent gathered the children to load the bus. She was told to take these students directly to school and forget the rest of her route. Word had gotten around about the delay and parents had taken the other bus children to school.

The bus arrived at school over ninety minutes late. Alice received phone calls from parents inquiring about what happened to the bus. When Mrs. Pearson heard her two daughters were so late, she chose to drive them to school herself from then on rather than put them in danger again. She filed a complaint against Mrs. Trent as an incompetent driver, but it was dismissed as the weather conditions were factors in the incident.

Having her daughters off the bus seemed to take Mrs. Pearson's focus off Matthew, but she still wanted him out of the school. She did hear back from Mr. Hall that there was no legal action to be taken against Matthew or his family. She noticed people in the community seemed to be unfriendly toward her, but she was waiting for the opportune time to complain again. With Mrs. Daniels no longer at the school, there was no one else who agreed with her.

CHAPTER 34

The sun's rays radiated warmth throughout the countryside. The temperature was ninety-five degrees and humid. It was haying time this July and conditions were favorable for mowing, raking, and baling hay. Jed got the farm machinery ready for the field. He needed to grease the equipment to make sure parts operated smoothly. Jed called Matthew to come see him.

"Matthew, I want to show you something. This is a grease gun." He held it up to Matthew. "I use this to grease parts of the tractor and equipment to get ready for the field work. I'd like you to be my special helper today." Jed pointed to a bearing on the wheel. "This is a bearing," he explained. "It gets dry over the months when we don't use a piece of machinery. We need to grease it. Here's what I do." He put the grease gun against a bearing and squeezed the pump. "See. Look at the grease that's on there now. I need to do several more. I want you to try it."

Matthew observed Jed greasing some bearings. "Now, it's your turn, Matthew. Hold this." He handed it to Matthew. "Here, put this on here." Jed helped him hold it and showed him where to squeeze. Matthew squeezed the grease gun. Jed assisted him only the first few times then asked him to do the rest.

The July scorcher continued. It was a typical Midwest summer day. Jed hooked the John Deere tractor to the baler. Matthew sat on Jed's lap and steered the tractor to the hay field. They drove through a pasture and one corn field watching the land ahead of them. "You're driving good and steady. You have a knack for driving."

They stepped out of the tractor. "Look at all this hay on the ground. See how the hay is in bunches and rows? These rows are called wind rows. I line the baler up to them. I drive slowly as the hay goes into the baler and makes small bales."

Matthew reached down and felt the coarse, pokey hay. He put a bunch to his nose and sneezed.

"It's dusty. Some people, like your sister, have allergies called hay fever. They can't be around it without being miserable." Jed climbed the tractor and said, "Time to bale."

Matthew climbed up and sat down next to Jed's seat. He looked behind him as one square after another dropped on the ground. He said, "Dad, Dad. Stop. Stop. Broke. Hay broke."

Jed looked back and saw a bale that was bunched up instead of in a packed bale. "Good eye. We need to get out and take care of it, but first, I need to turn off the baler for safety. We don't ever get near the baler when it's running." Jed showed Matthew where to turn off the baler before getting off the tractor. "We need to spread the hay in another wind row, so it can still be baled. It happens sometimes." They picked up bunches and spread out the hay.

"There," said Jed. "It's time to get going again."

Jed had Matthew try lining up the baler to the hay to make bales. A small line of hay didn't get into the baler, but Jed wasn't concerned. He wanted Matthew to have the experience. Jed went back over the rows where some hay was left.

In the evening, when Jed was done baling, he helped the hay crew load the bales on a trailer, unload them, and stack them in the barn. Matthew walked along with the crew and tried to lift the heavy bales of hay, which weighed sixty to seventy pounds. He couldn't lift one yet. The crew smiled as Matthew attempted to help them. During haying season, there were many late hours, and Matthew stayed out late with Dad, Brad, Rick, and the crew. Mom came out often during the day to replenish the water jug, serve treats, and check on them.

CHAPTER 35

After Matthew completed third grade, distant cousins from Seattle, Washington, came for a three-week visit to their grandparents. Eric and Pam Sorenson stayed with Grandpa Ken and Grandma Flora, who lived only two miles away from the Parkers. Eric was twelve years old and medium height. He was solidly built with blond curly hair. Pam was fourteen years old and had dark brown wavy hair dropping to her shoulders. She liked spending time inside with Flora while Eric wanted to be outdoors.

Jed invited Eric and Pam to the farm to show them the cows and farm life. They rarely got out of the city. The wide open spaces thrilled Eric. Pam came reluctantly. All of the children piled into the back of the pickup. Jed had his window rolled down and asked, "Have you two seen a tame cow before?"

Eric answered, "I've never been around cows. We are always in the city. We never see open country like this. It's all buildings, stores, and houses."

"You are in for a treat. I want to show you the best cow on the farm. Her name is Bonnie, and she belongs to Matthew. She always walks up to him and lets him put his arms around her."

The pickup slowed as Jed watched for Bonnie, and he saw a black cow coming toward them. "That must be her." Jed pointed to the cow "There she is."

He stopped the pickup. Matthew and the rest of the children climbed out. Matthew stood still as a statue as his cow came closer and held his hand out. Bonnie gradually eased up to him and sniffed his hand. Matthew remained still. Bonnie rubbed her nose against him. He carefully lifted his arm and put it around Bonnie's neck. He gave her a big hug. Then, he took off his cowboy hat and put it on her head.

Eric laughed out loud. He walked toward Matthew, but Bonnie nervously backed up at the sight of this stranger.

Jed remarked, "Bonnie is shy with strangers. I can't get as close to her as Matthew does. Neither can Brad or Jenny. We think it's because we move too fast that it spooks her. We're amazed how she responds to Matthew more than anyone else."

Eric was impressed. "Why would a cow let him put a hat on her head? That's just too funny!"

Pam stood there without expression and her arms folded across her chest. It looked too filthy to her. She thought it was sweet, however, for Matthew. She was glad he had something that made him happy. She wanted to get to her grandma's house.

Jed continued, "The most amazing thing is that she survived a tornado which made her quite nervous. The storm had an impact on several cows even though they were unharmed. I was hoping she would calm down. And she did. We bought several cows from the same man and had to sell two already because they were too spirited. We didn't feel safe around them. The case isn't so with Bonnie. She got some quiet attention, and it calmed her down thanks to Matthew."

"Matthew, that's great. You sure have a way with animals. I'm glad you showed her to me. Can I help you on the farm this week?" asked Eric enthusiastically.

"Tanks. Me cow. Me cow like me."

"If your grandma lets you, you're more than welcome to come and see what we do around here," Jed said.

"I don't see it as a problem," Eric responded.

"Ask her tonight and let us know."

"Here are the bean fields. We walk them and use a bean hook to cut out all the weeds. We are starting this week. We always hire a crew. Do you want to join us? We'll pay you an hourly wage."

"I'd love to help. I don't know what a bean hook is."

"We'll show you tomorrow. It's easy to use," Jed said. "We'll see you bright and early tomorrow morning."

"How early do you mean?" Eric asked.

"Be here by seven o'clock. We like to work in the cool of the day."

"No sleeping in for me then," Eric said. "But, I'll be there."

As a treat to their city guests, Glenda invited Flora, Ken, Eric, and Pam to their farm out by the creek to have a bonfire with a weenie roast. Flora accepted immediately. The day of the weenie roast, Eric had been on the farm all day. He watched Jed, Brad, and Rick do mechanic work on the tractors.

"What's a weenie roast? I never heard of one," Eric inquired.

Matthew smiled widely. He nodded and said, "Good. Cook. Eat. Run. Play."

Jed said, "We go out to the creek by the corn field and clear a place to start a fire. The boys gather wood to burn. We cook hot dogs over the fire."

"I can't wait," Eric said enthusiastically.

Jed instructed, "Boys, you go up and down the banks of the creek and gather a huge pile of sticks for me. The small sticks burn quickly. If you find some big ones, that would be good too. Bring them back here so we can get this fire started before the rest get here."

Eric followed Matthew and Brad up and down the bank looking for sticks. Matthew hurried along and checked out the tiny fish in the creek. It was dusk, and Eric was ecstatic with the adventure outdoors. He saw some deer far away in the field. The boys came back several times with an armload of sticks. Matthew pointed out some nests in the trees and showed him a beaver dam further down the creek. Eric had never seen a dam before and was amazed at the craftsmanship a wild animal possessed.

It was almost dark by the time Ken brought the ladies out for the roast. Jed called the boys to come. He had lit the fire, and it was glowing in the dark. The bright flame's warmth surrounded them. Glenda, Flora, Pam, and Jenny got the food out of the pickup. Ken and Jed spread two large picnic blankets on the ground several feet away from the fire. The extra pile of sticks was placed near the fire, providing plenty of wood for the night. Jed passed out the roasting sticks to the children as Glenda opened a package of hot dogs. The children held their sticks over the fire.

Eric got his hot dog too close to the fire and cooked it black as coal. "I'm sorry," he said. "I don't want this one. It's burnt."

"I'll eat it," Ken said. "I like my hot dogs black."

"You do?" Eric asked.

"Yip, that's how they're good. They have that burnt taste. I like it that way."

"Okay, Gramps." Eric slid his hot dog off into a bun and handed it to Ken.

Pam barely heated her hot dog. She saw what Eric did and didn't want hers to get that dark. She held hers high above the flame and quickly put it in a bun. "How is it?" Flora asked. "It doesn't look like you hardly got it hot."

"It's okay," she answered politely even though it wasn't quite warm enough.

The stars filled the twilight and shone beautifully. Eric and Pam gazed at the night sky. They had never seen the stars so vividly. "Remarkable," Eric observed. "I didn't realize we would be able to see so many stars in the sky."

"Me like stars. Me see light. Me see lots." Matthew studied the stars with his cousins. Then he got up to run down the creek. A howl sounded through the field.

"What's that?" Pam shuddered.

"It's just a coyote. A coyote is like a small wolf. It lives in the wild and hunts at night. We hear them all the time. Our dog, Mitzi, barks at them through the night. They won't hurt people. The coyotes won't come near the fire either."

"Me sleep fire. Me okay. Me see stars. Me dog stay me."

The children got up and ran around the creek, staying close to where they could see the fire. They played a game of tag. Matthew tiptoed close to the creek to look for animals.

"It's so scary out here," Pam said.

"I think they are lucky," Eric spoke up. "I think the country is an amazing place to be. The freedom to run and play. Privacy. Having a place for a picnic. It's the best. I could live here."

Brad agreed, "It does feel carefree. I'll always stay here."

"Me too. Me here me old. Me like farm." Matthew opened his arms to show the whole area.

"Matthew, buddy, I'll trade you places." Eric teased. "I'll stay here while you go back to the city."

"No. No. Me stay here. Me like. Me cows, dog, hay, work. Me happy here."

Eric chuckled. "I thought I'd give it a try to switch places with you. You have a great life here."

Matthew nodded his head in agreement.

As it got later, everyone fell silent and listened to the sounds of the night—hooting owls, bellowing cows, splashing fish, and howling coyotes. The fire was crackling as wood was burning. Smoke reached the sky. Eric breathed in a deep sigh and smelled the fresh scent of clover and the rich black soil.

Jed let the fire burn. The glowing fragments turned to ash. He dumped a bucket of water on it. "Time to call it a night," he told everyone. "We have a long day ahead of us. Thanks for coming. I hope you had fun."

"Did I ever," Eric piped up. "I'd like to do this again. Can we? It was a blast."

"Eric, don't invite yourself," Flora warned. "It isn't polite."

Matthew laid on the blanket as everyone picked up the food and garbage. Matthew was on his back and making deep breathing sounds. Eric saw him and shook him a little, "Matthew, wake up. It's time to go home. Wake up."

Matthew didn't flinch. Suddenly, he began snoring.

"Wake up," Brad ordered. "It's time to go back to the house."

Eric came up to him again and slightly shook him, "Time to go back home to bed."

Matthew snored louder and deeper. A big, mischievous grin spread across his face while his eyes remained closed. At last, he opened his eyes. He teasingly said, "Me sleep here. Me like here. No me real sleep. No real."

"Matthew, you sure got me there. I thought you did fall asleep. You looked rather convincing." Eric laughed.

Matthew smiled broadly. "Me tease you. You okay. Me silly."

"That's okay," Eric laughed.

The next week, Glenda and Jed invited Ken, Flora, and the grandchildren for grilled hamburgers and homemade ice cream. The children couldn't wait for another evening.

After supper, Brad asked them if they wanted to play some cards before dessert. Brad introduced the first game. "This game is called Pit. Your Grandma Flora and your great-grandmother played this. It was a favorite." Flora nodded in agreement as Brad explained. "This is a very quiet proper game, just like your great-grandmother." Brad shuffled and dealt the cards as he explained the directions.

"It's easy, kids," Flora said. She winked at Brad. "And listen to Brad. It's a mellow, calm game."

"Everyone, look at your cards," Brad instructed. "See what you have and what you want to trade for starters." He paused a few moments. "Okay, is everyone ready?"

Matthew, Flora, Jenny, and Brad were all set. Eric and Pam looked a bit confused but were ready to try it.

Brad said, "Does anyone have a question?" He looked around and no one spoke. "When I ring the bell, the game will begin." Each player was set with cards ready to trade with other players. Ding! The game began.

Matthew shouted, "Two, two, two!"

Flora yelled loudly, "Three, three, three!"

"One, one, one!" Brad hollered over the other two.

"Two, two, two!" Jenny shouted and quickly traded with Matthew.

Eric and Pam's eyes widened. "I've have never seen Grandma like this," he told Pam. "She's loud and wild in this game."

"This is a quiet game?" she questioned.

As they joined in the game, the yelling and hollering continued until Matthew rang the bell, saying, "Oh yeah. Me corn. Me good." Everyone moaned over the loss.

Eric piped up, "I have a question. I thought you said this was a calm and quiet game? It was wild and crazy."

Brad snickered, "We tell every guest that this is a quiet game. It's our family joke."

"I liked it," Eric said. "It was more fun than I expected."

Pam lit up, "I agree with Eric."

"Are we ready for another round?" Brad asked.

After a couple of rounds of Pit, they all enjoyed the creamy, lemony taste of the ice cream. It was Eric and Pam's first try of the family recipe.

At ten o'clock, Ken came out of the family room and said, "Okay, break up the fun. It's time to get you younguns' home and get some rest before we take you to the airport tomorrow." Eric and Pam thanked the Parkers again for another fun evening.

CHAPTER 36

At ten years old, Matthew was active and danced merrily around the house while he listened to music. He especially liked his dad's country music and played it on the record player. In August, the Parkers chose a popular vacation spot of Branson, Missouri, for their summer vacation.

The Parkers planned only two nights in Branson and bought tickets for a Carson Family Music Show. The singers and musicians, dressed in country western attire, performed musical numbers with comedy breaks. The hillbilly comedians told jokes that got the audience roaring in laughter. The Parkers sat halfway back in the auditorium. After each song, Matthew held his hands in front of his face and clapped fervently. He said, "Good. Real good."

At the end of the show, every musician was introduced. When the band bowed and left the stage, the crowd stood and cheered for more. The lead singer stepped back on stage and said, "Thank you. You've been a grand audience tonight. We have one more number for you." Everyone sat down as the curtain opened, and one more was performed. After the song, the announcer said, "Come on down and meet us. We'll be mighty glad to say howdy. We'll autograph programs or pictures. Have a great night and thanks for coming."

"Whew, what a show," Jed said. "I heard this one was great, but this was over the top."

"Me go. Me go down. Him sign." Matthew took his fingers and showed writing.

Glenda just wanted to go back to the motel since the line for autographs went all the way to the back of the auditorium. "Are you sure he can wait that long? It's getting late, and it'll be quite a while before he meets them."

"If he really wants to go, I'll take him," Jed said.

"Me see. Me see people. Sign." He made the motion to indicate autograph again.

"I'll take him down. You just wait here, Glenda. Does anyone else want to go with us?"

Brad curled upon the cushiony seat and stayed with Glenda, yawning and closing his eyes. Jenny took Matthew by the hand and walked him to the end of the line. He clutched the music program tightly, anxious to see the performers.

Glenda warned Jed, "If he gets too rambunctious in line, make sure you get out of line right away. We don't want a scene."

"He'll be fine. Jenny has already started walking him to the back."

Jed caught up to Jenny and Matthew where they made their way through part of a crowd that was leaving and another group that was in line for meeting the performers.

"How'd you like the show, kids?"

"It was fantastic," Jenny said.

"Me like. Real good. Me play. Me do that. Me play."

A retired couple stood in front of Jed and the children. The man said, "The concert was great." Looking at Matthew he asked, "What would you play?"

"Me play…" He pretended he had drumsticks in his hands and mimicked drumming.

"That's a great instrument," he said. "I like the drums too."

"Me boom, boom, boom. Me like."

The man and Jed spent a few minutes chit-chatting about where they lived. The couple lived in Dodge City, Kansas, only an hour from Jed's cousins who raised lots of wheat and fed cattle. Jed told him about Matthew's cow and how tame she was.

"You're a real cowboy," the man told Matthew. "Good for you."

"Yes, me cowboy. Me help cows. Me hug cow. Me cow like hat. Funny."

"That is something. You don't hear about that every day. You continue to take good care of her," the man replied.

As they got closer to the stage, Jed wished the couple a good vacation while Matthew waited patiently the rest of the time. The lead singer greeted them warmly and shook each of their hands. "Thanks for coming. Did you enjoy the show?"

Jenny nodded her head yes.

Jed said, "We've never been here before. That was an outstanding performance."

Matthew put his thumbs up and grinned widely in pleasure. The lead singer put his hand on Matthew's shoulder and said, "Thanks. Come again." He signed his name on the program.

The drummer had his drumsticks by him on stage as he signed his name. Matthew eyed them temptingly, "Me boom, boom. Cool."

"Perhaps you can play for us someday. We can always use more musicians," the drummer told Matthew.

"Me do. Me like."

"We go on a bus and sing lots of places."

"Me boom, boom. Me go bus."

"Maybe we'll see you one day."

Jed took Jenny and Matthew back to the seats where Glenda and Brad were tiredly waiting.

———✳———

At the motel, Matthew picked up a suitcase and said, "Me go. Me play boom, boom. Me play. Me go man. Me go bus. Me good."

"You want to be in a band?" Jenny questioned Matthew.

"Man say me play. Me go. Me boom, boom. Me go."

"No," Glenda explained, "You are not going to play in the band."

"Man say. Me go. Me good," Matthew spoke determinedly.

"He was being nice to you. You don't even know how to play the drums," Jed explained.

"Man show me. Me good. Me do. Me see him."

"It's time for bed," Jed spoke. "Change into your pajamas and go to bed."

"No sleep. Me go now. Me boom boom."

Glenda and Jed shot each other a look of concern. They didn't have good luck convincing him he wasn't going with the band. Glenda looked at the motel door, knowing Matthew was quite capable of unlocking the door and unlatching the chain.

Seeing Brad watching television gave Jed an idea. Perhaps, if Matthew got focused on something else, such as an entertaining television program, he might get his mind off the band. Jed picked up the television remote and turned the channels. Jed saw the Flinstones were on the television.

Matthew heard, "Yabba, dabba, doo." He recognized this cartoon as one of his favorites. He went to the bed and laid on his stomach, looking up at the television. Matthew laughed at Fred, Barney, and Dino the dinosaur. "Show good. Me see Yabba Dabba doo." He watched Fred slide down Dino's neck and clapped his hands. "Whee," he said.

Jed thought this worked to distract him from taking off. Glenda motioned for him to come over to the table and chairs near the door. Jed tiptoed over to her, careful not to distract Matthew from the show.

"Why does Matthew think he's going away?" Glenda asked.

"Matthew saw the drumsticks when the drummer signed his autograph. The drummer saw Matthew light up and said that perhaps he could join the band. He meant no harm. He was trying to be kind."

"He doesn't realize how impressionable Matthew is. He's distracted now, but once he has something in his mind, it's hard to remove the idea. I'm concerned about his insistence."

"He is stuck on the idea," Jed stated. "But I think the cartoon has gotten his mind off of it. He may have forgotten already."

"I hope you're right," Glenda whispered. "But I won't take any chances. I want to make sure we keep him safe tonight. He sleeps so light and is so quiet when he awakens. I don't want him sneaking off."

"He's sleeping the farthest from the door. He should be okay."

Glenda pursed her lips and looked around the room. She decided to push chairs against the door to block it. She whispered to Jed, "Have Matthew get on his pajamas while he watches the cartoon. Have him lie down and see if he'll go to sleep. We'll turn off the TV after the cartoon is over. I'll turn out the room lights and see if he goes to sleep." It was already 11:30 p.m.

Jed searched the suitcase for the pajamas as Glenda pushed two chairs against the door. This way, if Matthew woke up, they would at least hear the chairs move before he could get to the door. She checked to see if the door was locked and chained.

Jed saw that Matthew was asleep. He would forget about the band by morning. Glenda slept light as a feather as she heard the traffic pass by the highway near the motel. She looked at the window and saw the street light through the curtain. Although Glenda shut her eyes, she tossed and turned and looked at the clock. It was 12:30 a.m. She looked over at Matthew who seemed to be sleeping soundly.

---*---

Jed slowly eased out of bed at six in the morning, careful not to wake anyone. Glenda sat up quickly and was relieved it was only Jed.

"I hope he forgot about the band," she whispered. "We'll have to keep an extra close eye on him today."

Jed lathered the shaving cream on his face. "Glenda, he doesn't forget things. Let's stay away from big crowds so he can't get lost. We can go putt putt golfing and to the Laura Ingalls Wilder home. Jenny wants to see that. She loves the Little House books."

"Those places won't be as crowded as Silver Dollar City. That sounds good. Let's get cleaned up before he wakes up."

"Did you sleep well?" Jed already knew the answer.

"Not at all. I woke up frequently to check on him. I wasn't sure about him."

"He was determined about leaving. He doesn't realize he'd get lost. The musicians were so friendly and talked to him. Some remarked about his cowboy boots and belt buckle. Matthew felt so good talking to them. He'll cherish the autographs."

"I'm glad they were so kind to him. It's better than how people stare at him. Everywhere we go, someone's turning up their noses at him, yet most people are nice."

When the sheets rustled, Jed and Glenda looked toward the sound and saw Brad sitting up in his cot. "Good morning," Glenda greeted softly. She put a finger to her lips and pointed to Matthew still sleeping silently.

Matthew woke up without mentioning the band but turned on the television to watch cartoons. Jenny woke up squinting her eyes from the light in the room. "Oh," she groaned. "I want to go back to sleep."

"You need to get showered so we can eat an early breakfast," instructed Glenda.

Matthew saw Jenny and greeted, "Morning, Sis. You miss me. Me go. Me play. Me boom, boom."

Everyone raised their eyebrows and said, "Oh, no. Here we go again."

The rest of the vacation was spent at the Laura Ingalls Wilder home and putt putt golfing. They all kept an extra close eye on Matthew. Matthew spent several weeks after arriving home talking about playing the drums. He didn't talk about leaving home which was a great relief. He hung the autographed program on the bulletin board in his room so he could always see it. He looked at it and said, "Me go. Me play. Me good. Some day." The someday was a long ways off. He played the record of the music group over and over again, learning all of the songs by heart.

Glenda and Jed were glad to be home and back to routine. Once school started, Matthew spoke less and less of the band.

PART 5

HIGH SCHOOL

CHAPTER 37

As Matthew went through upper elementary and junior high, the gap widened between him and his peers academically. He was integrated in art, music, gym, social studies, and lunch. His peers had noticed a significant deficit in his speech. However, most of them had a protective instinct. They had grown up with him and gradually become aware that he had a disability that they were unaware of in earlier years. His peers cared about him and included him whenever possible at school.

His speech did not reflect the skills he did possess. His mechanical skills on the farm were strong. He did not read more than Dr. Seuss unless it was something he memorized. He did memorize some difficult words such as names of professional teams and the players. For Christmas, he looked at the quantity of his gifts rather than price. He thought one expensive gift was a small Christmas, so Glenda and the rest of the family gave several little stocking stuffers to please him. He learned his basic addition facts, but learned to use the calculator for any other calculations. Math was a difficult class for him. However, he could keep track of baseball statistics and numbers on the farm.

Matthew continued to have a happy demeanor with a smile on his face every day, feeling confident about who he was. It was not known if Matthew realized he had Down syndrome or not. He knew he couldn't always express himself. When he couldn't get a word said, he used his hands, a rhyming word, or learned to spell it. He eventually got his point across.

Matthew's high school life began with many changes such as going to the big building and having a new teacher. Mr. Hanson, the high school special education teacher, used to own the local grocery store and sold it to become a teacher. He knew the Parker family from the community and was excited to work with Matthew.

Mr. Hanson had a small group of special education students and was all prepared for his first day of high school. Dressed in dark green slacks, a white shirt, and green tie, he met Matthew as he stepped off the bus. He grinned at him, "Hello, Matthew. I'm Mr. Hanson, your teacher."

Matthew recognized the stocky man and knew he was nice. "Hi," Matthew said.

"Matthew, I'm going to take you around the building. Of course, you've always been here, but I want to show you where you will go and at what times. You'll spend most of the day with me and Mrs. Jones, my helper. Both of us will work with you and our other students."

"Okay," Matthew replied.

Mr. Hanson took Matthew to the classroom where Mrs. Jones waited. Matthew got a locker with a combination lock just outside of his classroom near the home economics room and the cafeteria. "Here's your locker. You'll put your backpack, gym shoes, and coat here. You're welcome to decorate the locker with posters if you wish."

"Good. Me team baseball. Me John Deere."

"You'll also learn the combination to your locker. I'll show you today, but you'll have to do it yourself. First, you turn left to the number fifteen. Then, you turn right once around to the number eight. Turn left back to the number twenty. You try it. We'll practice so you'll be able to do it in a week."

"Me okay. Me work. Me do. Me lock."

Mr. Hanson handed Matthew a copy of the daily schedule. Mr. Hanson said, "Here's a copy of where you need to be each day. You're expected to learn it."

Matthew looked at the schedule. "Me no know. Where go?"

"I'll take you around now. It will be easy once you learn it."

Mr. Hanson led Matthew to the art room. "Hi, Matthew. Good to see you again. I'm glad you'll be in class. As you can see, you'll get to do several different projects," Mr. Rich explained. Matthew saw clay models, paintings, wood carvings, and pencil drawings. There were approximately thirty tables and high stools for students to sit and work on art projects.

"Me happy. Draw. Paint."

"You'll do fine. Thanks for stopping by. We'll see you tomorrow," Mr. Rich said as he shook his hand good-bye.

Matthew and Mr. Hanson went to the automotive shop to meet Mr. Stevens. Matthew had one class of mechanics where he would learn the basics of automotive care. There were a couple of cars and lots of tools in the shop.

"Hello, there," Mr. Stevens greeted. "I'm the shop teacher. You'll learn mechanics here."

"Me do. Me dad. Me help farm."

"Then this class will be easy for you. Are you a football fan? I coach football."

"Me friends play. Me like. Me clap me friends."

"I'll see you at the games then."

Back in the classroom, Matthew bonded with Mrs. Jones and Mr. Hanson. The room was filled with cheerfulness, but one thing bothered Matthew. Mr. Hanson had a tendency to leave his closet and desk drawers open. While Mr. Hanson was talking to Mrs. Jones, he went over and closed the closet door and shut the drawers of the desk. Mr. Hanson saw him and chuckled. "I heard you liked things neat, Matthew. I see it for myself. I guess you can be my helper in keeping things organized. Thanks for closing those."

Matthew liked the way Mr. Hanson reacted to things and knew this was going to be a good year. He looked around the room some more and saw four posters of the Kansas City Royals, which had been his favorite team since he watched them in the

World Series a few years ago. Matthew saw the chalkboard and a kidney-shaped table surrounded with chairs. Mr. Hanson had a large metal desk with a black swivel office chair and a filing cabinet beside it. There was a bouquet of multicolored carnations on his desk to make the room colorful. Matthew went up to them and touched the soft, silky petals. He smelled their sweet fragrance and said, "Me mom. Mom like."

Mr. Hanson told Matthew it was time to see the home economics room. "We'll be spending lots of time in there. You'll learn to cook and do laundry. The room also has a sewing area where you'll learn to sew on buttons or repair tears in clothes. The room has a dishwasher. We'll teach you how to do dishes by hand and with a dishwasher."

Matthew rolled his eyes at this since he helped Mom at home with laundry and dishes. However, he didn't measure the detergent for either one. Mom and Jenny did the cooking at the house while he worked outside with Dad. There were four kitchens in the enormous room. He wondered why it needed four kitchens when one kitchen was all that was needed for cooking. He saw the washer and dryer along one wall and the ironing board nearby. He remembered that he was to stay away because the iron was hot. Would he learn that too?

The home economics room had cupboards and drawers for pots, pans, and silverware. Nonperishable food stocked the shelves. He walked around looking at each kitchen and the appliances.

"I see you look happy about this room. We get this room to ourselves for one hour every day. This is your second classroom." Mr. Hanson observed Matthew studying the layout of the room.

"Me like. Me cook. Me work. Me good."

"You'll be surprised what you will learn. We start tomorrow. When you cook, we will share the food with teachers and staff."

"Me happy. Me cook people."

"I know."

Matthew started to follow Mr. Hanson from the room, but then he saw some cupboard doors slightly ajar. He went to shut them and saw a couple of tea towels crooked on the towel bar from an earlier class. He straightened the towels so they didn't look bunched up.

Mr. Hanson patiently waited as Matthew got things in neat order and was ready to get started. Over three periods a day were in special classes where he would use his hands. He felt as if he had found a buried treasure.

CHAPTER 38

When Matthew started high school, Brad had already graduated and had been on the farm a few years working with Jed. They raised cattle and grew wheat, soybeans, corn, alfalfa hay, and a few oats. Brad was proud to be the fifth generation to continue the tradition of farming the land.

Jenny was a sophomore in college when Matthew started high school. She lived two hours away from home. Jenny took a while to adjust to the college life but adapted within the first year by getting involved in student ministries and doing lots of social activities. Jenny was a leader for the student ministries to reach out to the college community and met several good friends who served with her.

It was mid-term exam time, and Jenny studied especially hard for the tests. She called home and wondered if she could be picked up for the weekend. She didn't have a car and couldn't afford one. She was just thankful to be able to go to college at all. When Jenny called, Jed answered the phone. "How are you doing, my college girl?"

"Good. I'm done with midterm tests on Friday. I was wondering if I can come home this weekend."

"I think that should work. When do you want to be picked up?"

"Friday afternoon sometime. I haven't seen you guys for a long time. I can't wait to see Matthew. How's he doing?"

"He's doing amazing in school. He painted an impressive picture of a blue jay perched on a tree limb. We hung it on the kitchen wall."

"I can't wait to see it. Any more news?"

"Well, let me think. He made pancakes for us last Sunday morning. He also made cookies with Glenda the day before. He understands measuring and following directions on recipes."

"I hope he makes something for me. I'm excited to hear more about his school year. I can't wait to praise him for his new skills."

"He's growing and learning in independent living skills. He learned emergency and family numbers. He may call you one day just to talk. He's proud of knowing how to call people. He calls Grandma Kate, Gordon and Trudy, and friends from church. They love it when he calls. Of course, the conversations are short."

"He says little, but he thinks deep," Jenny chuckled.

"That's for sure."

"So are you coming to get me on Friday?"

"Count on it. I don't see any reason why not. We look forward to seeing you. We'll bring Matthew with us so you two can catch up on the way home. He'll be so glad to see you."

Jenny was anticipating Friday without homework or tests to study for on the weekend. She would go home and relax with her family. She had lunch with her friend Kurt who spent lots of time with her studying for accounting tests. Jenny told him how excited she was about going home.

"I haven't seen you this happy all semester," he remarked. "Your family must be something. I'd like to meet them."

"If you stop by the dorm, you can. I can't wait to see my brother. He's learning so much in school this year. I have so much to talk to him about." Kurt was so handsome and outgoing that Jenny thought he'd get along great with her family.

"So, what classes is he taking? Is he in algebra?"

"No, he isn't in algebra. He's working on independent living skills and mechanical skills at the high school."

"Why is that? That isn't doing much."

"Oh, yes it is. He has a disability called Down syndrome. But we don't focus on the disability. We like to be positive and focus on his abilities he was given."

"That's crazy. Down syndrome children have no abilities. They are like puppy dogs – cute and playful. All the value they have is to play with them like a pet. There's no intellect there."

"I happen to think there's a lot more value to him than that. He's learned so many skills, he—"

"Stop, Jenny. You don't get it, do you? Do you believe he can function in society? You're dreaming. He can't do more than be trained and do tricks like a dog. He can't think for himself."

Jenny's muscles tensed as she heard her good friend speak of her brother in this way. She tried to calm down as she wanted a way out of this conversation. He might be muscular and smart, but she now realized how shallow Kurt actually was. She was stunned to hear him speak in such a way. Where did he get his arrogance? Jenny bit her tongue and tried to control the volcano brewing inside her.

"Look, Kurt, I need to go back to my room and pack. They'll be here in a couple of hours. You don't need to stop by and meet my family. They'll be in a hurry to get back to the field work as soon as we get home. Have a great weekend."

"You too, Jenny. Uh, Jenny, I do hope that college teaches you to discern the realities of life."

"And what are those realities?" She wondered what he considered reality.

"That there's no place in life for the lowly."

"The lowly?"

"Yes. What counts in this world is intellect. Your brother will never read a classic or be college material. The college community is where it's at. We are the movers and shakers in this world. We're the ones who will make a difference in our world. Your brother will only exist and have little purpose."

"You think so?"

"I think that there are people who won't go to college and work in factories, but they are still beneath the college population."

Jenny was infuriated now. "Look, some of the hardest-working, most honest people I know couldn't afford college or didn't want to go. I grew up a farm girl, a respectable farm girl. I love my country roots. I'll always favor the heart of the country and the people there. And Matthew is a human being, pure and simple, not shallow or arrogant like you. I can't believe how you think you're so above others. Matthew is loved by his classmates and community. Something you could never understand. Don't bother to stop by my room today."

"Jenny, you need to be enlightened."

"Enlightened? I was today. My eyes were opened plenty by this conversation." She stood up and walked away. She felt disillusioned by this handsome, popular guy. She was completely blindsided by his attitude. She had thought he was a kind and compassionate person before today.

Jenny started packing her clothes and toiletries in her dorm room. She slammed the clothing into her duffle bag and stormed around the room. Her roommate, Diane, was studying at her desk and was surprised to see Jenny's stormy behavior. She asked Jenny, "What got your dander up? I've never seen you this way."

"Of all the jerks. I thought Kurt was a real gentleman. He's a snob."

"Why do you say that?" asked Diane sweetly. "Did you two have a fight?"

"I told him about my brother who has Down syndrome. He had the gall to say that he's only like a puppy dog. That makes me so mad. How can he say that?"

Diane spoke slowly, "Some people want everything to fit into a neat, tidy box. They criticize or put down what they don't know or understand."

"He thinks he's above hardworking, uneducated people that live good, honest lives."

"Haven't you run into this before? Didn't anyone else show fear or disgust for him ?"

"Only one or two. We didn't have many people that did. I do know that most of my brother's schoolmates are wonderful to him. They didn't treat him as though he was unworthy. They treated him like an equal. There has been some adversity, but the acceptance he has experienced has been so overwhelming. Our community's the best."

"That's so cool. He's most fortunate to grow up there. And it sounds like he has taught the people there lessons about life."

"He brings out kindness in others. But, I can't consider Kurt a friend when he has such an outlook on life."

"Ditch him. He isn't worth it."

There was a knock at the door. Diane opened the door and warmly greeted, "Hi. Come in. You must be Jenny's family. I've heard so much about you. I'm Diane. Nice to meet you."

"Hi," greeted Glenda. "We've heard a lot about you too. We're so glad to hear Jenny has such a good roommate."

Diane laughed, "It sounds like Jenny puffed me up too much. I'm not surprised. She always looks at the best in others." She turned to Matthew. "And, you must be the little brother I hear about all the time. You sure are special."

"Me miss sis. Me love sis."

"So how's school this year, kiddo? I hear you're learning a lot."

"Good." Matthew smiled from ear to ear at her.

"What do you like best?" Diane inquired.

"Me cook. Me pancakes."

"Can I come visit you? I'd love to have someone make me homemade pancakes." Diane smiled sweetly at him.

"Me do. Me cook you. You like. Mm good." Matthew and Diane chatted a bit. Matthew was so happy to meet Diane that he hugged her. He thought she was pretty with her long wavy brown hair. She was tall and slender. The top of his head reached her waist.

Jenny picked up her two pieces of luggage and was ready to go. "I'm all set. I'll be back Sunday afternoon. Thanks, Diane. You're the best."

"You're too kind," Diane laughed. "Nice to meet all of you. Have a safe trip and a good weekend."

Jed and Matthew offered to carry her luggage. Jenny opened the door and saw Kurt standing there and ready to knock. He smiled kindly. It almost softened Jenny, but she remembered the conversation they had.

He spoke to Jenny, "I wanted to stop by before you left for home. Aren't you going to introduce me?"

Jenny cleared her throat. "Mom, Dad, Matthew, this is Kurt Johnson. He's another student here."

"And, if I might add, good friends with Jenny." He held out his hand to greet Jed then Glenda with his polish and charm. They each admiringly shook Kurt's hand. Diane sat back at the desk and rolled her eyes at his finesse.

Matthew stepped behind Jed when he saw Kurt, not wanting to say hi to him. He had an agitated look on his face, and his lips turned in disgust. He kept his distance from Kurt, sensing something.

Jed instructed, "Matthew, step up and shake hands with Kurt. He's a real nice guy."

Matthew refused, but Jenny defended, "It's okay, Dad. Matthew must be tired from the long car ride." She went over and hugged him. "I missed you so much. I can't wait to see your painting." Matthew remained silent in Kurt's presence and wouldn't leave his spot behind Jed.

Kurt observed Matthew's withdrawal and nodded toward him. "I told you so, Jenny." Then, he turned to Jed and Glenda. "Have a wonderful weekend. Nice to meet you Jed, Glenda."

As he left, Jed commented, "What a nice young man."

Diane made a coughing sound. Jenny said, "Not as nice as you'd think. Look at Matthew's reaction. He saw Kurt for who he was. He isn't what he appears. I've learned that."

"Whatever do you mean?" Glenda inquired.

"I'll explain it to you later, Mom. Now isn't the time. Let's get home."

Jenny and Matthew sat together in the back of the car talking all the way home. At home, the first thing Jenny saw was the painting that hung on the kitchen wall. She loved the detail in the painting Matthew had made. "Matthew, it's beautiful. I'd like you to paint a picture for me to put in my room."

"Me do. Tanks, Sis. Me like do. Me good." He demonstrated how he held his brush and made strokes on the canvas.

"I'm amazed. You did a fantastic job."

Glenda added, "Mr. Rich had a sample painting that he showed Matthew. He let Matthew use it to copy, but he did this on his own. Matthew does a great job looking at a picture and painting a replica."

"Copy or not, it's wonderful. Can you make pancakes for us tomorrow morning?"

"Me do. Me like cook." Matthew left the room and went upstairs to put some laundry away.

Jenny told Glenda the story about Kurt and how she used to see him. "Mom, I didn't want to date him, but I thought he was so cool. I thought he had high integrity. I can't even think of someone like him as a friend. If he can't accept Matthew as a person, he isn't worth my friendship."

"I'm glad to hear you say that. Brad's neighborhood friends don't mind if Matthew tags along part of the time. In fact, the guys usually ask Brad if he wants to bring Matthew along when they go bowling or out to eat. We tell Brad that he doesn't always have to take Matthew with him, but he likes to do it."

"I won't stand for anyone treating him badly. He deserves better than that. Isn't Diane wonderful? She's so sweet all the time."

"Yes, and I noticed that Matthew really took to her. He thought she was something."

"See?" said Jenny. "Matthew does have good instincts about people. What you see is what you get with her. She's the best. She told me to ditch my friendship with Kurt."

"Good for her. I agree."

"I'd better unpack, Mom. I'll be back down. It feels good to be home."

Saturday morning, Matthew made a batch of pancakes from scratch for everyone and set the table with butter, two kinds of syrup, and five place settings. He did every step by himself, except that Glenda made sausage links. The pancakes were perfectly golden brown and delicious.

"This is the best breakfast I've had in weeks. It tastes so yummy. Thank you for making this." Jenny said, thinking how she missed a home-cooked breakfast.

"Me good. Me like cook. Mr. H. say me good cook. Me do all alone."

"I wonder what your next surprise will be when I come home for Thanksgiving."

"Stay calm, sis. Wait and see. Me 'prise you. Me cook you. Me do lots school."

"Well, Mr. Hanson must be quite a teacher. I like him already."

"Him cool man. Me friend. Like him. Him tell me do this, do that. Him okay. Him teach me."

"I'm glad you like school." Jenny winked at him. "I want to play some board games tonight. We need to have fun this weekend."

"Go bowl. You, me, Brad, go bowl. Fun. Me do." Matthew mimicked walking with a bowling ball and throwing it.

"That sounds good too," Jenny said enthusiastically. "I haven't bowled since last Christmas. Let's do it."

Brad, Jenny, and Matthew went bowling and ate pizza at the local pizza place. The weekend passed all too quickly for Jenny. The college felt so far away. She was sad as she went back to college.

When Jenny got back to college, she distanced herself from Kurt. Diane was a great help in blocking the phone calls. Jenny hid in the closet if he stopped by the room while Diane told him she wasn't there. He tried to spend time with her for a couple of weeks, but finally got the hint that she didn't want to be around him anymore. It was awkward for a while with both of them attending the same ministries group. Diane invited Jenny to a dynamic Bible church that believed in the value of human life no matter what the circumstances. Jenny attended with her and found a new social group of friends. She felt so at home at this church and did many social activities with them.

One evening, Jenny sat in her dorm room and held Matthew's freshman picture. Aloud she said, "You're so important. I won't tolerate anyone who doesn't see the wonderful person you are." She set Matthew's picture on her bed stand. Jenny smiled and went to her desk to study.

CHAPTER 39

The high school had dingy tan lockers with metal doors and a place where students put their combination locks. Matthew got his own locker in the hallway near the special education room, the cafeteria, and the home economics room. Once he mastered his combination, he never forgot.

Matthew kept his coat, backpack, and gym shoes in his locker and decorated it with pictures of Michael Jackson, a John Deere tractor, and the Kansas City Royals taped on the inside of the door.

One day as Matthew grabbed his nylon duffle bag with his gym shoes, the locker door banged against the next one, surprising him. He looked up and saw Billy, who was dressed in a ripped t-shirt and faded jeans. Matthew shrugged his shoulders when Billy pounded his fist into the locker, glaring at him. Billy ripped off the Kansas City Royals poster and tore it to shreds.

Luke and Brian were several feet away and saw Billy approach the locker. They exchanged glances and stood motionless as they watched the episode. They both knew there was trouble.

"Stop. Stop. Me picture. You bad. You bad man. No take me stuff," Matthew said firmly.

Billy reached for the John Deere poster and ripped it off. He laughed mockingly. "You can't tell me to stop, you retard. I can do whatever I want."

As Billy tore the second poster, Matthew sternly said, "You stop. Stop. Me stuff. No you stuff."

Billy laughed with a sense of superiority.

Luke and Brian continued to watch. Brian whispered to Luke, "I think we'd better go and put a stop to this."

Luke put his fingers to his lips. "Sh. Let's see how Matthew deals with it first. He's holding his own so far. I want to see what happens. If there's a chance he could get hurt, we'll help out."

"I don't know, Luke. Billy is a rat. I think we should get involved now."

"Wait," Luke said. Brian didn't agree and started to walk closer to the scene. Luke put his arm out to stop him.

Matthew reached for his locker door, attempting to shut it to protect his belongings. Billy put his black boot against the locker door, holding it open. He reached into the locker again, but Matthew didn't shy away. He stood strong and firm. He asserted, "You go. You go. You bad man. You stop."

"Ha, ha, ha," Billy mocked. "What can you do? Do you think you can stop me?"

"Me say, you bad news. Keep away. Me stuff." Billy threw his chest against Matthew's body. Matthew rolled up his shirt sleeves. "See. Me tough. Me muscle. Me stop you. Go!"

"Ha, ha, ha. You can't stop me. You aren't strong."

Matthew hesitated and dropped his shoulders. He fell to his knees and hung his head down low.

"I knew you were a wimp."

Brian tensed up. "This is getting serious, Luke. We need to help him."

Luke shook his head, not wanting to see what would transpire next. Brian didn't like this at all. He thought that Luke was crazy to wait it out. They heard a loud grunt when Matthew dropped to the ground. Billy heckled, "I knew it. You frightened little mouse."

Suddenly, a large growly sound came out of Matthew's mouth as he leaned forward and wrapped his arms around Billy's legs. He yelled, "Argh! Argh!" He lifted Billy right off the ground.

Billy was taken aback and lost his balance. He grabbed for the locker door, but his hands were slick, and he couldn't grasp it. "Put me down. Put me down," he yelled before he fell down on the hallway floor. Billy's hands braced the fall, but he hit his nose against the locker. "Ow! Ow!"

Luke started laughing hysterically. He thought Billy got exactly what was coming to him and was surprised that Matthew went to that extent to defend himself. Brian began laughing also, but covered his mouth so Billy wouldn't hear him.

"Is Matthew in trouble?" Brian asked.

"What for? He only lifted him off the ground to protect his belongings."

Brian pointed to Billy and watched as he sat up and covered his nose. Billy looked dazed. Matthew stooped down and asked, "You okay? You hurt?"

"Of course, I'm hurt. Look what you did. Leave me alone, you retard," Billy yelled.

Mr. Hanson heard someone yell and stepped out of his classroom. He saw Matthew stooped down and Billy's blood-stained face. "What's going on here?" he asked sternly.

Billy stood up carefully and removed his hand from his nose. "See what this retard did to me. I was minding my own business and look!"

Mr. Hanson turned to Matthew, "Can you tell me what happened?"

"Me stuff. Me locker. Me stop him. Him no stop. Him bad news."

Mr. Hanson looked quizzically at both boys and ordered Billy to go to the nurse's office. "When the nurse has seen you, go to the principal's office. He'll want to ask you some questions." Mr. Hanson scanned the locker area and saw shreds of paper strewn on the ground.

He recalled that Matthew had several posters hanging in his locker. He asked Matthew, "Where are your posters?"

Matthew pointed to the ground. "Him rip. Rip, rip, rip. Me tell him stop. No stop. Him rip. Him bad news."

"I see. I think we will visit with Mr. Clark. He'll want to see you. Come on."

Luke and Brian hesitantly approached Mr. Hanson. "Mr. Hanson," Luke gulped. "This is all my fault. I shouldn't have let this go so far. I watched the whole thing."

"What do you mean, Luke?" Mr. Hanson inquired. "What happened here?"

"I told Luke we needed to stop it," Brian added, "but he wouldn't listen."

"Boys," Mr. Hanson directed, "let's all go down to Mr. Clark's office, so you can tell him the whole story."

Brian and Luke nervously nodded their heads. Mr. Hanson led Luke, Brian, and Matthew to the office.

Mr. Clark pursed his lips and wrote down Billy's account of what happened. Something didn't sound right. He felt there were holes in the story. "Are you sure Matthew punched your nose while you were minding your own business? That isn't typical of him."

Billy fidgeted in his chair. "I told ya already what happened."

Looking down at his notes, Mr. Clark doubted this was true. Billy was known for lying and instigating trouble. He couldn't do anything until he got to the bottom of this. He dismissed Billy to class and told him he would call him up later if necessary. As Billy left the office, Mr. Hanson escorted Luke, Brian, and Matthew into the main office. Billy looked astonished and wondered what Luke and Brian were doing there. He didn't think that anyone had seen the incident.

Mr. Hanson had Matthew sit in the board room and gave him some paper to draw. He would talk to Matthew while Luke and Brian visited with Mr. Clark.

Mr. Clark knew that parents had to be contacted. He thumbed through his phone directory to find the numbers of both parties, but he still needed more information before calling. He heard a knock on the door. "Come in," he snapped, exhaling a long, deep breath.

"Am I interrupting something?" Mr. Hanson asked calmly.

"Not right now, you aren't. What's up? I've had quite an ordeal today."

"I think I know what it is," Mr. Hanson said confidently. "I have two young gentlemen who need to speak with you."

"Really?" Mr. Clark said in disbelief.

"Yes, sir. I have two boys who saw something that's important for you to know."

"Okay, tell them to come on in," Mr. Clark said reluctantly.

Luke and Brian filed into the principal's office. Luke felt guilty he didn't get involved and wondered if Matthew was in deep trouble. Brian wished he had ignored Luke and intervened immediately. He felt Luke was responsible for what Matthew had done. He didn't want to be in trouble when he wanted to help. He let Luke be in control.

Mr. Clark observed the emotions on the faces of the boys and knew they were struggling. He didn't know why, but he attempted to put them at ease by beginning, "Boys, it's so good to see you. I want to say that neither one of you is in trouble. Mr. Hanson only brought you down here to inform me of something that occurred a little while ago. I don't have much information and need you each to tell me every detail. Don't leave anything out."

He studied the boys again. They breathed a sigh of relief. Both boys had reputations for their honesty and character. He knew they would tell the truth, but he needed them to relax. "Would either of you like something to drink?" Both boys shook their heads no. He waited patiently for one of them to begin.

Both Luke and Brian told a detailed account of what happened. Mr. Clark knew they were telling the truth as they retold many vivid details. He paused a few moments after listening to their accounts. "Thank you boys for sharing this."

"Is Matthew in trouble?" Luke asked, concerned.

"I can't answer that yet. He acted in self-defense. It was an accident that Billy lost his balance and hit his nose. I'll see. Don't you worry about it. You did what you did. There's nothing wrong with allowing Matthew to stand up for himself. Thank you again. You may go back to class."

The boys left the office, and Mr. Hanson, who was still in the board room with Matthew, peeked into the principal's office and asked, "Can we see you now?"

"Sure. I can't spend a long time. I need to make parent calls before the end of the day. Then I need to determine how to handle this. Billy's parents will be furious. Matthew acted in self-defense, yet he needs to have consequences for lifting him up and causing a bloody nose." He laughed out loud. "Well, I don't blame him for what he did. I do see that Matthew has skills to protect himself."

Matthew was still doing an activity in the board room while Mr. Hanson stood in the doorway of the office and chuckled. "Well, Leo, I guess he'll be okay. He can use his resources of strength." The two men saw eye to eye. When they stopped their laughter, Mr. Hanson got Matthew from the board room. Mr. Clark frowned and looked serious.

Matthew came in with Mr. Hanson and sat down at the chair. Matthew wouldn't communicate what happened. "We realize that Billy was destroying your property and saying hurtful words. It's okay to defend yourself, and we don't blame you for picking up Billy," Mr. Clark explained. "However, Billy was hurt."

Mr. Clark kindly told Matthew, "I'm sorry to tell you, Matthew, that even though you didn't mean for Billy to get hurt, you will have a consequence for his injury."

Matthew nodded his head in agreement.

"You weren't wrong in protecting your property. We aren't angry with you at all. We understand why you defended yourself," Mr. Hanson assured Matthew. "Let's get back to class."

Mr. Hanson put his arm around Matthew as they walked back to class.

"Me no hurt. Me no like rip, rip, rip. Me stop. No boo boo."

"We know. Billy had no right messing with your stuff. You did what you thought was best."

"Him okay? Him hurt?"

"He's fine. His pride's hurt, but he's good."

"Me no happy him hurt."

"I know." Mr. Hanson got out some school work for Matthew as they settled back in the classroom.

Mr. Clark deliberated the issue before calling the parents. Both Matthew and Billy would have consequences. Billy provoked the situation and did intentional damage to property. Mr. Clark didn't want to punish Matthew at all, but he knew that Billy's parents would create havoc if there wasn't something done.

The next morning, Mr. Clark was ready to talk to each of the boys. He talked to Billy first. "Billy, you have a one day in-school suspension for damage to property, and you'll sweep the halls of the school thirty minutes each day after school for a week."

Billy guffawed, "It was only a couple of dumb posters."

"But they were not your property. And you harassed Matthew with harsh words. That is unacceptable."

Billy shrugged it off and complied, knowing he couldn't convince Mr. Clark he had done nothing wrong. Billy appeared nonchalant and unaffected by Mr. Clark's stern voice. He didn't mind the in-school suspension because it kept him out of class for a day.

Mr. Clark then met with Mr. Hanson and Matthew. He had a brilliant idea that would appease Billy's family. He leaned forward and folded his hands together. "Matthew," he said softly. "I have some extra work for you to help us with at school and—"

"Me good work. Me work hard. Me muscle."

He smiled. "I have two new jobs for you. First, you'll be my assistant for one hour a day for a week. You'll come to my office and do whatever work I need you to do."

"Okay. Me help you. You nice man. Me like help you."

"I'm glad you feel that way. I have a second job for you that you'll do for the rest of the school year. It will teach you work skills. You'll be a cafeteria helper from 11:00 until noon every day. Barbara will be your boss and tell you what to do. Do you understand?"

Matthew nodded his head in affirmation.

"Matthew," Mr. Hanson said gently, "working in the kitchen will teach you many new skills. You'll learn a lot."

"Okay," Matthew agreed.

"Mr. Hanson, I'll have Matthew come to my office after his work in the cafeteria."

"Yes, sir," Mr. Hanson replied and winked at Mr. Clark.

At last, Mr. Clark was alone in a quiet office, put his feet up on the desk, and leaned back in his chair. He reflected on the day's events and how he had handled them. Billy's parents were angry until they learned all that Matthew was expected to do. They felt it was satisfactory, yet Billy had a vengeance brewing in his soul. He felt at some time he'd get payback for being humiliated.

Matthew's parents were relieved that Matthew had such an easy punishment and felt it was good for Matthew to work with the cafeteria staff. They were a bit concerned because Barbara was aloof and often unfriendly. They knew the other ladies in the kitchen, however, and felt Matthew would do just fine. Mr. Clark was content because little did anyone involved know that

Matthew was going to learn work skills anyway by working in the school cafeteria.

Word spread around the community about what Matthew did to Billy, and most of the locals felt Matthew was most justified in defending himself. At the café, gossip spread quickly and people retold the story over and over, making Matthew out to be a little celebrity.

Mr. Clark received a phone call from Mrs. Pearson. He dreaded hearing Alice announce that she was on the line. "Hello," he answered cheerfully.

"Mr. Clark, this is Meredith Pearson."

"How are you today, Meredith?"

"Just wonderful! I was calling to tell you I'm so happy how you handled the situation with Billy and Matthew. I know you're aware that I don't want Matthew in the school, but making him do work is a wonderful idea. He can work off his aggression. I think that's the perfect punishment. Perhaps he will learn something at least, which I doubt."

"Well, uh, thank you. I'm glad to hear your comments on the situation." Mr. Clark was befuddled.

"I'm also glad Matthew isn't with the other students as often now that he's in high school. At least he's more segregated than when he was younger. He needs to be isolated." Mrs. Pearson didn't know of his integration in gym, art, and music. Mrs. Pearson's two daughters were both out of high school, and she wasn't aware of what all went on at school.

"Thank you for calling, Meredith. Is there anything else I can help you with?"

"No. I'm still keeping my eyes open."

"Thank you and have a nice day." Mr. Clark didn't trust how sweet Mrs. Pearson acted. It wasn't her normal self, and he knew she would stir up trouble again when she felt she had reason. But, for now, he would enjoy the peace. He sipped his coffee and went to the file to get some forms from the state.

Mr. Hanson led Matthew to the cafeteria to introduce him to all the ladies. They knew Matthew, of course, since they watched him grow up, and a couple of the ladies were good friends with Trudy. Ethel, Marlene, Ann, and Barbara greeted Matthew with big grins while they mixed food, wearing their plastic gloves and hair nets.

"Matthew, this is Barbara. She's the kitchen boss. She'll explain what work you need to do," Mr. Hanson explained.

"We need good help," Barbara said.

"I'll turn it over to you, Barbara." Mr. Hanson turned and left the cafeteria.

Barbara began her instructions, "Matthew, I want you to wash your hands with soap first. We always wash our hands before working here." Matthew went to a sink in the kitchen and washed his hands with soap and water. "Next, I have a stack of napkins here. Here in these buckets are clean forks and spoons. Take one spoon and one fork. Set each down in the napkin and roll up the napkin. Put the silverware on this tray." She demonstrated what to do. "Now you show me what to do."

Matthew did as he was told and set the napkin with silverware in the gray plastic tray. "Good job. That's exactly it. Finish the silverware from these buckets. When you're done, come to the kitchen to get me." Matthew sat down at a cafeteria table to get the silverware ready. He carefully wrapped each napkin around the silverware. After finishing the job, he went to get Barbara.

"I didn't expect you to get done so fast." She inspected the work and saw how neatly he had done it. "Good work. I have one more for you to do." She looked at the clock. It was ten minutes before the younger students had lunch. "Matthew, in a few minutes, the little kids are coming in for lunch. You'll put milk on a tray for them. Until then, I want to show you where the soap and water is to clean the tables. You'll wash off all of the tables when lunch is over." She went to the kitchen and showed him where to get the soap and water bucket. "If you forget where to get it, ask me. I'll help you today."

"Okay."

Matthew waited a few minutes until a long line of children came through the lunch line. Matthew said, "Here you go, Ashley. Here you go, Ben," He called each of the children by name. If he didn't know a name, he asked and soon learned the names of all the elementary students he served.

As Matthew passed out milks, each boy and girl said, "Thank you, Matt."

He responded with a big smile and replied, "Welcome. Happy day."

When the younger children were dismissed, Matthew got the bucket and squeezed out the cloth. He washed each table and made sure every spot and crumb was off of it. For the last fifteen minutes, Matthew went back to the dishwashing area where his pal Bobby worked years ago. Mildred was the woman in charge of washing student trays. She stood hunched over the trays with a sprayer. The metal sprayer cleaned off the trays, which were then steam-cleaned in a dishwasher one rack of trays after another. Matthew was told to take out the clean trays, pile them up, and take them to the kitchen. Matthew recalled seeing his friend do this years ago when he was little. He was glad to do the same job Bobby had done. Matthew piled load after load and took them into the kitchen for the cooks to fill with food. Since Matthew worked so hard, he had additional duties of taking out garbage. He also mopped floors and lifted heavy items for the cooks. It was noon at last, and he removed his apron. "Fun. Easy. Me like work."

"You have a good work ethic," complimented Barbara. "You were particular with everything you did. I'm glad to have you helping us."

"Me fun. Me like help. Me happy work hard."

"Thanks for your help. You may get your lunch now and have seconds on anything you want. No limit. We appreciate all you did," Barbara told him.

"Tanks. Me like cookie. Me like apples." Matthew got seconds on both items. He set his tray down a minute and gave Barbara a big hug. "Tanks. Me like you."

Barbara hugged him back. She had never been around him before and was so impressed with his attitude toward work.

"Barbara, you're turning into an old softie," Ethel teased.

"Before you know it, you'll be giving him a free lunch," Marlene joked.

"We actually saw you smile? Couldn't be," Ethel said.

"Enough, ladies," Barbara barked. "Get back to work."

Matthew took his tray and sat down with his high school friends who had gathered in the cafeteria for lunch. Luke asked, "Hey, Matthew, how'd you get two cookies?"

"Me work. Me clean. Me get milk kids. Cook give me. Cook happy me work hard."

"I wish I could help in the kitchen," Luke teased. "I'd like extras. You're lucky."

"Me work hard. Me real hard. Me like work."

"I know you're a hard worker. You do all kinds of work on the farm. They must've worked you real hard to give you extras," Luke said.

"No. Easy. Me easy work. Me like help school."

Brian said to Matthew, "You work harder than most of us."

Matthew answered, "Me tough. Me do. Me pick up hay. Me pick up seed. Me work hard." He flexed his arms to show off how much muscle he had. They all laughed with him.

David said, "You don't have to lift weights like the football guys. You keep lifting bales of hay, and you build muscle."

Matthew nodded his head in agreement.

"Yip, bales are heavy," Brian affirmed. "I think they weigh over fifty pounds each. Maybe more."

"Do you like the hard work in the kitchen?" asked Luke.

"Me okay. Me muscle. Me help old ladies."

The boys at the lunch table laughed. Brian said, "They're old. Some of them are older than my grandma."

"Me too," Matthew agreed. "Raw old woman. She flabby arms."

"Mine has flabby arms and lots of wrinkles too." Luke chuckled.

Lunch with friends he had had since kindergarten ended all too soon for Matthew. Now that lunch was over, it was time to spend his first day with Mr. Clark at his office. When Matthew arrived, Alice greeted him with her million-dollar smile and told him that Mr. Clark was out a bit, but to go ahead and sit in his office and wait for him to come.

Matthew went into the dark, vacant office. Matthew flipped on the light switch. He saw the office in disarray. Papers were all over the desk, drawers open, pens scattered around, and chairs misaligned against the wall. He wasn't used to seeing a disorganized office.

First thing he did was shut desk drawers. As he closed one drawer, he saw paper clips scattered all over, took them out, and placed them in the paper clip holder. Then he found several pens and pencils lying around. He sharpened dull pencils and put them in a pencil cup. He got the office all tidied up for the principal. Mr. Clark saw Matthew cleaning his office and decided to watch him for a bit.

Mr. Clark walked into the office enthusiastically. "Hello. What happened here? It looks different from how I left it."

Matthew responded, "Me clean. Mess. Icky mess. Me help you. Me work you."

"It looks great. I'm impressed how organized everything looks now. That was on my list of things to get done this week. Thank you."

"Welcome. Me help you."

"You did. Now, I have some jobs for you to do this week. The first job is to sort the mail that came a little while ago. Each day you come, go to Alice. She'll give you the stack of mail. You will match the name on the mail with the name on the staff box. Do you understand?"

"Me do. Me read. Me read names teachers. Me know read." That is one thing Matthew memorized over the years. He could read and spell all of the names of staff at the school plus perfectly spell the first and last names of his classmates.

Matthew went to the front. "Here's the mail," Alice explained. "The mailboxes are over here. Read the name on the envelope and put it into the correct box."

"Me okay. Me do alone." Matthew put the mail into the boxes. When he was done, he asked, "What do now? What work?"

"Matthew, I'm taking you to Mrs. Carmen to practice counting money. She'll help you. You go back to the board room where she'll work with you."

"Okay."

Matthew came into the room and sat next to Mrs. Carmen. He saw the pile of play money. "Me rich. Money. Me rich." He picked up a ten-dollar bill. "Ten dollars. Me rich. Me pay house. Me pay car. Me rich."

Mrs. Carmen looked at him. "No, you aren't rich with ten dollars. I want you to count how many are here."

Matthew counted the ones. There were twenty-eight. "Big money. Me rich."

Mrs. Carmen realized that he didn't have a concept of what he could buy with money. She thought it sure would be nice to be rich on twenty-eight dollars. She worked with Matthew for fifteen minutes and sent him back to Mr. Clark's office. She felt like it was difficult to teach him about money.

"Alice, please show Matthew how to use the copying machine. Show him where to put the paper and select the number needed," Mr. Clark ordered.

"Sure thing. Matthew, come with me." Alice led Matthew to the copying machine and modeled what to do.

"Easy. Me do." Matthew put a sheet of paper on the glass, put the lid down, and made one copy.

"Great. You'll get lots of experience. The teachers always like someone making copies for them."

---*---

Mr. Clark sat back in his office one morning having coffee with Alice. "Can you believe this is the same boy who used to take off at school and run all over? Look how much he's grown. He's able to do so much. He doesn't read or do math like other students, but he's energetic and persevering. What a role model for other children. He's quite determined to learn. I can't believe what he memorizes when he doesn't read at a high level."

"I understand. He can do so many tasks. I'm glad he's still here. Mr. Hanson has taught him to cook at least two dozen recipes. Matthew is so pleased with himself and his new skills. I'm glad to get a taste of the treats he makes. That's a fringe benefit." Alice patted her stomach with a broad grin on her face.

"He has grown a lot this year. He'll do fine in life," Mr. Clark said.

CHAPTER 40

Jed and Brad were unable to do field work one April morning due to the heavy rain soaking the ground. Matthew stayed inside and spent time in his room. He pulled a large suitcase out of the closet and opened it to sort his collection of professional baseball shirts. He got his caps from the shelf and matched each shirt and cap. Matthew neatly put back the clothing. He got a piece of paper and wrote down a list of which team shirts and caps he wanted Jenny and Brad to give him for Christmas. He spelled every team correctly in capital letters.

After Matthew made out his Christmas list, he went downstairs to the kitchen where Glenda was preparing homemade rolls for dinner. Matthew opened the dishwasher and put the clean dishes away. He washed, dried, and folded clothes.

By dinner time, the rain had subsided and totaled two inches. Matthew knew it was too late for the men to go to the field, but he wanted to take Gator and check the cows. Birthing season was in full progress, and it was Matthew's after-school and weekend responsibility to drive Gator out to the pasture near the home place and check if there were any new births or any cows needing help.

Matthew wrapped himself in a gray hooded jacket and tall rubber boots. He pulled a stocking hat on his head and went to the shop to start up Gator and fill it with gas. He headed out to the wet, soggy pasture careful to avoid mud puddles and stay where the ground was the least saturated.

Matthew eased up slowly to the cattle, checking for signs of birth. Bonnie walked toward him and followed Gator. In the distance, he saw a Hereford cow with two legs sticking out its back end. Before Matthew drove closer, he petted Bonnie's face and wet nose. She licked his hand. Bonnie backed up as Matthew drove away, but she continued to follow him. Matthew stayed several yards away from G28, the Hereford cow whose calf was being born.

"G-2-8," he muttered to himself, "is having baby." Matthew drove every part of the fifty-acre pasture. He spotted two new calves. He identified each cow's tag number. One was a red white-faced calf, and the other was a black calf with a white tail. Matthew made a mental note of the new calves.

Mud spit out of the tires as Matthew drove through the pasture, and his clothing became speckled with mud. He carefully drove back to the shop through the pasture that seemed like a swamp.

At the shop, Matthew hollered, "Dad, Dad, you go?"

Jed came out from under the pickup where he was changing oil. "What's up, Matthew?"

Matthew reported, "Two new babies. R45 and R26. Okay baby calves. One red and white face and one black face and white tail. G28 baby come now. Me see two legs stick out."

"Oh," Jed rubbed his chin. "Let's check on her in thirty minutes. Go get the grease gun. You can grease the 4020." Matthew got the grease gun and left the shop to grease the tractor in the machine shed.

Jed drove Gator to the machine shed a few minutes later. "It's time to check on G28. Take Gator and go now. Let me know what happens."

Matthew drove back to the field where the cow was all alone. He observed that she hadn't made any progress in the birth of the calf. The cow looked as if she were in pain. "Me tell dad she need help," Matthew said aloud to himself.

Matthew drove right up to where Jed was working.

Matthew spoke breathlessly, "Cow G28 same. Need help. Baby no come. Baby same. Cow hurt. She pain."

Jed called, "Brad, we may need to pull a calf. Come on."

Brad came to the gator and sat in the back. Matthew drove up to the cow. Jed put on a pair of gloves and crept up to the cow, softly saying, "Easy, girl. We're here to help that calf of yours." He got close enough to stroke her head. "Easy."

The cow stood still and moaned. Jed and Brad went to the back of her and inspected the situation. It looked as though the calf needed to be pulled. Matthew stayed in front of the cow, stroking the cow's face. He said to her, "Stay calm. You calf come. Stay calm."

While Jed and Brad got ready to pull on the calf's legs, Matthew continued to talk to the cow, calming her. Jed began pulling. The cow moaned loudly. He pulled more as the cow pushed. Matthew stood gently next to the cow and remained calm. The cow bellowed louder in agony, and Matthew heard Jed grunt as he pulled again. The calf appeared at last. The cow instinctively turned toward her new calf and licked the body. The calf got to its feet. Jed and Brad put their arms around the newborn and helped it stand. The calf was still feeble from such a hard birth. With the calf in his arms, Jed walked the calf toward the udder of the cow, knelt down, and guided the calf's mouth to the udder, and the calf began sucking milk. He held on to the calf a few more minutes. As the calf stood there and drank, its legs became less wobbly and looked stronger. Jed released his arms and let the calf stand on its own. After the first feeding, the calf walked steadily, circling its mom. The guys made sure the calf was strong and went back to the shop.

CHAPTER 41

Matthew continued his cafeteria job during his sophomore year and energetically greeted the young elementary children by name every day. Mr. Hanson instructed him in life skills, and Matthew was still integrated in mechanics, art, and gym. One day, Matthew was walking down the hallway. "Me go this way. Me gym. Me play game. Me like," Matthew said to himself.

Billy laid low the rest of Matthew's freshman year and didn't go near him, except for one time. Billy and his friend Doug crept up behind Matthew in the hallway and caught him off guard. They backed him to a corner entryway of the school near the home economics and special education room. No one was in the hall since classes had already started. Billy hovered over Matthew's short, stout stature and sneered, "Hey, Matthew, how about sharing a beer with me? You want some, don't cha?"

Matthew's eyes widened, and he turned up his nose. He firmly denied the offer, saying, "No. Me no do. Bad stuff. Me no like."

Billy paced in front of Matthew, heckling. "Oh, Matthew, c'mon. It'll make you feel so good. It won't hurt you. You won't know if you like it or not if you don't try."

Matthew remained calm. He stood his ground firmly, "Go away. Me good. No do bad stuff."

Doug, who was watching the hall for passersby, laughed teasingly at Matthew's response. Billy pushed himself up against Matthew and pulled out a beer from the inside of his loose jacket.

He pulled the tab and held it up to Matthew's lips. "Drink some, Matthew. You'll like it."

Matthew shook his head no and pushed the beer away. It dropped to the ground, spilling beer all over. Billy yelled out, "Oh, crap. Look what you did. I told you to drink it."

Matthew tried to sneak around Billy's body to escape, but Billy overpowered him. He didn't know what to do except yell. "Help! Help!" He ducked away from Billy, but the boy and his friend grabbed his arms. Matthew couldn't get away.

Matthew tried to yell again, even louder. "Help! Help!" He sounded more desperate this time.

Nicki, Kathy, Amy, and Sheila, football cheerleaders, heard the yelling from inside the home economics room. They recognized the voice as Matthew's. Amy went running out of the room with the other girls following behind.

Mrs. Moore, the home economics teacher, was oblivious to Matthew's plea for help. She scolded them. "Girls, you get back here this instant. You may not leave this room without permission."

The girls were focused on the commotion in the hallway. Billy and Doug were still restraining Matthew, and then they saw Sheila. They immediately let go of Matthew. "What's going on, Billy?" Sheila demanded.

Kathy suspected something. "What are you doing with Matthew?"

The other two girls moved closer. Billy thought Amy was gorgeous with her petite build, sparkling blue eyes, and long blonde hair. He spoke charmingly to her, "Nothing's going down, Amy. How are you?"

"Baloney, nothing's going down. What's up with you two?" Amy asked firmly.

Billy said, "Come on, sweetheart. I mean no harm." He tried to slip his arm around Amy's waist.

Amy pushed his arm away. She thought he was a slime ball who was nothing but trouble. She observed the beer spilled all over and asked, "So, what's this beer doing all over the floor? Explain that."

Billy said smoothly, "We saw Matthew carrying a can of beer and followed him. Matthew opened it and tried to drink it. I had to stop him."

Sheila doubted his story. "Where did he get it in the first place?"

"Heck if I know," he lied. "He can get it anywhere. I knew it wasn't good for him."

"Really? You expect us to believe that?" Kathy was irritated.

"What do you expect from a retard? He doesn't know a soda from a beer."

"Uh, yeah, Billy's right," Doug said, defending him.

Kathy disappeared. Amy told Billy and Doug, "You honestly think we're stupid enough to believe your line of baloney? We love Matthew, and you'd better not ever mess with him."

Sheila put in her two cents, "Matthew is cool, and we love him."

Billy rolled his eyes.

Matthew's eyes lit up. The girls loved him. *Ah, girls love me. Me happy girls think me cool.*

Kathy came walking down the hall with Mr. Clark. Billy and Doug saw him approaching and ran away from the scene. Mr. Clark barked, "What's going on here?

"Mr. Clark, Billy tried to get Matthew to drink beer. Look at it. It's all over the floor," Sheila said.

"Go after those two and tell them to report to my office. Now!" Mr. Clark said, "Kathy, get the janitor to clean up this mess."

Amy ran after Billy and Doug. "Stop, you two! Stop. Get back here." Two burly football players, Ray and Andy, stepped out of study hall to see what was happening. "Get them." Amy pointed in their direction. "Get Billy and Doug."

The football boys sprinted after Billy and Doug. They were at arm's length from the two perpetrators when Ray reached out and grabbed Doug by the collar and wrestled him to the ground.

Andy caught Billy, grabbed his arms, and pulled them behind his back in an arm lock.

"What's going on?" asked Andy.

"Nothing. I don't know why you're chasing me," Billy said defensively.

Amy came panting up to the group. "These two had Matthew cornered and were forcing him to drink a beer. There was beer spilled all over the floor."

"What jerks," Andy snarled. "Why would you do that?"

Andy pulled back harder on Billy's arms. Billy winced in pain. He wanted to get away but couldn't move. He tried to kick Andy, but Andy shoved his foot against the wall and stepped on his feet. Andy slammed Billy against the wall and threatened, "If you ever cause the slightest bit of trouble again, I'll come after you."

"Ditto," said Ray. "That makes two of us. Matthew's our buddy. We won't stand for trouble like this."

"Not only will we," continued Andy, "but the entire senior class and football team will hunt you down. Do I make myself clear?" He spoke the last words slowly with emphasis.

Billy's arrogance shrank to fear, but he had to save face for the sake of his reputation. He responded, "You don't scare me. Just cuz you're a football player doesn't make you so tough." He spat on the floor near Andy. Andy seethed and clenched his fists.

"He's not worth it, Andy," Ray warned him. "He wants you to fight. It isn't worth it. Hold him until Mr. Clark comes."

Andy took a few deep breaths. Ray was right. They were used to watching each other's backs in football and in school. Doug surrendered to Ray's grip and sat defeated on the floor in exhaustion.

Silence. Footsteps were heard from a distance. Mr. Clark found them at last. "What do we have here?" Mr. Clark was furious.

Amy and Andy told Mr. Clark the whole story.

Mr. Clark talked to Billy, "The beer you had is illegal for your age."

Mr. Clark decided to call the authorities before escorting Billy to the office. He walked into the nearest classroom and pushed the intercom button for Alice. When she answered, he asked her to call the police and have them send someone immediately.

Mr. Clark stepped back into the hallway. "Andy, Ray, help me escort these two losers to my office. Thanks for your help." They walked the guys to the office and held them in the board room.

Back by the home economics room, Kathy, Nicki, and Sheila put their arms around Matthew to comfort him. They asked him if he was all right. He got hugs and pats on the back. The girls showed much concern and Sheila said, "Are you okay?"

Kathy added, "We won't let anyone hurt you. We like you."

"And," Nicki added, "the football team will look out for you. Are you coming to the game tonight?"

"Me go. Me do."

"Good," she answered. "We have a treat for you. We all love you."

Matthew's heart raced as he felt so pampered and special. The pretty girls liked him. Sheila squeezed his hand and said, "We'll see you tonight."

Matthew almost forgot about what Billy tried to do. He was so engrossed in the attention of these girls. His mind was on how they loved him.

Mr. Clark called Matthew's parents as he always did when there was a negative situation. He knew this wasn't going to be a pleasant call. Glenda was at the sink with her hands in the soapy water when the phone rang. Mr. Clark explained the incident. He commended the four girls and two football players who helped resolve things. He suggested that Matthew have the rest of the day off. Glenda said that they would pick Matthew up as soon as possible and hung up the phone.

Someone had attempted to force Matthew to drink. How could someone be so cruel? She hunched over sobbing until her stomach hurt. Her heart hurt for what Matthew experienced because of that scoundrel Billy. She was thankful he wasn't harmed, but what if…no, she wouldn't go there. Jed came in the back door and saw Glenda's pain.

"What's wrong? What happened?"

Glenda stammered, "It's Matthew. We need to pick him up."

"I'll go get him," he said softly.

Jed let Rick and Brad know they needed to pick up Matthew from school.

"Why?" asked Brad.

Jed shrugged his shoulders. "I don't know. Your mom is shocked about something."

"Do you want me to stay with Mom and have Grandpa ride with you?" asked Brad.

"That's a good idea. I think I need to ask your grandmother to come down and be there for her. Trudy will talk to her."

Brad went inside the house and saw that his mom had gone to the couch to lie down and rest. Her thoughts raced to how Matthew would never be safe in this world because he was a target for trouble makers.

Jed headed to the Rogers' home. "Trudy, please go see Glenda. Something happened at school today, and she won't say anything. I need to go get Matthew."

"Oh my," Trudy gasped. "I'll go right down. I hope everything's all right."

"I hope so too. Where's Gordon?"

"I believe he's in the barn. Otherwise, he's in the hay field." She got in the car and went down to Jed's home.

Jed found Gordon at the barn. "Would you ride with me to get Matthew from school? Something happened today, and Glenda's shook up about it. She wouldn't tell me what happened."

"It must be serious. I'll come right now and stay in these chore grubs."

"Thank you. I wonder what happened," Jed said with concern.

"Well, let's get going and find out," Gordon said calmly.

Mr. Clark had Matthew sit in the board room while waiting for his ride home. Matthew seemed to be okay despite the situation. Word spread across the school about what had happened, and students were riled up the rest of the day. Teachers had a hard time teaching because students wanted to discuss it.

Gordon and Jed went inside the school office. Alice looked somber. Marie kept her eyes on her typing instead of greeting them. Mr. Clark came out and greeted them sadly. "Good morning, Jed, Gordon. Come on back. I suppose you already know what happened today."

"I have no idea." Jed explained. "Glenda was so upset, she wouldn't talk. I could barely get her to tell me to get Matthew. She was shocked and speechless."

Mr. Clark was afraid that would be her reaction. He looked at Jed and Gordon, who were impatiently waiting to hear about the morning. He cleared his throat and began retelling the occurrence. Jed was angry and relieved at the same time. Gordon was expressionless.

"To conclude, Billy will have charges pressed against him for underage possession of alcohol. You may also press charges. It's up to you. If he gets off easy, I'm personally going to the school board with a recommendation to expel him from school."

Jed sat still, speechless. He was beside himself and wished he was there to comfort Glenda. He understood her grief and had taken off without being there for her.

All he could say was, "I want to see Matthew."

"Of course. I have him waiting in the board room."

Matthew was seated at the board room table doing a puzzle with Mrs. Carmen. She smiled at the men and politely excused herself.

Matthew looked happily at Dad, Papa, and Mr. Clark. He ran up and hugged his family. "Dad! Papa!" he eagerly said.

"How are you, buddy?" Gordon hugged Matthew. "I hear you had a tough day."

"Me good day. Girls help me. Girls stop bad boy. Love me. Girls love me." He put his hands to his heart and smiled.

Jed and Gordon looked at each other in surprise. They had thought Matthew would be more troubled by the morning.

"Me love. Me love girls. Girls say me cool. Love me."

Jed let out a sigh of relief. Gordon boomed in laughter. "Well, when you have pretty girls on your side, life is good."

Jed said, "I agree. Who wouldn't like that?"

"Let's go home, Matthew," Gordon said.

Mr. Clark shook hands with both men. He was glad Matthew was okay. Never a dull moment at the school. There was something new every day. He smiled that it had ended well.

———*———

When they got home, Glenda was sitting on the couch talking to Trudy. Trudy sat next to her with her arm around Glenda's shoulders. When Matthew came in, Trudy asked, "How are you, sweetie?"

"Me good. Girls like me. Say me cool. Girls love me."

Trudy asked, "What do you mean?"

"Girls say me cool. Say me cute. Me good man. Me no do bad. Girls like me. Hug me." He put his hands to his heart.

Glenda was amused by Matthew's story about the girls. She was thankful Matthew had handled the day so well. She seethed angrily, however, at the boys who were responsible for this. But at least there were some caring students who got involved. They sure made an impression on Matthew.

At school lunch, the football players sat together at the same table. Ray spoke to his friends, "What do think about what happened today? Billy sure was a scum to force Matthew to drink alcohol."

Andy added, "Yeah. Except for the girls, it could have been much worse. I'm thankful they weren't afraid to get involved."

"This should never happen again," Ray remarked. "It's wrong for a person to harm anyone, let alone someone with a disability."

"I think we need to keep a closer eye on things going on around us. We don't want the losers to take control. They cause trouble in and out of school."

"What should we do?" Trevor, another football player asked.

Ray thought a moment. "We need to be secret protectors for him and keep our eyes open when Matthew is passing in the halls. Most of time, he'll be safe, but today was a fluke because he was running late. We can each take turns to see he gets where he needs to go. I think I'll hang out at my locker until the halls clear during the first period when I have study hall. We can talk to Mr. Clark about our plans. Is anyone else with me?" There were sounds of agreement at the table.

Andy had another idea, "Matthew is going to be at the game tonight. Why don't we let him cheer us on as we enter the football field? He would love that. This way he knows we're behind him while he supports us at the game."

"Good idea," Trevor affirmed.

"Do we all agree?" Ray asked. All agreed.

Game night. Fans of the school team were filling the stands. Nicki, a cheerleader, came up to the stands and greeted Matthew and his parents. She politely asked, "May we have Matthew come down on the field until the game starts? We want his help."

Glenda hesitated, but since she and Jed knew Nicki's family, they agreed.

Nicki led Matthew to the football field. She explained to him, "Matthew, you stand here. I want you to hold out your hand and give each of the players a high five when they run out to the field. Wish them luck. They'll feel lucky seeing you there to cheer them on.

Matthew followed directions and got ready. The first player to run out on the field was Andy, the team captain. Matthew gave him a high five and said, "Good luck."

"Thanks," he replied.

One by one, Matthew wished each player good luck. He stood tall and held up his head. Nicki came over to Matthew after the players were on the field. "Here's a megaphone. We want your help. We'll yell a cheer. You repeat. I mean yell the words into the megaphone."

"Okay. Me do."

"Great. Stand here." They did a simple cheer that Matthew was able to chant. The cheerleaders jumped and cheered. Matthew yelled loud and clear. He joined his mom and dad after the cheers and watched the game as he drank a cup of hot chocolate with marshmallows. This was the best school for him.

High school continued to be eventful and mostly positive during Matthew's sophomore year. Billy was suspended only for a few days of school and put on probation. The football players watched the halls. Only Billy and his two friends ever bothered Matthew, but that stopped when the football team kept an eye on things. Everyone else treated him in a friendly and cordial way. Matthew was invited to sit with the football boys at lunch.

Mr. Hanson and Mrs. Jones worked with Matthew on a variety of skills. Matthew gained much knowledge about independent living. He learned about changing oil, checking belts, testing tire pressure, and changing tires during mechanics class. He got an A in mechanics and art class. His teachers expected the same of him for his projects as they did of their other students. He still wasn't able to understand money concepts other than basic shopping, such as spending ten dollars in a store. He didn't know how much to expect for change. He read at a lower elementary level, but still spelled anything he wanted to memorize. His phone skills were good and he learned to take messages. He learned the emergency numbers and took a list home with him.

CHAPTER 42

Jenny had a surprise for her family. She was bringing home a friend whom she had met five months earlier. Jenny met Ed before finals in December. He was a teaching major. They hit it off instantly. She had already told him about Matthew, and he said he grew up with a Down syndrome boy in his home church. He said it wasn't any big deal. They were human beings. Jenny was impressed with what she had in common with Ed and his outlook on life.

Jenny was putting Ed through a test. She was eager to see how Matthew and Ed got along. She knew Matthew had good instincts. Ed and she were beginning to get serious but didn't talk of marriage yet. They both were determined to complete college first.

At home, Glenda was frantically cleaning the house, wanting everything spotless for this new guest. Matthew helped her with the housecleaning. He swept carpets, dusted furniture, did laundry, and put dishes away while Glenda prepared several dishes for the Easter weekend feast.

On Friday afternoon when Jenny drove in the driveway, Matthew peered out the window and saw a person in the passenger seat. Matthew hadn't been told that anyone was coming with her and thought the cleaning was for the Easter meal with Gordon, Trudy, Flora, and Ken.

Jenny parked where the bus used to stop. Her passenger stepped out. He was medium height and slender. He had dark brown hair. He wore a black zipper jacket, blue jeans, and dingy white tennis shoes. He reached into the back seat for his duffle bag. Jenny got out of the car and retrieved her luggage. She put her duffle bag over her shoulder and locked the car.

Ed and Jenny walked down the long sidewalk toward the house. Matthew cautiously came up to the two of them and eyed this stranger. Jenny was glowing. Ed whispered something to her, and she giggled. As Matthew got closer, Jenny introduced them. "Matthew, this is Ed. He's a good friend of mine." Matthew extended his hand and they shook hands firmly.

"Nice to meet you. Jenny told me all about you. She said you love baseball and the farm."

"Me like Royals. Good team. Hit balls hard."

"I like the Chicago Cubs myself," Ed said.

"Team okay. Me Cubs shirt."

"I like the Twins too," Ed added.

"Twins good. Me twin calves. Me lots cows."

"Can I see them this weekend? I'd like to see them."

"Yes. Me lots cows. Bonnie number one. She babies have babies."

"So they are all related?" Ed asked.

"All one big family." Matthew spread his arms out wide.

"Let's get unpacked, and I'll show you where to put your things." Jenny motioned toward the house.

"Me help you. Me take bag." Matthew offered.

"No thanks. I'm okay," Ed said appreciatively.

Inside, Ed settled into his weekend room. It was an older room with aged wallpaper, a cracked linoleum floor and furniture that was over sixty years old.

In the kitchen, Matthew and Jenny were having a snack of chocolate chip cookies. Matthew talked quietly to Jenny. "Me like him. Him nice man. You marry him?"

"We're good friends. We haven't known each other long."

"Him nice man. Me say like him. You keep him."

"He's a nice guy," Jenny said. "I'm glad you like him." When Ed entered the kitchen, Matthew offered to take him on Gator and show him his cows. Ed expected to drive, but he saw that Matthew quickly revved up Gator and drove into the yard to pick him up. Matthew and Ed checked cows and looked for newborns. Matthew stopped and pointed to Bonnie. Bonnie walked up to him and rubbed her face against his. Ed was surprised to see a cow this tame. He didn't know cows were like pets.

"Me cow. Me like cow." Matthew wrapped his arms around her. Bonnie stood perfectly still as usual. He took off his hat and put it on the cow, and Ed laughed.

"Me nice cow." He turned to Bonnie and said, "Okay, baby. Me go. See you." He stroked her one more time. Matthew drove confidently back to the shop and parked Gator.

Jed wiped the grease off his hands and came up to Matthew and the guest. "Welcome, I'm Jed, Jenny's dad. I hear you're a good friend of my daughter."

"Yessir, I'm Ed. Jenny and I met a few months ago at college."

"While we go in for supper now, tell me about yourself."

Glenda had the table set with two more place settings. She served a platter of fried chicken, a bowl of mashed potatoes, sweet corn from the freezer, strawberry fluff salad, homemade rolls, apple pie, and angel food cake.

Ed remarked, "Mrs. Parker, this reminds me a lot of my mom's cooking. You went to too much work."

"I like to serve guests plenty. I hope you enjoy the meal."

"I have no doubt that I'll love it," Ed said as he looked at the table.

Jenny wanted to sit by Ed, but Matthew refused. He sat in between the two of them. Ed asked Matthew questions about the farm. Ed surprisingly comprehended most of what Matthew had to say and patiently listened to Matthew talk.

After supper, everyone went into the family room to visit and watch a family movie. Jenny sat next to Ed on the love seat.

Matthew came and squeezed between the two of them, making the love seat crowded.

"Matthew, move!" Jenny exclaimed. "It's too crowded here. We were here first."

"Me here. You get off, Sis. Me stay here." He crossed his arms across his chest and refused to budge. Jenny got up and left the room.

———*———

After the movie, everyone except Ed and Jenny went to bed. They stayed up late to spend some time together and sat on the floor watching some more television. Ed moved closer to Jenny and slipped his arm around her waist. Jenny leaned back as she heard a noise behind the couch. Matthew had sneaked in and hidden there. He leaped over the couch in between the two of them. He told them, "You two no sit close. You move. Keep arm off me sis. Mine. No you. Me love sis."

"Go to bed," Jenny said in a bossy tone. "You should be in bed now."

Matthew left the room and Jenny and Ed scooted close together again. A few minutes later, Matthew quietly sneaked into the room. Jenny and Ed knew he was hiding and moved apart from each other when Matthew peered over the top of the couch.

"We know you are back there. Leave us alone and go to bed. It's past your bedtime!" Jenny was agitated.

"Me stay here." Matthew was insistent. "Me keep eye on you."

Glenda heard the fuss and told Matthew to go to bed. He dashed out of the room knowing she meant it. Jenny and Ed sat close to each other again. Ed grabbed Jenny's hand and held it in his as they heard Matthew's footsteps coming toward them.

Jenny moaned. "This is getting old. He is back spying on us."

"It's all right, Jenny. I think it's time for me to go to bed."

"No, he needs to learn we like each other and want to spend time together." She firmly squeezed Ed's hand. She said aloud through gritted teeth, "We want to be alone. Good night, Matthew."

"Me see you. You two hold hands. No. No hold hands."

"Look, I'll go to bed now. Matthew isn't sure about us yet. He doesn't want someone to compete with him. He's protective."

"He's being annoying. Good night, Matthew." Matthew stayed in the family room until Ed went to bed.

"Next time, give us some privacy," Jenny scolded.

During the summer, Ed and Jenny got engaged. "Look at my diamond with rubies everyone," she held up her hand for everyone in her family to see.

"It's beautiful. I'm so happy for you," Glenda said.

"Looks like someone else will have to put up with you," Brad teased. "I'm off the hook now."

"You two marry. Honeymoon. Love. Babies come," Matthew added.

Jenny blushed and said, "Slow down. We aren't married yet."

"Come soon. Marry. Honeymoon. Love." Matthew hugged himself.

"That's enough. Don't talk about it." Jenny rolled her eyes. "Good grief," she muttered to herself.

CHAPTER 43

Loud screeching sound came from the shop. Jed whistled as he sharpened the blades on the bean hooks. A small crew of teenagers was hired to walk beans with the Parker family.

The crew gathered around Jed for instructions at seven in the morning. "Okay, folks. Here's a bean hook." He held one up for all to see. "You'll each get one. Your job will be to cut all the weeds in the rows. You'll walk between four rows of beans, two on each side of you." Jed demonstrated getting the hook around the lowest part of the weed's stem as possible and pulling the hook to cut the weed. "I want you to cut the weeds like that. Only carry your hook to your side with the hook facing away from you or in front of you. Don't carry the bean hook over your shoulder. Brad nicked his neck a few years ago and got stitches."

Brad pulled down his shirt collar. "I have the scar right here to prove it. See where I was nicked?"

Everyone looked at Brad's scar.

"That's why you need to hold the hook on the ground. Also, watch for tangled beans and weeds. We don't want anyone tripping. Any questions?"

David, one of the crew members asked, "How long will we be in the field?"

"We'll be out there from 7:30 until just before noon. Glenda has filled water jugs and packed treats for whenever we need a break. Okay. All set to start."

The crew piled into the two pickups and rode out to the first soybean field. The beans had a vast number of pods on them. The crew lined up, each taking four rows. "Let's start," Jed commanded. "Make sure you don't chop the beans, just the weeds."

The crew walked through beans, reaching down and removing the weeds. Grasshoppers hopped on their arms and faces. "I'm hot," Amy cried. "I can't stand those grasshoppers. It feels as if needles are poking me."

"They won't harm anything," Jed said. "They're just pesky. But, they do eat into the leaves of the soybeans."

"Yuk! A bug went up my nose and down my throat," shouted Nikki. "My nose feels itchy."

The boys laughed at the whining girls.

"What was that?" asked Amy frightfully. "Something ran across my feet."

"It ran in front of me," Tyler said. "It's just a scared little field mouse. They're all over the field."

"Yikes!" yelled Amy. "I hope another one doesn't run across my feet."

"You girls are such wimps," Tyler said as he laughed. "It's more afraid of you than you are of it."

"No me yell. Silly. You silly girls." Matthew laughed at them.

The crew walked the beans, placing the curved hook around the base of the weeds. Tugging at the bean hook, weeds fell down, leaving stubble on the ground.

Matthew had on his Stetson hat to shield his face from the sweltering sun. His shirt was drenched.

"Break time, folks!" Jed waved his hand toward the pickup where there was water and homemade cookies.

"I can't stand the bugs," Nikki complained.

"Do you want to quit?" Jed asked.

"No," Nikki replied. "I don't mind the walking or the cutting weeds. The bugs are just a pain."

"Bugs okay," Matthew said.

"They taste awful," Amy said as she cringed. "I wonder what kind of bug is on me now." She slapped a bug on her arm.

Bean walking continued until noon. The crew went home, and Glenda prepared a quick lunch for everyone. Jed ate quickly and rushed out to bale hay. Brad and Matthew waited for the next crew to come for afternoon work. Brad hooked the hay wagon to the 4020 and drove out to the hay field. The crew came in the pickup and put on haying gloves. Matthew drove the tractor for the crew. Willie and Todd stood on the wagon while Luke and Brian threw the bales up to them. Matthew listened to the blaring radio, moving his head to the music, looking forward and not watching the boys in the back.

The hay crop was so abundant that the boys missed some bales as the tractor kept moving. Everyone yelled to Matthew to stop the tractor. He had the music on so loud he didn't hear. Finally, Brad ran up to the side of the tractor, waved his hands, and hollered to Matthew. "Stop! Stop!" He climbed onto the tractor. "Turn off that radio. You can't hear us when we want you to stop."

"Me look bales. No hit them. Me drive good."

"You are a good driver and are watching ahead of you, but we have so many bales, we need you to stop once in a while to catch up."

"Okay. Me listen you. No music."

"Thank you. Also, it's your turn to switch with Willie and stack the bales on the wagon. Everyone will drive some today."

When the wagon was full, Brad drove to the barn where the hay was unloaded. Two boys stacked hay in the barn, and two boys loaded the elevator. Matthew threw bales off the wagon. After unloading, the boys' faces were masked in dust.

Glenda brought treats while the boys took a break.

"It's hot in that barn," Luke said.

"At least you weren't in the sun," Willie replied.

"I'll be ready for football." Luke flexed his muscles. "I already feel stronger."

"Tell me about it," Willie added. "This is harder than lifting weights. I'm not going to the weight room when I'm putting up hay."

"No reason to go this week. We're lifting enough weight," Brian said.

"Me muscle. Hay. Help me strong," Matthew said as he flexed his muscles.

The boys went back out and loaded several more wagons and worked late into the evening.

———— * ————

Sunday was a day of rest for the Parkers. Matthew loaded Gator with fishing gear and water and drove to his favorite relaxing spot at a creek surrounded by a few acres of natural grass. The shallow creek had steep banks and a blanket of trees covering the summer sunlight. Matthew wore his straw hat and a t-shirt with jeans when he left for the creek, which he called his wilderness.

Matthew cast the fishing line into the water and propped his pole against a tree. He sprawled across the log as he watched for a tug on the line. He felt a few tugs, but no fish. Getting bored with fishing, he ran up and down the banks of the creek. He crossed the creek on a log that had fallen off a tree. He stepped one foot in front of the other, balancing his body. Matthew spent several hours at the creek for his restful Sunday afternoon.

CHAPTER 44

Mr. Hanson leaned back in his chair and yawned after a long day of parent conferences. The last meeting was in thirty minutes, concerning the future of Matthew Parker. As the door opened, Mr. Hanson was startled and quickly sat up in his chair. He rose to greet Mr. Terry Porter, a regional educational consultant and advisor for Matthew's future goals and placement. As Mr. Porter greeted Mr. Hanson, he stroked his reddish beard and said, "We need to talk before the meeting."

"Of course. What's on your mind?" Mr. Hanson asked.

"Our team of specialists believes Matthew needs to be removed from his home. He's done with school this year, and he needs to be in an environment where he'll learn and thrive."

"Oh?"

"There are some spectacular group homes in the city. Matthew's tests don't show much academic growth or potential. He gained in life skills, but it would be better for him to be in a group home where he can work in a recycling business sorting cans. That's what many of our disabled students do."

"And you believe this is best? What about his parents?"

"His parents are nice people, but they don't have the education to know what's best for him. They can't keep him living on some isolated farm sitting around all day. It would be crippling."

"You think so?"

Mr. Porter continued, "Admit it. There isn't opportunity for him to be independent. His life would be so stifling without work or socialization."

Mr. Hanson looked at Mr. Porter, doubting the wisdom of his suggestion. "Do you plan to share this at our meeting?"

"Not in the way I told you. Now that Matthew is eighteen, it's our job to place him where he's at his best. Like I said, his parents are well-meaning people, but they aren't equipped to work with him as an adult. They can only do so much. And besides, they'll die one day. Where will that leave Matthew?"

"Have you ever visited his home? Are you sure you know what you're saying?"

"I haven't visited, but yes, I know what I am saying. It would be so stifling to have him in that home where he'll will be dependent on them. He needs more than that."

"Did you think to ask the parents what they think is best? What about their input?"

"Studies support the proper placement for adults with disabilities. Adults thrive in group home settings where socialization, activity, work, and life skills classes are provided."

"I think you ought to visit the Parkers before deciding what's best for Matthew," Mr. Hanson said, irritated that the specialists had decided what would be best for Matthew before they had even observed his life at home. "You might be surprised what you'll discover."

"I'd like to visit them and solidify my opinion. Trained people are hired at the workshops. They will have the skills to help Matthew."

"I agree that's an option for many families, but Matthew is different. He works on the farm. He's surrounded by friends and family constantly. To remove him from there might prove to be devastating."

"Oh, he might feel homesick at first. If he's to remain here, he isn't being monitored by educated people. It may be all talk about what he can do. You know how it is. Parents always inflate their children. Most Down syndrome children have limited abilities. His math and reading placement tests show he's quite deficient in his skills. I hardly believe the stories his parents tell. I'm not saying they're lying, but I think they omit how much assistance they actually give him when he does the tasks they claim he can do. He needs supervision by a government-funded workshop to help him. He'll be required to work, exercise, and eat healthy."

"Terry, I think you're wrong about what Down syndrome children can do. Given the right care and education, they are capable of doing much more. Also, Terry, you're acting as if his parents have no say in the matter. They're still his parents. They have a plan for Matthew's life and want what's best for him."

"What they believe is best doesn't mean it's in his best interest. We are basing our placement for him on research and successful experiences of others like him."

"Terry, research doesn't fit every situation. Please, keep an open mind in the staffing today. There are exceptions to every rule. Research is only that. You know from experience that as educators we cannot lump every situation as the same."

"I'm firm in my professional opinion."

Mr. Hanson was firm in his conviction that Terry was wrong. He sided with the wishes of Jed and Glenda. Mr. Clark agreed also. Jed and Glenda were caring, supportive parents who had taught Matthew so much and believed in hard work. Matthew would be treated well and have a strong social support system. Brad lived there and would look out for him. The remark about what would happen when Jed and Glenda passed away was unfounded. Brad would be there. Jenny and Ed were actively involved in his life, and there were several neighbors and friends who would be there as well.

Terry felt frustrated with Mr. Hanson. He couldn't believe Mr. Hanson's subjective opinions on Matthew's future. Terry finally spoke. "So, whose side are you on? I'll emphasize that our agency pushes for independence for children with disabilities. It means placing them out of their homes and in a group home living situation. We stand strongly on this. I hope you'll agree with us."

Mr. Hanson ran his fingers through his hair. "I'm on Matthew's side and the rights of his parents. I want what will work best for him."

"Look at all he can't do. He'll be expected to do nothing and will wilt like a flower rather than flourish. I repeat, his parents don't have the skills to care for him properly."

"Terry, we don't focus on what he can't do here in this community. We look past that and see his ability. His family has helped us all do that. He achieved far more than expected because his parents expected it. No, he isn't a scholar, but he is capable of so much. Believe me, I have visited the farm and been his teacher for four years."

Mr. Hanson dismissively started attending to paperwork and ended the conversation. Terry had been with the regional agency for only one year and didn't have any background knowledge about the family. Mr. Hanson knew Terry so much wanted to control Matthew's fate that he was inconsiderate of the parent's rights. Mr. Hanson knew this wouldn't be resolved until the specialists visited the Parkers on their farm.

Jed and Glenda entered the school office. Alice lit up when she saw them and engaged in small talk. She winked at them and asked, "Are you ready for this meeting?"

"We are, but they're not going to like what we have to say. We're firm in what we want to do," Jed whispered.

"You are the parents. No one can tell you what to do. And you love him. You know what's best."

"Thanks, Alice," Glenda said graciously. "You're the greatest. We've appreciated you all these years."

Alice grinned. "These students are my family, and Matthew has a special place in my heart." Alice winked again. "Good luck. Remember, most of us support your decision."

Jed and Glenda confidently walked into the board room. They sat down at one end of the long conference table. Jackie Stephens, a school-to-work coordinator, was seated next to Terry. Terry and Jackie had determined looks on their faces. Mr. Hanson smiled at Jed and Glenda but they sensed that Mr. Clark was uneasy about something.

Mr. Clark cleared his throat to begin, "Let's get this meeting under way. We're here to discuss the plans for Matthew once he completes this year of school. We're here to come to an agreement concerning Matthew's best interests." He looked firmly at Terry and Jackie.

Jackie began adjusting her finely tailored blouse, rose from her chair, and cleared her throat before explaining their findings "Terry and I have discussed this issue in depth. We have looked at Matthew's school records and skill levels. We have evaluated Matthew extensively. Based upon the data that we have compiled, our analysis for his placement shows that he should be…"

Jed and Glenda looked at each other, and Jed shook his head. They could tell that this consultant had only looked at a bunch of statistics, not Matthew.

Jackie continued, "…in a group home where he can train at the recycling plant. He'll have an apartment with supervised care. This facility provides opportunity for learning more life skills and socialization, which, we believe, he will lack living here on the farm. We intend for you, Mr. and Mrs. Parker, to see that this is the only option in Matthew's best interest."

Terry broke in, "We researched several options extensively, and based upon Matthew's disability, we see this as the best option. It was a long process."

Jed and Glenda were prepared for this suggestion. However, they were the parents and had the right to choose what was best for Matthew. Jed spoke. "He lives for the freedom of the farm. He's able to do multiple tasks. I've shared this with you before, and Mr. Hanson and Mr. Clark know I'm right. He has a variety of skills. He has a support system on the farm and in the community. Where you are suggesting, his work would be doing only one task all day. That would bore him. He belongs on the farm where he will thrive."

Mr. Clark observed Jackie looking at her red fingernails and brushing lint off her red skirt. She obviously thought the Parker family were uneducated and wasn't going to compromise on this.

Mr. Clark decided to mediate, "I can see we don't agree here. Both sides have expressed their viewpoints. It's time for Mr. Hanson to share his observations."

Mr. Hanson began, "I have taught Matthew for four years now. We talk about life. Matthew talks about the farm daily and is passionate about it. He has knowledge about it I don't have. The cows have enhanced his number recognition. He uses problem solving skills daily. He drives cautiously. He has a gentle nature with animals, which is necessary when caring for them. I agree whole heartedly with Jed and Glenda. Taking him away from this stimulating environment would be detrimental."

Jackie sat down in her chair, but was not to be defeated. "Staying at home only stunts growth. He can't possibly do all that. His reports indicate strong deficiencies in the area of problem solving. He can hardly read or do math. He won't function productively there."

Terry added, "We are set in our opinions. He needs to have adequate supervision. You've been loving parents, but he needs educated people working with him now that he is almost done with school."

There it was. Jed knew this was going to be said. Both Terry and Jackie acted like he and Glenda were not capable of enhancing Matthew's learning. Jed thought, *Who else taught him to drive, do mechanics? Little do they know.*

Jackie went on, "I'll reserve his apartment immediately following graduation. He may remain with you until then. It's in his best interest. Don't be stubborn. We know what we are doing. We have studied this."

Jed was beginning to lose patience, but he contained his emotions. He spoke firmly, "You will not make any such accommodations. We are the parents. We have the right to choose Matthew's future."

Jackie was fuming and argued back, "You are being unreasonable. I have the education and training to transition handicapped children. I do this all the time. I have never dealt with such oppositional parents." She pressed her lips together, not at all convinced that farm life would be beneficial to Matthew.

Mr. Clark held up his hand to stop Jackie. She had crossed the line of being professional.

Jed stood, "Come on, Glenda. This meeting is over. These experts don't care about people. They only care about their studies."

Mr. Clark thought Jed had said it accurately. Jackie, especially, had tried to air her expertise only to burn bridges. She had a lot of growing to do in her profession.

Jed and Glenda walked angrily out of the office. Alice saw their flushed faces and knew things had not gone well. She shot them a sympathetic look.

Jackie was fuming and felt humiliated by Mr. Clark's gesture to stop her from speaking the truth. He had no right to intervene. She was up against unreasonable people. She would find a way to get Matthew removed from his home. He was an adult. In a few weeks, his senior year would be over. She spat out, "Don't those people realize the training we've had and that we know far better than they what is best for that boy?"

Mr. Clark was appalled. He sternly told her, "You have shown unprofessional behavior when they were here in this meeting and right now. You have no idea what you're saying. I've worked with this family and Matthew for over fifteen years. I know all of their children, and I know how well Matthew's done on the farm. You were out of line. I'm disappointed that you are here representing options for placement."

She replied, "I'm doing what's best."

"I don't think you are. There's more to life than statistics. People cannot be fit into tight little facts and figures. In your job, you help families with decisions that seriously impact their lives. You need to gather all of the information before you dare to make any recommendations. A great leader cares about others; they do not merely overpower them."

She turned red with rage. "I've never had anyone question my judgment on placement. I know my area."

"You don't know people," Mr. Clark said. "You need to see the hearts and character of those you are supposed to help. You are hindering more than helping. The next time you come to this building, I expect to see some change. You are young, inexperienced, and arrogant. It's time to look beyond your opinions."

She stood up and left without saying good-bye. Terry let her walk ahead and told Mr. Clark, "I apologize for Jackie, sir. She was out of line. Good day."

"Good day, Terry."

Terry caught up to Jackie. He understood what Mr. Clark was saying, yet he still agreed with her. He had an idea. Everyone said how Matthew had so many skills. There was no documentation other than subjective hearsay. He thought if he did a home visit, then he could prove Matthew's parents exaggerated his skills. He thought this was a great way to triumph. He would call Mr. Clark in the morning and see about making arrangements. Mr. Clark would schedule the day for the home visit, and he'd prove Jackie right.

Terry and Jackie had a thirty-minute ride back to the agency office. He revealed his idea to her. "Give me a chance to prove you are right. I think this is going to work. The parents are embellishing his abilities on the farm. We both know that Down syndrome children don't excel in much at all. I'll prove them wrong, then they'll have no choice but to go along with us."

Jackie grinned. "I like that idea. Those people won't have any clue what you are doing. I think it might work."

Terry added, "He can barely communicate. He has done okay, but he is so deficient in so many areas. I'll pretend to advocate for them. I'll observe his home routine and take mental notes."

Jackie said, "Good luck. I think we found a way to get him away from his home and into the best place for him."

Mr. Clark sipped a cup of coffee as he thought about the meeting he had had concerning the plans for transitioning Matthew Parker from school to work. He felt most displeased how Jackie exhibited arrogance and disrespect toward Jed and Glenda. Jackie was all too eager to show her academic expertise and prove that she was right. Mr. Clark had seen this arrogance from several young professionals who were wet behind the ears. Eventually, they learned from experience that not all their knowledge comes from a textbook. Yet, he wanted to communicate that Jed and Glenda Parker were the experts in regard to their son. He knew they had a keen sense of his abilities and would only choose the option that was in the best interest for him. His thoughts were interrupted by a call from Terry, who asked if he could make a visit to Matthew's home.

After his conversation with Terry, Mr. Clark called Glenda. "I have a quick question for you. Terry just called and wondered if he could do a home visit to see what Matthew has going for him on the farm."

"I…uh…I don't know. He's determined to have Matthew leave us."

"I understand your concern after yesterday's meeting. However, I believe he'll see things differently if he spends a day with all of you. It will open his eyes."

"Do you really think it will help? He wasn't as cruel as that know-it-all woman, but he didn't think Matthew should stay here."

"I know. He is the key, though. If he's convinced that Matthew has independence and skills, he'll side with you. I think you should consider it."

"When does he want to come?"

"As soon as it works for you."

"I can be ready by tomorrow. I think that'll work. Do I have Matthew stay home from school then?"

"I think that's a good idea."

"He can come early. We'll have lunch for him."

"I'll tell him to arrive around 9:30 in the morning. Thanks, Glenda. Let me know how it goes."

Glenda cleaned the house to perfection for the visit. The morning of Terry's visit, she prepared a barbecued minute steak recipe, baked potatoes, homemade rolls, and two salads. She made an apple pie for dessert. She was working on breakfast clean-up when Terry arrived.

"Matthew, get the door please," Glenda hollered.

Matthew politely opened the door and shook Terry's hand. "Welcome. Come in. See me home."

Terry removed his Kansas City Royals hat and said, "You have a big home."

Matthew looked at the hat. "Me like hat. Me team. Baseball. Me like."

"I'm a big fan of theirs. I go to their games a few times every summer."

Terry was impressed by Matthew's manners, but it didn't demonstrate anything significant. Terry stood in the brightly painted dining room with its cheerful green color. He saw the outdated, plain carpet in the living room and lots of family pictures hanging on the walls. Matthew led him to the living room to have a seat on the couch that faced a painting of an old mill. The detailed watercolor painting captured his attention, and he studied it intensely while he waited for the adults.

Glenda and Jed came in to greet Terry. Jed told him, "I'm glad you were able to come and visit. We're happy to have you here."

"Thank you," Terry replied. "It's my pleasure."

As Jed talked, Terry observed that Matthew seemed more subdued and less communicative at home. He felt smug about this and knew Matthew wouldn't thrive here. Jed small talked about farming. Terry had not grown up near the rural areas, so this was like listening to another language. Matthew smiled and nodded as the two men talked.

"Jed," Terry interrupted, "This is all great to hear about the farm, but what you tell me about Matthew is unlikely. It's most unusual. Unbelievable."

"Terry, I see where you may not comprehend all of this. That's why we're glad to have you here. I think it's time that Matthew takes you on the farm tour. It might teach you a thing or two."

"What do you mean? The three of us will see the farm?"

"No, I mean Matthew will drive you around to show you our operation."

Terry felt reluctant. "Well, he isn't really able to."

Jed turned to Matthew, "Check the gas tank for Gator and take Terry through the pasture to the hay field and by the creek to the back eighty. Let him see the farm."

"Okay. Me do. Me take him. Him see cows. Him see corn."

Terry followed Matthew to the gator and watched him check the fuel tank and pull it up to the gas barrel to fill it. He instructed Terry, "Get in. Me take you see cows."

Terry felt quite uncomfortable riding with Matthew driving. If the ride was too scary, he would make an excuse to get back to the house.

Matthew drove off through the pasture looking for cows that gave birth. He told Terry, "Me see cows. Cows have babies." He saw that G28 had a calf. The calf was still on the ground and being licked by its mother. Matthew eased close to the cow and calf. He said, "G28. Me tell Dad."

Terry sat silently as Matthew drove through the pasture. A cow started following them. Matthew stopped the gator, and the cow came close to Matthew. Bonnie sniffed him and licked his hand. Matthew put his arms around her and said, "Easy girl. Stay calm." Bonnie stayed close, and Matthew told Terry, "Me cow. Cow like me."

Terry wasn't impressed. *So what if he had a pet cow? There were stranger pets than that.*

Matthew went to the corn field where the creek was and drove on the road real close to the creek. Terry was skeptical. He observed that Matthew was able to drive near the creek without letting the tires get too close. There were some holes along the road that Matthew avoided. At the hay field, Matthew pointed to the big bales of hay. "Me hay. Me line hay. Me drive tractor. Me take hay."

"Oh, I see," Terry said doubtfully.

Matthew drove Terry back to the pasture and saw a cow with legs sticking out of its back and made a mental note. "Red fifteen. Cow need help."

He pulled up to the calving shed to clean out the pens. He spread a fresh bed of straw. "Me keep cows warm. No cold. Help them."

Matthew drove back to the house to report the birthing situation. Brad was in the shop and wanted to go see if the calf needed to be pulled. Matthew and Brad took Terry to the pasture with them. Brad saw the cow was struggling. He told Matthew, "Stand by her and keep her calm. I'll see if I can get the calf out."

Matthew fearlessly spoke softly to the cow. "Easy. You okay. Stay calm." The cow remained calm while Brad pulled the calf. It took twenty minutes to get the calf out. Terry had never seen the birth of an animal, let alone a human being assisting in the birth and watched in admiration at the new life.

Back at the shop, Jed needed some greasing done on his planter before going to the field. "Matthew, get the grease gun and work on the planter so I can get to the field."

"Okay, me do."

Terry watched as Matthew carefully prepared the planter for field work. When he was done, Matthew started up the lawn mower and mowed the lawn around the shop.

While Matthew mowed, Terry remarked to Jed, "He certainly can get around here."

Jed replied, "Yes, he can. Next, I want him to start up the tractor and take you to the hay stack and get a bale for the cows. He does this all alone. He has for two years now."

"Sure." Terry cordially agreed. Matthew finished mowing and started up the tractor. He drove Terry to the haystack with the bale carrier attached. He backed up to a bale of hay and carried it to the pasture. At the pasture, he let down the bale of hay. Terry was surprised he was able to do this independently.

After dinner, Jed told Matthew, "Load the gator with bags of bean seed. Meet me at the field by the pasture." Matthew opened the machine shed door and loaded the seed. While he loaded it, Jed took the planter to the field. The weather was perfect for planting. Jed and Matthew loaded the planter, and Jed said to bring another load later.

Before going back for the second load of seed, Matthew went to the shop where Brad was working. Brad needed some wrenches. Matthew went to the collection and quickly found the sizes he needed. Brad asked him to check the tire pressure in the pickup. Matthew checked it and said the front left tire needed air. He pulled the air compressor hose to the tire and filled it.

It was time to load more seed and take it to the field. Matthew counted the bags of seed as he loaded each one in the back of gator. He drove Terry out to the planter again for refilling the seed. Jed asked, "How has your day been?"

Terry was speechless, which was uncommon. He had to think about what to say.

Jed continued, "I would like to take more time to visit, but we need to plant while the weather's good."

"I understand. I have to admit that Matthew can do much more than I expected. I personally don't know anything about farming, and he by far surpasses me in his ability here. He does many tasks, as you stated in the meeting. I see for myself why you feel he belongs here."

"There's never a dull moment here. He has different jobs each season of the year. I wish you could stay late enough to see him fill buckets of feed for the cattle."

Terry looked at his watch. "Actually, I must be going. I have a long drive ahead of me."

"Thank you for coming. I'm glad you were able to make it."

The two men shook hands, and Matthew drove him back to the house. Terry said, "Thank you, Glenda, for the outstanding meal. I enjoyed myself today."

"I'm glad you enjoyed your day, but I hope you discovered why we know that this farm is the best option for Matthew's future. Good-bye." Glenda went back into the house to finish her dishes.

As Terry drove back to the agency building, he thought about how Matthew had lots of independence and responsibilities on the farm. He had no doubt that he had seen only a smidgen of the skills Matthew possessed and thought how this life would keep Matthew's mind busy. He saw Matthew drive and work without supervision. Matthew's parents were being honest with them. Terry felt a bit guilty when he reflected on the day's experience.

"You're crazy," Jackie said after Terry told her the events of the day. He knew it was difficult for her to admit they had been wrong. "What possessed you to side with them?"

"I saw the independence Matthew demonstrates there. He's quite skilled and able to work on his own. He's thriving. I will no longer be part of trying to change their minds."

"They prepared him for this. They knew you were coming and wanted to put on their best."

"I went on a day's notice. I was alone with him when he performed many skilled tasks. He'll do fine there."

"He's still very low-skilled."

"That's because he does many tasks that are not measured on educational tests. A person has to observe it to understand. His dad has taught him so much. The skills he learned weren't assessed because they use hand/eye coordination. We don't test for this. For being uneducated, the family sure had much patience and ability to teach Matthew so many things."

Jackie scowled at Terry. "You were supposed to prove that he belonged in a sheltered workshop. Now you've changed your mind?"

"In most cases, it is beneficial, but Mr. Clark and this visit helped me realize we need to look at individual situations and at the people."

"A collection of data is the basis for indicators of ability and placement choices."

"Not always. There are many other factors to consider. I think data is great, but it needs to be used appropriately. It doesn't determine everything."

Jackie turned her back to Terry and left the room. She had the expertise and education, but lacked the heart and understanding she needed to serve her clients well. Terry watched her and thought how just yesterday he had seen things her way. He realized that she was too set in one way of thinking. He was glad he listened to Mr. Clark's advice and made his home visit. Mr. Clark was an amazing leader who used his education for the benefit and well-being of the students and community.

Mr. Clark smiled triumphantly as he hung up the receiver. Alice stepped into his office. "What are you beaming about?"

He looked at her and accepted the reports she had brought for him. "Good news. Very good news."

"Does this have anything to do with the Parkers?"

"Yes, it does. Terry was impressed with his visit. He was impressed with all that Matthew knew. He has decided to accept the decision of the parents."

"Glory be! That's good news. Jed and Glenda will be delighted to have that support."

"You know what, Alice?"

"What?"

"I've been here from the time Matthew started kindergarten. I've have raised my own children here. I'm not looking forward to the end of the school year."

"I know what you mean. I feel the same way."

"We've watched Matthew grow and change from kindergarten until now. The school staff and students have benefitted from his life here. They have learned to accept and love a person with a disability. I know we'll see him in the community, but it won't be the same."

"He's a great kid. We all have been touched by him here. He kept us in our running shoes." Alice laughed and then said, "He has many strengths in spite of his academic limitations."

"And I wish most of the students were as hardworking as he's been. He has a hard work ethic and doesn't complain."

"We've all been inspired by that."

Mr. Clark confided in Alice, "I ordered a diploma for him. I know there will be some people who disagree, but he deserves to go through graduation. He completed the program that was specially designed for him and successfully completed it."

"He does deserve to graduate with his class, sir. It will mean a lot to him and his classmates."

"It's a special occasion. I hope Jed and Glenda allow him to participate in the ceremony."

"I'm sure they will. If not, it's worth convincing them." Alice had a faraway look in her eyes. She thought about the day when Matthew was missing, and he was on the bus. She also thought about how he was falsely accused in the food fight. She thought of the students who had graduated years before him, how they gave him high fives and lit up when they saw him. Memories flashed before her eyes. She excused herself to get back to work.

Mr. Clark reflected back on all the times Matthew spent in his office. There were many humorous times and some challenging ones. He had accomplished his vision for the school. He wanted the student body to accept a child with Down syndrome. Most of the students over the past twelve years had embraced the opportunity to get to know Matthew. He set a model for acceptance and saw hearts changed. He sat back in his chair, feeling peace about the past years. It was worth every minute, and his life was touched. Graduation needed to be special for Matthew as well as his classmates.

CHAPTER 45

Three weeks after the visit, Terry Porter called Glenda. "Hello, Glenda. Terry Porter here. I wanted to call you myself and let you know I was pleased with the farm visit. Matthew definitely belongs there. I want to wish him the very best and keep in touch. I'd like to visit in a year or so to see how he's doing."

"Thank you, Terry," she said in disbelief. "You're welcome to come again."

Terry hung up the phone, and Glenda went outside to tell Jed about Terry's call. She approached Jed as if walking on air.

"What's up?" Jed asked.

"Terry was impressed with the farm visit," she said elatedly. "What a relief."

"I knew he'd be impressed once he saw all that Matthew did. It's so evident to visitors that he belongs here." He slipped his arm around Glenda and held her.

———✳———

It was prom night, and Matthew came downstairs in his black suit, green tie, and shiny black shoes.

"My, my, aren't you a handsome one," Glenda said proudly. "Look how grown up you look."

"Mom, no say me. Girls tell me. No you."

"Come over here and let me pin this red rose on you. Did you comb your hair?"

"Me okay. Me comb upstairs. Me clean me glasses."

Glenda pinned the rose on Matthew's suit coat when there was a knock at the door. Mr. Hanson and his wife, Cheryl, were waiting to pick Matthew up and drive him to Oakwood to prom.

The students and guests arrived at the hotel banquet room which was dimly lit. Each couple entering the banquet room stopped at the sound of a trumpet and waited to be introduced by an announcer.

The trumpet went, "Da-da-dada-daaaaa." The announcer introduced, "Luke Jensen and guest. The faculty and students already seated applauded. Luke and his girlfriend walked elegantly down the stairs.

The trumpet sounded again. "Da-da-dada-daaaaa. Brian Wilson and Sheila Larson." Everyone applauded as they walked in like royalty. A photographer took pictures as each couple or person was introduced.

Alice and her husband were next. Alice hollered, "All right, party time!" The students and staff cheered loudly.

"Mr. Hanson and his wife, Cheryl." Cheryl waved to everyone bubbling with joy.

"Da-da-dada-daaaaa. Matthew Parker." Matthew walked in with his shoulders thrown back and head held high. As people clapped, he put his hand across his waist and took a bow. Students whistled and shouted at him.

After all of the introductions were done, the waiters and waitresses served a chicken parmesan dish with baked potatoes, corn, fruit salad, and rolls. Relish trays were set on each table as well as a basket for extra rolls and butter. The dessert came out on a cart.

Once the meal was over, the sophomore servers performed skits about the seniors and reminisced about funny things that happened over the years. They told about Matthew taking the teacher's whistle and blowing it. They also included the story about him picking up Billy, who had graduated two years earlier. All of the senior class had memories about humorous times. The sophomores had a prophecy of what each senior would be doing in ten years. They predicted Matthew being a cowboy with his one hundred cows.

The senior parents put together a surprise for the prom. They had a photo slide show of pictures of the class from kindergarten through their senior year. It included teacher and activity photos. The students made sounds of admiration as they saw the slides. The Master of Ceremony spoke, "As the school year's ending is near, many of us here are graduating. We're either getting jobs or going to college. We all have dreams of what we want to achieve. The sky's the limit. We need to reach for the stars and follow our dreams. We only have one chance. Let's do it!"

The disc jockey was behind the podium and began playing music. The couples went onto the dance floor with the strobe light turning and stars glowing on the ceiling. Matthew sat with Luke and his date from Oakwood, Brian, Sheila, David, and Nicki. The girls all took turns dancing with Matthew. Matthew asked Alice to dance, which she eagerly accepted. Alice went on the dance floor riling the dancers up with her flamboyant moves and clapping to the music. Matthew did his version of the moonwalk. Other students joined them.

"Ray, will you excuse me? I want to have a special dance with Matthew," Amy told him sweetly.

Ray kissed her cheek. "Amy, that's what I love about you. You're so kind and loving. Go out there and have fun."

Amy danced a fast and a slow dance with Matthew. He danced with Mrs. Clark and Mrs. Jones and hardly sat down during the evening. During the few songs he didn't have a dance partner, a group of six or eight students got in a circle to dance. Matthew shook his hips and swung his arms rhythmically. Other students joined them. Alice got in the center of the group and danced wildly, clapping her hands and shaking her whole body. She yelled, "Groovin' time!"

Matthew was taken home at midnight. He was so happy to dance most of the evening with friends, he couldn't stop talking about it. It was a highlight of his senior year.

CHAPTER 46

It was two weeks prior to graduation. The seniors counted down the days of school left. Mr. Clark hoped that Jed and Glenda realized that even though Matthew didn't study the same subjects, he was a part of the graduating class and achieved his goals for school. He felt Matthew deserved to graduate.

While Mr. Clark was doing some paperwork, Mrs. Pearson stormed into the office. It had been a long time since he had seen her because her two girls were out of high school.

Mrs. Pearson hovered over his desk. He was baffled at what brought her to school now. She began, "Mr. Clark, I've heard rumors around town that you plan on allowing Matthew Parker to graduate from high school and partake in the graduation ceremonies."

"That's correct."

"This is unacceptable. He hasn't taken the rigorous academics that other students have had. His getting a diploma cheapens the value in receiving a diploma at all."

"I respect your point of view, Meredith, but our school board has already made that decision."

"He doesn't deserve the recognition that the other students deserve who worked so hard for this day. He isn't the quality of the others."

"Mrs. Pearson, we have made our decision that he rightly deserves to graduate with his class. He has learned far more than what was anticipated. This will be a good closure for him also."

"Then let him attend the ceremony and wish his classmates well. I don't agree with him receiving a diploma and being recognized. What an insult to our school."

"I know you don't agree. We've had conversations about him in the past. His classmates are happy that he is part of it."

"I guess you won't listen any more to what I have to say."

Mr. Clark felt relieved this conversation was about to end. "I think we've summed things up. Thank you for stopping in today. By the way, how are your daughters?"

"Tina's engaged to be married this summer. She graduated with her BSN in nursing, and she'll live in Denver. We're so proud of her, and she has the sweetest fiancé. Tiffany's studying engineering and makes all As. She's determined to have a career before getting serious with anyone. They're both such wonderful young ladies."

"You definitely do have sweet girls. What nice and ambitious young ladies," Mr. Clark replied.

Mr. Hanson thought about graduation day. True, Matthew had a different academic program, yet he was challenged and gained so much during high school. Almost everyone in the school and community saw that Matthew deserved the honor of walking on stage and receiving a diploma. Since this was an occasion of great celebration, Mr. Hanson needed to discuss this with Jed and Glenda. He wanted to convince them to allow Matthew to walk across that stage. He had a vision of Matthew confidently accepting his diploma and had talked to Matthew what graduation meant and how it rewarded him for his accomplishments. He decided it was time to make a call.

"Glenda, Mr. Hanson here. How are you this morning?"

"Okay," she spoke hesitantly. "Is everything all right?"

"Things are great. I want to find a time when I can have a short meeting with you and Jed. I have something to discuss with both of you. It would be better in person."

"And what's this concerning?" she asked.

"It concerns Matthew."

"Mr. Hanson, you know that we are firm in our decision that Matthew will stay on the farm once school is over."

Mr. Hanson abruptly said, "No, Glenda. It isn't about that. It's about graduation. I wanted to have a little chat. When works for you to meet?"

Glenda thought about it. "Jed's in the field getting the crops planted. He needs a day this week when it will rain. I believe the forecast predicts rain on Thursday. Let's meet Thursday. If it doesn't rain, we may have to wait."

"Sounds good. What time?"

"The earlier the better. I think nine will work out."

"Great. I'll put it on my calendar. See you then."

Glenda hung up the phone and thought there was no reason to speak to Mr. Hanson about graduation because Matthew had a different academic program than those going through the ceremony. They felt Matthew deserved a small party to celebrate his school career being completed. Matthew had spent his whole school life there, and these were students he knew since kindergarten. Glenda highly respected Mr. Hanson and felt obligated to visit with him. He had made a positive difference in Matthew's life.

———✻———

On Thursday, Jed and Glenda went to Mr. Hanson's room. Mr. Hanson greeted them at the door. "Come on in. Have a seat. Do you want some coffee or water?"

"No thank you," Glenda said.

"Coffee please," Jed said.

"I'm glad that you were able to make it today," Mr. Hanson said as he poured Jed a cup of coffee. "Thank you for coming despite your busy schedules." He put Jed and Glenda at ease right away. "I do want to inform you that Matthew was measured for a cap and gown, and his name appears on the graduation program as a graduate."

Jed and Glenda glanced at each other.

"I know we've discussed this once before, but Matthew is looking forward to this day. He is so deserving. He's exceeded our goals for him."

"This school was such a good place for him. He couldn't have had a better experience. He is part of this wonderful class, but he didn't take the same classes," Glenda spoke softly to Mr. Hanson.

"Glenda, the school board, student council, staff, and even the student body agree that Matthew deserves this honor. He's taught us all so much. He's modeled outstanding character. He's an amazing young man."

Glenda got defensive, "I don't want a spectacle made of him. So many visitors won't understand him being there."

"Please, let's all celebrate the years we've had with him. It's for us also."

Jed and Glenda sat silent a few minutes. They were at a loss for words.

Mr. Hanson added, "Matthew completed the individual program that was written specifically for him. It isn't the same as the program for other students, I agree, but it fit his needs. We're all so proud of him."

Jed at last said, "I think it's okay for him. If it means that much, he can. He's accomplished a lot."

"Thank you, Jed. And you know that I would never ask anything of you that would in the slightest be hurtful to him."

As Jed and Glenda left the short meeting, Fred breathed a sigh of relief. It was much easier than he thought to convince them to have Matthew participate in the graduation ceremonies. They wouldn't regret that decision. He was certain of it.

On graduation day, the Parker family attended church and ate out at Oakwood. Soon, Matthew would go to school to graduate with his class of thirty-six students. At home, everyone dressed in their Sunday best. Matthew brushed off the lint on his black suit and looked in the mirror proudly. Brad took pictures of Matthew and his parents.

Gordon and Trudy were unable to attend due to health issues that confined them to their home. Matthew stopped by to see them on the way to school. They both hugged him and congratulated him for his accomplishments.

"We couldn't be happier for you than we are today. You've done well," Trudy said.

Matthew frowned as he left their home. "Me sad. Raw. Papa home. No go see me. Me love."

At school, Matthew quietly went to the music room where the seniors gathered before entering the gymnasium. The rest of the family looked for seats in the gym. It was packed full of friends and families of the graduates.

The high school band was set up at the back of the gym and began playing. Two by two, the graduates walked into the gym and down the center aisle. Matthew stood straight as he walked in with a serious look on his face, focusing directly ahead of him. Glenda opened her purse for a tissue. Brad and Jenny rolled their eyes at their mom, thinking it was silly to cry at graduation.

The graduates stood in front of their chairs. Mr. Duncan, the superintendent, stood at the podium and directed them to be seated. "Today is a day when a journey ends and another begins. We celebrate the accomplishments of each graduate seated before me. Each one has obtained various achievements."

After Mr. Duncan concluded his comments, Andy gave the valedictorian speech. Ray spoke second.

The choir sang a song about memories. A slide show was presented displaying pictures of all of the students from kindergarten through high school. The graduates moaned and laughed at the memories projected before their eyes.

Mr. Peters, the school board president, approached the podium. He announced, "It is now time to introduce the graduates. I will call each one by name."

After each student received his or her diploma, the crowd applauded. Mr. Peters read, "Matthew John Parker."

Matthew walked up on stage. He firmly shook hands with Mr. Peters as he received his diploma. Mr. Clark shook his hand with a long, firm shake. As he stepped down, he held the diploma high in the air, waving it and radiating with pleasure.

As the crowd applauded, students and staff stood up. All of the visitors in the gymnasium, except for one person, were standing and clapping. Glenda scanned the crowd and felt a lump in her throat. As the cheering continued, she saw Mrs. Pearson in the bleachers with her arms wrapped tightly across her chest. Tears ran down Glenda's cheeks. Matthew was loved and accepted in the school and community. What a blessing he was in her life and in the lives of so many.

Mr. Clark went to the microphone and asked everyone to sit down. He commented, "I have never seen a standing ovation at graduation ever in my years as a principal. This is incredible." He said one last comment before concluding the graduation. "Matthew, you have had an impact on this school and community in so many ways." More applause.

CHAPTER 47

Ed and Jenny married in August after Matthew graduated from high school. The small, simple wedding was held at Oakwood Christian Church. Matthew was poised in his gray tuxedo as he ushered the guests to the pews. He greeted each of the guests with a big smile. "Me sis marry Ed. Happy day."

Matthew teased Ed and Jenny by telling family, "Jenny. Ed. Honeymoon. Babies come. Me uncle."

Jenny heard Matthew telling that to people and felt embarrassed. She urged Matthew, "Please talk about something else. You can tell others about your cows, not about Ed and me."

---*---

When Ed and Jenny came back the first time after the wedding, they put their luggage in the room where Ed had always stayed as a guest. Matthew saw Jenny walk into the room with Ed. He was agitated and told her, "No. No same room. Sis, you go that room. No sleep here."

"Matthew, we're married now, and that's what married people do," Jenny explained.

"No," Matthew insisted. "No same room. You go here." He pointed to another room.

Jenny firmly said to Matthew, "I'm staying here tonight with Ed. He's my husband now. We're married."

Ed said nothing. He knew Matthew liked him, but it seemed Matthew didn't understand what changed once they were married.

Ed did suggest one thing to Jenny. "You know, perhaps you should sleep in the other room for tonight until Matthew understands things. He's getting upset, and it isn't worth it."

"He needs to learn sometime," Jenny argued. "We'll visit several times a year."

"You listen Ed, Sis. Him right. Him tell you," Matthew said to her.

Brad came in the house from doing chores. "Brad, Matthew won't let us sleep in the same room. It's quite upsetting to him. We tried to explain that we're married now," Jenny complained.

"I'll have a talk with him. Once I talk to him, he'll be quiet about it."

"Good luck," Jenny said. "I can't explain it."

"That's what brothers are for," Brad teased. "We'll have a man-to-man talk."

PART 6

ADULT YEARS

CHAPTER 48

A few years after her marriage to Ed, Jenny worked out of her home doing accounting for a firm. She had two children, Devin and Amanda. She wanted to be at home with them, but her desire was to work also. She was fortunate to have a firm that allowed workers to do work from home.

One day, Jenny had a meeting with her boss, Doug, a Christian man who had a large family. He had a Down syndrome nephew. "I have some questions for you about your brother. What does he do now that he's been out of high school for several years?" Doug asked.

"He works on the farm full time. He gets out there and has lots of responsibility. He's quite independent as a worker."

"What kinds of things does he do?"

"This winter, he's been feeding cattle, even during the frigid days we've had. He helps in the shop with maintenance of equipment. Dad has taught him quite a bit about mechanics. He also helps my mom with many household chores. Her back isn't good, so he does dishes, laundry, sweeping, dusting, and some cooking."

"It sounds like he works all the time. Does he have a social life? It sounds like he's stuck on the farm."

"Oh, he has quite a few friends. He makes friends everywhere he goes. Some of the neighborhood guys get together to play Monopoly, Pit, or rummy. They go bowling occasionally or out for pizza. They celebrate birthdays together and have New Year's Eve parties. Luke, his friend since kindergarten, drives truck for a local company. He stops by to see Matthew a couple times a year. They've remained friends after all these years."

"It sounds like he has a good support system. Anyone else from high school keep in touch with him?"

"He has a friend, Brian. Brian stops by once a year when he comes home for Christmas. He's a great guy. He makes himself at home. If I go home and see people, I tell them who I am. Lots of people have forgotten me, but when they hear my maiden name, they know I'm Matthew's sister. I guess he's unforgettable."

"My brother has a Down syndrome boy who's two. He says he's always smiling and laughing, but he can be stubborn at times."

Jenny laughed, "That about sums it up. Matthew was so much fun, but he had that same stubborn streak. He isn't stubborn often. Sometimes, he gets upset if he can't watch a particular television show when there's farm work to do."

"What does he do during the spring and summer months on the farm? Is there much he can do then?"

"Oh goodness, yes. He gets the farm equipment ready for field work. He's responsible for checking cows during birthing season and hauling feed sacks to the field. He has fifty-five cows now. All of them are descendants of his very first cow. He keeps statistics on each one of them. He writes down information on a poster board to keep track of each one. I don't know how he remembers so much about them. Matthew knows their tag numbers and the names of all the calves that have been born. He keeps most of the female calves to increase his herd. His original cow, Bonnie, has died now. It was hard on him, but he has her daughters, granddaughters, and great-granddaughters."

"That keeps him busy just to keep track of all of those cows and take care of the others. It sounds like he has a full life."

"He also keeps the calving shed clean and bedded with fresh straw so the cows can have a warm place to be when they calve. He bottle feeds calves that need it. That doesn't happen very often, but once in a while there's a calf that can't feed off its mom."

"How does your family do it with all those cattle and the crops? I realize your brother is a great help, but that's a hefty work load they have."

"Dad hired a neighbor guy as a hired hand. He put up hay for them when he was a teenager and loves farm work. He didn't have an opportunity to farm on his own, so he wanted to work for a farmer. His name's Jeremy Jensen. He spends over sixty hours a week on the farm. Mom considers him another son. She spoils him rotten. Jeremy is Matthew's best buddy. They do chores and field work together. He's a great guy."

"At least they have some good help. Farming's a busy life and such hard work. How're your parents doing?"

"Mom's back is weak. She can't do what she used to do. My dad's slower in his work, but he's in good health. They're so lucky."

"What else does Matthew do?"

"In the summer, he puts up hay, fences, and continues to do cow chores. He also mows lawn and helps Mom garden."

"Does he have any fun in the summer? It sounds busier than the winter."

"Rodeo time's a big deal. He gets autographs every year from the clowns and fair queens. He keeps these in an album. Dad takes him to the Pirates games, the nearest minor league baseball team. The regulars know him by name. He also goes to the car races a couple times each summer with friends."

"His social life's better than mine," Doug laughed. "I thought he'd be more isolated and sheltered by not being in a group home. Not so with your brother. He gets out quite a bit."

"It just worked out that he had another opportunity than a group home. I know it might be best for most kids with disabilities, but he loves the farm. He has friends who take him to the Cloverville High football games. The students almost all know him by name since the high school students are the ones he served in the cafeteria. They remember him."

"What a community you're from. How fortunate to have so many friendly and kind people."

"Let me tell you that Matthew gets attention everywhere he goes. Even the sale barn. The auctioneer announces his presence every time he's there. Farmers come up to him and talk to him about his cattle. They always tell Dad the farm's a great place for him."

"I'll have to share this with my brother. He lives in town, but it'd be good for him to hear what your brother's like in his adult life. Can he drive at all?"

"Mom and Dad don't let him drive on the highway for liability purposes, but he drives the tractor on the farm. He goes to the hay stack and picks up big bales to feed to the cattle. He also gets the hay from the field and lines up the hay. In the fall, he drives the grain cart to help Dad out when the combine needs to be emptied. Then, he empties the grain cart on the semi."

"I can see why he doesn't drive on the highway. But, he gets around wherever he wants to on the farm. That's wonderful. I'm glad to hear of his individual successes. He doesn't just sit around expecting others to do everything for him."

"Definitely not. My parents expected a lot out of all of us."

"I can tell by your work ethic," Doug said.

"I try to do my best in all my work for you and as a mom. I can't begin to let you know how much I appreciate your flexibility in letting me work from home. I like being a mom first, yet I like working. Thank you so much."

"My wife stays at home with our kids. She sells Pampered Chef. She gets out and meets lots of people and has an online business. It keeps her schedule flexible where the kids are first. It works for us. I respect those who choose to be at home. My mom was always there for me. And, you do your job accurately and in a timely manner. It doesn't matter that you work out of your home."

"Thank you so much. Well, I need to get going."

"See you later when the next project's due."

"It'll be sooner than later."

Doug sat in his desk chair and thought about Jenny's brother. He could do so much. He made a mental note to call his own brother to tell him about Matthew. Doug's brother and his wife were occasionally discouraged having a child with Down syndrome and weren't sure what to expect.

Matthew was cleaning his room. He was dusting the furniture and picked up his picture of Bonnie. He said, "You good cow. Me miss you. Me cows you family." Next to the picture of Bonnie was one of Mitzi. "Me miss you. You good dog. Me friend." He dusted it and set it down.

He dusted his desk above which hung a calendar. There were many names written on it to remind him of birthdays. He often called his friends and family on their birthdays. From his desk, he pulled out a sheet of paper. "Me give Ed. Me give Jenny. Me Christmas. See me want." Setting the wish list aside, he dusted the shelf where he kept his video collection. The movies were shelved in a way that Matthew knew where every single one could be found. He had a collection of classic Disney and John Wayne movies.

Matthew finished working in his room and dressed for chores. Jeremy, his best buddy, was going to feed the cattle with him. The pickup was parked at the end of the sidewalk.

"Hey there, buddy. I've been waiting for you. They're hungry up there. We don't want them to starve," Jeremy said teasingly with his sparkling blue eyes.

"Me here. Cows okay. Time eat. Me best buddy help cows."

"You bet. We'll get them what they need. How's it going today? What have you been up to?" Jeremy ran his fingers through his sandy blonde hair.

"Me clean room. Me look me dog, me cow. Me miss. Me see Luke birthday come soon. Me call him. Tell him Happy Birthday."

"Who's Luke? I don't believe I know him."

"Him me friend long time ago. Him good man. Him married. Him kids. Nice kids."

"I'll have to meet him sometime. Sounds like a great guy."

"You, me best buddy," Matthew said.

They pulled into the Rogers' homestead that had a cattle lot with several bunks lined up for feeding. The cattle were standing by the bunks waiting to be fed.

CHAPTER 49

At Christmas time, Matthew, Jed, Glenda, Ed, Devin, and Amanda went to a farm acreage that displayed thousands of colorful Christmas lights strewn on fences, a barn, a combine, and windmill. A Santa's workshop and Disney characters were displayed along with luminaries lining the sidewalk of the farm house. Thousands of sightseers drove by during the holiday season to view the elaborate display.

Brad and Jenny had stayed alone by the Christmas tree with its blue lights illuminating the darkened living room. Jenny slowly sipped a mug of hot chocolate with mounds of marshmallows and licked her lips as she tasted the rich chocolate flavor.

Brad chugged down a plastic bottle of Mountain Dew as Jenny said, "Can you believe it? Matthew's turning forty this spring. Here I am, with a family of my own. The years have passed quickly."

"You know," Brad thought aloud. "I think we ought to have a fortieth birthday party for Matthew. He loves parties, and we haven't had anything big since he graduated."

"I like the idea. I can do most of the preparations."

"Let's do an open house. No telling how many will come, but he's worth it," Brad said.

"Forty's a landmark. We'll go all out with catering and decorations. I'll get it planned and keep you posted."

"Mom and Dad don't need to know until the day of the open house. They can be surprised too. With Mom's back, she can't do as much. I don't want to burden her," Brad said with concern.

They ended their conversation when a vehicle drove into the driveway.

Jenny spent the next three months making out the to-do list, planning for the decorations, ordering food, and calling Brad several times a week. Jenny's twelve-year-old son, Devin, used his creativity for designing banners and posters. Nine-year-old Amanda helped making special mints in molds and several dozen cookies. Glenda had taught Amanda cooking skills from the summer weeks she and Devin spent on the Parker farm with their grandparents.

The Saturday morning in March was full of sunshine and warmth, making it a perfect day for Matthew's party. Ed and Jenny met Jeremy at the community center to decorate. The men set up rectangular tables while Jenny covered them with black tablecloths and silver confetti with the number forty on it.

When Ed and Jenny were finished decorating, they met with the rest of the family at a fast food restaurant. They were eating when Matthew asked, "Why you gone long time? What you do? Me miss you."

Ed swallowed and attempted to avoid the question.

Matthew asked again. "You come see me. No you here. Where you go?"

Jenny smirked and put a napkin in front of her face to stifle the giggles.

"You date? You honeymoon?" Matthew asked.

"We had to go somewhere," Ed answered. "But we have the rest of the weekend to spend together."

"Me no see you. Me talk you. Show you cows."

"Sorry, buddy." Ed apologized. "We'll spend time together."

"What you do?" Matthew insisted. "You come here, you go. What you do?"

Jed and Glenda were sitting at a separate booth from Brad, Matthew, Jenny, and Ed since the restaurant didn't have tables for eight while Devin and Amanda sat with their grandparents. Jed and Glenda knew there was something more happening today than Brad had revealed. They suspected something when Brad and Jenny were gone all morning. Brad had told his parents that the neighbor guys and their wives were coming for a quaint little party with refreshments and games. Now, Jed and Glenda didn't believe this story. Jed said, "Ed and Jenny were gone all morning. What would take them so long if this is a small get-together?"

Glenda agreed, "I wonder how big this thing's going to be. Do you know anything about this, Amanda?"

Amanda didn't want the pressure of saying anything. She had promised to keep it a secret, so she went over and sat by her mom. Jenny went up front to refill her soda. Amanda went with her. "Mom, Grandma and Grandpa asked me how many people they thought were coming to the party. I couldn't sit there and keep a straight face. They suspect something."

"They can suspect, but they don't know yet," Jenny said. "We have a little longer to keep this secret. Remember, it'll be the best part to see everyone's faces."

Amanda smirked and stayed close to her mom the rest of the meal, avoiding any more inquiries about the day.

The party was scheduled to start at five in the afternoon, and Jenny arrived one hour early to meet with the caterer and the servers. Jenny set out table service and napkins when she noticed the first two servers, Ann Jones and Sharon Dean. Ann immediately started filling trays with mints and cookies. Sharon began mixing and pouring the beverage in the punch bowl.

"The cake is so perfect," Sharon remarked. "It depicts Matthew so well."

"Does it ever!" Ann exclaimed. "We'll cut into the picture last. We want as many guests as possible to see it."

"Everything's so nice," Sharon added.

"Couldn't have a better day." Ann turned and went back to work.

When Matthew came in, his eyes scanned the room full of decorations. The first thing he noticed was a round table with a guest book and a vase containing a red rose. Looking over at the food table, he saw a large white cake with mounds of frosting. But, what really caught his attention was the center of the cake. It was a picture of him with his cow, Bonnie. Matthew's tongue slipped out of his mouth as he wiped a tear. "Me party? Me four-oh? Me miss me cow."

Glenda came over and slipped an arm around him. "Happy Birthday, sweetie."

"For you, Matthew. We are here to celebrate your fortieth birthday," Brad told him.

Matthew hugged Glenda and Jed and said, "Tanks."

"Don't thank us," Glenda informed him. "Brad and Jenny did this."

"Me happy. Me family do this. Me happy day. Me four-oh."

Ed said, "You're getting to be an old man."

Matthew looked at him and said, "Me young. Me live old man. No old now."

"I guess you are young," Jed said. He turned to Jenny. "How many people are you expecting?"

Jenny pretended not to hear and went to check on the kitchen ladies as Jed and Glenda shot glances at one another.

"Look at the posters. Devin made them for your party. All these decorations are for your special day," Ed explained. "Here's a table with a guest book. The people that come sign this book. You'll want to remember who was here."

"Nice, real nice," Matthew answered.

"Once people sign, invite them to have something to eat. Jenny and Amanda made dozens of mints and cookies so there'd be plenty to eat."

"Lots food. Me party."

"You'll have a great time," Ed said as he patted Matthew on the back.

"Number people come?"

"We don't know. It's an open house. Anyone can come."

"Me friends see me."

"I'm sure you'll have many people stop by for you."

Brad explained to Matthew, "It's okay to hug people today because this is a very special day."

"Me okay. Stay calm."

Janet, a family friend, was the first guest to arrive. She said, "Matthew, Happy Birthday."

"So good to see you, Janet. It's been a long time," Glenda said.

"My, things look beautiful and look at that food table. You went all out."

"We had nothing to do with it. Jenny and Brad did it all."

As she went to the food line, a few more guests arrived. Derrick and his wife, Kim, hugged the family. When he saw Derrick, Matthew said, "Fun. Grandma Kate. Baseball. Sing. Play outside."

Derrick said, "Yes. We have lots of good memories at Grandma's house. Those were great times. Happy Birthday."

Matthew said, "Good party. Nice. Me happy people come see me."

One by one, friends, family, neighbors, and school staff lined up to greet Matthew. There were people waiting outside the building. Matthew blinked tears from his eyes from time to time.

He saw Miss Evans. She gave him a bear hug and teased him. "Forty. You're getting old. But I'm sixty-eight."

Matthew shook his head and said, "Me okay. No old."

Several of the hay crew workers from years ago attended the party. Willie asked Matthew, "Are you still putting up hay?"

Matthew flexed his muscles and said, "Me do. Me muscle. Me work hard."

The community center filled to capacity. Ray and Amy, high school friends, were in line. Ray said, "Hey, buddy. Happy Birthday."

"Thank you," Matthew smiled.

"Happy Birthday," Amy said as she gave him a big hug. "I want you to meet our children. This is Calvin. He's fifteen. This is our daughter, Brittney. She's ten."

Matthew shook both their hands. "You mom, dad real nice. Me friends. Long time ago."

"We never forgot you," Amy said. "We drove two hours to be here for you. We miss you."

"Miss you too. Thanks. Me happy you come. Eat food. Cake. All you want."

Luke arrived with his wife and children. He hadn't seen Matthew for a while. "What have you been up to? Happy Birthday, pal." Luke patted Matthew on the back.

"Me happy day. Me work cows. Me work hay. Babies come."

Luke reminisced, "Remember how we talked about the rodeos? Do you still go every year?"

"Me do. Me cowboy. Me like bulls."

"You always did like the bulls. That's the most exciting part," Luke said. "Happy Birthday. We'll get together and go to a rodeo this summer if it's all right with you."

"Me say yes. Okay me."

"Look at this! What a party! You deserve it, buddy," Luke said.

"You eat. Lots food. Not too much. You thin man." Matthew patted his stomach.

Nick, one of the older boys from Cloverville School, shook Matthew's hand. "Hey there. Do you remember me?"

"Me do. You climb bars."

"I sure did. You were a daredevil in school. I'll never forget when you swatted Mr. Clark with the flyswatter. We thought you were so cool. Of course, you still are."

Matthew nodded his head. "You too. You cool man. Me okay. Me cool."

Nick commented, "I remember when you also liked blowing the whistle. You kept Mr. Clark and the teachers in their running shoes. We thought Mr. Clark had lots of work keeping up with you. Happy Birthday."

Dale, whose wife Ann was helping, told Matthew, "This is quite a party. Look at all the friends you have. You're one lucky guy."

Matthew nodded his head. "Big party. Me four-oh."

"We'll celebrate more birthdays this summer. Maybe we can go bowling and play board games."

"Good news." Matthew said.

"Hey, best buddy," Jeremy said loudly. "What's going on here?"

"You come see me. Me big party. Big 'prise."

"It sure is a surprise. Have you had any cake yet?"

Matthew put his hand to his stomach. "Me wait. Party over."

"I'll try to save you some," Jeremy said jokingly. "I have a big appetite."

"You tease me." Matthew laughed.

Over three hundred people attended the party. When guests dwindled, Matthew approached the food table. He made a ham sandwich, got a big piece of cake, and a glass of punch.

Ed and Jenny cleaned up the building with the kitchen helpers.

———＊———

When everyone was settled back at the house, Glenda asked, "How did all of these people keep from telling us?"

Jenny answered. "I guess our friends are good at keeping secrets."

Glenda was amazed. "I had no idea that so many people could keep quiet. That's shocking."

"I guess it shows how important this was to make it a surprise," Brad commented. "I was concerned someone would tell you, but no one did."

"This was so wonderful and went off so well. Thank you all for doing this. It'll never be forgotten," Glenda said graciously.

"Me good time. People see me. Me party. Me happy." Matthew put his hands to his heart. He kept every decoration and card in his room. He looked at them over and over again. Jenny gave him a photo album of pictures of the party. Matthew often flipped through the pictures, treasuring this day as he did his old high school annuals and videos of prom and graduation.

CHAPTER 50

When Matthew was forty-two years old, Jeremy was still working on the Parker farm. He was an asset to them since Jed was getting older and working at a slower pace. Jeremy had worked with Matthew's family for fifteen years and put in long hours. He lived and breathed the farm life, especially during spring planting and fall harvest. Jeremy was part of the family and considered Jed and Glenda his second set of parents. He often ate with them at dinnertime and went to fairs and rodeos with Jed, Brad, and Matthew.

Jeremy dated a few girls over the years, but none were serious until he met Emily. She was tall, slender, and had beautiful hair down to her shoulders. Emily was raised a farm girl and had much in common with Jeremy. Jeremy brought Emily out to the farm to spend time with Glenda, Jed, Brad, and Matthew. Emily sat on a wooden rocker and visited. Matthew pulled up a chair and leaned over close to Emily. She smiled at him and said, "Jeremy says you're his best buddy."

"Me buddy. Him good man. Me work him. Him nice. Him tease me."

"Jeremy teases me too," she said. "He likes your family."

"Him lots time here. Him help cows, hay."

"He loves it here."

"Me happy here." Matthew leaned over and put his arm around Emily. "You two marry? You nice girl."

"We'll see. We're good friends," Emily replied.

After Emily had spent a few times with the Parkers, Jeremy asked Emily to marry him. They decided on an outdoor wedding near a country church. It was going to be small with a reception to be held in town at a fair building. Over four hundred guests were invited.

Jeremy told Matthew, "Well, Matthew, I'm getting married. You're my best buddy. I wondered if you'll be in my wedding. I want you to be a groomsman."

"Me happy you. You marry nice girl. Her pretty blue eyes and red hair. You two honeymoon. You two babies come soon."

"Don't rush things." Jeremy laughed. "I have to get married first."

"Me happy you. Me help you."

"Thanks, buddy. I'm glad you will. Brad's standing up with you also and so is my brother, Jason."

"You, Emily, love." Matthew put his hands over his heart. "You two huggie, huggie. You two kiss." Matthew chuckled teasingly.

"Matthew, that's a little personal." Jeremy laughed heartily.

"You two real love? You have party?"

"We're having a dance. You can get out there and show your moves."

Matthew put up both thumbs. "Me do moonwalk. Me shake me booty." Matthew imitated a moonwalk and shook his behind.

"Dance however you want," Jeremy said. "There'll be several people dancing. Thanks, buddy, for being there for me."

"Okay," Matthew said.

---*---

When the wedding day arrived, Glenda saw Matthew looking spiffy with his silky tan tuxedo and polished brown cowboy boots. "My, you look handsome."

"Thanks Mom. Me do good. Me help Jeremy."

Glenda moved closer and straightened Matthew's tie and his shirt collar. "You'll do fine up there. You're my grown-up young man."

When Matthew and his parents arrived, Matthew looked for the groom. He was nowhere to be seen. Matthew went inside the church and found Brad waiting inside the entryway with Jeremy's brother Jason. They looked around for Jeremy, who was hiding out in the bathroom looking at himself in the mirror. He nervously paced back and forth. Brad wanted to check himself in the mirror, but the door was locked. He knocked and called, "Jeremy, are you in there?"

"Yes. I'm here."

"You okay, me buddy? You marry now?" Matthew inquired.

Jeremy took a deep breath and wiped his sweaty hands on a towel. "I'm okay. I'm just nervous."

"Stay calm," Matthew called. "You okay. Emily nice girl. Stay calm. Me help you."

"Thanks, buddy," Jeremy answered. "I need to step out and see who's here." Jeremy opened the door, and Matthew saw that sweat was trickling down Jeremy's face.

Matthew and Brad went into the bathroom to check their tuxedos and comb their hair. Jeremy stepped outside to see people sitting on the hay bales. Glenda and Jed felt honored to be seated as parents of the groom and next to Jeremy's parents.

Jeremy saw Lois, a relative of Emily's, who said to him. "Jeremy, darling, I have a question for you."

"What's up?" he asked.

"I was wondering where the handicapped man is."

Jeremy was taken aback. "I don't know who you mean."

"Of course you do, darling. You know, the friend of yours who has a mental disability."

"If you are referring to my buddy, Matthew, I see a man, not a disability."

Lois huffed and shook her head in disbelief. Jeremy watched her march off when his Aunt Sophie approached. She was a special education teacher who introduced Jeremy and Emily. She told Jeremy, "That was so kind of you to say what you did. You're such a good friend for Matthew."

"Aunt Sophie, I honestly don't see a disability. He's my friend."

Sophie hugged her nephew. "Jeremy, you're an amazing young man. I wish you and Emily much happiness."

---*---

Jeremy swallowed hard as he saw Emily perfectly poised in her white satin gown trimmed in intricate lace and a short train draping behind her. At thirty-two years old, he had found the perfect woman whose beauty mesmerized him. Emily sweetly smiled at her handsome groom. Jeremy grasped her hand gently as they turned toward the pastor. The pastor shared stories about the relationship between a man and woman. He read the love chapter from the Bible and spoke about the importance of marriage. The couple lit the unity candle and exchanged rings. When the couple exited, guests began chattering with one another. Matthew told Brad, "Real nice. Honeymoon. Babies come."

---*---

The disc jockey introduced the couple. "Here's a special song for the newlyweds. Jeremy and Emily, this dance is for you. Congratulations."

The guests clapped as Jeremy and Emily danced, their arms wrapped around each other. Glenda was sitting at a table chatting with some neighbors when Jeremy walked over to her. He cleared his throat and asked, "Mom, may I have this dance?"

"I'm not much of a dancer, but I'll do it for you."

Jeremy offered Glenda his arm, and they walked to the dance floor. Matthew danced with Sophie and moved his feet to the beat of the country songs playing. He slid his feet backward imitating the moonwalk. Sophie followed Matthew, then one guest started some line dancing so people could dance without having partners.

Matthew said at the end, "Happy, happy day. Honeymoon. Babies come soon."

Brad looked at him and replied, "Thanks for not saying that to anyone at the party, but wait and see."

"Me do. Me stay calm. Me wait babies come. Jeremy happy day. Him dad."

"That's enough," Brad told Matthew. "Let's talk about something else."

Ten months later, Jeremy and Emily were blessed with a baby girl.

PART 7

PRESENT

CHAPTER 51

Brad and Jenny had been sitting on the porch a long time listening to the sounds of the country and looking at the old barn with its green roof and white tin siding.

Jeremy was finishing feeding the cattle with Matthew. His three children often visited Jenny and played in the yard just as the Parker children did years ago. Jenny made lunch and Trudy's sugar cookies several times a month for them. Her three grandchildren visited several weeks during the summer months and were the sixth generation to enjoy the farm.

At fifty-four years old, Matthew continued caring for his cow herd, which now totaled sixty-five cows. Matthew operated much of the farm machinery and particularly helped with haying and harvest. Brad and Matthew were the fifth generation of farmers to till the land. They raised plenty of hay to feed to the cattle and to conserve the rich soil. It was important to them to be good stewards of the land.

Glenda had Alzheimer's and had a room in a local nursing home. She told stories about the days of raising the children and about her own childhood. She didn't recognize Brad or Jenny. They weren't sure if she recognized Matthew or not, but when he visited, she always had a big hug for him. He felt some peace getting the affection from his aging mom.

Jed shared a room with Glenda in the nursing home. He had had a massive stroke one year ago and was in a wheelchair. He was unable to do daily tasks. Brad and Jenny had tried to take care of Glenda in her home with home health care as long as possible, but with Jed's stroke, it was too difficult.

Jenny cooked the meals for Matthew and Brad. Ed worked in the city and helped with the farm work on Saturdays. Jenny spent a few hours every day at the nursing home. Brad and Matthew tried to visit every evening. It was important to Matthew to spend that time with his mom and dad. He remembered when his grandparents passed away and couldn't imagine losing his own parents. He still had many friends who stopped by to see him and went places with him, such as the rodeos and baseball games.

Jenny moved back to be there for her parents and brothers. That move proved to be good for her as well. She felt an inner peace being home where her roots were.

Brad looked at Jenny, "Do you think that we should have another big bash for Matthew when he turns fifty-five?"

Jenny smiled. "It might be good for him. There has been so much change. We could just have close friends. I think it would be a great idea, especially since he's having difficulty dealing with Mom and Dad in the nursing home. Something could happen anytime."

"I know," he said sadly. "It's so sad for Matthew and for us to see them like this."

"I can't believe all that has transpired here since we were kids." Jenny limped slowly across the porch to limber up her legs.

"Life changes. I'm glad Matthew can still see them."

Ring! Ring! Brad and Jenny looked at each other. Ring! Ring! Jenny slowly walked toward the door. She opened the screen door to the house and stepped inside the entryway where the phone was mounted on the wall by the roll top desk. Jenny reached for the receiver, but Brad had followed her inside and answered the phone. "Hello." He listened in the receiver for a few moments and responded, "We'll be right there." He slowly hung up the phone and ordered Jenny, "Get in the pickup. We're going to town."

"What is it?" Jenny asked.

"Jeremy took Matthew to the hospital. We need to meet them there."

"What? Why? What did he tell you?"

"Just that Matthew had passed out after carrying the last bucket of feed," Brad calmly explained.

"Oh my!"

Brad parked in the hospital parking lot and raced into the emergency waiting area with Jenny. Jeremy bolted to his feet when he saw them.

"Any news?" Brad asked.

"He's in the examining room now. The doctors are with him. It'll be a while before the doctor comes out."

"Oh no," Jenny spoke frightfully. "I hope he's all right."

Jenny and Jeremy went to the cafeteria to get a drink. Jenny got a large glass of iced tea to take with her to the waiting area. "So Jenny, how're Devin and Amanda doing?"

"Devin's working as an engineer. They're expecting their third child. Amanda's got one child and just completed her master's degree. Her husband works evenings, so they don't need day care."

"I've enjoyed watching them grow up when they came during the summers," Jeremy said.

"Those summer visits are some of their best childhood memories."

Finally, the doctor came out. He addressed them seriously. "Hello, I'm Dr. Carson, the regional cardiologist."

"I'm Brad Parker. This is my sister Jenny." They all shook hands.

"I'll be honest with you. Matthew suffered a massive heart attack. This is not unusual for Down syndromes. He has been most fortunate never to have had any heart issues in the past. He lived an unbelievably healthy life. However, this heart attack has weakened his heart too much to do surgery. His heart is extremely weak. I'm sorry. He may die at any time."

Jenny gasped. "My baby brother."

Brad asked, "Can we see him?"

"The sooner, the better. He may live a few minutes or a few hours. I'm so sorry."

"I'll call Ed first," Jenny said. She opened her purse and pulled out a business card where Ed could be reached. He worked one hour away, and she knew he wouldn't be here anytime soon.

Brad and Jenny crept into Matthew's room. His eyes were closed and the sound of a heart monitor beeping was all that could be heard. Wires from the monitor and an IV pump were hooked up to Matthew. He breathed slow, shallow breaths. They stood and watched him a few moments.

Brad said, "He's sleeping now. We don't want to disturb him."

At the sound of Brad's voice, Matthew opened his eyes and smiled weakly. "Hi, Sis," he said hoarsely. "Brad."

Jeremy opened the door and came into the room.

"Me best buddy. You here."

"Hello, Matthew. Where else would I be but here with you?"

Matthew groggily responded, "Me sleepy. Me nap. Me home soon."

Everyone breathed a sigh of relief and smiled at Matthew. He seemed weak, but he was himself.

Jenny held his hand and said, "I love you so much."

Brad stood on the other side of the bed and held Matthew's other hand. "We love you, buddy. We want you to get better."

Matthew looked up at Jenny, smiling. "Me go home. Me see Jesus. Me happy. Me see Raw, Papa, Kate, Gary. Hug me. Love me. Me happy see Jesus."

They all smiled at this. Jeremy and Brad fought back tears.

"Why you cry?" Matthew whispered. "Me see Jesus."

Matthew closed his eyes. His hands felt cold and clammy. His best buddy and beloved brother and sister stood in silence unable to believe they were losing him. Suddenly, the heart monitor beeped long and steady. There was a straight line on the screen. The nurse and doctor rushed in and asked them to step outside while they tried to revive Matthew.

Dr. Carson came out a few minutes after they left the room, and announced, "I'm sorry. He's gone. Believe me, I know this is hard."

They were numb with shock. Only a few hours earlier, Matthew was working vigorously and in good health. Now, he was gone.

---*---

Arrangements were made for Matthew's funeral at Unity Christian Church, the church he had attended for over thirty years after White Chapel, their country church, had closed. Pastor Burt had been there since Matthew was in his twenties and knew the family well. He often visited Jed and Glenda in the nursing home.

Jenny and Brad decided not to tell Glenda and Jed about Matthew's death. They didn't feel that they would comprehend the loss. Jed wasn't coherent much of the time. He told stories of his younger days, but he didn't recall current details of life. Glenda wouldn't remember it either.

Neighbors and friends stopped by both Brad's home and Jenny's home to offer their condolences. They brought food for the family. Ed took a few days off work. Devin, his wife, and two young children came to Jenny and Ed's house. Devin's son, Gary, was seven years old, and his daughter, Kate, was four years old. His wife, Chelsey, was expecting a third baby. Amanda arrived with her husband and their three-year-old son, Matthew. She also was expecting another child. The old Rogers' home had plenty of bedrooms to house all of the family. Jenny was comforted by the presence of all of her family. She was so blessed with her children and grandchildren. They loved to see Grandma Jenny, Grandpa Ed, and Brad. Jenny vowed to be as wonderful as Grandma Trudy and Grandma Kate had been for her. She had a beautiful family to love.

At the funeral, Matthew's casket was open in the back of the church in the fellowship area. The family sat in a side prayer room of the church and spoke to Pastor Burt before the funeral. He said, "This is a celebration of Matthew's life. We are gathered here in grief but also joy. We know that Matthew knew the Lord. He was a man of simple faith. It says in Psalms that if you have the faith of a mustard seed, you can move mountains. Matthew moved mountains. Let us pray."

The family closed their eyes for prayer. Pastor Burt continued, "Lord, thank you for life and every breath we take. You are the giver of life. Thank you for sharing the blessing of Matthew with so many lives. We were able to see your love and goodness through him. He loved you simply and heartily. He knew that at the end of his life he was going to heaven to see you. We know that Matthew is there with you, dancing and celebrating. His memory in our lives is forever imprinted on our hearts. Amen."

They all wiped their eyes and felt joy in the life that they had with Matthew. Matthew had been a gift from God. They were given the opportunity to love unconditionally and learn patience. They were ready with the strength God had given them to go inside for the funeral.

The sanctuary and balcony were full. An intercom system was set up to broadcast the funeral in the basement. The funeral attendants closed the casket and rolled it up to the front of the sanctuary where there were numerous flower arrangements emitting a sweet fragrance.

Pastor Burt stepped up to the podium. He looked at the family and the number of people there. He prayed silently to God for strength and the right words. Brad, Jenny, Ed, Jeremy, and Emily were seated in front. Jenny's children and grandchildren were right behind them. Jenny's eyes had dark circles under them. Brad's eyes were swollen. Jeremy and Emily fanned their faces with the obituaries, fanning off tears. Jenny's grandchildren stirred in their seats.

Pastor Burt put his hands on the sides of the podium and held on tightly. The organ played "In the Garden" and "What a Friend We Have in Jesus." The congregation sang along. He opened with prayer and scripture.

"We are gathered here today to celebrate the life of Matthew John Parker. Matthew went to heaven on August 22 at the age of fifty-four after suffering a massive heart attack. Matthew was born to Jed and Glenda Parker. At birth, they learned he was born with a disability called Down syndrome. Jed and Glenda were told he might not be able to do much at all. However, with the support of both sets of grandparents, they vowed they would love, support, and teach Matthew all that they could. Jed and Glenda faced many obstacles, challenges, and prejudices. Yet, they never gave up on their son. They persevered, and the whole family showed unconditional love. His family looked at his strengths, not his weaknesses. Matthew lived his whole life in this community. As people got to know him, they saw beyond an outward disability. They saw a happy person who made them smile. He brought joy to others and learned far beyond what others thought possible.

"Matthew took pride in working hard on the farm doing various jobs throughout the year. He was proud of his cow herd and took great care with them. He knew about every one of them. He loved rodeos, baseball, bowling, and board games. He had an enormous number of friends as we see here today.

"Matthew had impeccable manners, good social skills, and a hard work ethic. Those are strong character traits to possess. Matthew had a meek, simple faith and intuitive sense of other's feelings. His gentle, calm manner touched many lives."

Pastor Burt cleared his throat. "Did we touch his life as much as he touched ours? I believe God used him as an instrument to affirm a simple faith and to teach us all that every human being has value and a purpose. Each one of us here has our weaknesses.

Our weaknesses aren't always visible. We must remember not to focus on our weaknesses, but to focus on the strengths and talents that God has given us."

The organist began playing a song. The pastor took a deep breath and wiped his brow. He hoped his message had gotten across. He saw many tissues being used throughout the congregation and heard stifled cries.

He began again, "Life has a way of throwing us curveballs. Do you know what I mean? It's hard to get a base hit, let alone a home run with a curveball. It's an unpredictable pitch. Matthew and his family played the game of life like a baseball game. They went to bat daily and were thrown many curveballs. Matthew's birth was a curveball. It was something they didn't expect, but they persevered anyway. They had struggles and doubts, but they put their faith in God to be their guide. Matthew's life was one of uncertainty, yet he stepped up to home plate with his bat and hitting stance. He eagerly awaited whatever pitch was thrown at him. He gave each pitch his whole effort and never complained. He stayed in the game of life with gusto, never quitting when challenges came. He struck out; he got to base and scored. He never quit the game. The final pitch was thrown, and he hit a home run to heaven where he met with our Savior. What do we do when curveballs are thrown at us? Do we cower and quit the game? Do we pout and become angry? God wants us to trust in him no matter what pitches come our way. Be like Matthew and his family. Stay in the game of life with determination, trusting in God, no matter what obstacles come your way. Let us pray."

Jenny was trembling, yet she knew she needed to be strong for her family and friends. Many joined the family at the cemetery while others stayed behind to console them later on. The procession to the cemetery was fourteen miles. The closed casket represented a heartbreaking finality for Jenny. Ed, Jenny, Brad, Jeremy, and Emily sat in chairs while other people stood. Several friends put their hands on Jenny's shoulder, and she thanked them for coming and honoring Matthew with their presence. Pastor Burt spoke some final words of comfort and prayed.

When everyone had gathered at the church again, Pastor Burt said a blessing, and a wonderful luncheon prepared by the ladies of the church was enjoyed. People, of course, were grieving over Matthew, but soon laughter could be heard more and more. People told stories about how loving and clever Matthew had been. Jenny left the church that afternoon amazed and moved by how many lives Matthew had touched. His life truly was an EXTRA ordinary life.

EPILOGUE

Two years after Matthew's death, Jenny sat on the porch all alone while Brad and Jeremy were at the barn doing chores. She looked thoughtfully at the yard where she played with her two brothers so many summers long ago. She felt sad a minute. She realized Matthew was happy in heaven with Glenda and Jed and wanted her happy too. She smiled at the legacy he left behind and felt blessed for every day they had together. It was bittersweet, but the best thing she could do was press on and love others as he had loved them.

Jenny focused her energies on spending as much time as possible with her grandchildren. She modeled herself after Grandma Trudy and Kate. She loved her grandchildren and shared stories and pictures of Matthew.

Brad kept Matthew's cow herd and its descendants. The family line of cattle continued. Brad used a portion of the profits to give to adults at the local group home to purchase tickets for baseball games, rodeos, and car races. The adult residents were thankful for these tickets and had good times going to the events.

Jeremy and Emily adopted a Down syndrome child and felt honored to raise this boy.

Jenny's daughter, Amanda, was an elementary teacher and got her master's degree in special education. She worked with children of varying disabilities and worked to bring out the strengths in each student.

Jenny's son, Devin, worked as an engineer. He had five children and took two Down syndrome children under his wing. He invited them to family get-togethers. He wanted his own children to love and see the preciousness of life. He donated money every year to an agency that trained disabled adults for jobs.

AUTHOR'S NOTE

This book is fictionalized, and the characters are not intended to reflect anyone. However, this story was inspired by true events.

The development, abilities, and skills resemble those of my brother. He learned so much thanks to the loving adults surrounding him who taught him to work hard and achieve his best.

I hoped that you enjoyed reading this book. Having a Down syndrome person in my life has brought my family so much joy and laughter. My brother truly was a special gift from God.

Down syndrome children all have unique abilities, interests, and gifts. The content in this story does not reflect every child born with Down syndrome. There are many varying abilities and personality traits.